A Proper Pursuit

LYNN AUSTIN

A Proper Pursuit

BETHANYHOUSE
MINNEAPOLIS, MINNESOTA

Published by Bethany House Publishers
11400 Hampshire Avenue South
Bloomington, Minnesota 55438

Bethany House Publishers is a division of
Baker Publishing Group, Grand Rapids, Michigan.

Printed in the United States of America

Paperback: ISBN-13: 978-0-7642-2891-9 ISBN-10: 0-7642-2891-9
Hardcover: ISBN-13: 978-0-7642-0440-1 ISBN-10: 0-7642-0440-8

Library of Congress Cataloging-in-Publication Data

Austin, Lynn N.
    A proper pursuit / Lynn Austin.
        p.   cm.
    ISBN 978-0-7642-0440-1 (alk. paper) — ISBN 978-0-7642-2891-9 (pbk.)
 1. Young women—Fiction. 2. Chicago (Ill.)—Fiction. 3. United States—History—
1933–1945—Fiction. I. Title.
    PS3551.U839P76   2007
    813'.54—dc22

                                                                                    2007023563

To my family
Ken, Joshua, Benjamin, Maya, and Vanessa
I love you all.

Books by
Lynn Austin
FROM BETHANY HOUSE PUBLISHERS

All She Ever Wanted

Eve's Daughters

Hidden Places

Wings of Refuge

A Woman's Place

A Proper Pursuit

REFINER'S FIRE

Candle in the Darkness

Fire by Night

A Light to My Path

CHRONICLES OF THE KINGS

Gods and Kings

Song of Redemption

The Strength of His Hand

Faith of My Fathers

Among the Gods

LYNN AUSTIN is a three-time Christy Award winner for her historical novels *Hidden Places, Candle in the Darkness,* and *Fire by Night.* In addition to writing, Lynn is a popular speaker at conferences, retreats, and various church and school events. She and her husband have three children and make their home in Illinois.

Chapter

1

Saturday, May 20, 1893

I couldn't imagine more shocking news.

I sat at Widow Maude O'Neill's dining room table and stared at my father as the overcooked mutton on my plate grew cold. I would have cried out in protest and begged him to reconsider, but as a recent graduate of Madame Beauchamps' School for Young Ladies, I'd learned that a proper young lady never caused a scene at the supper table, especially if she was a guest.

Father looked immensely pleased with himself. He leaned back in his chair, his hand thrust inside his suit coat as he played with his watch chain. Maude, dressed in widow's black for the last time, wore the phony smile that she reserved for my father and did her best to blush like a maiden. She had won a valuable prize in my father, John Jacob Hayes, and she knew it.

I glanced at her unpleasant children, Horace and Harriet, and knew by their smug expressions that my father's marriage proposal wasn't news to them. Maude had scrubbed their piggy pink faces so thoroughly it looked as though she had boiled them. I wished she had.

My father's smile faded as my silence lengthened. "Well, say something, Violet. Have you forgotten your manners?"

I looked down at my hands, folded primly in my lap. "No, Father. I haven't forgotten." Good manners prevented me from telling my father that he was a fool. Or from smacking the smile off Maude's pinched face.

"Congratulations, Father," I said in my sweetest voice. "And best wishes to you, Widow O'Neill." I had learned the proper responses from Madame Beauchamps: *"Never congratulate the bride; offer her your best wishes."*

"Thank you, Violet," Maude replied. If her narrow rat face had whiskers, she would have preened them.

"We hope to be wed this coming fall," my father continued. "It will be a small, private affair at home with only a few relatives and guests in attendance."

"Excuse me, Father," I said politely, "but aren't you forgetting something?"

"What's that?"

"You already have a wife—my mother."

He cleared his throat. "Yes ... well, perhaps I neglected to explain it to you, but the fact is, I've been free to marry for some time." He sawed off another rubbery morsel of mutton and chewed it vigorously, as if unaware that this second piece of news had shocked me even more than the first.

"Free to marry?" I echoed, careful to keep my tone mild. Young ladies never burst into tears in public.

"Yes. You were away at school, and I didn't want to upset you with the news."

I quietly wadded Maude's damask napkin into a ball as I pondered his words. Why did people always tiptoe around me as if I reclined on a bed of violets that might be crushed beneath their feet?

"Poor, pitiful Violet. Her mother became ill, you know, when she was only nine. She's an only child, always daydreaming. . . ."

"When did Mother die?" I had to struggle against the lump in my throat.

"We'll talk about it later, Violet."

"Excuse me once again, Father, but I believe I should have been informed of her passing. You might have——"

He cleared his throat, interrupting me. "This is hardly the proper time to discuss the matter." He nodded discreetly toward Horace and Harriet, who had stopped gnawing their mutton to gaze at me with their round piggy eyes. "I realize, now, that I should have explained everything to you ahead of time, and I apologize for that. But let's not spoil Maude's wonderful supper or this momentous occasion with details that can wait until we're home, shall we?"

Evidently, my mother's demise was a detail. I would have excused myself from the table in order to allow my tears to fall, but I was a guest in Widow O'Neill's home. Leaving midmeal would be unspeakably rude. Weeping at the supper table would be rude as well. Besides, my tears were more for myself than for a mother I barely remembered. Even so, Father might have mentioned her death.

Maude lifted the platter of meat and offered it to my father. "Would you care for more, John?"

Maude had poisoned her first husband—I was certain of it. I had read about women like her in my favorite dime novels and pulp fiction magazines. My best friend, Ruth Schultz, smuggled copies of *True Crime Stories*, *The Illustrated Police News*, and *True Romance Stories* into our dormitory at Madame Beauchamps' School for Young Ladies along with dime novels in bright orange jackets. We hid them beneath our mattresses so we could read them after lights-out. Of course, proper young ladies never read such trash—but Ruth and I did.

What would become of me after Maude poisoned my father the same way she had poisoned her first husband? Would she drive me from my home to beg for alms in the gutter? I pictured myself on a street corner as snow swirled around me, a tattered shawl clutched around my shivering shoulders, my gaunt hand outstretched in supplication. Then the image faded as I realized that I was much too old to beg for alms. As a pretty young woman of twenty years, a much worse fate awaited me: I would have to become a woman of the night! A warm blush spread across my cheeks at the prospect.

While it may sound vain to call myself *pretty*, I had heard enough people use that adjective when describing me to convince myself that it must be true. My thick, curly hair was the color of strong coffee, my eyes just as dark. And even though Madame Beauchamps had referred to my complexion as a bit *swarthy* and had cautioned me to stay out of the sun lest I resemble *une paysanne*, she had also described me as *très jolie*. A careful examination of my face in a hand mirror confirmed to me that I was, indeed, quite pretty.

"Would you like some more meat, Violet?" Maude offered the platter to me next, her teeth bared in a grin. What if she planned to poison me along with my father, so that Horace and Harriet could inherit our entire estate? I declined politely, then pushed away my dinner plate, my appetite suddenly gone. For all I knew, Maude may have begun the slow, poisonous process this very evening.

"I believe our news has upset you, Violet," Maude said, her head tilted to one side in sympathy. "We were so hoping that you would be happy for your father and me. And that we would all become one big family." Horace and Harriet had laid down their forks as if waiting for me to graft them into the family tree with my butter knife. They would have a very long wait. I felt a greater kinship with the poor dead sheep on the serving platter than I did with them.

In the long silence that followed I heard a horse trotting up the street. If only it were a young, fair-haired lieutenant, newly arrived from the western Indian wars, riding to my rescue . . . *He had been gravely wounded by a native's savage arrow, his uniform in bloody tat-*

ters, but his undying love for me had kept him alive, and now we would be reunited at last, and . . .

The horse cantered past the house, followed by the unmistakable rumble of carriage wheels over the rutted street. Maybe it was a sign from Providence. Perhaps the passing carriage had been sent to tell me that I must run away from home at the first opportunity.

Did twenty-year-old women run away from home? And if so, how did they accomplish it? Did they tie their belongings in a shawl and sling the bundle over their shoulder? A steamer trunk would be much more convenient, considering how many belongings I possessed. The trunk I had taken to school with me would suffice, although I doubted if proper young ladies pushed their own steamer trunks through the streets. Madame Beauchamps had never specifically addressed the subject of proper etiquette when running away from home, but I was quite certain she would consider pushing one's own trunk through the streets of Lockport, Illinois, unacceptable.

"Violet . . . Violet. . . ?" I looked up when I heard Father addressing me. "Daydreaming again," he muttered. "Kindly pay attention, Violet. Mrs. O'Neill has asked you a question."

"Oh, pardon me. Would you be kind enough to repeat it, Mrs. O'Neill?"

Maude's smile may have appeared innocent to the untrained eye, but I thought I detected the proverbial "gleam of malice" as she said, "I understand that Herman Beckett has been courting you. He is such a fine young man, isn't he?"

"Yes, ma'am. Mr. Beckett is certainly above reproach. But I would hardly regard our two Sunday afternoon outings to Dellwood Park as a courtship."

I searched for a way to change the subject. It seemed obscene to discuss my own courtship so soon after hearing the shocking news about Maude and my father. Old people had no business courting, much less getting married. But Maude seemed determined to engage me in a verbal tennis match. I knew the rules of polite conversation, but I lacked the will to play.

"I happen to know that young Mr. Beckett is quite serious about your courtship," Maude said, leaning closer. "I know his mother very well, and it seems that he is absolutely smitten by you."

She had lobbed the ball into my court, but I let it lay there. If Herman Beckett was truly smitten with me, he hid the evidence well. I longed for a suitor who would gaze deeply into my eyes the way the heroes in Ruth's romance stories always did. Someone who would kiss my ivory fingertips and whisper endearing words in my ear. The beau in one story had even nibbled on his beloved's earlobe. That didn't strike me as romantic at all, but perhaps my imagination had been tainted by an adventure story I had read the same week that had featured cannibals.

"Herman comes from such a fine family," Maude insisted.

"Yes, ma'am."

"You would be wise to encourage him before some other girl snatches him up."

"Yes, ma'am."

I had no idea what else to say. I wished Madame Beauchamps had spent less time teaching me the proper way to consume a dinner roll—*"Delicately tear off one small morsel at a time, girls, and apply butter to each individual piece with your butter knife"*—and more time teaching me how to rid my life of scheming widows with romantic designs on my father. I had no heart for meaningless conversation after Father's absurd news. I wished I were a child of nine or ten, like Horace and Harriet, who were expected to be seen and not heard.

After supper, good manners required me to play the piano for everyone's enjoyment. Maude's piano sounded as out of tune as a hurdy-gurdy, but I poured all of my sentiment into the music—and I had a great deal of sentiment that evening. If only a world-famous impresario would chance to walk down the street on his evening constitutional and hear my earnest performance and pound on Maude's door, declaring that my song had touched his very soul!

"Let her come with me," he would beg. *"Let me nourish her budding talent until it blooms and flowers!"* We would travel the world together, and I would perform before the crowned heads of Europe. Later we would be married, and—

"It's time to go home, Violet." My father stood beside the piano, holding my wrap.

"Thank you for a lovely evening," I said dutifully as I rose from the piano stool. I scurried through the door as Maude lunged to embrace me.

"I would like to know where Mother is buried," I said as soon as Father and I started walking up the hill toward our home. "I would like to visit her grave."

"Listen, Violet—"

"I know that everyone considers me fragile and frail, someone who must be protected from every unpleasantness in life. But I'm no longer a schoolgirl, Father. I'm a woman."

"Yes, I'm well aware of that." His voice sounded flat and emotionless. The village streets were too dark for me to see his face and discern if he was grieving for my lost childhood or if I had angered him with my demands. I plowed forward.

"And you had no right to hide the news about Mother from me. I have every right to grieve and mourn her death, even if I haven't seen her in years—"

"She isn't dead, Violet."

"I should have attended her funeral, at the very least, and . . . w-what did you say?"

"Your mother isn't dead." He stopped, winded from the uphill climb.

I stared at him, stupefied. "Then how can you possibly marry Mrs. O'Neill?"

Father exhaled a long, slow sigh like a train releasing steam at the end of a weary journey. "Our marriage has been dissolved by the

15

courts. Your mother and I are divorced."

"But that's so heartless! Marriage vows promise 'in sickness and in health until death do you part.' How could you even dream of abandoning Mother when she's ill? That's so cold and . . . and cruel . . . and—"

He gripped my shoulders and gave them a gentle shake. "Stop the theatrics, Violet, and listen to me. Your mother was never ill. She left home of her own free will."

"Never ill? Of course she was ill! She—"

He shook his head. "She hated her life with me, hated living in a small town like Lockport, hated being tied down. So I let her go."

"That means . . . That means you lied to me?"

"You were a child. I thought at the time that it would be kinder to lie than to tell you the truth. But the fact of the matter is, she abandoned us."

"I don't believe you," I said in a whisper. Then my voice grew louder and louder as my shock turned to anger. "If you admit that you lied eleven years ago, why should I believe anything you tell me now?"

"I'm sorry, Violet. I'll show you the divorce papers when we get home, if you'd like, but I'm telling you the truth."

I demanded to see them. We went straight into Father's study the moment we arrived home, still wearing our cloaks. Father removed a sheaf of papers from his desk drawer. The top one bore the official seal of the State of Illinois, and I saw several sentences that all began with *Whereas*. Then I saw my mother's name: Angeline Cepak Hayes. Beneath the printed type was her signature—bold, flamboyant.

Alive.

I remembered her then—the woman she had been long ago when I was very young, not the tired, sad woman who had gone away. Her dark, untamed hair, so like my own, had been a wild tangle of curls. I'd inherited my dark eyes from her as well. She had worn bright, silky clothing that had blazed with color, and I remembered how she had danced with me, lifting me into her arms and laughing as we whirled breathlessly around the parlor. She smelled like roses.

"I'm sorry, Violet," Father said again. "I should have told you the truth years ago."

I glimpsed a Chicago address beneath Mother's name before Father whisked away the papers and stuffed them into the drawer. I stared at my father as if at a stranger as I struggled to grasp the truth.

"Why didn't you tell me?" I murmured.

He took a moment to reply, silently fingering his watch chain. When he spoke, his voice sounded hushed. "I'm sorry. . . . I think . . . I think I always hoped she would come home to us again."

Chapter

2

I couldn't fall asleep that night. I had too much information to digest along with Maude's indigestible mutton. My stomach ached in protest.

Father's engagement to Widow O'Neill had shocked me badly. But to suddenly learn that my real mother hadn't been ill all these years but had abandoned us to live in Chicago—I couldn't comprehend it. My mother was a traitor, my father a traitor *and* a liar. Where did that leave me?

I had to stop Father's wedding, of course. I'd always thought of the two of us as happy, living a quiet, comfortable life in our home on the hill overlooking the canal in Lockport. We had Mrs. Hutchins to keep house for us and cook our meals—wasn't that enough for my father? How in the world could he expect me to share him with a stringy widow and her dreadful children, Homely and Horrid? I had decided I would secretly refer to Harriet and Horace by those more appropriate names. Yes, I must stop the wedding at all costs. But how?

I climbed out of bed and lit the gas lamp, then retrieved my journal from under my mattress and opened it to a clean page. I wrote *PREVENT FATHER'S MARRIAGE!!!* in bold letters across the top and underlined it three times, breaking the pencil point in the process. I found another pencil and numbered the page from one to ten.

What to do? What to do?

Perhaps with a little detective work I could prove that Maude had murdered her first husband and send her and her odious offspring to prison for the rest of their lives. Homely and Horrid had been accomplices—I was certain of it.

I wrote:

#1. Investigate Mr. O'Neill's death, then added: *(Re-read* The Adventures of Sherlock Holmes *and* Allan Pinkerton's *detective book for inspiration.)*

I spent the next ten minutes drumming the pencil against the page as I searched in vain for another idea.

When my head began to ache from thinking too hard, I turned off the lamp, climbed beneath the covers again with my journal and pencil, and pondered the second piece of shocking news I'd received: My mother had abandoned us.

For eleven years, I'd imagined Mother pining away in a stark sanitarium as she valiantly struggled to regain her health and come home to us. The scene always scintillated in dazzling light: *White hospital walls, white sheets, white-clad nurses, and Mother in the middle of it all, her skin as pale as alabaster, clothed in a frothy white nightgown. She kept a photograph of Father and me at her bedside, and she wept with longing whenever she gazed at it.*

Now, with three cold, blunt words, my father had shattered that ethereal image.

She abandoned us.

It couldn't be true. Why would Mother do such a thing? What

was wrong with me that had made her decide to leave? I couldn't recall being a demanding or difficult child, but perhaps my memory was faulty.

I closed my eyes, trying to remember what life had been like before my mother left us. Days and days would go by when she wouldn't get out of bed—which surely meant that she was ill, didn't it? Father hired a young Swedish girl who barely spoke English to take care of me during that time, and Mrs. Hutchins had cooked and cleaned for us for as far back as I could recall. But I remembered crying one day and throwing a temper tantrum because it was Mrs. Hutchins' day off and I was hungry. I escaped from my Viking jailer and tugged on Mother's limp arm as I tried to rouse her from her lethargy, demanding that she get out of bed and fix me some lunch. What I really wanted was for her to get dressed in one of her rainbow-hued gypsy dresses and whirl around the parlor with me, laughing the way she used to do. Had my tantrum driven her away that day? I wished I knew.

In the wee hours of the morning, after covering my diary page with dark, impassioned doodles, I realized that if I found my mother I could solve both of my dilemmas at the same time. She would see that I was a young woman now, a graduate of Madame Beauchamps' School for Young Ladies and no longer prone to temper fits. Once I convinced her to come home, Father would have no reason to marry Murderous Maude. And if Mother still wouldn't come home, I could escape from my father's impending marriage by moving to Chicago to live with her.

But how in the world would I find her?

Getting permission to travel alone to Chicago would be my first hurdle. I would figure out how to find Mother once I arrived.

I remained in bed until eleven o'clock the next morning. When I finally did rise, I refused to write Maude a proper thank-you note for last night's dinner. I also refused to speak to my father for an entire day.

I was sitting alone in the parlor after supper, reading a proper, boring novel, when Herman Beckett came to call. Herman was an earnest young man of twenty-three and my only suitor, so far. I hadn't decided if I would allow the courtship to continue or not. Herman worked as a clerk for a shipping company, and on our first outing I made the mistake of asking him which commodities his company shipped and where he shipped them. His answer proved so long and boring that I actually dozed off for a moment. Madame B. would have poked me with her parasol for committing such a social *faux pas*.

"Good evening, Miss Hayes," Mr. Beckett said upon arriving at our door. He bowed as if his dark, dreary suit was too tight and might split at the seams. "I was taking my evening constitutional and thought I would pay you a visit. We could get to know one another a little better—that is, if you're free to accept callers."

If he hadn't explained his purpose, I would have guessed by his somber expression and sober attire that he was on his way to a wake rather than paying a social visit. I weighed the merits of my boring book against an hour spent with Herman and decided to invite him to come inside. Father came out of his study to chat with Herman while I fetched glasses of cider for Herman and me. My traitorous father could fetch his own cider.

When I returned, Father retreated into his study across the hall from the parlor, leaving both doors wide open, of course. It took only a few minutes of idle chitchat to discover that I had made a poor choice; Herman was even more boring than my book had been. I had to do something—and quickly—in order to stay conscious.

"If you could choose," I asked him during a long, embarrassing pause in the conversation, "would you rather be a horse or a carriage?"

My friend Ruth and I used to entertain each other for hours debating questions such as this one, but Herman gripped his cider glass with both hands and bolted upright in his chair as if the fate of the world might depend on his reply.

"I-I don't understand."

"It's a simple question. If you could choose, which one would you rather be? There are advantages and disadvantages to each, you see. A horse is alive and can fall in love with another horse and have baby horses—"

"Oh my! Miss Hayes!" His face turned a remarkable shade of red.

"A carriage can't fall in love, but it has the advantage of traveling to exciting, faraway places and conveying interesting people—perhaps even royalty. So which would you choose?"

He gulped a mouthful of cider, as if stalling for time, then said, "I-I wouldn't care to be either one."

Herman didn't get it. I would have to make the game simpler. "Okay, then. Would you rather be unbelievably handsome but poor, or enormously rich but disfigured?"

This time his reply came quickly. "I'd rather be myself, thank you." He frowned in a way that made his bushy black eyebrows meet in the middle, forming one long caterpillar-like eyebrow. I wanted to point out that the frown was quite unbecoming, but the resemblance to a caterpillar reminded me of another one of Ruth's favorite questions.

"What's the most disgusting thing you've ever eaten, Mr. Beckett? I hear that in some countries people eat things like insects and dogs and cats. Would you sample one if given the opportunity?"

"No."

"What if you were *starving*? Or if you were a missionary to a pagan country and they offered caterpillars to you, and you had to accept them in order to be polite? What if your missionary endeavors would suffer if you didn't eat one?"

"I hardly think—"

"At Madame Beauchamps' school she once served snails because she wanted us to learn what the special fork was used for and how to handle it properly. Madame is from France, you see, and snails are a delicacy over there. As soon as Madame tugged one from its shell my friend Ruth gagged at the sight of the slimy thing and had to leave the table. None of the other girls wanted to eat one, but I removed my snail from the shell with great ease and gulped it right down. It wasn't so bad. The only thing I could taste was the garlic butter. The snail was so slippery that it slid right down—"

"Please, Miss Hayes."

"What's wrong?"

"I'm beginning to feel quite ill."

I refused to give up. "So what was the most . . . *adventuresome* . . . thing you've ever eaten?" His mouth hung open, but no sound came out. "How about buffalo, Mr. Beckett? Would you eat a buffalo steak? They serve them out west, you know."

Herman didn't reply. He obviously had no imagination at all. I could see that a lifetime with him would be uneventful and predictable. Surprises would fall into the same category as typhoid fever: something to be avoided at all costs. I felt grateful to have discovered this truth about Herman now rather than after I'd consented to marry him. I would sooner become a spinster than spend a lifetime with a boring, unimaginative man.

Had that been the reason my mother had left us? My father could be boring and pedantic too. *"She hated her life with me,"* my father had said, *"hated living in such a small town."* Had the monotony so wearied her that she simply had to leave? But then why not take me with her? *"She hated being tied down,"* Father had said. That must have included me. I must have tied her down.

"Miss Hayes?" Herman was staring at me as if I had devoured an entire bucketful of snails.

"I'd much rather eat buffalo," I told him, "than dine on—" I nearly slipped and mentioned Maude O'Neill's mutton, which had been as tough and tasteless as horsehide—not that I've ever tasted horsehide, mind you. But just in time, I recalled Maude's friendship with Herman's mother. I remembered the plans I had outlined in my journal last night to investigate her husband's death and decided to steer the conversation in a different direction.

"That reminds me, Herman. I understand that we have a mutual acquaintance, Maude O'Neill?"

"Why, yes. My family knows her very well."

"It's so tragic that she was widowed at such a young age, isn't it? I was away at school when her husband died, so I'm not sure I ever heard the cause of his demise."

"It was most unfortunate, I'm sorry to say. He tumbled down the cellar stairs and struck his head."

Ah ha! Just as I thought! Murderous Maude had pushed him! Homely and Horrid had probably strewn objects in his path to aggravate his fall, and greased the handrail for good measure. I masked my glee with what I hoped was a look of horror.

"How perfectly awful for Mrs. O'Neill! I hope she wasn't home at the time."

"I'm afraid she was. She sent poor little Harriet to fetch Dr. Bigelow, but he arrived too late."

Probably *hours* too late—and only after Maude had caved in his skull with a sledgehammer for good measure. I was deep in thought, pondering these highly suspicious circumstances, when Herman cleared his throat again.

"Did I mention that I'm going to Chicago to see the World's Columbian Exposition?"

"Really? When?" I handled the abrupt change in topics with finesse, taking care not to reveal the fact that I was investigating Mr. O'Neill's murder.

"I plan to go next month, when the weather warms up a bit."

Herman blathered on and on about the fair's architectural marvels and educational wonders until, once again, his monotone began to induce a hypnotic stupor. My eyes watered from stifling yawns.

"Are you and your father planning to visit the fair, Miss Hayes?"

His question gave me a brilliant idea: I could use the Exposition as an excuse to travel to Chicago and find my mother! I would begin badgering my father to go immediately.

As soon as Herman finished his cider—I didn't offer him a refill—and I'd closed the front door behind him, I turned to my father, who had ambled out to the foyer to bid Herman good-night.

"Herman is going to Chicago to visit the Exposition this summer. I would very much like to go as well."

"It so happens I've planned a trip to Chicago. I thought that we all could go."

"*All* of us? You don't mean Maude and her children?"

"Well, yes—"

"Father, please—no! I don't want to go with them. I'm a grown woman, not a child like Homely and Horrid." I didn't realize that I had used my secret names for them until I saw Father's shocked expression.

"Violet! I'm surprised at you."

"Sorry," I muttered.

"It's unlike you to be cruel, Violet. Are you . . . might you be . . . a bit jealous of them?"

"Certainly not! They're children and I'm a grown woman—and that's the point I'm trying to make, don't you see? Maude spoke last evening as if we will all settle down and become one happy family, but her expectations aren't realistic. I won't be linking hands with her little urchins as we skip through the Exposition with a picnic basket. I would much rather see the fair with companions who are my own age."

"I understand. But it's out of the question for you to accompany Mr. Beckett without a chaperone."

"What about Grandmother? Why couldn't I spend a few weeks in Chicago visiting with her?" The idea came to me in a flash of genius. My father could hardly argue that his own mother was an unfit chaperone. Grandmother kept quite busy working for several charitable causes, so I was certain that I could slip away from her for a few hours to search for my mother once I was in Chicago.

"I don't think that's wise, Violet. Your grandmother doesn't need the added responsibility of watching over you. She has enough to deal with as it is, with her sisters."

"But I wouldn't be any trouble at all. There's plenty of room for me in that huge old house. Please, Father? Grandmother is always inviting me to come and stay with her every time she writes. Why won't you ever let me go?"

Father paused as if carefully phrasing his reply. "You're a very . . . impressionable . . . young lady. I fear that the Howell sisters would have a disruptive influence on you."

His words intrigued me. Here was another mystery to solve. How could my devout grandmother and her three aging sisters possibly have a bad influence on me? I was more determined than ever to go—just to find out. I chose my next words with care.

"You began courting Widow O'Neill while I was away at school and never breathed a word of it to me. Instead, you've sprung the news of your engagement on me without any warning and without ever asking for my opinion on the matter. Next, I discover that you've been lying to me about Mother for more than ten years, telling me that she's ill when it seems she isn't ill at all. Taking all of this into consideration, one might say that you've been extremely unfair to me. And faced with such lies and betrayals, one might simply decide to leave home unannounced—*and* without a chaperone." I had delivered a threat without raising my voice. Madame Beauchamps would have approved.

"I never intended to hurt you, Violet, I thought that—"

"Then you might show your remorse by treating me as a grown woman instead of a child. I'm merely asking to take a brief trip away from home to see the World's Columbian Exposition. Perhaps the time away will help me accustom myself to the new state of affairs here at home. And I'll be in the company of your own mother during that time."

"That's what worries me," he mumbled.

"Why? What's wrong with Grandmother?"

He gazed into the distance, slowly shaking his head. His eyes wore the vacant gaze of a stuffed elk.

"Father, why is it that we so rarely see Grandmother when she lives a mere train ride away in Chicago?"

"It's complicated, Violet. . . ." Father groped for the comfort of his watch chain, as if reaching for a weapon to defend himself.

I refused to back down. "May I travel to Chicago to visit with her or not?" He opened the watchcase and stared at the dial before snapping it closed again. I was quite certain that he couldn't have said what time it was.

"Let me think about it, Violet."

"Very well." I turned and glided regally up the stairs. "I will write a letter to Grandmother while I await your reply."

Chapter

3

I settled onto the stiff, velvety train seat, adjusting my skirts before waving a curt good-bye to my father, who stood outside on the platform. Then I turned my back on him. Maude O'Neill and her ill-behaved brats had accompanied us to the train station, and I had no wish to gaze upon them for another moment. She was not my mother and never would be. Homely and Horrid, who had entertained themselves by making ugly faces and rude noises at the other passengers, would never be my siblings. All in all, my send-off had been nearly unendurable. Maude talked on and on about Herman Beckett until I wanted to scream—in spite of everything I'd learned in school about proper manners.

"Mr. Beckett will be *so* lonely without you," she'd insisted. "I understand Mr. Beckett is eager to accompany you to the fair . . ." *Mr. Beckett this . . . and Mr. Beckett that!* If she had mentioned how "smitten" he was with me one more time I would have lost control and smitten her.

I had managed to hold my tongue by imagining what my real

mother would be like, and how she would handle my courtship to a bore like Herman Beckett. I convinced myself that any gentleman Mother picked out for me would be infinitely more exciting than Herman.

The more Maude had hovered over me, the more determined I became to find my real mother—even if it was the last thing I ever did. Once I found her, I would convince her to come back to Lockport to live with Father and me. Wouldn't Maude O'Neill be surprised when she invited herself to my welcome home reception and met the *real* Mrs. John Jacob Hayes?

Of course, I hadn't told Father that I intended to find my mother or he never would have allowed me to go to Chicago. I didn't inform Grandmother of my true plans either.

I wiggled in place, trying to make myself comfortable on the hard train seat, willing the whistle to blow and the train to hurry up and steam out of the station. I sensed Father's worried gaze on me through the window, and I feared that at any moment he would change his mind and charge onto the train to yank me off. It had required prodigious efforts of persuasion on my part before he allowed this trip in the first place. And he had nearly postponed it when no one could be found to accompany me on the train.

"A woman needs a gentleman to watch over her," he'd fussed. "Her husband or father or brother . . ."

"What for?" I had asked him. "I can watch out for myself well enough."

"It just isn't right. Who will handle your trunk and so forth? And what if there's a problem? You wouldn't know what to do."

"I know everything I need to know. I'll board the train in Lockport, sit in my seat—watched over by a very competent conductor—and get off at Union Depot, where Grandmother will be waiting for me. What could go wrong? Besides, the world is on the brink of a brand-new era, Father. We're about to enter the twentieth century, and young ladies are being allowed a bit more freedom. After all, I am twenty years old."

I'm not sure if I truly convinced him or if I simply wore him out. Either way, I was pleased when he'd finally consented and purchased my train ticket. I was slightly less pleased when he agreed to Herman Beckett's request to meet me in Chicago later in the month so he could take me to see the Columbian Exposition, accompanied by his married sister. I doubted if I ever could convince a man as unimaginative as Herman to help me find my mother. Besides, Herman's mother was Maude's friend, and they were certain to gossip about my activities in Chicago.

At last the train lurched forward and began to move. I risked a final glance out of the window and saw Maude cheerily waving her handkerchief as if I were a soldier leaving for the battlefield. Father looked very worried and sorry he had ever agreed to let me go. Little Horrid stuck out his tongue at me. I resisted the temptation to return the gesture.

As soon as the beige limestone train station was out of sight, I heaved a sigh of relief. Madame Beauchamps would have been appalled.

I was leaving Lockport, Illinois, behind and speeding toward Chicago. I felt like pinching myself to see if I was dreaming. I was riding the train into the city—alone! For the first time in my life I felt like an adult. I closed my eyes and imagined that I was running away. I had already decided that if I couldn't prevent Father's wedding, I wouldn't return home. After all, Father had lied to me—all these years!

It didn't take long for the view of flat, monotonous prairie land to bore me. I wondered if God had run out of ideas after creating the mountain ranges and the mighty Mississippi River and had nodded off when He was supposed to be designing the middle portion of America. Was Illinois the result of an unfortunate catnap? Or perhaps, in a gesture of beneficence, the Almighty had delegated the task to a less imaginative underling. If so, I hoped the underling had been fired for his lack of creativity.

As I continued to gaze at the uninspiring terrain, I tried to think of it as a symbol of the larger journey on which I had embarked. Our literature teacher had labored to interest us in things like symbolism and similes, but I confess such imagery bored me when compared to the graphic, lurid details I read about in Ruth's *Illustrated Police News*. But maybe it would help to think of my journey as symbolic: I was leaving my boring life behind along with the terrain and embarking on an exciting new life in Chicago.

To be honest, my stomach churned quite unpleasantly whenever I thought about what might lie ahead. Many of those shocking *True Crime Stories* I used to read had taken place in cities like Chicago, and I was keenly aware of the dangers that might await a young woman such as myself.

Eventually I grew tired of trying to dredge up symbolism from a boring view and I pulled a book from my satchel, settling back to read. I had barely begun the first chapter when I felt the train's momentum begin to slow, and a few minutes later we made a brief stop at the train station in Lemont. The village held little interest for me, but I spotted an intriguing traveling salesman—more commonly referred to as a drummer—waiting to board the train with his suitcase full of wares. I guessed his age to be about the same as Herman Beckett's, but the similarities began and ended right there. Herman dressed like an undertaker's assistant, while this man's unbecoming suit was as garish as a circus clown's, sewn from cheesy plaid material that sagged at the knees and had been worn to a shine on the elbows and rump.

I would have described him as good-looking if his smile wasn't so phony or his hair so slicked-back with Macassar oil that it reflected light. I watched him climb aboard and search for his seat, and he seemed to have absorbed the greasy oil through his scalp until it lubricated him from within. His movements were so smooth that he glided when he walked, as if his bones were as pliable as cheese. A

31

dime novel would have described him as "a slippery character."

I thought him wonderfully dangerous! Everyone warned innocent girls such as myself to stay far away from unsavory men like him. In fact, he was exactly the type of man that my father had worried about when I'd embarked on this trip. In short, the drummer fascinated me.

His restless eyes roved all around the passenger car as if searching for a hidden compartment or a clue to a mystery, and I saw his gaze slide over me a few times, lingering a trifle too long to be proper. I immediately looked away, pretending to read, but I confess that my heart raced with excitement.

He spoke in a very loud voice to the conductor and the other passengers—who seemed reluctant to converse with him. He laughed much too loudly. Once the train resumed its journey, he couldn't seem to settle down, stirring restlessly as if unable to sit still, crossing and uncrossing his legs. He opened his newspaper and began to read, making such a racket that the rustling pages sounded like a forest fire. He finally put the crumpled pages down again. He shifted the position of his sample case three times, opening it briefly to glance inside before stowing it beneath his seat again. At length, he removed a cigar from inside his jacket and left the coach.

I wondered if his unease was caused by a guilty conscience. What crime might he have committed to make him so unsettled? Murder? I must try to look for bloodstains beneath his fingernails when he returned. Theft? It seemed unlikely since he'd boarded the train with no luggage except his sample case. But diamonds were small—might he be a jewel thief?

Ten minutes later the drummer returned from the smoking car, bringing the aroma of cigars with him. I made the mistake of watching him glide down the aisle, and when he saw me he nodded in an overly familiar way. His manners were exceedingly improper and much too forward. His smile was what Madame Beauchamps had called a "candelabra grin."

"Never overdo your enthusiasm, girls, especially with members of the

opposite sex. A slender taper of light is all that one needs to send forth. Be mysterious and enigmatic." Ruth and I had practiced our *enigmatic* smiles in front of a mirror every night until we could no longer suppress our giggles.

I quickly looked away from the salesman's frank gaze, but once again, a thrill of excitement shivered through me. His crime must be adultery. He had what the romance novels referred to as "charisma." He probably knocked on weak-willed women's doors with his suitcase full of samples and sidled his way into their parlors . . . and their affections.

I didn't dare look up again. Instead, I rummaged through my satchel, pretending to search for something, and spotted my mother's address. I had tiptoed into Father's office while he was at work and found the divorce papers, then carefully copied down the address printed beneath Mother's signature. Tears filled my eyes at the memory of her flamboyant signature. It wasn't the handwriting of an invalid, but of a woman who was very much alive. And healthy enough to be a mother to me.

"She abandoned us," my father had said. The more I pondered the truth of her desertion, the smaller and more worthless I felt. No one discarded a treasure, did they? Only worthless things were left behind. Before I could stop them, my tears began to fall.

"Are you in distress, miss?"

I looked up to find the drummer hovering in the aisle beside my seat. My heart began to race, outpacing the train.

"I-I seem to have something in my eye," I lied, quickly applying my handkerchief. Lies must be a family trait.

"Want me to have a look and see if I can fish it out?"

"Um . . . no, thank you." The last thing I needed was a mysterious man gazing deeply into my eyes. I stole a quick glance at his face and saw that his eyes were as flashy as the rest of him, their color such a bright, clear shade of blue that they made me thirsty.

"My name's Silas—Silas McClure." He held out his hand for me to shake, evidently unaware that a gentleman always waited for a lady to offer her hand first—if at all. I couldn't be rude and leave it hanging in midair, so I briefly grasped his fingertips for a dainty shake.

"Violet Hayes." I hated my name the moment I spoke it. *Violet.* It sounded old-fashioned and as limp as velvet. I longed for a more dramatic name and decided that I would change it when I arrived in Chicago. I would introduce myself as Athena or Artemesia or maybe Anastasia. "How do you do, Mr. McClure?"

"I do just fine. . . . Say, don't tell me, let me guess—I'll wager you're going to Chicago to see the fair. Am I right?"

"Um . . . yes. Are you going as well?"

"I've already seen it—three times, in fact. But I'm going again, first chance I get." He propped one foot on the seat that faced mine and folded his arms on his raised knee. "The fair is really swell. I could give you some pointers—what to see and what's a waste of time—if you want me to."

Before I could reply, he dropped his leg and slid into the seat facing me, perching on the very edge so that our knees were practically touching. His manners were outrageous! I imagined Madame Beauchamps flapping her hands as if shooing away pigeons and saying, *"No, no, no, Miss Hayes! You must never, never accept advances from such a creature."* Anyone unsavory was a *creature* to Madame B.

But in the next moment, I found myself wondering whether to believe Madame or not. If my father had lied to me my entire life, why should I obey anything else I'd been taught? Anger swelled inside me, making it difficult to speak. I had felt it growing in strength since the night I'd first learned about Maude and about my mother, slowly rising and expanding like bread dough in a warming oven. The more I thought about the wedding, the deplorable stepchildren, and my father's lies, the more I wanted to punch something the way Mrs. Hutchins punched the rising bread dough so she could shape it into loaves.

The safe cocoon in which I'd been wrapped all my life suddenly felt suffocating. Madame had taught me to be a proper young lady, demure and sedate, but beneath the surface I longed to fly as freely as a butterfly, to do something bold and daring. I scooped up my satchel and placed it on my lap to make room for Mr. McClure on the seat beside me. I even patted the cushion lightly, beckoning him to sit there.

"I would love to hear all about the fair. But please, tell me all about yourself first, Mr. McClure."

"Well, I'm a drummer, as you can probably guess," he said, dropping into the seat. "I sell Dr. Dean's Blood Builder—a nutritive tonic."

"Is it really made from *blood*?"

"No," he said, laughing. "Our specially patented formula is made from the highest-quality beef extract, fortified with iron and celery root. If you're suffering from extreme exhaustion, brain fatigue, debility of any kind, blood disorders, or anemia, our Blood Builder will enrich your blood and help your body throw off accumulated humors of all kinds. It's guaranteed to stimulate digestion and improve blood flow, or we'll give you your money back. Why, we have testimonials from thousands of satisfied customers, people who've suffered all sorts of maladies from nervous exhaustion and weakness to general debilitation. You can find inferior goods anywhere, these days—at twice the price of our tonic, I might add. But only Dr. Dean's Blood Builder offers a thirty-day money-back guarantee. You should try it, Miss Hayes. I'll wager you'll feel renewed, or I'll refund your money."

"Your presentation is quite convincing, Mr. McClure. Do you use the tonic yourself?"

"Of course."

He did appear unusually healthy and robust, and so filled with energy that he could scarcely stay in his seat. Hoards of army ants might have been crawling up his pant legs. I wasn't sure I wanted to have that much vigor. I imagined it would feel quite uncomfortable to be so energetic—and completely unladylike.

"Do you enjoy the life of a traveling salesman, Mr. McClure?"

"Oh, I love riding the rails. There's a new adventure around every corner. I could never stand being a clerk, cooped up in an office all day."

I thought of Herman Beckett.

"And you mentioned the fair—did you find it as exciting as you had hoped?"

"Oh, boy! And then some! Make sure you ride Mr. Ferris' wheel when you go. What a thrill! I happened to be there on the day they gave it the very first test run. They had only attached the first six cars, you see, and nobody had ever ridden it before. It wasn't even open to the public yet, and nobody knew if passengers would even live through the experience. But Mr. Ferris' wife volunteered to be the first one to try it, and she climbed into the first car like she was going for a Sunday afternoon carriage ride. Well, when we saw her going up in the air, the whole crowd of us pushed forward to get onboard the second car— even though the wheel's operators were hollering at us to get back."

"How did you know it was safe if it had never carried passengers before? Weren't you frightened?"

"I was having too much fun to be scared. Although I did have second thoughts for a moment when a bunch of loose nuts and bolts started showering down on us like hailstones. And the gears made a terrible racket at first, crunching and grinding like they were about to give out. But then the car started climbing, up and up, until I had the best view I wager I'll ever see." He gazed into the distance as if seeing it all over again.

"You can see the whole fair from up there, Miss Hayes, all laid out like a little toy village. Lake Michigan is in the distance, and the skyline of the city . . . Well, it takes your breath clean away. As soon as I reached the bottom and stepped off, I wanted to get right back on and ride it all over again. Everyone else had the same idea, and there was a huge rush to get on board—even though the wheel wasn't officially open. Like I said, they had only attached the first six cars at the time. But I managed to squeeze my way forward and go for a second ride—and I would have jumped on and gone around a third time, but the men operating it finally said that if any more people forced their way on board, they'd run us up to the top and leave us there for the night. That wheel is one of the Seven Wonders of the World—or are there eight wonders? I forget . . . Anyhow, nothing like it has ever been attempted before."

"It sounds exhilarating!" I wondered if Herman Beckett would dare to go for a ride. I made up my mind that I would ride the wheel, with or without him. "You should have been an explorer, Mr. McClure!"

His daring proved so contagious that in the next moment I found myself asking, "If you could choose, would you rather perish in a terrible cataclysm such as a train wreck or a collapsing Ferris wheel and die amid twisted iron and splintered wood, hearing the screams of trapped and suffering humanity—or would you prefer to die a long, slow death at home in your bed, your body growing ever thinner, your breath leaving you in painful gasps?"

His eyes widened, slightly, and I saw him lean almost imperceptibly away from me. "You have quite an imagination, Miss Hayes."

I was too caught up in my own drama to notice that I had shocked him. "I think I would rather die quickly and spectacularly," I said. "If I were given the choice."

"Would you, now? Well . . . let's hope today isn't the day. Anyhow, it looks like we're getting close to the city." He nodded his glossy head toward the window where the view of the prairie had changed to one of factories and warehouses and the backs of buildings. While we had been conversing, the brilliant sky had gradually dimmed to a dull gray, like tarnish on fine silver, and the air had taken on the unmistakable odor of the stockyards.

"May I ask, Miss Hayes—if I'm not being too pushy—would you consider going to the fair with me the next time I'm in Chicago? I'd love to show you around."

"I would enjoy that very much." Father would be scandalized, but I didn't care. I gave Silas McClure an encouraging smile, but he seemed to be waiting for something more. "Was there anything else you wanted to ask, Mr. McClure?"

"I'll need to know where you're staying, Miss Hayes."

"Oh, how silly of me." He gave me one of his calling cards, and I copied down Grandmother's address for him on the back of it. Then the conductor entered the car, toddling down the aisle, punching tickets. Mr. McClure returned to his seat and his suitcase full of tonic as the train slowed. My heart raced with anticipation as I glimpsed Chicago's towering buildings.

I gathered my belongings and crowded into the aisle with the other passengers once the train stopped. The conductor placed a small stool below the passenger car, and he offered me his hand to help me down. The air stank of rotting garbage and hot metal as I hurried down the long platform, following the others.

As soon as I entered the cavernous Union Depot, I began looking around for my grandmother. I heard joyful salutations and saw warm embraces and even tears as the other passengers met their loved ones, but there was no such greeting for me. Even Mr. McClure had been welcomed by two unsavory-looking men in dark coats and bowler hats.

Where could my grandmother be? I visited so infrequently that perhaps we'd failed to recognize each other. But eventually the lobby cleared as porters and baggage agents hefted suitcases and trunks, conveying them to waiting carriages and drays. My fellow passengers hurried away to their destinations. And there I stood, quite alone.

"Is this yours, miss?" I turned to find a baggage porter pointing to my steamer trunk, now loaded onto a cart. He was waiting for his tip, no doubt, but I had no idea how much money to offer him. I had only a few dollars to my name.

"Yes, that's my trunk. My family should be along any minute to fetch me." He rolled his eyes before drifting away.

My earlier euphoria vanished as I realized my helplessness. I had been abandoned. I was lost and alone in an unfamiliar city with little money. I didn't know what to do. Madame Beauchamps may have taught me proper social etiquette, but I was thoroughly unprepared for real life.

I wandered as far as I dared without losing sight of my trunk and saw people rushing to catch their trains, newsboys selling papers, and ragged urchins who probably were waiting to pick pockets or snatch purses. Where could Grandmother be?

Time passed, and still she didn't come. I stood alone, guarding my trunk, for what felt like hours. What if night fell and I was left here with no one to protect me from the ravages of beastly men? What if a stranger abducted me at knifepoint or even gunpoint! I recalled one of Ruth's true crime stories where a man assaulted an innocent maiden in the most dreadful way and—

"Miss Hayes?" When the male voice spoke close behind me I nearly leaped from my skin. "Hey, sorry. I didn't mean to scare you." It was the drummer, Silas McClure. If he hadn't gripped my arm I would have run straight out the door and into the path of an on-coming train. "You need a lift somewhere?" he asked.

"My family is supposed to be here to fetch me." I looked around again as I battled my tears and tried to slow my galloping heart. "I can't imagine why they're so late."

"I'll wager they're stuck in traffic. I've seen snarls so bad it takes ten policemen to unravel them. You get a bunch of wagons and car-riages and streetcars all trying to go one way, see. And they crowd right up against each other like freight cars. But the cross traffic is trying to go forward at the same time and so they meet in the mid-dle." He gestured with his hands to show the resulting collision. "There's no room for anybody to go around because you got wagons and carriages parked along both sides of the street. Then you toss in a bunch of pedestrians trying to get across the road, and pushcarts and newsboys, and—well, you can see that you got a real mess in no time at all. Once they all get jammed up in the middle of the inter-section like that, nobody can move."

"That sounds awful."

"Yeah, I'll wager that's what happened. But I'd be happy to help you hail a cab, if you'd like."

"What happened to your two friends?"

"Huh? Oh . . . don't worry about them. They had business elsewhere."

My fear battled with my anger. I had been cruelly abandoned once again. First my mother had deserted me, then Father had decided to shove me aside for Maude and her impertinent imps, now my grandmother was taking her turn. My fury made me courageous. I would leave the whole lot of them behind and go straight to my mother's house. I pulled her address from my satchel and showed it to Mr. McClure.

"Are you familiar with the city—do you have any idea where this address might be?"

He studied it for a moment, scratching his glossy head. I hoped his fingers didn't leave grease marks on the paper and cause the ink to run. "It's not too far from here, Miss Hayes. I believe it's in the downtown area."

"Would it cost much? To take a cab there, I mean. I don't have very much money, and I have no idea what a cab would cost." Once again, I wished Madame B. had taught us practical information.

"It can't be more than two bits or a half-dollar. But you can always take a streetcar if you're worried about money."

"What about my trunk?"

He turned to look at it and made a face. "I'll wager you won't get that thing on a streetcar. You'll need a cab for sure. Listen, do you want me to tag along?"

"Would you? Don't you have your own business to attend to?"

"Nothing that can't wait. I'm always happy to help a lovely damsel in distress."

He grinned his wide candelabra grin as he offered me his arm, reminding me of a picture from one of my childhood storybooks: a wolf, dressed in a nightgown and floppy cap, smiling at Little Red Riding Hood. *"Grandmother! What big teeth you have!"*

But what other choice did I have?

"Thank you, Mr. McClure. I'll accept your kind offer."

I tossed all of my common sense to the wind and took Silas McClure's arm. I was about to hail a cab with a traveling tonic salesman and drive to an unknown address. But before we could get the baggage porter's attention, someone called my name.

"Violet! Violet Rose!"

My grandmother hurried toward me out of breath, towing my great-aunt Bertha by the hand. Relief settled over me like warm bath water the moment I saw them. Grandmother drew me into her embrace, obviously as relieved to see me as I was to see her.

"I'm so sorry, dear. We made a terrible mistake and went to the wrong train station. And the traffic gets so tangled up this time of day. Thank goodness you're all right."

She finally released me and waved to the baggage agent. He raced over to fetch my trunk and his long-awaited tip. Mr. McClure watched the drama in bemused silence as if viewing a theatrical production. Then I saw my grandmother looking him over and I remembered my manners.

"Grandmother, I'd like you to meet a friend of mine, Mr. Silas McClure. . . . This is my grandmother, Mrs. Florence Hayes, and her sister, Mrs. Bertha Casey."

Grandmother nodded politely. "How do you do, Mr. McClure."

"I do just fine."

Aunt Bertha gave me a fervent hug. Then, much to Silas' surprise, she proceeded to hug him too. She was opening her arms to embrace the baggage agent when Grandmother said, "No, no, Birdie, dear. That gentleman isn't an acquaintance of ours."

My aunt Bertha's sisters had nicknamed her Bertie, but when I was a child I thought they were saying *Birdie*. The name seemed to fit her, and she had been known as Birdie ever since. She always wore a dreamy smile on her face and a faraway look in her eyes, her brows raised in gentle surprise, as if she were listening to a pleasant conversation that only she could hear. Her expression was so unchanging that I often wondered if the faint smile and uplifted brows were there while she slept. She had seemed childlike to me when I was younger, more of a playmate than an adult. Now that I was older, she just seemed odd.

"Are you heading off to the war?" she asked the baggage clerk, "or returning home from it?"

"That's a railroad uniform he's wearing," Grandmother told her, "not an army uniform."

"Oh, how nice. My husband, Gilbert, is fighting with General McClellan in the Peninsula Campaign, you know. He wants to help Mr. Lincoln free the slaves."

I waited for my grandmother to correct her. I knew that Aunt Birdie's husband had been killed in the War Between the States. But Grandmother linked arms with her sister and said, "Come, Birdie, we need to take Violet home. She must be exhausted from her trip."

How could she deceive poor, naïve Aunt Birdie? Father had lied

43

to me the same way, and it infuriated me. But before I had a chance to speak up, my grandmother turned to Mr. McClure and said, "Thank you so much for accompanying my granddaughter. It was kind of you to wait here with her when I'm sure you must be anxious to see your own family. I trust we'll be seeing you again soon?"

Grandmother had mistaken Mr. McClure for Herman Beckett! My father must have told her that a suitor would be escorting me to the Exposition and she thought Silas was the one. I decided to let my grandmother assume whatever she wished. Fortunately, Mr. McClure's mouth had dropped open in surprise and he hadn't responded.

"Yes, Mr. McClure will be calling on us in the very near future. Isn't that right?" I asked him, gently nudging his arm.

He smiled his ornate grin and said, "I wouldn't miss it for the world."

We arrived home an hour later to find my great-aunt Matilda pacing in the front foyer like a circus lion. "I was beginning to think something terrible had happened. Was the train late? If women ran the world, the trains would all run on time, you know."

"The train was on time," Grandmother told her. "Birdie and I were the ones who were late. We went to Dearborn Station instead of Union Depot."

Aunt Matilda glared at Grandmother as if she deserved a rap on the knuckles with a hickory stick. To tell you the truth, I had always been a little afraid of my great-aunt Matilda—Aunt Matt for short. She was the oldest of the four Howell sisters and still a spinster. She always wore a look of displeasure, as if spoiling for a fight, her eyebrows knit together, her mouth downturned. She seemed perpetually disgusted with life in general and with men in particular. To Aunt Matt, men were the chief perpetrators of everything unfair.

"If women ran the world . . ." she would insist, *"tea wouldn't be so expensive . . . the politicians would be honest . . . the sun would set at a more convenient hour . . ."* She held her hands curled tightly into fists,

her knuckles white, as if she needed to be prepared at all times to punch someone.

"Well, dinner's ready," she said with a sniff. "We'd better eat it before it's thoroughly ruined."

"Dinner can wait five more minutes," Grandmother told her. "I believe Violet Rose would like to freshen up after her journey."

"Well, don't blame me if the food is stone-cold."

"We won't, Mattie, dear. It's my fault entirely. I had no idea there were two train stations in Chicago."

"If women ran the world, there would be only one station so people wouldn't get confused." Aunt Matt marched into the dining room like a general charging into battle, shoulders set, head thrust forward.

"Come, Violet," Grandmother said, steering me away. "I asked the driver to carry your steamer trunk up to your room." As she led me down the front hall, Aunt Birdie stopped us.

"Would you like to stay for dinner?" she asked me in her fluttery voice. "I'm sure we have plenty of food."

"I am staying for dinner, Aunt Birdie. I'm staying for a month, in fact."

"Oh, how nice."

The tall case clock in the foyer chimed six o'clock as I followed Grandmother upstairs to the guest room. I loved this grand old house. My great-grandfather, the Honorable Judge Porter C. Howell, had built the graceful Greek Revival-style home in 1830 and raised my grandmother and her three sisters here. Grandmother, Aunt Birdie, and Aunt Matt still lived here, while the fourth sister, Aunt Agnes, lived across town with her husband.

According to my father, this house had narrowly escaped the Great Fire that destroyed much of Chicago more than twenty years ago, the flames halting a mere city block away. Great-grandfather Howell had deeded the house to Aunt Matilda, who had never married. Aunt Birdie had moved in after her husband died in the war, and my grandmother joined them when her husband died. It remained a mystery to me why my grandmother hadn't moved in with Father and me, since my mother had already left us by then.

I was very hungry, so I washed quickly using the pitcher and bowl on my washstand, then tidied my hair. On my way down to the dinner table, I paused to peek into the other bedrooms, glimpsing how very different the Howell sisters were from one another. My grandmother's room resembled a monk's cell, with bare wood floors, a simple dresser and mirror, and a plain white spread on the narrow bed. A spare wooden cross was the only wall decoration.

Aunt Birdie's room across the hall was packed to the ceiling with color and pattern and ornately carved furniture. A scarlet Turkish rug stretched across the floor; pink floral wallpaper clashed with framed botanical prints and lush landscapes; a red floral bedspread and dozens of tapestry pillows covered the bed; and gold brocade curtains hung on the windows. Jammed into the room beside the four-poster bed were two dressers, a wardrobe, a mirrored dressing table, two end tables, two slipper chairs, and a washstand, barely leaving room to walk.

Aunt Matt's bedroom on the first floor had once been my great-grandfather's study—and it still resembled one except for the quilt-covered daybed shoved against one wall. A massive desk, buried beneath piles and piles of papers, took up most of the room. Glass-fronted barrister's shelves filled with my great-grandfather's books lined two walls. I had no idea where Aunt Matt kept her clothing; the room had neither dresser nor wardrobe. I suppose it didn't matter because she always looked the same to me and might well have owned only one dress: high collared, ankle length, prim, and black.

The three women had filled the remaining rooms of the house with the accumulated possessions of all their lives, and I had fun trying to guess which items belonged to whom.

I slipped into my place at the mahogany dining table, where the Howell sisters sat waiting for me. We bowed our heads as Grandmother said grace.

"Did Father tell you he's planning to remarry?" I blurted moments after Grandmother said "Amen."

"Oh, how nice," Aunt Birdie said. "I love weddings."

Aunt Matt huffed in disgust. "I'll never understand why any woman in this modern era would feel the need to subject herself to a man's control."

"Yes, your father told me he'd met someone," Grandmother said with a sigh. She rested her hand on my arm in a gesture of comfort. My grandmother used her hands more than any person I knew—touching, caressing, or gently laying them on someone's shoulder or arm. When her hands weren't soothing they were working: scrubbing, baking, cleaning, cooking. Then when her other work was finished, she would sit in the parlor to do her darning, mending, crocheting, or knitting. *"Idle hands are the devil's playthings,"* she often insisted.

I took another bite of mashed potatoes and returned to the subject of my father, hoping to win my devout grandmother as an ally. "Have you given his marriage your blessing?" I asked. "I would think that divorce and remarriage are against your religious principles."

"Your father didn't ask for my opinion, dear—or my blessing."

"Well, did you know that he's been lying to me all these years, telling me that my mother was ill? I learned only this month that she hasn't been sick at all. And now he has divorced her!"

"I gather you don't think much of his decision to remarry. Do you know this Mrs. O'Neill very well?"

"I hate Maude O'Neill!" I said, banging my fist on the table and rattling the silverware. There. I'd spoken the truth. Grandmother laid her hand on my arm once again.

"The Bible says we mustn't hate anyone, Violet Rose."

"Hatred is what's causing this terrible War Between the States," Aunt Birdie added.

I might have known my grandmother would react this way. She was the walking embodiment of the fruit of the Spirit, carrying love, joy, peace, and all the rest around with her as if toting an invisible basket, passing them out freely to everyone she met.

"Please don't let hatred overtake you, Violet." Jesus' eyes must have looked just like my grandmother's: kind, loving, sorrowful, or sometimes filled with righteous indignation—over the very same things that moved my grandmother. She turned her woeful Jesus eyes on me now until I had to look away in shame.

"I'm sorry," I mumbled. "But I can't help disliking Maude. Father gave me no warning at all. I arrived home from boarding school one day, and he announced his engagement the very next evening."

"Marriage is bondage," Aunt Matt declared. "This widow ought to think twice before sacrificing her freedom. Did she inherit any property from her late husband?"

"She has a house . . . and two perfectly wretched children."

"My husband adores children," Aunt Birdie said dreamily. "We plan to have a large family once he returns from the war. He has to conquer Richmond and defeat Robert E. Lee first."

"Maybe I should have a word with this Widow O'Neill," Aunt Matt said. "Someone needs to tell her how much she stands to lose if she remarries."

"Oh, I wish you would speak to her, Aunt Matt." If anyone could frighten Maude into canceling the wedding, it was my militant Aunt Matt.

"Now, Mattie," Grandmother said, "you know John would never allow you to interfere with his life—"

"Did you know," Aunt Matt continued, "that when a woman marries, her property, her wages, and her inheritance all become the property of her husband?"

"No, I didn't," I said in surprise. "I think someone had better warn Maude right away before—"

"There are poor women in this city who labor for twelve hours a day in sweatshops and factories, yet by law, their drunken husbands can take their wages straight to the saloon and indulge themselves with what she's earned by the sweat of her brow, leaving her and her children to starve."

I had never heard Aunt Matt express her views so strongly. Perhaps it was because I'd never visited my grandmother's house alone before. My father always accompanied me. He was probably the reason my aunts never talked about my mother. I decided to steer the conversation back to her.

"I think I deserve to know something about my mother."

"She was ravishingly beautiful," Aunt Birdie said, gazing into the air above our heads. "She was Juliet to Johnny's Romeo." I waited to hear more, but Aunt Birdie seemed to have lost her train of thought. My grandmother and Aunt Matt fell silent, eating their food without looking up.

"Is that true?" I finally asked. "Were my parents like Romeo and Juliet, living in feuding households?"

"I never met your mother's parents," Grandmother said quietly. "There was no feud. . . . Listen, Violet. I know you're upset with all this secrecy, and I don't blame you. But asking about your mother will only lead to more grief in the end. Sometimes it's best to leave the past in the past—and this is one of those times. Besides, we're all tired tonight. Supper was later than usual, thanks to the station mix-up. And right now it's time for our evening devotions."

She rose to fetch her Bible from the buffet and rustled through the fading, onionskin pages until she found her place. I didn't comprehend a single word that she read as I battled tears of anger and frustration. I would learn nothing more about my mother tonight.

Ten minutes later Grandmother ended with a lengthy prayer, thanking the Almighty "for safely delivering our Violet Rose" and finishing with "Amen."

"Amen," Aunt Birdie echoed. Grandmother rose quickly again.

"I believe we've lingered here long enough for one evening. Mattie, it's our turn to do the dishes. Violet, why don't you go upstairs and unpack?"

She didn't wait for a reply but gathered up as many dishes as she could carry and headed to the kitchen, her steps brisk and purposeful as if unwilling to waste a single one of them. My grandmother believed that waste of any kind offended God, especially wasting time.

I lacked enthusiasm for the task of unpacking, but I dutifully went upstairs and removed my dresses from the trunk and hung them in the empty wardrobe, which smelled of mothballs. I arranged my comb and brush and other toiletries on the dresser top and tossed my stockings and undergarments into the empty drawers. I spent the longest amount of time searching for a place to hide my journal, finally deciding to stuff it underneath my mattress, as usual.

Grandmother and Aunt Matt were still in the kitchen when I went downstairs again. Aunt Birdie sat alone in the parlor, gazing into space with a contented smile, her hands folded loosely in her lap. She had soft, limp hands, like aging goose-down pillows with nearly all of the stuffing gone. I sat beside her on the horsehair sofa, hoping for a few minutes alone with her before the others joined us.

"Aunt Birdie, did you know my mother?"

"Of course. I knew her very well."

My hopes soared. "Would you tell me something about her, please?"

"I'd be happy to. Let's see now . . ." Her pause lasted a very long time. I waited, thinking that she was searching for a place to begin. But finally she looked up at me and asked, "Who are you again?"

"I'm Violet Rose Hayes. Your nephew, John Hayes, is my father." When Birdie still seemed puzzled, I added, "I'm Florence's grand-daughter."

"Why, what a coincidence! I'm Florence's sister."

"Yes, I know. Aunt Birdie, you said that my parents were like Romeo and Juliet. Do you remember when they got married?"

"Like it was yesterday. I even have a picture. Would you like to see it?"

"I would love to!"

She rose gracefully to her feet and removed a framed photograph from the curio cabinet in the corner, wiping a layer of dust from it with her sleeve, then blowing on it to remove the rest. I held my breath in anticipation as she handed the photo to me. My hopes plummeted quickly when I saw that the bride in the photograph was Aunt Birdie.

"I think this is you, Aunt Birdie. You and your husband."

"Gilbert is off fighting in the war, you know. He's with General McClellan in Virginia on the Peninsula Campaign. I miss him terribly." Tears filled her gray eyes.

I fumbled for something to say. "He's . . . he's a fine-looking man."

"Yes, isn't he, though? Is there someone special in your life, dear?"

"Not really. Herman Beckett from back home asked my father for permission to court me, but he's my only suitor so far." Unless I wanted to count Silas McClure, the traveling salesman—which I didn't.

"Do you love this Mr. Beckett?"

"Certainly not!"

"Well, then. That says it all, doesn't it? Make sure you marry for love, dear."

"I really don't know much about love, Aunt Birdie. My friend Ruth and I used to read *True Romance Stories* and they made falling in love sound like a bad case of influenza. Your stomach goes all aflutter and your palms sweat and your head starts spinning. I'm not sure I would like the sensation, to tell you the truth. Does love really feel that way?"

"My husband fell in love with me the moment he first laid eyes on me. He saw me across the room and he said to his brother, 'Look! Isn't she the most beautiful woman you've ever seen?' He couldn't take his eyes off of me. 'I'm going to marry her,' he vowed, 'if it's the last thing I ever do.' He begged my father for permission to court me, but it wasn't enough for Gilbert to win Father's permission or even my consent to marry him. He was determined to win my love. And so he did." She sighed and wiped away the tear that had rolled down her soft cheek. "Then this terrible war started, and we've been apart ever since."

"I'm sorry," I said, gently squeezing her hand. "I hope I meet a gentleman who loves me that much."

"Make certain you marry for love. My sister Agnes married for money, and Florence married so she could serve God, and poor Mattie never married at all. But I was the fortunate one. I married for love."

"Do you know why my father and mother got married? Their names are John and Angeline Hayes."

"Oh yes. That was true love. Deep and passionate. Like my husband's and mine."

"Won't you please tell me their story?"

"Their passion was ignited the night of the Great Fire, and the fervor of their love was as all-consuming as the flames."

Wow! Aunt Birdie could write True Romance *stories!* But was it the truth? I knew that the Great Fire had occurred in October of 1871. I was born in April of 1873. Allowing a few months for courtship and marriage, and nine months for pregnancy, the timing did seem to make sense.

"What happened then, Aunt Birdie?"

"It began to rain early on Tuesday morning and the fire finally stopped. If it hadn't been for the rain, this house would have burned up with all the others."

"I mean what happened with my parents? Do you have a photograph of their wedding?"

"Yes. Would you like to see it?" She lifted her wedding photo from her lap and showed it to me again. I was disappointed but not surprised.

"I think this is you, Aunt Birdie."

"Darling Gilbert. He's the love of my life. He's fighting in Virginia to help free the slaves, you know. Make sure you marry for love, dear."

I gave up. Trying to get information from Aunt Birdie was probably a lost cause. A few minutes later, Grandmother and Aunt Matt finished the dishes and joined us in the parlor.

"Unpacked already?" Grandmother asked. "That didn't take long."

"I'm letting my dresses hang in the wardrobe for a while before I press them."

"Well, if you'll excuse me," Aunt Matt said, "I have an article to write. Good night." She crossed the front hall to her room and closed the door.

"That reminds me," Aunt Birdie said. "I need to write a letter to Gilbert. It always cheers him to receive mail from home." She stood and floated to the tall secretary across the room, unfolding the drop leaf so it formed a desk. She sat down gracefully and took out her stationery and a pen. Meanwhile, my grandmother had retrieved a bag of yarn and knitting needles and settled into a rocking chair.

"What are you making?" I asked.

"Socks. They're for the children down at the settlement house. Some of those poor little dears run around in the snow all winter with bare feet in their raggedy shoes. Do you know how to knit, Violet?"

"I learned how to once, but I'm not very good at it. I can't say that I enjoy it."

"Well, if you ever feel like helping me, I have extra knitting needles and plenty of yarn. I could use all the help I can get."

I sat watching the women work. The only sounds were the steady ticking of the clock in the hallway, Grandmother's knitting needles clacking rhythmically, and Aunt Birdie's pen scratching across the page. I wondered if I'd made a terrible mistake in coming to Chicago to live with a spinster and two widows. Was every evening going to be as boring as this one? I missed my friend Ruth from school, and I especially missed her exotic reading material.

I would have to come up with a plan to find my mother soon— before I died of boredom.

Chapter

5

Tuesday, June 6, 1893

I slept late the next day. By the time I came downstairs for breakfast, the others already had eaten. "Where's my grandmother?" I
asked Aunt Matt. She was trying to fasten a hat to her head with a
long hatpin, stabbing it into the straw so fiercely I feared she would
draw blood.

"Florence left the house hours ago to do her charity work," she
said. "She told me to let you sleep, so I did. She also told me to fix
you some breakfast when you finally woke up, so what do you want?"

Judging by Aunt Matt's expression and tone of voice, it was going
to be a terrible imposition for her to wait on me. She obviously had
more important things to do.

"Thank you, but I'm not hungry. I never eat much for breakfast."

"All right, then. I'm off to do the shopping." She strode through
the back door as if heading off to war, marching to the grocery store
to conquer the cabbages. Once again, I was alone with Aunt Birdie.

I found her in the parlor, daintily scattering dust as she skimmed a feather duster over the room's bric-a-brac. Neither she nor the feathers did much good, as far as I could see. Dust motes danced in the slanted sunbeams for a few seconds, then settled back into place on the cluttered furnishings. When Birdie saw me she hurried over to embrace me, as if I had just arrived home from a very long journey.

"Good morning, dear. Did you sleep well?"

"Yes, very well."

It wasn't exactly true. I hadn't slept well at all. But Madame Beauchamps had insisted that most people really didn't want to know the answer to polite questions such as "How are you?" or "Did you sleep well?" The inquirers were simply making small talk, and so the proper reply should always be something like, "Fine, thank you. And yourself?"

In truth, my grandmother's refusal to discuss my mother had upset me a great deal. I had spent a portion of the night tossing and turning on the lumpy guest-room bed, trying to devise a way to escape from the house so I could search for my mother. I then wasted a few more hours trying to figure out how I could get Aunt Matt to deliver her lecture on remaining free from domineering husbands to Maude O'Neill. When I finally did fall asleep, I dreamed that Chicago was on fire again and my father and I were racing through the flames to find my mother.

"I'm so glad you slept well, dear," Aunt Birdie said. "We have a big day ahead of us, you know. It's a good thing you got your rest."

"Pardon me . . . ? Um, what is it, exactly, that we're supposed to be doing today?"

Aunt Birdie leaned close to me and whispered, "It's a secret!" She winked.

I had no idea if she was making sense or not. My grandmother hadn't mentioned a "big day" or a secret. A moment later, Birdie returned to her dusting, and I spotted the wedding picture she had shown me last night still lying on the parlor sofa. I picked it up and studied this younger and surprisingly pretty Aunt Birdie.

"Do you have any more pictures, Aunt Birdie? Maybe a scrap-book of photographs that we could look at together?" I would rec-ognize my parents, even if Aunt Birdie didn't.

"Oh, yes. I have quite a collection of photographs. They're not in a scrapbook, though."

"That's okay. I would still like to see them."

"You would?" She smiled her dreamy smile. "Oh, how nice."

Birdie went to the secretary and removed an entire drawer brim-ming with photos and other mementos. She carried it over to the sofa and sat down beside me with a sigh. I wanted to root through the pictures quickly, searching for my parents, but Aunt Birdie seemed to have all the time in the world for this task. Shielding the drawer from my grasping fingers, she patiently pulled out each picture, one by one, and described it to me in excruciating detail.

"This first one is my sister Agnes and her husband, Henry. She married Henry in 1847 . . . or was it 1848? His last name is Paine—Henry Paine. His people are very well-to-do, you know. Those are their two boys, Henry Junior and Michael. They're grown now, of course, with children of their own. But aren't they darling in this picture? I think little Michael must have been about twelve . . . or was he older? Let me think . . ."

At the rate she was going, I would be grown and have children myself by the time we reached the bottom of the drawer. I decided to hurry things along.

"It doesn't matter how old he was, Aunt Birdie. Who is that in the next picture? Is that my grandmother?"

"Yes, this is Florence and her husband, Isaac. Too bad he isn't smiling—he looked much nicer when he smiled. But, then, Isaac never did smile very much. He was a minister, you see. One of those fire-and-brimstone preachers you hear so much about, and he never seemed to think there was much in this life worth smiling about. Now in heaven, on the other hand . . . He would preach about heaven too, once in a while. . . ."

I gritted my teeth, struggling to be patient. We had reached only the third photo—one of Aunt Birdie's father, taken shortly before he died—when I heard a horse and carriage drawing to a halt out front. I was afraid that it was my grandmother and that she would take away the photos or hide all the ones of my mother before Aunt Birdie could show them to me. I jumped up and parted the front curtain to peer out.

An enclosed carriage, complete with a driver and a matched team of horses, had parked by our front walk. I couldn't see the occupants, but the elegant vehicle was a far cry from the run-down hansom cab and old nag that my grandmother had hired to fetch me from the train station yesterday.

"Does my grandmother—Florence—ever hire a carriage and driver?" I asked, ready to yank the drawer full of photos from Aunt Birdie and stuff it back into the secretary.

"Florence rides the streetcar, dear."

"Well, someone is here to pay us a visit in a very expensive-looking rig."

"Oh, how nice."

The driver dismounted from his seat and hurried to open the carriage door. My suspense ended as I watched my great-aunt Agnes climb down. She was a stout woman, the most full-figured of the four sisters—and also the wealthiest. Prosperity, respectability, and the aura of riches hung from her like diamonds. She swept regally up the walkway, as if balancing a crown on her head. I could easily picture an invisible entourage of velvet-clothed pages rolling a red carpet before her and lifting a long, elegant train in her wake.

"*Bonjour*, my dears," she sang as she flowed through the front doorway. An engraved calling card dangled from Aunt Agnes' gloved fingertips. Madame Beauchamps would have praised the way she held her pinkie finger daintily outstretched. Aunt Birdie hurried out to the foyer to give Agnes one of her bone-crushing embraces.

"Where is the tray, Bertha?" Agnes said, smoothing the wrinkles from her gown again. "I know you own a perfectly fine silver tray for receiving calling cards. I'm the one who bought it for you."

Madame Beauchamps had drilled into us at some length the importance of the calling-card ritual. I felt compelled to search for the lost tray immediately and correct this horrendous oversight. Since I had no idea what it looked like or where to find it, I turned in useless circles, peering beneath the hall table and into the coat closet while Aunt Agnes waited and Aunt Birdie stared dreamily into space.

"Never mind," Agnes finally decided. The card fluttered from her fingertips and landed on the hall table. "Come here and let me look at you, Violet."

She held me at arm's length, studying me with a keen, critical eye. I feared she would find fault with my dark eyebrows and dusky complexion, but my great-aunt's round, regal face broke into a genial smile.

"Why, you're quite lovely. You should do very well—very well indeed. I'll introduce you straightaway."

"Oh, how nice," Aunt Birdie said.

"Introduce me to whom, Aunt Agnes?"

"Why, to Chicago society, of course. You do have calling cards, don't you? Properly engraved?"

"Yes, ma'am." Madame B. had made certain of that.

"And suitable apparel, I presume? A proper hat? Gloves? Well, I can remedy that easily enough, if you don't. I hope you speak French. I understand that you attended that boarding school in Rockford? What was it called?"

"Madame Beauchamps' School for Young Ladies."

"That's the one. You may not be aware, but I was the one who recommended it to your father. I assume they taught you French there?"

"*Oui, Tante Agnes. Je parle très bien français.* Madame wouldn't have allowed me to graduate unless I'd mastered French along with the rules of etiquette and other social necessities."

"Wonderful."

"Madame also insisted that we learn a smattering of Italian in case the need ever arose to converse with a Venetian count; that we played the piano and sang; that we knew how to find her French homeland and other important countries on a map; and that we had a passing knowledge of poetry and literature."

"*Très bon*, Violet," Aunt Agnes said. "You seem very well prepared. It's about time that your father decided to do right by you and send you to Chicago to find a proper husband."

I stopped breathing.

"A-a husband?"

"Yes, certainly. Why do you think you were sent to Chicago? To see the fair?" She laughed at her own joke. "Mind you, I told your father it was almost too late, that you were almost too old. But I shall endeavor to make up for lost time."

Was this really the reason my father had agreed to let me come? I was so astounded by Aunt Agnes' news that I had no idea what I was supposed to say. Fortunately, Madame Beauchamps had taught us that expressions of profuse gratitude were suitable for nearly every occasion.

"Thank you, Aunt Agnes. *Merci*. I'm so very grateful." But in truth, the idea of shopping for a husband made my heart pound—though whether from fear or excitement I couldn't have said. Perhaps a bit of each.

"I'll call for you tomorrow at two o'clock," Agnes said. "Make sure you tell your grandmother that I'm coming. Bertha won't even remember that I've called, the poor dear. And wear a hat. And gloves."

She turned toward the door in a swirl of swishing taffeta, calling "*Au revoir*, Bertha," as if poor Aunt Birdie were deaf as well as simple. To me she said *sotto voce*, "Don't forget your calling cards. *Au revoir*."

I must have looked like Aunt Birdie as I stood staring dumbly into space, completely flabbergasted by Aunt Agnes' visit. The scent of her perfume lingered long after she left, along with her tantalizing words.

A *husband!* I could well imagine what Aunt Matt would have to say about that.

I was still standing in the hallway in shock when I heard someone coming through the kitchen door. I quickly raced into the parlor and stuffed the drawer full of photos back into the desk. Now that I knew where Aunt Birdie kept them, I could browse through them on my own another day. I picked up the feather duster and pretended to dust—just as my grandmother walked in from the kitchen to hang her hat on the hall tree.

"Did you mail my letter to Gilbert?" Aunt Birdie asked after greeting her with an embrace.

"I took care of it."

It surprised me that my grandmother, a good Christian woman, would be deceitful. Evidently I came from a long line of accomplished liars. I knew firsthand the pain and disillusionment of being lied to for years and years, so I gave the feather duster to Birdie and followed my grandmother into the kitchen.

"Why don't you tell Aunt Birdie the truth about her husband and the war?" I asked in a hushed voice.

"We have told her, dear. Countless times. And every time, when she finally grasps it, she grieves inconsolably for days and days. Then, by God's mercy, she wakes up one morning and has forgotten what year it is and she's happy again—writing letters to Gilbert, awaiting his arrival. We don't intentionally deceive her, and whenever she asks me for the truth I don't lie to her. But it's so much kinder for her this way, don't you think?"

"I'm not sure. My father might have thought he was being kind by sparing me the truth about my mother, but my shock upon learning the truth has been truly upsetting. It's one of the reasons I needed to get away from home for a while."

"I'm so sorry." She rested a soothing hand on my shoulder. "I told John how displeased I was when he first invented his lie. That's probably why he never allowed me to see much of you over the years. He knew I wouldn't lie if you asked about your mother. But he made me promise not to talk about her. I may be John's mother, but he made it clear that his marriage was none of my business."

"Well, I would like to know the truth now."

"What good can that possibly serve, Violet?" She slid her hand down my arm and took my hand in hers.

"I already know that Mother was never really sick, was she."

"Not unless you count being sick at heart."

"But what was she like? I barely remember her."

Grandmother paused as she released my hand and picked up her apron, tying the strings behind her back. "In the beginning . . . ? Your mother was full of life. Vibrant. Vivacious. And very beautiful. You resemble her, you know."

I shook my head. "I hardly remember what she looked like. Why aren't there any pictures?"

But just as I was learning some useful information, Aunt Birdie interrupted us. She walked into the kitchen carrying Agnes' calling card in the palm of her hand as if it were made of glass.

"We had a social call, Florence—and I couldn't find the silver tray!"

"Was it Agnes? Let me see that." She lifted the card from Birdie's hand.

"Aunt Agnes is coming for me tomorrow at two o'clock," I said.

"Oh, dear." Grandmother's shoulders sagged. "I was hoping she'd be too busy to subject you to her social rounds—unless you want to be subjected, that is. You're a grown woman, so I suppose it's your choice."

"What's wrong with making social calls with Aunt Agnes?"

"Nothing. It's just that she hobnobs with people like the Palmers and the Pullmans and the Fieldses, drinking gallons of tea, and I see no point in all of that social folderol. There are so many more important things to do in this brief life."

"Aunt Agnes said my father sent me here to find a husband." Unfortunately, Aunt Matt picked that moment to march through the back door. She nearly dropped all of her parcels when she overheard me.

"Agnes said *what*? Over my dead body she will!"

I felt like I was standing in the middle of one of those traffic snarls Mr. McClure had described, with vehicles colliding all around me.

"But where is the silver tray, Florence?" Aunt Birdie asked. "I can't find it anywhere."

"I put the tray away in the buffet, dear. It was badly tarnished and I didn't have the time or the patience to polish it—especially when Agnes is the only person who ever comes calling these days."

"Now, Florence," Aunt Matt said sternly. "Promise me that you won't allow Agnes to sell your innocent granddaughter into servitude!"

"Don't be melodramatic, Matt. You make it sound as if Agnes wants Violet to be an indentured servant instead of a wife."

"There is very little difference," Matt said with a sniff.

"Are we all out of silver polish?" Aunt Birdie asked from inside the pantry. "I can't find it."

"Look on the shelf behind the ammonia," Grandmother called to her. She turned back to Aunt Matt. "Besides, it's up to Violet and her father to decide whether or not she marries, not us."

"Well! We shall see about that." Aunt Matt dropped her parcels on the kitchen table and stomped off.

I worried that I had made her angry, and I couldn't afford to do that. I needed Aunt Matt to talk Maude out of marrying my father. But at the same time, I wanted to go visiting with Aunt Agnes. How could I turn down the opportunity to hobnob with Chicago's high society—not to mention, find a husband?

"I think I'd like to go calling with Aunt Agnes tomorrow," I told my grandmother. "Would you mind?"

"That's entirely up to you. Just watch out or she'll quickly take over your life with her nonsense."

"Here it is!" Aunt Birdie announced. She emerged from the pantry looking disheveled but triumphant, waving a very tarnished silver tray and the container of silver polish. "Now we'll be prepared when callers arrive at our door!"

And if Aunt Agnes had her way, one of those callers just might be my future husband.

Chapter

6

Wednesday, June 7, 1893

I tried on three dresses before deciding which one I would wear to make social calls with Aunt Agnes. I finally chose one that accentuated my small waist, even though I couldn't cinch myself very tightly without my friend Ruth's help. She had been able to make me quite svelte—and quite breathless.

Ruth Schultz had been an expert on what a girl could do to improve her figure, and everyone at school had come to her for help. When it came to nipping, tucking, and reshaping, Ruth's knowledge of corsets was second to none. She also recommended daily doses of an Egyptian elixir that promised to provide "a graceful plumpness" to poorly endowed girls if taken regularly. It tasted like bile. Fortunately, my endowments didn't need plumping.

"*Small-waisted girls who are too top-heavy always look as though they're in danger of falling over,*" Ruth had counseled me. "*Especially if they have tiny feet.*"

I took a long time pinning up my hair, unable to get it just right.

I felt absurdly nervous, as if I were about to take an examination at school and all of the skills and lessons Madame B. had taught me would be put to a final test. What if I tripped over a rug and fell flat on my face in front of everyone? What if I dropped my teacup and it turned out to be a priceless heirloom that had been rescued from the Great Fire, the only surviving item of a precious family inheritance, absolutely irreplaceable and—

I stopped, took a deep breath, and told myself to think of all the good things that might happen today instead of the bad. What if I met a man who was everything I've ever dreamed of: handsome, charming, rich . . . but most of all, daring, adventuresome, imaginative? What if he fell in love with me at first sight, the way Aunt Birdie's husband had fallen in love with her? My dream man would set out to win my heart, courting me in all of the most romantic ways, just like the heroes in Ruth's *True Romance Stories.* Our story would be so touchingly beautiful that it would become a classic, read by millions of envious girls for decades to come. In fact, we would—

"Violet?" Aunt Birdie interrupted my flight of fancy, calling to me from the front foyer. "Agnes is here. Her carriage just arrived."

"Coming." I quickly pinned on my hat, gathered my gloves and calling cards, and hurried downstairs.

I couldn't recall ever riding in a carriage as fine as my aunt's, but a lesser vehicle would have looked completely out of place stopping at the elegant townhouse we visited first. A uniformed servant met us at the door and received our calling cards on a Chinese enameled tray. I wanted to gaze all around at the lavishly appointed rooms as he ushered us inside, but good manners forbade me to gawk. The small glimpses I did steal convinced me that this was the finest home I ever had visited. The servant led Aunt Agnes and me to the drawing room, where a handful of well-dressed women gathered around the tea cart.

I walked into the room with practiced grace and faultless posture: back erect, shoulders straight, and head held high. I had spent hours at Madame Beauchamps' school walking with a book balanced on top of my head before being allowed to graduate to the next level of difficulty. I then was expected to gracefully sit down while holding a cup of hot tea and still balancing the book on my head.

"Ladies," Aunt Agnes said in her cultured voice, "I would like to introduce my great-niece, Violet Rose Hayes. She's visiting my sister Florence Hayes and our fair city of Chicago this summer."

The ladies greeted me with pleasant smiles and a chorus of lilting voices: "Hello . . . How nice to meet you . . . Welcome, Violet. . . ."

"Thank you so much."

I paid very close attention as our hostess introduced each of the women to me, recalling Madame B.'s stern warning: *I cannot emphasize strongly enough the importance of remembering the name of each person to whom you are introduced.* She would place strangers' photographs on a row of chairs and make fake introductions so we could practice recalling names.

I had perfected my own secret system of memorization, fabricating scandalous stories about each person based on her name or physical attributes. For instance today, when our hostess introduced a Mrs. Smith, I imagined that the dear woman was having a secret romance with a large, muscular blacksmith.

Our hostess served tea to everyone from an engraved silver teapot, and we all sat down to drink it. A thrill of anticipation coursed through me. So many of the things one learns in school are quickly forgotten and never used, but now, in this very room, all of my hard work and diligent study would finally be put to use. I had always feared that my impeccable training would languish from lack of use back home in Lockport and eventually go to waste. But thanks to Aunt Agnes, I had finally found my place in life.

I spread the miniscule napkin on my lap, balanced the delicate teacup just so, and took the tiniest of sips. The afternoon sun dappled across the beautifully polished furnishings and exquisite carpet. I could get used to this life. I sat among some of Chicago's most prominent women, the cream of society from one of America's premier cities. Excitement filled me as I anticipated a discussion that would be both edifying and stimulating.

"Beautiful weather we're having, isn't it?" our hostess began.

"My, yes. I cannot recall another June in recent years that has begun as lovely as this one has."

"Let's hope the summer continues to be as nice."

"Mmm . . ." the ladies murmured in chorus, plumed hats bobbing. "Let's hope so."

"I so dislike the hot, muggy summers we sometimes have in Chicago."

"I believe everyone does."

"Fortunately, we have a home on one of the Finger Lakes in New York State, so we can always escape."

"Yes, you are fortunate."

The conversation seemed to be rolling along nicely when suddenly, a brief lull occurred. I stopped breathing as the silence lengthened into several tense seconds. *"One must never allow the conversation to lag,"* Madame B. had instructed. *"A lengthy silence spells the death of every social event."*

But just as a bead of sweat began to trickle down beneath my hat, our hostess asked the other women, "What did you think of the thunderstorm we had the other evening?" My admiration for her abilities soared.

"I found it rather frightening," someone replied.

"Did you? I quite enjoy thunder."

"As do I—providing it isn't too loud."

"I don't mind *loud* thunder as long as it isn't accompanied by *wind*."

"Oh, yes. Wind!"

"Too much wind can be quite vexing."

The ladies went on and on this way for some time, delicately sipping tea and discussing the merits of thunder and wind and several other weather-related phenomena, until I feared I might nod off. I hadn't slept well the previous night as I'd nervously anticipated meeting my future husband. My eyes actually may have fallen closed in a prolonged blink when the hostess suddenly decided that the proper time had come to include me in the conversation.

"Do you enjoy the summer months, Miss Hayes?"

I felt the way I had in school whenever I'd been caught daydreaming—which was often. I gripped the teacup in my shaking fingers so it wouldn't rattle. My heart raced as I formulated my reply.

"Yes. I've always enjoyed summer. But then, I enjoy all of the seasons equally well. It's so nice to live in a climate that offers a variety of seasons, so one doesn't become bored with any of them. Don't you agree?"

I could tell by their smiles and nods of approval that I had answered well. I had spent hours practicing the art of conversation at school, and I knew that simply answering the question was insufficient. One must always add a question of one's own to keep the conversation alive. Madame had compared a proper conversation to an elegant tennis match: *"One must not only keep the ball in the air, but also return the serve with grace and finesse."*

I knew I had passed my first test. But by the time Aunt Agnes and I finished our tea and took our leave—and I had bidden farewell to each woman by name, of course—I confess that I felt a bit disappointed. I hadn't encountered my future husband.

"That was for practice, Violet," Aunt Agnes said as we settled into the carriage once again. "You did very well, by the way. But this next call is much more important."

"Oh? Why is that?"

"Our next hostess, Mrs. Kent, has better social connections, for one thing. But more important, she has a very eligible grandson, as do some of the other ladies who will be calling on her. Mind you, there also may be young ladies your age present, so stay focused and make sure you don't underestimate the competition."

"You mean we'll be competing for the same suitors?"

"Why, of course."

I couldn't help smiling at the challenge. I realize that it was extremely unfeminine of me, but I enjoyed competition of any kind. I once tried to organize a betting pool at school where each girl would contribute two bits and the "pot" would be awarded to whoever scored the most points on an upcoming exam. But only one other girl besides Ruth and me had been willing to risk expulsion by taking part in a gambling ring—and none of us would risk it for only seventy-five cents. It was probably my competitive streak that contributed to my lack of interest in Herman Beckett; no other girl in Lockport seemed to want him.

Aunt Agnes and I called at a stately mansion on Prairie Avenue next, and this time the conversation took a much more interesting turn, even if it did revolve around my appearance for a while.

"Your niece is lovely, Agnes," our hostess, Mrs. Kent, announced. "Where have you been hiding her all this time?"

"Violet has been studying at one of the finest boarding schools in Illinois. She speaks French as if she'd grown up in Paris. And wait until you hear her skills on the piano. She'll take your breath away!"

Since my aunt had never heard me play the piano, her boast struck me as an astonishing leap of faith. I decided it would be prudent to begin practicing on my grandmother's piano in my spare time.

I was the center of attention as the ladies gathered around, sizing me up as if I were merchandise on display at Mr. Marshall Field's famous store. Their comments were all complimentary until Mrs. Grant joined the discussion.

"Don't you think her complexion is a little dark? Violet has a bit of a gypsy look to her."

Mrs. Grant had come calling with two daughters of her own, Hattie and Nettie, who were close to my age. Her unkind remarks had the same effect on me as a shot from a starting pistol at the beginning of a race. I remained composed as I sized up my competition. Neither of the Grant sisters was as pretty as I was, even with my dusky skin. And their assets could have used a little plumping from Ruth's Egyptian elixir. But we were in a race to the altar, and I wasn't about to offer any advice to my rivals.

"Violet is well aware that she needs to stay out of the sun," Aunt Agnes said. "Aren't you, dear?"

"A parasol is an essential summer accessory for every woman," I replied.

"I find that her unusual coloring adds to her mystique," my aunt said.

"What about suitors?" my hostess asked. "Do you have any gentlemen callers, Violet?"

I didn't dare tell them about stodgy Herman Beckett, the shipping clerk from Lockport. Then, to my horror, I recalled giving the traveling salesman, Silas McClure, permission to call on me at Grandmother's house. What on earth would I do if he showed up at my door with his garish plaid suit, flashy grin, and oiled hair? I couldn't invite him in! His head would leave grease stains on our upholstery! Why, oh why, had I given him Grandmother's address?

"I've arrived in the city only recently," I replied, dodging the question. "I've been away at Madame Beauchamps' School for Young Ladies in Rockford."

"That's a fine institution."

"Yes, wonderful reputation."

"Agnes, dear, why don't you bring Violet to the fund-raiser for the Art Institute? I would like my grandson, George, to meet her."

My heart sped up.

"And I would love for her to attend my *soirée*. My grandnephew Edward will be in attendance."

One of the Grant sisters gave me a malevolent glare at the mention of Edward. But soon the women lost interest in me, and the conversation shifted—or dare I say degenerated—into gossip. No one's private life seemed off limits as they talked about who was courting whom, how the courtship was progressing, which gentlemen had proposed, which ones were never likely to, and so on. I stayed alert, cataloging the information, aware that my future success might depend on it.

Later, as Aunt Agnes and I were taking our leave along with the other women, our hostess caught my arm and whispered, "Stay for a moment, Violet. There's someone I'd like you to meet." She beckoned to a serving girl, who hurried over. "Katya, please ask Nelson to come downstairs for a moment."

The serving girl hesitated as if she hadn't understood the command. But her questioning eyes met mine, not Mrs. Kent's. I had the distinct feeling that she was sizing me up the same way that I had sized up the Grant sisters. Katya was young—no more than seventeen or eighteen—and very pretty, with slanted blue eyes and wheat-colored hair and sharp, Slavic cheekbones. She dropped her gaze and curtsied.

"Yes, ma'am. Right away, ma'am." I could have sworn I saw tears in her eyes.

Of course! She was in love with her employer's grandson, this Nelson whom she had been sent to fetch. Maybe he was in love with her too, but their love had to be kept secret because she was an immigrant serving girl and totally unsuitable for a man of his social standing.

They met on back stairways and in the darkened garden after midnight, exchanging tearful embraces and passionate kisses. Katya had begged Nelson to run away with her, but he was torn between his love for her and his love of money. Then, one stormy night—

"Katya emigrated from Poland," Mrs. Kent explained while we waited. "She didn't speak a word of English when we first hired her, but she is improving every day."

A few minutes later, Nelson arrived—without Katya. I imagined her weeping in the linen closet, using the spare blankets and bed sheets to muffle her jealous tears.

Nelson Kent ambled out to the foyer dressed for the tennis courts, and I had to bite my bottom lip to keep my mouth from dropping open. He was the living embodiment of every romance story's hero: tall, slender, fair-haired, and handsome. And if this home was any indication, he was also extraordinarily rich.

"Nelson, dear, I'd like you to meet Miss Violet Hayes. She is my dear friend Agnes Paine's great-niece and has just arrived in Chicago. She needs to meet some other young people her age. Violet, this is my grandson, Nelson Kent."

"How do you do?" I breathed. I was grateful that I'd practiced my mysterious smile so I wouldn't appear too eager. It wouldn't do for me to greet him with a grin like the Cheshire cat from *Alice in Wonderland*. Too bad Madame B. had never taught us how to speak when we've just had the wind knocked out of us by a handsome, wealthy man.

"I'm pleased to meet you," Nelson replied. He seemed cordial but cool. Unlike Aunt Birdie's husband, it wasn't love at first sight for young Mr. Kent.

"Be a dear, Nelson, and take Violet for a stroll around the garden, would you? There's something I need to discuss with Agnes."

"I would be delighted." He offered me his arm and escorted me down the hallway toward the rear of the house.

If I had to describe my first suitor, Herman Beckett, in one word, it would be *stodgy*. Silas McClure's word would be *slippery*. But the only word that could possibly sum up Nelson Kent was *smooth*. He seemed so at ease with proper etiquette, so casual with the trappings of wealth and his elevated social standing, that it was as if he had never been required to learn such things but had emerged from the womb with them.

I imagined him socially at ease the very first time guests arrived to view him, mere days after his birth. I could picture him smiling casually and confidently from his cradle and passing out his own cigars: *"Mr. Mayor, how are you? Mr. McCormick, so nice of you to visit. Would you care for a drink? I'll have one of the servants fix you one."*

"How long have you been in Chicago, Miss Hayes?" he asked as we walked through a set of French doors onto a veranda.

"Only a few days—and you?"

"I've lived here all my life, except for the years I was away at university. How do you like the city so far?"

"It seems like a very nice place."

My heart skipped a beat when I realized I had just halted the conversation. It was hard to concentrate when strolling on the arm of a man like Nelson Kent.

"What lovely gardens," I said, since that had been the pretense for the stroll.

"You are by far the loveliest flower in them, Violet." Something about his words sounded phony. I quickly glanced at his face to gauge his sincerity. His pleasant smile hadn't changed, but his eyes seemed very sad.

"Thank you for the compliment, Mr. Kent."

"Please. It's Nelson."

As we made our tour around the garden, I waited for the influenza-like symptoms of true love to strike me: the dizziness, the heart palpitations, the fluttering stomach and fevered brow. If Nelson Kent was destined to become my true love, I should feel something immediately, shouldn't I? Instead, I felt disappointingly healthy.

"Have you been to the Columbian Exposition?" I asked him.

"Yes, several times. Have you?"

"Not yet, but I would like very much to go."

"Perhaps you would allow me to escort you there one day." This was my third offer. I wondered how Chicago's young lovers ever undertook a decent courtship before the fair was built. I gazed up at Nelson again and gave him my well-rehearsed, enigmatic smile.

"Perhaps I will."

I had been taught to act mysterious with suitors, to be shy yet flirtatious, to play hard to get. *"Men enjoy the pursuit,"* I'd been coached. *"Chase him until he catches you."* But I had the distinct feeling that Nelson Kent was playing the same game with me, acting charming enough to gain my interest while remaining coolly aloof. And he was a much better player than I was.

"Might I be seeing you at the fund-raiser for the Art Institute?" he asked.

"Yes, you might."

"Then I hope you will save one dance for me."

My only reply was another enigmatic smile. I longed to ask him one of my favorite questions just to get a sense of who he truly was: *"If you had to choose between being struck blind and never being able to see the face of your beloved again, or becoming permanently deaf, and being denied the sound of music and of a child's laughter, which would you choose?"* But I didn't dare ask Nelson Kent such a question. Madame B. had warned against the indiscriminate use of our imaginations.

"If you could visit only one pavilion at the fair," I asked instead, "which one would you choose?"

"The Electricity Building," he answered immediately. "It's a showcase of modern progress and innovation. I predict that electric lighting will make gaslights obsolete one day. Just wait until you see the White City all lit up at night. It's astounding. I'm trying to convince my father to invest in some of the modern inventions that are being introduced at the fair."

"Did you ride Mr. Ferris' wheel?" I asked, recalling Silas McClure's description of it.

"Not yet. I went to Paris for the previous World's Fair and saw Mr. Eiffel's Tower. There has been quite a controversy over which is the more impressive achievement."

"What is your opinion?"

He gave me his gentle, charming smile. "I'll let you know after I ride on the wheel."

We made a circuit of the garden—it wasn't very large—and arrived back at the French doors.

"Thank you so much for the garden tour," I said as we joined the others in the foyer.

"The pleasure was all mine, Miss Hayes. I hope to see you again soon." He gave a slight bow and strolled away, his hands slipping casually into his pockets.

"You carried yourself very well this afternoon," Aunt Agnes told me on the way home. "All the ladies seemed quite taken with you."

"Thank you, Aunt Agnes. I confess that I was a bit nervous. Did it show?"

"Not at all. In fact, did you notice how they all competed for you? You can expect several invitations to arrive in the coming weeks. The women are always excited when someone introduces new blood."

"New *blood*?" I shivered involuntarily, wishing I had never read Ruth's cannibal story.

"Yes. After a while, everyone ends up related to everyone else and it becomes a bit . . . unseemly, if you know what I mean. One could lose track of who is a first cousin and who is a second—and that would never do. But if we can manage to marry you well, then our families—the Howells and the Hayeses and the Paines—will all move up a notch or two in the social ladder."

I suddenly felt like the prize money in a betting pool—winner takes all. It was not a pleasant feeling.

"Young Nelson Kent seemed quite enamored with you."

"Did he? He was very pleasant and well-mannered."

"Be careful not to let him monopolize your time too quickly. I hope he didn't rush to fill your calendar already."

"He mentioned escorting me to the fair. And he asked me to save a dance for him at the fund-raiser."

"Oh, dear. He does move quickly. Mind you, he is an excellent catch as far as husbands are concerned, but take your time making your selection. One never knows when an even bigger fish might come along."

"Do society men and women ever marry for love?"

"Love!" She laughed. "My dear, you've been spending too much time with my sister Birdie. Do I dare ask how you answered Mr. Kent's invitations?"

"I gave him a very vague reply."

"Good. Good. Never appear too eager. Keep him in suspense awhile longer."

"But I would like to see him again," I said, thinking that perhaps a fire wasn't always kindled with one match. "Do you think he'll ask?"

"Don't worry—you'll see him quite soon. His grandmother told me that she plans to hold a party at her home and invite you and Nelson and all the young men and ladies your age, including some of your second cousins. I've always thought it such a pity that you don't know your extended family very well."

"Speaking of family, may I ask you a question, Aunt Agnes? Everyone commented on my skin tone, which is quite unlike my father's. Did I inherit my dark coloring from my mother, by any chance?"

"We will not discuss your mother, Violet Rose, under any circumstances. Do not mention her ever again." With that, Aunt Agnes' lips drew closed in disapproval, as if they were attached to an invisible drawstring.

Once again I had encountered a wall of silence from my relatives. I was beginning to wonder if there was more to my mother's story than I had imagined.

Chapter

7

Friday, June 9, 1893

V iolet ... Violet!"

I opened my eyes to find Aunt Matt standing alongside my bed, whispering my name in an urgent voice. I sat up in alarm.

"What's wrong?"

"You need to get up and get dressed, quickly. We don't have much time."

I swung my legs out of bed and sniffed the air. I had been dreaming about the Great Fire again, and I expected to smell smoke. Instead, I smelled bacon.

"Not much time? To do what, Aunt Matt?"

"There's going to be a march today, and I think you should see it. Your father is dead set against my work, and he told Florence and Agnes to keep you well away from it, but Florence left for the settlement house and won't be home until this afternoon."

I stared at her sleepily, trying to digest her words.

"Well, come on. Why are you wasting time? Don't you want to

come with me and help shape the future for all women?"

"Yes, of course. I'd love to go with you." Especially if my father had forbidden it. I was still angry with him for lying to me and for bringing Maude O'Neill into our lives. Besides, if I armed myself with Aunt Matt's ammunition, perhaps I could scare Maude away by myself.

I climbed out of bed and opened the doors to my wardrobe. What did one wear to a march for women's rights? I couldn't recall ever studying that in school. I decided to take my cue from Aunt Matt's prim attire and chose a long, dark gray skirt and a high-collared white shirtwaist. I pinned up my long hair in a tight bun. But when I came downstairs, Aunt Matt was so focused on the upcoming battle that I don't think she would have noticed if I were wearing only my muslin undergarment.

"Do you want breakfast?" she asked. "There isn't time for it, but I suppose if you're really hungry I can find you a hard-boiled egg."

After feasting on sugary tea cakes and watercress sandwiches the past two days with Aunt Agnes, I could see that the battle for women's rights was going to involve great personal sacrifice.

"No, thank you, Aunt Matt. I'm not hungry."

"Good. Let's go, then."

I barely had time to pin on a straw boater hat before we marched out the front door. I had a hard time keeping up with my aunt as she charged down the block to the nearest streetcar stop. I should have worn sturdier shoes. Thank goodness I hadn't laced my corset very tightly.

"Now the first thing I want you to do," Aunt Matt said when we reached the streetcar stop, "is to forget everything you were taught in that ridiculous finishing school you attended. Women aren't silly, delicate creatures, incapable of grasping intelligent ideas. They are not the weaker sex. The act of childbearing alone should tell you how strong we are. Women are perfectly capable of going to the same universities as men and getting an identical education. There is already a school for women physicians, and someday women will be scientists and judges and company presidents too."

My facial expression must have revealed my shock and disbelief because she quickly added, "I doubt if I'll see it my lifetime, but why not, Violet? It isn't a question of ability—it's a question of opportunity. Women aren't going to tolerate being tied down much longer."

Her words reminded me of my mother. Father said she had hated her life, hated being tied down. Could this be what he'd meant?

A streetcar approached, the horses' hooves clopping noisily and raising a cloud of brown dust. We climbed aboard and Aunt Matt paid our fares. I waited until we were seated and the streetcar had lurched forward before asking, "Is that why my mother left us? My father said that she felt tied down."

"I really couldn't say. But I doubt if she left in search of educational opportunities." I detected scorn in Aunt Matt's tone.

"Then why did she leave?"

My aunt gave an impatient wave. "Listen, you aren't paying attention to the bigger picture, Violet. That's what I'm trying to show you. Our individual lives as women aren't nearly as important as the overall movement."

"Will this march take long? I'm afraid that if Aunt Agnes comes—"

"Too bad for her. She had you all week, and now it's my turn. I want you to see that there are alternatives to the life my sister has planned for you. You don't need a husband in order to be fulfilled as a woman."

"Are you against marriage?"

"Certainly not. There are some very good men in the world who treat their wives as equals. Elizabeth Cady Stanton's husband is one of them. But marriage is not for me. I see no reason to surrender my independence for a life of servitude."

"Aunt Birdie says I should marry for love."

"I suppose it's possible. She and Gilbert did seem to love each other. But who knows what sort of a husband he would have turned out to be over the years if he had lived."

I suddenly realized that I should be paying attention to where we were going and watching the street signs we passed. I needed to learn my way around the city if I ever hoped to find my mother's address on my own. It had been impossible to see any signposts at all when riding inside Aunt Agnes' carriage.

"Every married woman is an actress," Aunt Matt continued. "Each time she's with her husband it's as if she is onstage, playing the part that he expects her to play. The only time she can stop acting is when he leaves the stage."

I thought of the act I had been taught to play, the delicate art of flirtation I had rehearsed with Nelson Kent the other day. Would I have to continue acting, continue smiling enigmatically even after I was married? What if I could never be myself again, reading detective novels and letting my imagination run wild? The thought made me shudder.

"But I want you to understand, Violet, that if you do marry, it should be to someone who allows you to be your own person, not his ornament or prize. Let me ask you this: do you enjoy all that socializing and calling-card folderol that you do with Agnes? Do you really want to get married and be like those women, serving tea and gossiping for the rest of your life?" My grandmother had asked a similar question.

"I confess that I did find it a little boring when we discussed the weather for twenty minutes. But Aunt Agnes says we're going to attend cultural events too. And book discussions."

"Book discussions," Matt said derisively. "Those women should read something with substance, like Mary Wollstonecraft's masterpiece, *A Vindication of the Rights of Women*."

I didn't say so, but I couldn't picture Aunt Agnes' crowd delving into a book with such a formidable title. "What is it about?" I asked.

"Mary Wollstonecraft was years ahead of her time. She wrote that book one hundred years ago, in 1792. She said it was time for women to rise up and revolt against the status quo—the way our ancestors rebelled during the revolution. The patriots protested against taxation without representation. But do you realize that, as a woman, I'm forced to pay taxes on my home, yet I cannot vote for the man who imposed those taxes?"

"That doesn't seem fair."

"Of course it isn't fair. As one woman in the suffrage movement has said, 'I don't know what women's rights are, but I have suffered under a sense of women's wrongs.'"

People were getting on and off the streetcar as Aunt Matt lectured, and at times the car became quite crowded. She paid no attention to the other passengers, nor did she seem to care if anyone overheard the controversial things she was saying. Her booming voice was filled with righteous indignation as she lectured me.

I was listening so intently to my aunt's speech that I almost missed the signpost as the streetcar rumbled past LaSalle Street. That was it! LaSalle was the name of the street where my mother lived. It would be easy for me to retrace my steps and find it again. All I had to do was board the same streetcar, ride it straight to LaSalle, and get off. I could figure out which direction to turn on LaSalle once I got there, but hopefully it wouldn't be a long walk to my mother's house from the intersection.

"Are you paying attention, Violet?" Aunt Matt asked. I had swiveled around in my seat to get a good look at the street, but I quickly turned back again.

"Yes, Aunt Matt. Please go on. It's very interesting."

"Thousands of women became involved in the abolition movement before the War Between the States, and we worked very hard to bring an end to slavery. It was easy for us to sympathize with the slaves, you see. We understand what it's like to be considered inferior and to be denied all of the privileges that white men take for granted.

"Then the Fifteenth Amendment was passed, allowing Negro

men to vote—but the women who had fought so hard to help them win that right were left out! The new amendment stated that no one could be denied the right to vote on the basis of race, color, or the fact that he was previously a slave. It said absolutely nothing about gender. Now tell me, Violet: If it was wrong for a Negro man to be held in bondage, to be considered the property of a white man, then why is it all right for a woman to be enslaved to her husband? To be considered his property? For her wages to go to him?"

"It doesn't make sense," I admitted. The more I listened to Aunt Matt, the easier it was to understand why she always looked so furious. I was starting to clench my fists too.

"Another of our leaders, Susan B. Anthony, made up her mind to register to vote in Rochester, New York, along with her sister and several friends. Of course the men tried to intimidate them, but on election day, Miss Anthony and sixteen other registered women cast their votes. The U.S. Chief Marshal served her with a warrant, charging her with voting illegally. The court fined her one hundred dollars. She refused to pay it. That was twenty-one years ago, and she still hasn't paid. Miss Anthony is the current president of the National American Women's Suffrage Association, by the way—at the age of seventy-three."

"What's the point of women voting?" I asked.

"What's the point!"

I knew by her look of horror that I'd asked the wrong question. "Madame Beauchamps told us that it isn't feminine for women to take an interest in politics," I quickly explained.

"What?"

I lowered my voice to a near whisper after my aunt's shout drew stares. "Madame said that ladies needed to know only enough about politics and things like that to attract a man's interest. She said men didn't like women who were too intelligent."

"Lies! Male propaganda!" she sputtered. "What a horrible thing to teach impressionable young girls! How could your father send you to such a ridiculous institution? He's just like all the other men, trying to keep women in subjection! I don't suppose they taught you anything about modern science or mathematics or . . ."

My aunt was raving. I knew she didn't expect me to reply, so I didn't. Besides, I was busy trying to sink down in my seat to avoid being noticed.

"I can see that you'll require an entirely revised education," she continued. "The question is where to begin? You've obviously been wrongfully indoctrinated already. But you seem very bright, Violet. Have you ever thought of furthering your education?"

"I have a high-school diploma," I replied. I remembered all the hard work it had required to balance books on my head and to memorize names, and I added, "I graduated from Madame Beauchamps' School for—"

"Not that moronic place! I mean a real college, where women are allowed to learn alongside men, studying the sciences and so forth, not how to bat your eyelashes and flutter your fan."

I felt hurt that she would insult my school. But in truth, I had been terribly bored there. My friend Ruth and I hated all of the restrictions we faced as "proper young ladies." And so we had rebelled by covertly reading detective stories and dime novels. *"If I were a man,"* I often told Ruth, *"and I could be anything I wanted to be, I think I would become a detective."*

"I must show you the Woman's Pavilion at the World's Columbian Exposition," Aunt Matt said. "All of the planning, as well as the daily operation, has been under the guidance of the Board of Lady Managers. Even the building was designed by a female architect, Sophia Hayden." Aunt Matt pulled herself to her feet as the streetcar slowed to a halt. "Come, Violet. This is where we get off."

We stepped off the streetcar and walked two blocks to where a crowd of women had gathered outside a brick building. A sign above the storefront read: *Women's Suffrage Headquarters*. A second sign in the window read: *Come in and learn why women ought to vote*.

"Hurry," Aunt Matt said, tugging me by the arm. "The speeches are about to start."

I watched in surprise as a woman stepped up on a raised platform in front of the building to enthusiastic applause. The idea of a woman delivering a speech in a public place was outrageous. I glanced around, wondering if the police would rush forward to arrest her.

"Men want to deny women the right to speak in public," Aunt Matt said, as if reading my mind. "But we won't be denied."

"As many of you know," the speaker began, "this July marks the forty-fifth anniversary of the first Women's Rights Convention in America. In July of 1848, our tireless colleagues Elizabeth Cady Stanton and Lucretia Mott gathered with a group of like-minded women to discuss their rights and protest their condition. They drew up our Declaration of Sentiments and Resolutions, stating that the Creator has endowed *women* with certain unalienable rights too. Our declaration calls for an end to the absolute tyranny of men over women; for equality in higher education and in economic opportunity; for the right to equal child custody provisions; the right to speak in public and to testify in court. Most of all, the declaration calls for a woman's right to vote. Ladies and gentlemen, that's why we're here today."

She paused, waiting for the cheers and applause to die away. "Fifteen years ago, in 1878, our leader, Miss Susan B. Anthony, persuaded one courageous United States senator to propose a Constitutional Amendment guaranteeing women the right to vote. It was defeated. And it has been repeatedly defeated every year for the past fifteen years. But we will not let those defeats stop us!"

This time I got swept away too and found myself applauding with Aunt Matt and the other women.

"Thousands of women have signed our petition once again," the speaker continued, "asking our United States senators to support a constitutional amendment granting women the right to vote. I urge you to join our demonstration as we march to our senator's office today and present him with our request. We *will* be heard!"

Before I knew what was happening, someone handed signs to Aunt Matt and me and we were swept along as the crowd marched down the street. One group of women carried a banner that read *National American Women's Suffrage Association.* I hadn't felt such a thrill of excitement since the night Ruth Schultz and I crept into the school's basement at the stroke of midnight, carrying a candle, in an attempt to divine who our future husbands would be.

Cross traffic came to a halt as Aunt Matt and I surged down the middle of the street with hundreds of other women. Heads turned and pedestrians stopped to watch as we marched past. Cab drivers and teamsters shook their fists at us in rage for blocking traffic. We were definitely attracting attention.

Then I spotted an expensive carriage similar to Aunt Agnes', and I stopped in my tracks. Neither she nor her wealthy friends would be caught dead at this rally. What if one of them saw me? Would it ruin my chances for a wealthy husband?

The woman behind me bumped into me, forcing me forward again. But I had lost my enthusiasm for the cause, knowing that I had a great deal more to lose. What did it matter if I won the right to vote if I never found true love?

I instinctively lowered my sign. I was afraid to look at the crowds of people lining the sidewalks as we marched past. I heard angry catcalls and wished I were shorter, or that I could hide in the center of the procession. If only I had worn a larger hat—or one with a veil.

Yet the rebel in me realized that Aunt Matt had made some excellent points. In spite of Madame B.'s indoctrination, I did balk at the idea that I was somehow inferior. Besides, on the train ride into the city I had decided to leave my suffocating cocoon and fly freely, and this certainly felt like flying. I lifted my sign again, proud to be supporting a good cause. And maybe, if I held my sign just right, I could fight for women's suffrage and shield my face from view at the same time.

I marched for several more blocks in this proud yet timorous state—until I spotted a squad of uniformed policemen armed with billy clubs moving into the middle of the street to stop us.

"Aunt Matt? Are . . . are the police going to arrest us?"

"It wouldn't be the first time. Honestly! The city officials should be ashamed of themselves for sending the police. This is a peaceful march. The constitution grants men the rights to freedom of speech and freedom of assembly; shouldn't women be accorded the same rights?"

"I-I guess so."

The parade halted. As I watched the policemen move in, I imagined what it would be like to be taken into custody by a handsome young Irish policeman with curly dark hair and Irish-green eyes. I made up my mind to struggle so that he would have to take me into his brawny arms to subdue me and carry me away, but of course he would fall hopelessly in love with me the moment he lifted me off my feet. He would try to find a way to spring me from jail, but I would refuse to accept his offer, preferring to suffer with my fellow suffragettes. What fun it would be—and so dramatic—to be arrested and locked inside a cell and forced to spend the night in jail! I might even have to share a cell with so-called "women of the night" and listen to their scandalous stories as we ate our meal of bread and water. I would have a prison record and—

I would have a prison record?

I saw all of my chances for a society husband going up in smoke. I tugged on my aunt's arm to get her attention.

"Um . . . Aunt Matt?"

"Yes?"

"While I clearly see the merit in what you're trying to accomplish, and I agree wholeheartedly with everything you've said . . .

um . . . I don't think Grandmother or my father would be very pleased if we got arrested."

She frowned as she considered my words. "I suppose you're right," she said in disgust. "Maybe another day. This is only your first march, after all." She grabbed my sign and gave it to one of the other women, along with her own. Then we stepped out of the street and onto the sidewalk to walk back the way we had just come. I could see that Aunt Matt was furious, but whether it was with me or with all the injustice she had endured in life, I didn't know. I decided to remain quiet.

We returned to the streetcar stop and climbed aboard the first car that arrived. Aunt Matt released an enormous sigh as she sank onto the seat.

"How did you get involved in the suffrage movement?" I asked her—just to let her know I was still on her side.

"One of my earliest memories is of my father's reaction when my sister Florence was born. 'If only she had been a boy,' he said over and over again. 'Why couldn't she have been a boy?' It seemed as though a great tragedy had occurred in our home, like a death in the family. He had the same reaction when Agnes and Bertha were born—deep, deep disappointment.

"As I grew older, I tried very hard to make him proud of me, to show him that I was just as good as any son. I began reading his newspapers, following his court cases, and discussing current events with him. I even learned how to research law cases for him. I wanted to be everything to him that a son would have been.

"But even as he lay dying, he told me, 'Too bad you weren't a boy. . . . It's my lifelong regret that I never had a son to carry on my work.' He was disappointed in me and there wasn't a thing I could do about it. It didn't matter how sharp my mind was or how well I could converse with him. He never forgave me for being trapped in a woman's body."

"That doesn't seem fair," I said.

"Nearly all men are the same. They want sons. And they blame their wives for failing if they produce only daughters. My mother had a very difficult time delivering Bertha and nearly died. She never should have had another child. But Father insisted that she produce a son for him. My mother died in childbirth along with her fifth child—her fifth daughter."

By the time Aunt Matt finished her story we were home. I didn't know what to say to her, but fortunately she went straight into her room and closed the door. Her story left me feeling very sad. I wondered if my father had decided to marry Maude so that he could have a son.

I went into the parlor and collapsed onto the sofa, exhausted and invigorated at the same time. Compared to sipping tea and discussing the merits of thunder, it had been an exhilarating day.

Could Aunt Matt and her friends be right? Were women just as smart and strong and deserving of a good education as men? And should women be allowed to vote? I had a lot to think about.

I hadn't seen my grandmother's hat on the hall tree, so I knew she was still out. I would have a few minutes alone with Aunt Birdie's photographs. I crept over to the secretary, opened the drawer, and had just picked up the first photo when Aunt Birdie came in.

"That's a picture of Matt," she said, peering over my shoulder. I had to look very closely before I could see that she was right. Aunt Matt was smiling. And slender. And pretty. She wore a light-colored dress. And jewelry.

"She looks so different," I said.

"It's her engagement picture. She had it taken for her beau."

"I didn't know Aunt Matt was engaged."

"We didn't think she would ever get married. She was thirty-one when she met Robert. He was one of my father's acquaintances, and he came to visit when Father was dying. The rest of us were all married and had left home by then. Matt lived here alone, taking care of him. His illness was very hard on her. But then Robert Tucker came to call, and Matt fell in love. Oh my, she was *so* in love!"

"What happened?"

"It turned out he was a thief," Aunt Birdie whispered.

"What do you mean, a *thief?*"

"Well, a thief is someone who robs people of their money and all their valuables and—"

"Yes, yes, I know what a thief *does*, but what kinds of things did this man steal? And how did Aunt Matt find out about it?"

"Why, she found out when he stole her heart, of course."

"But—"

"Oh, good. There's the postman," Aunt Birdie said as the daily mail suddenly fell through the slot in our front door with a plop. "I do hope I get a letter from Gilbert today. He hasn't written in ever so long."

I studied Aunt Matt's picture, unable to get over the enormous change in her. Aunt Birdie was right: Robert Tucker was a thief. He'd stolen Aunt Matt's smile and all of her joy . . . along with her heart.

Chapter

8

Madame Beauchamps had prepared us for a variety of occasions and circumstances, including how to eat snails and nibble caviar, but she had never warned us that being sociable could be so exhausting. I found out just how tiring it was on the evening of the fund-raiser for the Art Institute of Chicago. Aunt Agnes and Uncle Henry took me to the gala event, and from the moment we strode through the door, the evening felt like a test of physical endurance combined with one of Madame's grueling final examinations.

I also discovered the extreme pain involved in the life of a socialite. I acquired rows of welts around my middle from lacing my corset too tightly and bubbly blisters on my feet from dancing in delicate silk slippers all evening. My head throbbed from staying constantly alert, remembering dozens of names, and keeping the conversational tennis ball in play. But the part of me that ached the most was my face. Holding a mysterious smile in place for four or five hours was very hard work.

My evening did not get off to a very good start either. Aunt Matt happened to be standing in the foyer when I descended the stairs in my finery, and I knew from the frown on her face that I had disappointed her.

"So. I see you're still running around with Agnes."

"I'm sorry, Aunt Matt." I felt the need to apologize, but I didn't know why. "She and Uncle Henry are taking me to a fund-raiser for the Art Institute. Aunt Agnes says they've opened a new building on Michigan Avenue recently, and now they're raising money to expand their art collection."

Aunt Matt clucked her tongue in disapproval. "It's just a veiled excuse for Agnes to find you a rich husband. Listen to me, Violet. Agnes married Henry Paine for his money. So before you blindly follow the path she took, I suggest that you ask her how happy her marriage has been."

"That's a rather personal question, isn't it? I-I really wouldn't feel right asking her such a thing."

"Then I'll tell you. Henry keeps a mistress." If Aunt Matt intended to shock me, she had succeeded. She had also given me more information than I cared to know.

"Oh . . . I see."

"Wealthy society men all have them, you know. They marry a suitable woman—whom they don't love—for propriety's sake and keep a mistress on the side. Nobody ever talks about this dirty little secret, though, do they?"

"No," I said quietly. I could feel my cheeks burning.

"If you're going to run with Agnes' crowd, then you need to know the truth about them."

I wanted desperately to change the subject. "But the Art Institute is a good cause, isn't it? Art and culture aren't frivolous."

"No, they aren't frivolous. But I would be willing to bet that very few of the funds they raise will be used to support female artists. It's all right for a woman to be the *object* of art, but that's all she's allowed to be—an object. It's too bad, because there are some very fine female artists, you know. The American painter Mary Cassatt helped design the interior of the Woman's Pavilion at the Columbian Exposition."

"I'll be very eager to see it when you take me there, Aunt Matt. But I need to leave now. I think Aunt Agnes' carriage is here."

"Be very careful, Violet," she said ominously.

"I will." I hurried out the door.

I felt quite differently toward Uncle Henry after learning that he was an adulterer. Fortunately, it was dark inside the carriage, so I didn't have to face him. Aunt Agnes started dispensing advice the moment the horses began to move.

"Now, don't be nervous, Violet. I'm sure you'll do just fine. You've handled yourself splendidly so far. The other ladies have been very favorably impressed with you. But tonight will be an important evening for you. Everyone who is anyone will be there—and that includes several potential suitors, of course."

She went on and on this way for the entire carriage ride, so I didn't have to do much more than nod my head and murmur in agreement. Uncle Henry said nothing at all.

From the moment we arrived at the fund-raiser, the gaiety and glitter swept me away. The event was held in a private residence overlooking the lake, a mansion by anyone's standards. The party was already in full swing, and the magnificent ballroom, which occupied the entire third floor, echoed with music and the laughter of hundreds of vivacious guests. I soon discovered that Aunt Matt had been right; the event had very little to do with art but was all about gowns and jewels and hobnobbing with the elite. For Aunt Agnes, it was an opportunity to find me a wealthy husband.

The Grant sisters greeted me like a long-lost friend. Their real names were Hattie and Nettie, but I secretly called them Haughty and Naughty. They pretended to be nice to me, and they made a huge fuss over my gown, but I could tell that their comments were insincere. I'd spent hours learning how to make idle, insincere chit-

chat at Madame Beauchamps' school, so it was easy for me to recognize it. Haughty made such a show of fluttering her fan to command attention that I wanted to yank it out of her hand and toss it
into the fireplace.

Eventually a group of eligible bachelors joined us, and since mine
was a new face among these pitifully bored creatures, the men
accorded me a great deal of attention. Several of the women I'd met
during my afternoon teas eagerly introduced me to their nephews and
sons and grandsons. Naughty's fixed smile slipped into a narrow-eyed
glower of jealousy when one of the women introduced me to her
great-nephew Edward. It didn't take Sherlock Holmes to deduce that
Naughty had designs on him.

The orchestra kept the event merry, playing an endless variety of
waltzes, and I danced with dozens of young men. After a while, my
would-be suitors seemed as alike as peas and as phony as wooden
nickels. We might have been at a masquerade ball, where all of the
men wore the same mask to hide their true identities. I was disappointed that none of them fell in love with me at first sight the way
Aunt Birdie's husband had fallen for her. Nor did I feel the fever of
true love toward any of them.

After countless dances, several glasses of punch, and a few trips
to the buffet table with my pea-pod partners, I wanted to collapse in
exhaustion. I extricated myself from a conversation with one of the
peas and was trying to slip away for a few moments alone—mostly
to give my tired face a rest—when Nelson Kent came up beside me.

"This is quite a feat of endurance, isn't it, Miss Hayes? How are
you holding up?" His was the first sincere expression I had seen all
night. I took a chance and wiped the enigmatic smile off my face and
answered truthfully.

"To be honest, I'm exhausted. I was just sneaking away from it all
to rest for a few minutes."

"Good idea. Come on. I know where there's a balcony. We can
get a breath of fresh air. Well, as fresh as the air ever gets here in

Chicago." He linked arms with me and led the way outside to a spacious, third-floor balcony. A dozen other people already milled around out there, so I knew we would be well chaperoned.

"How do you like the view?" he asked, pointing to the night sky above Lake Michigan. "Whenever I get tired of all this rigmarole, I like to go outside and look at the stars. They remind me of what's real and true."

Handsome, elegant Nelson Kent intrigued me. He was so casual and comfortable with the socially elite and with all of this wealth, yet he didn't keep his mask in place like the others had. Of all the young gentlemen with whom I'd danced and sipped punch, he alone seemed genuine—and I felt at ease with him for some reason, as if we were old friends.

We talked for several minutes about real things, and I didn't feel the need to pretend. The only time Nelson's mask went up was when someone approached us. He would offer his charming smile as he greeted them, shaking hands, saying a personal word or two, and asking a question to show he was interested in them—obviously as well trained as I had been—but I could tell that his heart wasn't in it.

"Tell me who you really are, Nelson," I said between interruptions.

"What do you mean?"

"Well . . . for starters, do you work here in Chicago?"

"I just graduated from university last month. I'm taking some time off before I begin working with my father's firm."

"What does your father do?"

"Several different things—he's a property manager, a real-estate developer, an investor. He wants me to learn his business from the ground up, but he promised me an executive position alongside him once I've settled down."

"And do you want to settle down?"

"I don't know," he said with a shrug. "I'm his only son, so it's expected of me."

He looked so unhappy that I felt compelled to ask, "If you could choose to be anything you wanted to be, what would you choose?"

"That's a good question. I would have to think about it. . . ." His worried frown deepened, and he gazed out over the lake for a moment before saying, "I know I'd choose something challenging—that's for certain. I like the business world, but I doubt if working for my father will be very demanding. His business is well established. Safe. Secure. . . . But if I could choose for myself, I'd like to take more risks, branch out into something new and modern—maybe I'd invest in one of the new horseless carriages or a flying machine or some other novel invention."

"Why don't you do it, then?"

"I have no capital of my own," he replied, showing me his empty hands. "And my father is a very conservative investor. He would never take a chance on something unless it's tried and true. . . . But what about you, Violet? What would you like to do if you had a choice?"

"The proper answer to that question is to get married and have a family," I told him. "Women aren't supposed to dream of anything else."

He must have picked up a note of discontent in my tone or expression because he said, "I get the feeling that you're different. That you find this life rather boring. . . . Oh, don't worry—it's boring to me too. So tell me the truth, Violet. What would you really like to do?"

I took a chance and let my own mask slip a little further. "This is very scandalous, so please don't tell my Aunt Agnes, but I took part in a march for women's rights with my Aunt Matilda the other day."

"No kidding? Good for you. So what did you think? Are you going to join them and be a suffragette too?"

"I wouldn't dare," I laughed. "My father would tie me up and carry me back to Lockport in a gunnysack if he ever found out. But my aunt and all the others in the movement are dreaming of a future when women will be accepted as equals with men. She thinks women will be able to get an education and hold professional positions some-day. Do you believe that?"

"I don't see why not." He looked me right in the eye when he said it, and I knew he was one of the few good men that Aunt Matilda had mentioned. "So if things were different, Violet, and men accepted women as equals, what would you become?"

"A detective."

"Really." He smiled. A genuine one. He wasn't laughing at me or my idea. And he seemed very pleased that I had told him the truth.

"I would love to solve mysteries and help catch notorious criminals," I told him, though I realized that my career as a detective hadn't gotten off to a very good start. I had lived in Chicago for nearly a week and still hadn't found my mother.

"How is it that you became interested in detective work?" he asked. But I never had a chance to reply. We were interrupted again by one of the peas I had danced with earlier.

"There you are, Nelson. Hiding out here, are you? And with the prettiest woman at the party too. The Grant sisters are looking for you," he told Nelson. "They said that you promised both of them a waltz, and time is running out."

"I'll be there in a minute." He turned back to me with a sigh. When the pea moved on and we were alone again, he asked, "Have you met the Grant sisters?"

"Oh, yes—Haughty and Naughty."

Nelson broke into a wide grin. "What did you call them?"

I clapped my hand over my mouth. How had I allowed my secret names for them to slip out?

"Come on," he said, laughing. "Tell me what you just called them. . . . Please?"

"Promise you won't tell anyone?"

"Of course not. It'll be our little secret."

"Well, I invented a system for recalling names, you see. I make up a fake one that's similar to the real one, based on the person's attributes. I know the Grant sisters' real names are Hattie and Nettie—but I've nicknamed them Haughty and Naughty."

Nelson laughed so loudly that people turned to stare in our direction. "You are one of a kind, Violet Hayes." He took my hand in his and squeezed it. "And by the way, you look lovely when you blush."

Someone else interrupted us, looking for me, this time. "Your Aunt Agnes wants you right away."

"She probably found another bachelor to introduce me to," I mumbled, loud enough for only Nelson to hear. "I'd better go." He tightened his grip on my hand to prevent me from leaving.

"Wait. I want to ask you something first." He turned to the messenger and said, "Tell Mrs. Paine that Miss Hayes will be there in a moment." Nelson was still holding my hand when he asked, "Will you let me escort you to that silly party my grandmother insists on giving next week? I like you, Violet. You're different from all the others. You don't playact with me. I think we could become good friends. Besides, I don't think I have the energy to go through these phony dating rituals all over again next Saturday. Do you?"

I didn't care about playing the coquette. And I was no longer sure that I wanted a rich husband if he was going to turn out to be unfaithful like Uncle Henry. I was tired of flirting and very tired of smiling enigmatically. It was true that my heart didn't flutter uncontrollably when I was with Nelson, but he already seemed like a good friend, even though I barely knew him.

"I agree with you," I told him. "This is very tiring. I would be happy to let you escort me on Saturday."

"Good. I'll pick you up around seven o'clock. And I'll want to know what other names you've dreamed up for people . . . and what you call me."

"Now that you mention it, I've never made up one for you." I smiled—a genuine one—and hurried off to find Aunt Agnes. She would be disappointed with me for accepting Nelson's offer and not playing the game a little longer, but I think Aunt Matt would be pleased with my decision. Of course Aunt Birdie would remind me to make sure I married for love, and my grandmother . . . I had no idea what she would say. I had been ignoring her terribly while running around the city with her two sisters.

When I found Aunt Agnes, she had a smile of satisfaction on her face and another eligible bachelor in her clutches. I managed to hold up and keep smiling for the remainder of the evening, but I felt enormously relieved when it was time to go home.

Uncle Henry climbed into the carriage with us, leaned back against the seat, and promptly fell asleep. I sighed with relief. I had dreaded conversing with him, especially after watching him flirt with every attractive matron at the party. I wished that Aunt Matt had never told me about his mistress. I would have been content to ride home in silence, but Aunt Agnes wanted to review the entire evening in great detail.

"You certainly attracted a great deal of attention among the eligible bachelors tonight. I daresay you danced with every one of them. Did you enjoy yourself this evening?"

"Yes, very much. Thank you for inviting me." I tried not to sound as weary as I felt. "I met a lot of nice people. And the food was delicious too."

"Anyone in particular who struck your fancy?"

"No—not really."

"Well, I noticed that you spent a considerable amount of time in the company of young Nelson Kent out on the balcony." And if Aunt Agnes had noticed, so had everyone else at the ball.

"He's different from the others."

"I think I know why he is so eager to move quickly with you. His grandmother told me that Nelson's father promised him a place in his firm once he settles down."

"Yes, Nelson told me the same thing."

"You know what that means, don't you? He won't get ahead until he is suitably married. The sooner he finds a wife, the sooner he'll get his hands on his father's money."

Was that why he'd been so friendly to me? Had I misread him

completely? If what Aunt Agnes said was true, then Nelson wasn't being genuine with me at all; he was looking for someone he could court and marry quickly. I was new, with no suitors competing for my hand, and he probably considered me an easy catch. After all, I'd admitted that I didn't enjoy playing the flirtatious game of cat and mouse.

"I like Nelson, Aunt Agnes, but I'm not in a hurry to rush to the altar with him."

"Well, you should be in a *bit* of a hurry at your age. A woman's beauty fades very quickly after her twentieth birthday, you know. And her choice of suitors thins considerably too."

I didn't care if my beauty was fading—I wasn't ready to settle down yet. If only I could enjoy a little freedom before I went from being under my father's protection and supervision to being under my husband's rule. According to Aunt Matt, I would become my husband's property once I married, and I'd have to act the part he expected me to play for the rest of my life. Was I being naïve to want love? Was it only the stuff of romance stories or the musings of my addled aunt Birdie?

The carriage hit a bump in the road and Uncle Henry shifted positions, snorting loudly in his sleep. We happened to be passing beneath a gaslight and I saw the look Aunt Agnes gave him before she turned away; it was not a loving one. Except for the carriage ride to and from the ball, I hadn't seen my aunt and uncle together all evening. Aunt Matt had piqued my curiosity, but I would never dare ask someone about her marriage.

"I'm going to send over my seamstress on Monday morning, Violet. You're going to need a new gown for the party at the Kent home next Saturday."

"Thank you. That's very generous of you." But I knew that my aunt's offer wasn't entirely altruistic. She would move up the social ladder along with me if I married well.

The lights were still glowing in our parlor when I arrived home, and I was surprised to find my grandmother waiting up for me, knitting a pair of socks. She looked tired. According to the hall clock, it was nearly one in the morning.

"I'm sorry I'm so late."

"That's okay, dear. How was the party? Did you have a good time?"

"I guess so."

"You don't sound very enthused."

I watched her put away her knitting and slowly rise to her feet, leaning on the arms of her chair. I wondered if she was as disappointed in me as Aunt Matt was for getting so caught up in the social scene. Grandmother worked very hard for several charitable causes, yet I'd shown no interest at all in what she did. She had asked me to help her knit socks, but I hadn't taken time to do that either.

"To tell you the truth, Grandmother, a lot of what goes on at these high-society functions seems a bit . . . phony. I want to find a good husband but . . ." I shrugged and left the sentence dangling. She rested her hand on my arm.

"What is your definition of *good*? A wealthy one?"

"I don't know anymore. According to Aunt Agnes, Father sent me to Chicago to find a proper husband. So does that mean he wants me to marry into high society?"

Grandmother removed her hand and turned away. "I really don't know, dear. Your father doesn't tell me what he's thinking." Her voice sounded sad.

"But you're his mother. Why doesn't he—?"

"It's very late," she said, stifling a yawn. "We'd better go to bed. Will you be coming to church with me tomorrow?"

Attending weekly church services was a chore to me, and I longed to sleep until noon on Sunday. But I didn't want to hurt Grandmother's feelings—especially after she'd waited up for me tonight.

"Yes," I replied. "I would be happy to go to church with you."

Chapter

9

Sunday, June 11, 1893

Sunday morning dawned much too soon. I regretted my promise to attend church services with my grandmother the moment she tapped on my bedroom door to awaken me.

"Violet Rose? If you still want to come to church with me you'll need to get up soon."

"Okay," I mumbled. "I'm up." But I waited until the last possible moment to climb out of bed, just as I had in boarding school. I could get dressed faster than any of the other girls could. It helped that I always skipped breakfast—as I planned to do this morning.

Grandmother was waiting for me in the front hall when I finally descended the stairs. I still wore my hair pinned up from last night— a trick I'd learned that helped me get ready faster—but it looked very disheveled. I had also learned that I could avoid fussing with it by wearing a very large hat.

"Ready?" Grandmother asked.

I managed to nod in reply. I could barely keep up with her as she set off briskly down the street. Maybe I could squeeze in a short nap during the sermon.

"How far away is your church?" I asked, hoping it belonged to the steeple I saw on the next block.

"We'll have to take a streetcar. It's too far to walk. The church is downtown, on the corner of Chicago and LaSalle Streets." I perked up at the name LaSalle, the street where my mother lived. If only I had thought to bring her address.

We took the same streetcar that Aunt Matt and I had taken and got off at the LaSalle Street stop. Then we boarded another car that drove straight up LaSalle. I studied all of the buildings we passed, wondering if my mother was inside one of them at this very moment, a stone's throw away from me. Most of the buildings looked more like offices than residential dwellings.

My grandmother took me by the arm the moment we stepped off the streetcar and towed me behind her like a tugboat hauling an overloaded barge. She seemed flushed and excited and in a great hurry to get to church.

"What's the rush?" I asked as I stumbled along behind her. "Are we late?"

"Not yet. But there's someone I want you to meet before the service starts." She led me to an enormous brick building, several stories tall, with an even taller, castlelike tower.

"I can't believe this is a church," I said, gazing up at the imposing building.

"The first church that Dwight Moody founded was over on Illinois Street, but it burned down during the Great Fire. He dedicated this building five years later."

I was wide-awake now. My mother and father had met during the Great Fire. Maybe I could find another clue to the mystery.

"Did my grandfather preach at that other church?" I asked. "Did you live in Chicago at the time of the fire?"

"No, your grandfather's church was in Lockport—you know that."

I feared that my arm would come out of the socket as she pulled me up the stairs and into the building. She stopped once we reached the dim foyer and craned her neck to look around at the milling crowd, searching for someone.

"Ah, there he is!" she said with a smile of relief. "Yoo-hoo! Louis! Here we are!" She towed me by the arm toward a young man in his midtwenties who was kneading his hat in his hands.

"Louis, this is my granddaughter, Violet Rose." She beamed as if presenting him with the grand prize in a prestigious contest. "And, Violet, I'd like you to meet a dear young friend of mine, Louis Decker."

"How do you do, Miss Hayes? Your grandmother has told me so much about you. I've been looking forward to meeting you."

"Um . . . a pleasure, Mr. Decker."

I confess that I was much too surprised to say anything else. Was he the reason why my grandmother had been so eager for me to accompany her? Was she trying to find a husband for me too? I suppose it was only fair, since Aunt Agnes was doing the same thing, but I had never expected matchmaking from my grandmother.

Louis Decker was a compact, vigorous-looking young man with dark, discerning eyes behind his smudged, wire-rimmed spectacles. He was the first man I'd met in Chicago who seemed able to look at me rather than at my pretty facade. Nevertheless, I wished I had taken more time with my appearance.

"Louis is a student at the Chicago Evangelistic Society," Grandmother explained. "We've both been helping with Mr. Moody's campaign to win souls for the Lord while the Columbian Exposition is in town."

"Are you interested in Mr. Moody's work too, Miss Hayes?" he asked.

"I'm sorry, but I've never heard of him."

He blinked and his eyes widened in surprise.

"I've been away at boarding school for the past three years," I quickly explained, "and I've only been in Chicago for a week."

"I see. Well, Dwight L. Moody is a very famous evangelist who has traveled all over the United States and England, leading people to the Savior. And now that the whole world is coming to Chicago for the Exposition, he has organized a special campaign to preach the Gospel all over the city."

"Louis is very dedicated to Mr. Moody's work," my grandmother added, patting his shoulder. "And he also helps me with my work with the poor."

Louis held up his hands in protest. "It's all for the Lord's glory. After all, He has done so much for me." They might have been speaking a foreign language.

The best word to describe Louis Decker would be *intense*. He had a sense of urgency about him, as if a celestial clock was ticking away the seconds and soon he would have to give a thorough accounting of himself to the Almighty. Louis had longish hair and he wore a rumpled suit, but unlike my own tousled appearance, which was the result of my own laziness, Mr. Decker's dishevelment seemed the result of his having more important matters to attend to than his appearance.

"Why don't you take Violet Rose to see the Sunday school?" Grandmother asked. "There's time before the service starts. I'll meet you back here in a few minutes."

Louis nodded and led the way, plowing a path through the crowd for me. He was either too shy or too focused on his mission to offer me his arm, so I followed him as best I could. Nothing could have prepared me for what I saw.

The Sunday school children—and there were hundreds of them—were the poorest, most bedraggled souls I'd ever seen. Not one of them wore a decent set of clothing. I saw outfits that were many sizes too big or too small, ragged, worn out, falling apart at the seams. Most of the children were without shoes, and the shoes I did see obviously didn't fit—or were about to disintegrate. I thought of the cold winters in Illinois and knew that if Grandmother and I both knit from now until Christmas, we would never be able to make enough warm socks for all those dirty, callused little feet.

"Oh my!" My hands fluttered helplessly. "Oh, the poor little dears!" I looked at their matted hair and scabby faces, and I couldn't help comparing them to pudgy, well-scrubbed Horace and Harriet, who had probably never known a day of want in their lives. Louis Decker must have noticed the tears that had sprung to my eyes.

"We can always use an extra pair of hands around here," he said gently.

"Yes . . . I-I can see that you might."

"The Gospel gives them hope, Miss Hayes. Jesus was born into poverty, just as they were. And He loved these little ones. He said, 'Suffer the little children to come unto me, and forbid them not: for of such is the kingdom of God.' That's what our work is all about— building the kingdom."

"They seem very happy here." It was true. I saw smiles on nearly every little face in spite of their destitution.

"Mr. Moody started out as a shoe salesman," Louis told me. "He saw kids like these roaming Chicago's streets, and he made up his mind to start a Sunday school for them. His father had died when he was a child, and he understood what it was like to grow up desperately poor. But he also knew that God promises to be a Father to the fatherless."

"What about the motherless?" I murmured.

Louis bent his head toward mine and cupped his ear. "I'm sorry, I couldn't hear you above the noise."

"Nothing. Please continue."

"Mr. Moody's first Sunday school classes met in a converted saloon, but when that space became too small, he raised money to build his first church over on Illinois Street. He eventually had fifteen hundred children in his classes. President Lincoln heard about it and paid the Sunday school a visit. Mr. Moody is still a salesman—and I mean that in the best sense of the word. Only now he's using his talent to pitch the Gospel instead of shoes."

I could only nod, too moved by all of the ragged, exuberant

children to speak. I recalled the fervor of Mr. McClure's presentation aboard the train for Dr. Dean's Blood Builder, and I tried to imagine that same fervor applied in selling religion. Louis Decker reminded me of Silas McClure and of Herman Beckett all rolled together into one man; he had the same restless energy I'd seen in the elixir sales-man, combined with Herman's somber earnestness. If he had Nelson Kent's fortune, he could have transformed the world.

"We'd better find your grandmother," Louis finally said. He gen-tly led me away from the pitiful children, walking back the way we had come. I confess that I couldn't have turned aside on my own.

"Have you enjoyed your visit to Chicago so far, Miss Hayes? How have you been occupying your time?"

His question caused the tears in my eyes to overflow. I couldn't reply. My own superficiality horrified me. I'd spent my time sipping tea and preening to win a wealthy husband. I shuddered at the thought of all the wasted food I'd seen at Aunt Agnes' parties, at all of the money her society friends spent on gowns and jewels, and at the shallowness of my pea-pod dancing partners. Louis Decker lived a life that was meaningful, and mine felt banal and superficial in comparison. What good were all of the fine manners I'd learned at Madame Beauchamps' School for Young Ladies when children were shivering and hungry?

"I would like to help you with your work," I said, wiping a tear.

He smiled for the first time. "I'd be honored, Miss Hayes. Do you play the piano, by any chance?"

"Yes, a little. I haven't practiced in weeks though. Why do you ask?"

"We're desperate for a pianist for some of our evangelistic ser-vices. Mr. Moody rents theaters in various parts of the city and puts up tents in order to preach to the crowds wherever he finds them. You could be a tremendous help if you would be willing to accom-pany us on the piano for our song services."

"Oh, but I'm not a professional by any means."

"That doesn't matter. The music is quite simple—four-part

hymns, usually. I could give you a copy of Mr. Sankey's songbook so you could practice in advance."

"I-I guess I could give it a try." I was glad that at least one other thing I'd learned at Madame B.'s besides my enigmatic smile would be put to good use.

"I understand that your grandfather was an outstanding preacher—and that your father worked for Mr. Moody around the time of the Great Fire."

"What? Not *my* father. You must be mistaken. He owns a bunch of grain elevators in Lockport."

"I'm sorry. Perhaps I'm mistaken. I must have misunderstood what your grandmother told me."

What had she told Louis? And what other secrets was my family keeping from me? Anger boiled up inside me the way it had the night I'd learned the truth about my mother. I was trying not to let it spew out when Louis spoke again.

"I would love to hear your testimony, Miss Hayes."

"My what?"

"Your testimony—the story of your faith."

I drew a deep breath, not sure of what he meant. "There isn't much to tell. My father and I usually attend a small church in Lockport, but religion doesn't seem to interest him very much—which is why I'm certain you're mistaken about his working for Mr. Moody. When I went away to boarding school, the headmistress required all of us to attend church services on Sunday. It was our duty, Madame B. said. She called it our 'weekly obligation.' My grandmother is much more religious than Father and I are. She pours all of her energy into her causes, as I'm sure you know. My grandfather was a minister, as you also know, but my father seems rather indifferent when it comes to religion."

"What about you, Violet? I'm not asking about your father's faith or your grandmother's. I want to know about yours."

I had no idea what to say. Going to church was simply something everyone did on Sunday. The religious traditions were especially nice during the holidays. But Louis Decker seemed to imply that there should be more to it than that.

"I didn't mean to put you on the spot," he said when I didn't reply. "I'd just like to get to know you a little better." He removed his smudged spectacles and pulled a handkerchief from his pocket to clean them. I saw no difference at all when he'd finished rubbing them and had put them on again.

"I would like to know you better too," I said.

I longed to ask him one of my "If you could choose" questions, but I didn't dare. I didn't want him to know how frivolous and shallow I really was. My wild flights of imagination seemed immature compared to the serious work he did every day. For some reason I wanted Louis to like me, to approve of me—and I sensed that he would be shocked to learn that I enjoyed reading detective stories and dime novels. I had just met Louis Decker a few minutes ago, yet I cared very much about what he thought of me. Was it for my grandmother's sake or for my own?

We found my grandmother again, and she looked so hopeful as she studied our faces that I was certain she was indeed playing matchmaker. I never would have expected it of her.

"I look forward to seeing you again, Miss Hayes," Louis said as we parted.

"Yes. So do I." I meant it too.

The Sunday worship service in my grandmother's church was very different from the one back home in Lockport. The music was livelier, the preaching more passionate, and for once I had no trouble at all staying awake during the sermon.

"Is this where you come to do your charity work every day?" I asked her later as we rode the streetcar home.

"This is just one of the places where I'm needed. Why do you ask?"

"Mr. Decker asked me to come back with you some time and play the piano for the song services."

"And are you going to?"

"I told him I would try. I'm not a very accomplished player. And I'm horribly out of practice."

"Louis is a very fine young man. He works tirelessly for the Lord."

"He asked if he could see me again. He wants to get to know me better."

"I'm so glad." Grandmother and I sat side by side on the wooden streetcar seat and she rested her hand on top of mine. "I realize that Louis Decker can't compete with all of the wealthy suitors Agnes has lined up for you. But I think that in the long run you would find life with a man like Louis much more meaningful than a life of endless parties and teas."

I suspected that she was right. And I was quite certain that a man like Louis Decker wouldn't commit adultery.

"Can I ask you something?" I said after a moment. "Louis said that my father used to work with Mr. Moody. Is that true?" The streetcar rumbled down an entire city block before she replied.

"Your father was a volunteer with Mr. Moody's Yokefellows."

"What are Yokefellows?"

"It's a group of layman he started. They go around to saloons and bars searching for converts."

Now it was my turn to pause as I summoned the courage to ask my next question.

"Was that how he met my mother?"

"No," she said quietly. "I don't know all the details of the night they met, but I know that it wasn't in a saloon."

"Aunt Birdie said that my parents met during the Great Fire. Is that true?"

Again Grandmother hesitated for a long time, as if deciding whether or not to talk about my mother. I knew that she might not answer, but I also knew that she wouldn't lie.

"Yes, it's true," she said quietly. "Your father rescued her."

"Rescued her? How?"

"Your father had gone to the evening service at Mr. Moody's Illinois Street church. It was a beautiful building with Sunday school classrooms, an office, a library . . . He told me that Mr. Moody preached a sermon on the life of Jesus. The service was still in progress, in fact, when they heard all the fire engines rushing past. Then the great courthouse bell began to toll in warning, and the congregation started to grow restless, concerned about all the noise and confusion in the streets outside. Mr. Moody ended the service so everyone could leave. The fire swept through the city that night, burning Mr. Moody's church and his home to the ground."

"Did my father—?"

She shook her head. "I'm sorry, Violet Rose, but you need to ask him these questions, not me. . . . Now, you wanted to know what some of my other work projects are. I'm also involved with the Temperance Union. Our goal is to have all alcoholic beverages banned and all of the saloons closed for good. We want to put an end to drunkenness and to the lawlessness that goes hand in hand with it. We're trying to have the alcohol removed from patent medicines as well—or else have them banned outright. Most people don't even know that these so-called 'medicines' contain alcohol, but many of them do. They have caused untold sorrow when people unknowingly become addicted to them."

I wondered if Dr. Dean's Blood Builder contained alcohol. If so, Silas McClure better not try to peddle any of it to my grandmother.

"But I spend most of my time working at Jane Addams' settlement house," Grandmother continued. "Louis Decker works there too. He's wonderful with the children and very handy at repairing things."

"What's a settlement house?"

"It's not something I can explain easily—you should come down and see it for yourself. In fact, you're welcome to come with me tomorrow, if you'd like. We can always use an extra pair of hands. And Louis will be there too," she added with a smile.

I could hardly say no. I'd gone to the suffrage rally with Aunt Matt and to parties and social events with Aunt Agnes. How could I

refuse my grandmother? And when I remembered the pitiful children
I'd seen today, I knew I couldn't turn my back on them.

"I would like that," I replied.

I lay in bed that night, trying to imagine my father going into
saloons and talking to drunken patrons about God. I couldn't do it. I
found it impossible to imagine that he'd ever been as intensely passionate about religion as Louis Decker was. In fact, it was hard to
imagine my staid, unemotional father being passionate about anything. Had all of his feelings died when my mother left us?

My father rescued my mother from the fire.

I imagined him running down the street, flames licking at his
heels as he carried a load of Bibles in his arms. *Suddenly he heard
desperate cries. He looked up, and the most beautiful woman he had ever
seen stood before an open second-story window, trapped inside the burning building, choking on thick clouds of smoke. He dropped the Bibles,
knowing that God would surely understand, and urged—no, begged—the
beautiful maiden to leap from the window, promising to catch her . . .*

Or maybe my mother had been running in terror through the
flaming, smoke-filled streets—barefooted, fear-crazed, as burning
buildings fell into piles of rubble all around her. *Suddenly she twisted
her ankle and fell to the ground. No one would help her. People trampled
over her. And as the flames raced toward her along with billows of hot,
choking smoke, my father suddenly heard her desperate cries for help. He
dropped the Bibles he had been trying to save—certain that God valued
life more than mere paper, regardless of how holy it was. Giving no
thought to his own safety, he ran back through the flaming debris to rescue
her, heedless of the heat and smoke. He swooped her up into his arms and
carried her to safety, falling in love with her the moment he looked into
her fear-filled eyes. In fact, they both fell passionately in love. . . .*

What would it feel like to fall passionately in love?

I fell asleep thinking about Louis Decker and Herman Beckett
and Nelson Kent and wondering if I would ever know true love.

Chapter

10

Monday, June 12, 1893

I hadn't risen early enough to eat breakfast since coming to Chicago
a week ago, but I crawled out of bed on Monday morning determined to work at the settlement house with my grandmother and
Louis Decker. I staggered downstairs and found her and my two
aunts seated at the table, feasting on bacon and eggs.

"Good morning, Violet," Grandmother said. She was one of
those perennially cheerful people who managed to rise from her bed
with a smile on her face. I, on the other hand, was not one to rise
early—and certainly not cheerfully. At school, I considered myself
fortunate if I made it to my first class on time, let alone to the breakfast table.

"Morning," I rasped. Grandmother sprang from her seat, bouncing around the kitchen like an overfilled tennis ball.

"Come in and sit down, Violet dear. I'll fix you a plate."

"I'm really not hungry. I don't usually eat breakfast...." She
ignored my words and heaped a plate with scrambled eggs, several

rashers of bacon, and two thick slices of toast.

My eyes weren't quite open yet, and everything looked blurry, but I saw that my Aunt Matt was engrossed in reading a newspaper, her face hidden behind it. Madame Beauchamps would not have approved. In the first place, it was very rude to ignore the rest of us who were seated at the table with her, and in the second place, proper ladies weren't supposed to take an interest in such a masculine thing as a newspaper.

"What's the latest news on the war, Matilda?" Aunt Birdie asked her. "Has General McClellan conquered Richmond, yet?"

In the short time that I'd lived here, I'd changed my mind about telling poor Aunt Birdie the truth. She had such a gentle, loving heart that I could see how discovering the truth about her beloved Gilbert might cause her deep anguish. But I had also learned that Aunt Matt was very forthright and direct. I couldn't imagine her lying to Birdie about the war, anymore than I could imagine my grandmother lying. I held my breath, wondering what Aunt Matt would say. She lowered the paper and faced her sister.

"I didn't see any articles about General McClellan or Richmond, Bertha. But you're welcome to read the paper for yourself when I'm finished with it."

"The print is too small," Birdie said. "It hurts my eyes to read it."

"There is one article, however, that I think we all should pay attention to." The pages rattled as Aunt Matt folded the paper into a smaller square. She cleared her throat as if about to make an important announcement. "From now on we need to be very cautious about opening the door to strangers. It says here in the paper that ever since the Exposition came to Chicago, thieves have been roaming around posing as traveling salesmen. The phony drummer comes to the door, selling all manner of things from household brushes to patent medicines. He is friendly and amusing as he charms his way into the house, but whether or not he makes a sale is immaterial. . . . Are you listening to this, Bertha?" She tapped her finger against the page for emphasis.

Aunt Birdie focused on Aunt Matt once again instead of gazing into the air above her head. She nodded solemnly. But in truth, not only would Birdie let a thief inside, she probably would give him a hug.

"If the drummer does make a sale," Aunt Matt continued, "he uses the opportunity to make note of where the lady of the house keeps her cash. But the salesman's real objective is to observe the home's layout and the whereabouts of any valuables. He later relays the information to his partners, and they break into the house when no one is home and steal all of the family's silver and other valuables."

"Oh, I do hope they don't take our silver tray," Aunt Birdie said. "I worked so hard to polish it."

"I doubt if robbers would bother with our house," Grandmother said, patting Birdie's hand. "We really don't have much worth stealing."

I couldn't help wondering about the drummer I'd met on the train. Could Silas McClure be one of the thieves the newspaper warned against? He had seemed very friendly and charming—exactly the type of person the paper had described. I recalled how restlessly he'd behaved, and how I'd suspected him of being a criminal. Then I recalled giving him my grandmother's address! I would feel terrible if he came to call on me, then robbed us while we were all away. But more than a week had passed since I'd met Mr. McClure, and I hadn't heard one word from him. I hoped he had lost our address or forgotten all about me by now.

"I know that the Columbian Exposition has attracted a lot of unsavory people," my grandmother said. "But it also has provided an ideal climate for Mr. Moody to spread the Gospel. So you see? Every cloud has a silver lining."

"Well, I'm warning all of you to be careful," Aunt Matt said. "That fair has more than its share of sneak thieves, pickpockets, and purse snatchers. One of the women I know from the suffrage association had all of the money stolen from her purse. She thinks it happened while she was visiting the Woman's Pavilion, of all places. And she wasn't the first one to be robbed there either. At least two other women had the same thing happen to them."

"Can't they do something to make it safer?" Grandmother asked.

"We are doing something. The lady managers have hired Pinkerton's Detective Agency to help capture the thieves."

"The Pinkertons will catch those criminals—you can be sure of that," I said. I was wide-awake now. "I read all about it in Allan Pinkerton's book, which was based on his crime-fighting adventures. They're famous all over America for solving robberies. During the war, they helped arrest a bunch of spies, and they even foiled an assassination attempt on President Lincoln's life. Too bad they couldn't have prevented the second one, though."

Aunt Birdie suddenly looked alert. "What did you say about President Lincoln? Is someone trying to kill that nice man?"

"Not to worry," Grandmother assured her. "Have some more eggs. And, Violet dear, where in the world did you run across a book about detectives?"

"Um . . . at Madame Beauchamps' school."

"I'm surprised they would allow impressionable young ladies to read about robberies and murders and things of that nature."

"The book wasn't mine. It belonged to a friend." I hoped Grandmother wouldn't probe further. "By the way, Aunt Matt—how did your friends go about hiring the Pinkertons?"

"They have a branch office here in Chicago."

"They do? Does it cost much for their services?"

"I have no idea. Why do you ask?"

The directness of her question left me at a loss. I wanted to hire them to find my mother and to prove that Maude O'Neill had murdered her husband, but of course I couldn't tell Aunt Matt the truth.

And I didn't want to lie either. I should have kept my mouth shut altogether.

"I'm just curious," I said with a shrug. "It doesn't matter."

The clock in the front hallway struck eight and Grandmother sprang from her seat. "Come, Violet. We really must be on our way."

I hurried to the hall tree to fetch my hat, grateful for the timely escape. I was pinning it to my hair when someone knocked on the front door. I opened it cautiously, remembering Aunt Matt's warning. I half expected to see Silas McClure or some other thieving salesman on our doorstep. Instead, I saw a skinny birdlike woman carrying two bulging carpetbags the size of prize-winning hogs.

"Good morning. I'm Ethel Riggs." She dropped one of the bags and extended her hand. "Mrs. Paine sent me here to make a gown for Miss Violet Hayes."

"Oh no." I struck my forehead in dismay. I had forgotten all about Aunt Agnes' promise to send a seamstress. "I'm Violet Hayes—but I was just about to leave. Will this take very long?"

"Oh my, yes. At least two or three hours. And if I don't get started on your dress today, I'm afraid it will never be finished by Saturday night."

I saw no way out. I already had accepted Nelson Kent's invitation to escort me on Saturday night, and I had nothing new to wear.

"Never mind, Violet dear," my grandmother said. She had come out to the foyer to fetch her own hat and had overheard us. "We'll miss you at the settlement house, but you can come to work with Louis and me another day. I really have to run along now. Bye-bye."

Aunt Birdie smiled and waved good-bye to her, then greeted skinny little Ethel Riggs with a warm hug as she invited her inside.

Aunt Matt left the house a few minutes later, growling about the important suffrage meeting that I should be attending with her and how degrading it was for women to adorn themselves for the purpose of enticing a man.

"And remember, now, don't open the door to any traveling salesmen," she warned Aunt Birdie. The door closed behind her with a bang.

I spent all morning with the seamstress. One of Mrs. Riggs' carpetbags contained a pile of the latest fashion books from Paris. We paged through them for nearly an hour, searching for a style for my new gown.

"I've never seen so many beautiful dresses in my life. How in the world will I ever choose one?"

Mrs. Riggs gave me a long, appraising look, twirling one end of the measuring tape that was draped around her neck. Then she wet her forefinger and quickly paged through one of the pattern books.

"I think this is the dress we should make for you." She pointed to one with a low-cut neckline. "You have a wonderful bosom. Why not show it off?" Her mind was made up even if mine wasn't. She closed all of the other fashion books and stuffed them back into her satchel.

"It's a beautiful gown," I told her, "but I'm worried that my grandmother will find it immodest."

"Nonsense. I'll make sure it covers all of your essentials. These large, puffy sleeves are all the rage this year. And see these silk flowers on the shoulder and waist? I'll make an extra spray of them for your hair. You'll look lovely."

"I've never owned such a beautiful dress before."

"Mrs. Paine told me that you needed an outstanding one in order to attract a wealthy husband."

"She said that?" I knew my aunt's goal was to find me a rich husband, but Mrs. Riggs made us sound like cheap hucksters looking for a hapless victim to defraud.

"If this dress does the job, you can use it for your wedding gown," she added with a smile. "See these ruffled inserts in the sides of the skirt? They're called *godets*. We'll use a contrasting fabric for them— maybe a spotted voile." She opened her second bag, which fairly exploded with fabric samples in a variety of colors.

"I don't know how I will ever decide."

"May I make a suggestion? I think the dress would look lovely made from silk brocade. And the color should be . . . let's see . . . how about this gorgeous ivory, with pale blue for the accent color? It would be a magnificent contrast to your dark hair."

Mrs. Riggs measured every last inch of me—twice, it seemed. "I'll return tomorrow morning, bright and early," she promised.

My grandmother would have to go to work without me once again. Meanwhile, I hoped she wouldn't tell Louis Decker the reason I had stayed home.

I stood for hours the following morning while Mrs. Riggs pinned and basted the muslin pattern. Then I raced upstairs to change my clothes in order to make social calls with Aunt Agnes in the afternoon.

While I waited for my aunt to arrive I decided to spend a few minutes practicing the piano in case she asked for a command performance at one of our teas—and in case I ever made it downtown to play hymns for Louis Decker. I was practicing my scales so energetically, running my fingers up and down the keys, that I never heard the knock on our front door. I didn't realize that Aunt Birdie had gone to answer it until I played the final note—just in time to hear her say, "Why, yes, Violet is here. Won't you come in?" I leaped up from the piano stool and hurried into the foyer.

I almost didn't recognize the man who stood there until he smiled at me: Silas McClure, the traveling salesman. The very person I had worried about only yesterday.

"Good afternoon, Miss Hayes." A candelabrum was much too dim to describe his grin. His entire face seemed to glow as if lit by a spotlight. He had on a conservative brown suit this time instead of his garish plaid one, and he must have run out of Macassar oil since the last time we'd met, because his wavy brown hair looked clean and nicely combed. Except for his blinding smile, he might have been a different man altogether.

My heart began to gallop like a team of horses at breakneck

speed. "Mr. McClure!" I couldn't seem to draw a deep enough breath to say more.

"I was in town for a few days and thought I'd stop by like I promised."

"Oh, how nice," Aunt Birdie said. "I'm Violet's aunt, Mrs. Casey."

"Yeah, we met before. Great to see you again. Silas McClure's the name."

Aunt Birdie retrieved the silver tray from the hall table and held it out to receive his calling card.

"Here you are, young man . . ."

Mr. McClure took the tray right out of her hand and gave it the once-over, as if estimating how much cash he could get for it from a pawnbroker.

"Looks like good sterling silver," he said, tapping his forefinger against it with a resounding ring.

"Oh yes. It is sterling silver," Aunt Birdie assured him.

I couldn't breathe. What if he and his partners came back this afternoon while Grandmother was downtown and Aunt Matt was at her suffrage meeting, and I was making social calls with Aunt Agnes? Poor Aunt Birdie would be here all alone! Mr. McClure and his chums could tie her up and stuff her inside the pantry with a gag in her mouth and steal every stick of furniture in the house—and it would be entirely my fault.

"You rarely see one this shiny," he added, admiring his reflection.

"Why, thank you," Aunt Birdie replied. "I polished it myself. It's for calling cards. Do you have one?"

"Oh!" he said, as if finally catching on. "Yeah, just a minute." He handed the tray to Birdie and groped in the breast pocket of his jacket for one. His business card had the words *Dr. Dean's Blood Builder* on it in blood-red letters.

"Does your tonic contain alcohol?" I asked, groping for something to say. He found my question amusing, for some reason. His smile widened—something I wouldn't have thought possible—until he resembled a display of fireworks.

"Absolutely not. There's not even a trace of alcohol in it. Dr. Dean believes in strengthening the blood, not diluting it with alcohol."

"Let's not keep the nice man standing in the hallway, Violet. Won't you come in, Mr. McClure?"

I didn't want him to come in, but what could I do? Aunt Birdie hung his hat on the hall tree and led him into our parlor.

"Nice place you have here, Miss Hayes," he said, looking all around.

"It isn't my house," I said quickly—and emphatically. "I'm just visiting. My widowed grandmother and her two sisters live here." I wanted him to know whom he was robbing, so he at least would be conscience-stricken afterward. "They really don't have much that's worth stealing."

"Stealing?" he repeated. He seemed very amused. "It's a nice place. Reminds me of home."

"My husband is fighting with General McClellan in Virginia," Aunt Birdie told him. "Why aren't you in uniform, young man? Are you home on furlough from the war?"

For a horrible moment I feared that Silas would laugh at her or else try to convince Aunt Birdie that the year was 1893, not 1864. But my esteem for Mr. McClure rose immeasurably when he took Aunt Birdie's hand in his and replied, "I haven't received a draft notice, Mrs. Casey."

"Oh, how nice. . . . Well, I'll go fix us some lemonade—unless you'd prefer tea?"

"Lemonade's fine," I said quickly. Tea would take too long. Aunt Agnes was due to arrive any minute, and I needed to get rid of Silas McClure before she did. But as soon as Aunt Birdie left the room, he moved a step closer to me.

"You're even more beautiful than I remembered, Miss Hayes."

"Um . . . thank you . . ." I backed away, unaware that I was about to collide with the parlor sofa. I lost my balance and fell backward onto it with an undignified plop. My skirts flew up to reveal my ankles and ruffled petticoats. What on earth was wrong with me today? Madame Beauchamps would be horrified by my gracelessness.

"I-I'm sorry but our visit will have to be a short one," I explained as I rearranged my dress. I decided it was best to remain seated. I didn't think my legs could hold me. "I have an engagement with my aunt Agnes this afternoon, you see. She will be arriving momentarily and—"

As soon as the words left my mouth I realized my mistake. I had informed a potential thief that I was leaving soon. If Silas McClure was a thief—and I was almost certain that he was—then by the time I returned from my social calls, the house would be ransacked.

"May I call you Violet?"

"I-if you'd like." I didn't know what else to say. Everything I'd learned about making polite conversation seemed to have flown from my head. If the art of conversation was like a graceful tennis match, then I had lost track of the ball, the racket, and the score. Worse, I felt as though I'd become entangled in the net.

"Won't you have a seat, Mr. McClure?"

"Okay. Thanks. But please drop the 'mister' stuff and call me Silas."

He sank down on the sofa right beside me. I would have chided him for being too forward, but I remembered how I had invited him to sit beside me on the train. It was my own fault that he was taking liberties. I couldn't inch away from him because I was already sitting right up against the armrest. Besides, he was gazing deeply into my eyes with his bright spring-water blue ones and his charm began to have a mesmerizing effect on me, just as it had on the train. I couldn't have moved away from him any more than the poles of two magnets could be pulled apart. This must be how he charmed all of the other unsuspecting women he robbed.

"Was that you playing the piano a minute ago? You sounded really good."

"Yes . . . Thank you."

"I haven't stopped thinking about you since we met on the train, Violet."

For the first time in my life I was utterly speechless. I could tell by the soft look in his eyes that he was telling the truth. I seemed to have a hypnotic effect on him as well. We might have sat gazing at each other for an eternity if Aunt Birdie hadn't returned to the parlor just then.

"Here's the lemonade," she sang sweetly. "I do hope it's to your liking." She handed Silas a glass, and he took a sip.

"Perfect!" he said, smacking his lips. "Not too sweet and not too sour."

"Oh, how nice." From the way Aunt Birdie beamed, he might have come to call on her instead of me.

Silas set his lemonade on the parlor table and focused all his attention on me again. "I've also been thinking about the question you asked me when we were on the train. I couldn't get it out of my mind, in fact."

"Which question was that?" My voice sounded strange to me, as if I had climbed up a very steep hill.

"You asked how I would prefer to die if given a choice: in a terrible cataclysm or from a long, slow death at home in my bed. I've decided that I would prefer to leave this world quickly, in a flaming accident."

"Oh, how nice," Aunt Birdie said. Silas glanced at her with a nervous smile.

"Why an accident?" I asked him.

"Well, we all have to die someday, right? And I would hate to reach the end of my life feeling as though I'd never really lived. Life is for living and for taking risks, regardless of the danger. I guess I'd prefer to live each day as if it were my last and go out with a bang."

"Me too," I said. "That's exactly the way I feel about it."

"Speaking of flames," Aunt Birdie said. "Were you here in Chicago the night of the Great Fire, young man?"

"No, ma'am," Silas said. "Were you?"

"Oh yes. And for a while we all believed that the end of the world had come. I feared I might truly lose my life. It was a dreadful experience."

"You really lived through it?" Silas asked. "I would love to hear about it, Mrs. Casey."

"Me too," I added. "Didn't you say that my parents met on the night of the fire?" But she didn't seem to hear me.

"The fire started on a Sunday night," Aunt Birdie began, as if reading the words from an invisible script above our heads. "I went to bed early, but I woke up in the middle of the night to the sound of someone pounding on our front door. It turned out to be friends of ours. The entire family was running from the fire with a wagon full of their household goods. Oh my, you should have seen the sky! It was all lit up to the south of us, glowing like a furnace—orange and yellow and red. The wind was blowing very hard that night, which is why the flames spread so quickly.

"Well, of course we let our friends come inside—they had several small children, you see, and an aging grandmother. And their house stood right in the flames' path. They lost everything that night but their lives and whatever they had managed to fit into their wagon. No one ever imagined that the fire would jump across the Chicago River, but it did.

"By dawn the streets were filled with refugees, and we started handing out sandwiches and glasses of water to the poor souls. Many of them were acquaintances of ours but we hardly recognized them with their faces blackened from smoke and soot. They told terrible tales of the damage and destruction—the entire city was burning! And thieves had come out as well, looting homes and businesses. One man told me he had loaded everything he could fit into his wagon and then he simply left his doors open so scavengers could take whatever they wanted—it was all going to burn up anyway.

"The fire raged all day Monday, and by Monday night it was so close to our house that we began to pack our own belongings, imagining the worst. But how does one decide what to pack and what to leave behind? We could hear the roar of the flames a few blocks away and feel the heat. Flaming cinders flew everywhere, blowing toward us on the wind, and we soaked blankets with water to protect ourselves in case we had to flee. Oh, it was a terrible, terrible time!"

"Did my mother and father come here for refuge that night?" I asked. "Grandmother said that Father rescued my mother from the fire."

Aunt Birdie gazed at me for a long moment, and I immediately regretted interrupting her. I could see that she had lost the thread of her story. She gazed at Silas and me as if we were soot-covered refugees whom she didn't recognize.

"Were you living in this house at the time of the fire?" Silas prompted.

"I-I don't recall. . . . My husband, Gilbert, was . . . Where was Gilbert again? I don't remember. I was here, I think . . . But why would I be here with Matilda and not in my own home?"

Oh no. The fire had occurred six years after Uncle Gilbert had died and the War Between the States had ended. Aunt Birdie was about to remember that her husband was dead. I needed to change the subject—fast!

"It must be hard on you to relive such a terrible night, Aunt Birdie. Let's not talk about it any more. Isn't it nice of Mr. McClure to pay us a visit? Tell us what brings you to the city today, Silas."

"I came back to see you, and to ask if I could take you to the fair. Have you seen it yet?"

"No, I haven't."

"I would love to show it to you."

Silas McClure—thief or elixir salesman—was not a suitable

escort to the fair or anywhere else. Yet of the three men who had offered to take me, Silas was the most unconventional one—and the one I longed to see it with the most.

"I would love to go with you, Mr. McClure, but we would need to be suitably chaperoned. My grandmother would never allow me to go otherwise."

"I see. But . . . how does that work, exactly?"

"Well, couples are usually accompanied by another woman, often a family member. Chaperones protect a young lady's reputation, you see. I'm afraid I would be unable to step out with you unless someone accompanied us."

He looked crestfallen. "Could your aunt come with us?" he asked, gesturing to Birdie.

"I don't think she could endure the excitement of the fair," I said, then added softly, "She's rather fragile."

"It's just that today is my day off, and I was hoping you would be free to go to the fair with me right now."

"I'm sorry, Mister . . . I mean Silas." And I truly was. "But as I said, I have another engagement this afternoon."

"Gee, that's too bad."

I suddenly remembered that Mr. McClure knew how to find my mother's address on LaSalle Street. He had offered to escort me there the day I came to Chicago before my grandmother arrived. If we went to the fair together, maybe I could ask him to take me to my mother's place afterward.

"I don't suppose you have a female relative or other acquaintance here in town who could accompany us to the fair on another day?"

"Hmm . . . I'll have to think about that." He was gazing into my eyes again. If I didn't look away soon, he would hypnotize me into following him anywhere. I picked up my lemonade and took a long drink. I wanted to hold the glass to my burning cheeks to cool them. Silas emptied his glass in a few gulps and set it on the table again.

"Suppose I came back for you the next time I'm in town—with a chaperone. Would that work? Would you come with me?"

"Yes, that would be acceptable."

"Good. Well, I guess I'd better be going, then." He rose to his feet and offered me his hand to help me up. I took it without a thought for propriety. His palm was hot, his grip strong—and his touch so shocking it was like shaking hands with the wrong side of a flat iron.

"Thanks for the lemonade, Mrs. Casey," he said on his way to the door.

Aunt Birdie hugged him good-bye. "Please, come again."

"I will. I'm looking forward to it, Mrs. Casey."

Silas wouldn't need to pick the lock in order to break in with his cohorts—Birdie would throw open the door and embrace the entire gang of thieves.

Aunt Agnes' lavish carriage pulled to a halt in front of our house just as Silas was leaving. He let out an appreciative whistle when he saw it.

"Wow! That's quite a rig. With a matched team of horses, no less. Someone's got plenty of dough."

"That's my aunt's carriage. But she doesn't live here with us. She lives . . . Oh, never mind. Good day, Mr. McClure."

I quickly closed the door behind him, leaning against it for support. I needed to collect my hat and gloves and calling cards—not to mention my scattered wits. Why had he had rattled me so?

"What a nice young man," Aunt Birdie said with a sigh. "He's very sweet on you, you know."

"What makes you say that?"

"Why, he could hardly take his eyes off you the entire time he was here."

That was when I realized how quickly my pulse was racing—and that it had been racing for the entire time that Silas McClure had visited us. My heart might not survive an afternoon at the fair with him.

"I think you must be sweet on him too, Violet."

"No, I can't be sweet on him, Aunt Birdie. He's . . . he's dangerous!"

"Well, come here and look." She took my arm and pulled me over to the mirror that hung in the front hall. "Just look how pink your cheeks are."

"But . . . I-I think he might be a thief."

"Oh, how nice. Has he stolen your heart?"

"No, not that kind of thief, a *real* thief—a criminal."

Aunt Birdie gasped. "He didn't take our silver tray, did he?" Her eyes grew wide as she clutched her heart.

"No. It's still here." I held it up to show her, and she sagged with relief.

"Well, then," she said, smiling once again. "That says it all, doesn't it."

Chapter

11

Friday, June 16, 1893

I didn't have a chance to accompany my grandmother to the settlement house until Friday. Mrs. Riggs arrived for the final fitting of my dress on Thursday, and we arranged to have it delivered in time for the party on Saturday night. I couldn't imagine how much the dress had cost, but as Aunt Agnes had said, if we wanted to catch a big fish, we needed to use extravagant bait.

I wore old clothes to the settlement house. Judging by the simple way that my grandmother lived and dressed, fashion didn't matter where we were going. We rode on streetcars, switching lines twice until we finally disembarked in a section of Chicago that seemed worlds away from the gracious mansions and elegant townhouses that Aunt Agnes and I had visited.

The smell of the neighborhood assaulted me first, hitting me hard enough to make me gag the moment I stepped off the streetcar. The stench smelled like a combination of rotting garbage, urine, and the decaying remains of scores of rats. Everywhere I looked I saw a dead one—and I saw a few living ones as well, scurrying away into the shadows as we approached.

The warm, humid June morning intensified the odors. We passed the open door of a butcher shop, and the stink of blood and raw meat made me gag again. Then I saw a cow tongue hanging in the smeared window by a giant hook and I nearly left my breakfast in one of the overflowing gutters.

"Careful! Watch your step, Violet," Grandmother warned as I stumbled from nausea. She seemed indifferent to the stench.

"This place smells terrible! How can you stand it?" My words came out muffled. I had covered my mouth and nose with my hand.

"I suppose I'm used to it."

I walked the entire length of the busy, overcrowded street with my nose and mouth covered, trying not to retch. Hundreds of people, the poorest I'd ever seen, went about the business of buying and selling, visiting and arguing as if the neighborhood smelled of perfume and roses. Children swarmed everywhere. Every immigrant mother had at least four or five dirty-faced urchins buzzing around her skirts like flies on a horse's rump. The men we passed stank so strongly of sweat that I doubted if they ever had taken a bath in their lives.

"Try not to step in any puddles if you can help it," my grandmother said. "This neighborhood had a cholera outbreak not too long ago." I was beginning to understand why she always walked so briskly. I also knew that I had lived a very sheltered life.

The noise of the neighborhood overpowered me nearly as much as the smell. Most of the talking and bartering and shouting were in languages I couldn't understand. Pedestrians haggled with pushcart owners and shopkeepers for their goods—everything from cabbages and soup bones to squares of brown soap and bolts of cheaply made cloth.

I glanced down a side lane as we crossed at an intersection and saw dozens of drooping clotheslines strung across the alley from one rickety tenement to the other. Flapping diapers, undergarments, bed sheets, and work clothes, all in the same dingy shade of gray, dripped down on a gang of youths playing stickball in the dirt below.

I wanted to turn around and run home. I had uncovered my mouth to say so when my grandmother reached for my hand.

"We're nearly there, dear. That's Miss Addams' house on the next block."

She pointed to a large two-story brick home, the only decent house in this overcrowded immigrant neighborhood. It was a little run-down, but it stood out like a swan in a flock of circling buzzards.

"Why in the world would anyone choose to live here?"

"Jane Addams is a pioneer, of sorts," Grandmother explained. "Everyone thought it was outrageous for a single woman to live in the slums, especially an educated woman from a wealthy family. But she made up her mind to rent this house—named Hull House after the original owner—and live among the people she wanted to help. I would live here, too, if . . . well, if things were different."

I picked up my pace, running toward the house for refuge. If Jane Addams was rich and educated, then surely her house would be clean and fresh smelling inside, wouldn't it?

"How does she help these people? I mean, look at this neighborhood! I wouldn't even know where to begin."

"Miss Addams envisions her settlement house as a community center where everyone will be treated equally whether they are rich or poor." Grandmother paused on the broad front porch as she explained. "By living in the neighborhood, Jane was able to see what the greatest needs were and try to meet them. Feeding the hungry came first, and then her Jane Club, which is a safe, affordable boardinghouse for working women. Now she's adding English lessons and a kindergarten, and she hopes to start a day-care center and construct a safe playground for the children too."

My lungs felt as if they might burst from holding my breath. I reached behind Grandmother and opened the door to flee inside. I stood in the foyer breathing deeply. It smelled like heaven. I could see that it had once been a lovely, gracious mansion with elaborately carved fireplaces and a broad, sweeping staircase. The unusual wood-work that decorated all of the windows and doorframes resembled thick, coiled ropes.

"I've never heard of such a thing as a settlement house," I said after inhaling and exhaling a few times.

"Twelve years ago, Miss Addams visited a settlement house in London, England, called Toynbee Hall. The idea is that if educated people live and work among the poor, both classes of people will benefit by learning from each other. Jane decided to do the same thing after she returned to America. By getting to know these people—experiencing how they live—she can learn what the causes of poverty are and try to eliminate them."

"I'd like to meet Miss Addams. She sounds very dedicated." *But not quite sane,* I added to myself.

"Unfortunately she is going to be out of town all this week. Per-haps the next time you come."

The next time?

I started to remove my hat, but Grandmother took my hand again and said, "We won't be working here today. I just wanted you to see Miss Addams' house. We're needed in the public kitchen down the street."

I drew a deep breath before venturing back outside, as if I was about to plunge into deep water. Thankfully, the café was just a short walk around the corner on Polk Street.

"We've opened a small restaurant," Grandmother explained, "where we serve simple meals such as soups and stews along with home-baked bread. The neighbors can buy a nutritious meal for ten or fifteen cents."

We walked through a small dining room filled with mismatched tables and chairs and into the kitchen in the rear. Grandmother introduced me to the two immigrant women who were washing and drying a sink full of dishes, but they didn't seem to understand much English.

"You'll need this," Grandmother said, handing me a well-worn apron. She tied another one around her own waist.

"Um . . . what do I have to do, exactly?" I had never washed a dirty dish in my life, and I had no desire to disturb my record.

"Well, today we're serving a noon meal of soup and bread, so we'll need to get started on those right away. Do you want to help make the bread or cut up the vegetables for the soup?" I stared at my grandmother. "What's wrong, dear?" she asked, caressing my hair.

"I don't know a thing about cooking. Mrs. Hutchins did everything for us back home, and the cooks provided all of our meals at school."

"You mean they didn't teach you any practical homemaking skills at that school?" I shook my head. "How do they expect you to manage a household of your own when you get married and have a family?"

"Madame Beauchamps expected us to marry well and have servants," I said with a shrug. "In fact, she spent quite a lot of time teaching us how to manage a household staff."

"I see." Grandmother tried not to show how disappointed she was, but I detected it just the same. "Why don't you have a seat, then," she said with a sigh, "and you can just observe today."

Guilt draped over me like a very heavy coat. I recalled Aunt Matt's condemnation of the spoiled women in Aunt Agnes' crowd, and I rebelled at the notion that I was just like them.

"I-I'd be happy to help," I said with a gulp, "but you'll have to teach me how."

The back door opened and two more immigrant women joined us, chattering away in a very guttural language and toting large baskets filled with vegetables. My grandmother introduced the women to me, but their names sounded like gibberish. It shamed me to realize that I already had forgotten the names of the first two women.

Were my memory skills reserved for the rich? Had I not considered these women worthy of the effort? My shoulders sagged a few inches lower beneath my guilt overcoat.

The two newcomers washed their hands, then put on aprons and went to work as if they knew exactly what to do. One of them removed what appeared to be an elephant bone from a huge pot on the stove and began cutting off the cooked meat. The process looked so disgusting to me that I had to turn away. I would never be able to eat food that required so much handling on my part.

The other woman set the vegetable baskets on the table. I recognized carrots, onions, and potatoes, but there were several other lumpy things that looked as though they belonged in a witch's cauldron. I was quite certain that I had never eaten any of those things, nor did I want to sample them now.

"You would like to cut up?" one of the women asked. She offered me a knife.

"I guess so." I selected an onion since the skin was flaking off and it looked as though it would be the easiest thing to peel.

"I'm going to start the bread," my grandmother said. "If you need help with anything, just ask Magda." The vegetable woman smiled at me when she heard her name.

The onion's first layer came off fairly easily. Unfortunately, there were several more layers beneath it—and each layer proved more and more difficult to remove and more and more malodorous. The closer I got to the inside of the onion, the stronger the acid-like fumes became, until my eyes began to sting and stream with tears. I reached up to wipe them so I that could see what I was doing, but the onion juice was all over my fingers, and the moment I touched my eyes, the stinging turned to fire. They burned so badly that I dropped the onion and dug in my pocket for a handkerchief.

"Oh my! Oh dear!" Tears poured down my face as if my one true love had just jilted me.

I blew my nose and blotted my eyes—in time to see Magda turn away to hide a smile. I was not pleased at all to be the object of her amusement, so I picked up the onion again, determined to conquer it. The watering and stinging began in earnest the moment I did. If only my arms were longer so I could hold it farther away from me.

The last piece of skin finally slipped free and I set the brutish onion on the table with a victorious thump.

"Now you must chop," Magda said. "Like this . . ." She set one of the potatoes she had skillfully peeled on the chopping board and deftly hacked it into soup-sized pieces. I watched—and silently bid good-bye to my fingers.

But I refused to give up. I pinned the slippery thing to the board, drew a deep breath, and sliced into it. Fumes exploded from the cut onion like fireworks.

"Oh! Ow! Ow!" I gasped. I was quite certain that I'd been permanently blinded. I dug my fingers into my eyes, rubbing them—forgetting the important lesson I already had learned—and immediately made matters worse.

"Splash some water on your eyes, dear," my grandmother coached, leading me like a blind woman toward the sink.

I threw water on my face as if it were on fire, soaking my hair and the front of my shirtwaist in the process. When the burning and stinging finally stopped, I lifted my face from the sink—and there stood Louis Decker, offering me a towel, his brow furrowed in concern.

"Are you all right, Miss Hayes?"

"Where did you come from?" I asked in horror.

"I help out here sometimes. And these are two of my friends from school. I'd like you to meet Curtis and Jack. This is Mrs. Hayes' granddaughter, Violet."

Wonderful! More witnesses to my humiliation. Any pride I'd had in my appearance was thoroughly humbled as I greeted Louis and his two friends—soaked, red-eyed, and tear-streaked. I accepted the towel he offered and dried my face with it, wishing I could cover my head and run.

"It's wonderful to see you again, Miss Hayes," Louis said graciously.

"Yes . . . Nice to see you too." I sniffed. My nose wouldn't stop running. He gestured to the onion that sat waiting for me on the chopping board.

"I always leave onions to the experts."

It was a bit too late for that piece of advice.

"We need these many more," Magda said, setting two more of the unpeeled monsters on the board beside mine. "You like for me to chop?"

"Yes, please." I hung my head in defeat.

"Maybe you try this, yes?" She handed me an ugly brown lump with hairy tentacles sticking out of it. We could have played Animal, Vegetable, or Mineral? with the thing, but I wasn't in the mood.

"Is no smell in that one," Magda assured me.

"Good. Thank you."

Louis and his two friends donned aprons and began to work too. The sight of men doing women's chores astonished me. One of them added more wood to the fire in the huge kitchen stove. The other one began scrubbing out the pot that had held the elephant bone. Louis picked up another knife and began peeling potatoes for Magda now that she had taken over the onions. The fumes didn't seem to bother her in the least.

"I'm amazed that you would come here and help out this way," I said. "It's . . . it's so kind of you."

Louis dismissed my praise with a shake of his head. "It's not enough to call myself a Christian if my faith doesn't lead to action. In fact, that's exactly how Miss Addams herself describes this place: an experiment in translating Christian values into social action."

I looked down at the misshapen lump in my hand and was ashamed to admit that I lacked Louis' zeal.

"Miss Addams comes from a wealthy family," he continued. "She inherited quite a lot of money when her father died. She could be living in luxury, but she wanted to do something useful with her life. So she chose to live here and help make the world a better place. I want to do the same with my life."

I didn't want to interrupt Louis to ask what I was supposed to do with the mysterious mass, so I listened intently, nodding in all the appropriate places. I was willing to pitch in and help like the others—but I had no idea what the thing in my hand was, let alone what to do with it. When he finally set down the potato and took off his spectacles to clean them, I took advantage of the pause.

"Um . . . Louis? Do you know what I'm supposed to do with this?"

"You peel it—like a potato."

"Thanks."

I had watched him and Magda peeling things, and it didn't appear all that difficult. But as soon as I dug my knife into the tough outer skin, the wretched animal began to bleed all over me! The more I peeled, the harder it gushed.

"Miss Addams was raised a Quaker," Louis said, oblivious to the carnage I was wreaking. "They taught her to study society's problems and to work hard to correct injustice."

A beet! The cursed thing was a beet! And I knew enough about beet juice to know that it was as unforgiving as India ink.

"It's what Jesus would want us to do. 'What doth the Lord require of thee,'" Louis quoted, "'but to do justly, and to love mercy, and to walk humbly with thy God.' And the Apostle James wrote, 'For as the body without the spirit is dead, so faith without works is dead also.' Our Lord said that if we give even a cup of cold water in His name, we do it unto Him."

I had tears in my eyes again, but not from the sermon or the fumes. My hands would be indelibly stained from the beet juice by the time I finished, and I was supposed to attend a party with Nelson

Kent tomorrow night. But how could I lay the thing down and quit when Louis' soul-stirring speech was meant to inspire me to sacrificial service? I would be worse than a heathen.

"Jesus said, 'Blessed are the poor.' And if we turn aside and allow the poor among us to suffer, then the quality of all our lives suffers."

He went on and on, barely pausing for breath until he'd finished peeling and chopping the last of the potatoes. He tossed them into the soup pot with the meat from the elephant bone. By this time, Magda not only had dealt with all of the onions, but had scraped and chopped a basketful of carrots as well, and added them to the soup. My grandmother was covering a mound of yeasty bread dough with a towel and putting it into the warming oven to rise—and all I had to show for my morning's efforts were discolored hands and a few poorly peeled beets.

"Do you want help with those?" Louis asked, gesturing to the mound in front of me waiting to be peeled.

"Are they supposed to go into that pot of soup too?"

"No, I think one of the Russian ladies is going to make *borscht* out of them."

I nodded as if I understood, but I had no idea what he was talking about. "Yes, I could use some help," I admitted meekly. Louis picked up a beet and happily resumed his sermon.

"The settlement house helps people from a variety of races and backgrounds—Germans, Irish, Swedes, Italians, Poles, Russians, Greeks. Jesus looks past our ethnic and class differences and makes us into one new family—His kingdom, here on earth."

He continued in a similar vein as we attacked and conquered the beets together, but my mind drifted away from his lofty orations as I tried to think of a remedy for my stained hands. Lye soap, perhaps? It might remove the beet juice, but it would be at the expense of my skin. Which fate would be worse: red-stained hands or coarse, rough ones?

It sounded like one of the questions Ruth Schultz and I used to ponder: *"If your one true love took your hands in his, and you had to choose between having dry, scrub-maid hands or skin the color of beets, which would you choose?"* I tried to decide which fate Madame Beauchamps would tell me to choose, but she would be horrified that I'd found myself in this predicament in the first place. I would have to keep my gloves on tomorrow evening, which was not a socially acceptable thing to do when dining, but I saw no other way out of my dilemma.

We finally finished peeling the last beet. It seemed as though I had been in this kitchen for days. Louis removed his wire-rimmed spectacles again and polished them on his shirttail, which never seemed to stay tucked into his trousers. Once again, in spite of his vigorous efforts, the glasses looked just as smudged when he wrapped them around his ears again as when he'd started.

"It's almost lunchtime," he said. "We'll start serving the noon meal soon."

Indeed, the aroma of bread and soup had begun to fill the kitchen while we'd worked. My stomach rumbled with hunger. But when I recalled the nauseating smells that awaited me outside, I questioned the wisdom of eating anything at all. Hadn't I suffered enough humiliation for one day without losing my lunch in the street on the way home?

I helped carry stacks of bowls and spoons to the serving table while Louis and his friends lifted the soup pot from the stove.

"This is the part I love," he said. "Serving the needy, seeing their faces, offering that 'cup of cold water' in Christ's name. It makes all the hard work worthwhile, doesn't it?"

I glanced at my ruined hands and knew I couldn't answer his question truthfully. My stained nails looked as though I had murdered someone with my bare hands.

"I admire you, Mr. Decker. I don't believe I've ever met anyone quite like you."

"Please, Miss Hayes. God deserves all the glory, not me. I'm just His servant."

"You're a very good one, then."

As it turned out, my help wasn't required. When the doors opened and scores of hungry people came inside for a bowl of soup and a piece of bread, there were plenty of servers for the job. I watched my Grandmother and Louis and the others feeding the hungry and offering kind words of encouragement, and I doubted that I could ever dedicate my life to this work the way they were doing. What was wrong with me that given the choice I would rather be served than serve?

When the crowds left, we sat around the table in the kitchen where I had worked all morning and ate a bowl of soup for lunch. It was surprisingly delicious. I would have to write a letter to Ruth Schultz and tell her that my most adventurous meal might now be elephant soup. But when we'd all eaten our fill, I eyed the towering stacks of dirty soup bowls with dismay.

"We can help wash up another day," my grandmother said, resting her hand on my shoulder. "We have another job to do now. Let's go fetch our hats."

"Are we leaving?"

Grandmother nodded. I recalled my earlier experiences with onions and beets and didn't know whether to be happy that I'd escaped dishwashing or if an even worse fate awaited me.

"Where are we going?"

"A woman I know named Irina is ill. I've offered to bring some soup to her and her family. Louis is going to come with us. Here, you can carry this."

She handed me a loaf of bread wrapped in a kitchen towel. Louis already had the lunch bucket of soup in one hand, and he offered my grandmother his other arm. I drew a deep breath, inhaling the delicious aromas for the last time, then braced myself to walk outside.

The stench of the neighborhood had worsened in the afternoon sun. I usually reserved my prayers for bedtimes and Sunday church services, but I began to pray silently that this task wouldn't take too long or be very far away. Otherwise, my lunch was going to make a quick encore appearance.

I noticed the children as we walked. So many of them were ragged and barefooted, and so many of them were working rather than playing. Older girls aged eight or nine rocked babies and chased toddlers. Young boys, still in knee britches, hauled stacks of firewood on homemade carts.

"Where do they find wood in the city?" I asked Louis.

"They scavenge for it behind warehouses or along railroad tracks. Then they have to sell it all. They don't make much money, but every spare penny helps their families. A lot of our Sunday school boys work downtown all day selling newspapers or shining shoes."

Grandmother linked arms with me. "This is what hurts me, Violet—seeing all these children who have to work so hard when they should be in school getting a good education. Thank the Lord that you had a safe, happy childhood—these children certainly don't have one."

I thought I finally understood why my grandmother had moved to Chicago after my grandfather died instead of staying in Lockport and taking care of Father and me.

"Older children who should be in school are forced to find work in factories," she continued. "And much of the work that's given to women and children is either piecework or done in sweatshops."

"What's a sweatshop?"

"Any place besides a regular factory where work is done," Louis explained. "It's usually in a basement or a garage or a vacant tenement. Employers cram in a bunch of workers and treat them like slaves. Of course those places have very unsafe working conditions, and the workers have to put in long hours for very little pay."

"See that little boy?" Grandmother nodded toward a lad who couldn't have been more than eight years old staggering beneath an enormous bundle of fabric. "He's delivering piecework, probably to his mother and sisters. Those look like men's trousers. The family will finish all of the hand sewing at home, often after working all day at some other job. They'll get paid by the piece. Can you imagine little girls only seven or eight years old, sewing men's trousers day and night for seven cents a dozen?"

"That's all? Why so little?"

"Because there are hundreds of other destitute immigrants who are willing to work for those wages if they don't."

We turned down a crowded alleyway, and I had to pinch my nose closed again to block out the smell. I hadn't wanted to reveal my squeamishness in front of Louis Decker, but the entire lane reeked like an overflowing outhouse. I'd never seen so many flies in my life.

"Here, this is clean," Louis said, handing me his handkerchief. "The heavy rain we had the other night made all of the outhouses overflow. Is it any wonder that these neighborhoods have cholera and typhoid epidemics?"

"We're trying to educate people about the need for cleanliness," Grandmother added, "but there are just so *many* people. And, of course, language is a problem. That's why Miss Addams has added English lessons. . . . Well, here we are. This is where Irina and her family live."

The door to the tenement stood open, and I braced myself as we went inside, dreading how this dilapidated building might smell. It took a moment for my eyes to adjust to the dark, narrow foyer after the bright afternoon sunshine. I heard water running and identified the first odor as mildew.

A young boy stood at the base of the steps, filling an enamel basin with water from a sputtering faucet. He had spread a collection of cans, pots, and bowls on the floor, and he was slowly filling them, one by one.

"That's the only running water in the building," Grandmother said. "All of the people in these apartments have to share the same faucet—and they have to haul the water upstairs, of course."

"The tenants are probably thankful to have any water at all," Louis said. "Careful! Watch your step, Violet. . . ."

He took my arm to guide me across the slippery floorboards and around the boy's scattered containers. As I followed my grandmother up the rickety wooden stairs to the third floor, the odors changed from damp and moldy to the fragrant aroma of cooking food. I began to breathe more freely. I identified onions and boiled potatoes, but also the mysterious, spicy aromas of foreign foods. The air in the stairwell smelled delicious.

We climbed to the third floor and my grandmother knocked on one of the apartment doors. It opened a crack and a tousled boy with a dirt-smudged face peered out.

"It's me, Yuri—Mrs. Hayes," my grandmother told him. "I've brought your mother some soup."

"Yes, yes, let her come in, Yuri," Irina called from inside. He opened the door for us.

Irina was the thinnest woman I had ever met and also the palest. She sat propped up on one of the beds, her right leg immobilized by a bandage and wooden splint. She might have been a pretty woman, but the accident that had broken her leg had marred her face with purplish bruises. One eye was blackened and swollen shut, and her lips looked puffy and split. I wondered how she had been injured but knew enough about proper manners not to ask. She was top-stitching a man's suit coat; a pile of unfinished coats lay heaped on the bed beside her.

I counted three small children in the dismal room along with Yuri, and a fifth one asleep in a cradle that seemed much too short for her. I tried not to gape at the bare wooden floors, the lumpy beds, the chipped plates on the tilting table, knowing that it was just as rude to stare at the furnishings here as it had been in the mansions I'd visited.

"Irina, this is my granddaughter, Violet Rose. We brought you some soup."

"Thank you, thank you," she said, pronouncing it *tank you*. She set aside her sewing as one of the smaller children climbed onto the bed beside her. "How can I ever tank you? You would like to stay and visit? Yuri can make tea."

"No, we can't stay. Maybe next time, Irina."

"We're praying for you down at the church," Louis added. "I hope you'll soon be well again." He took the bread from me and set it on the table.

"Yes. Tank you."

"We miss you down at the kitchen," Grandmother said. "No one makes *borscht* as good as you do."

"Tank you." I saw Irina wipe away a tear as Grandmother closed the apartment door behind us.

"What happened to her?" I asked when we reached the stairwell. "How did she break her leg?"

"Her husband did that to her," Grandmother said.

I couldn't utter another word until we reached the foyer. The young boy was still standing at the water faucet, slowly filling a blackened teakettle.

"But—why would he do such a terrible thing?"

"He becomes violent whenever he has too much to drink. Irina would rather take the abuse herself than let him harm one of the children. I didn't want to stay and visit today for fear he would come home."

"Why in the world doesn't she leave him?"

"She has no way to support her children or pay the rent."

"Everyone at church is praying for her," Louis said. "And for her husband."

"Yes, Irina is such a dear woman."

Louis walked with us to our streetcar stop on a main thorough-fare. Finally, I dared to breathe deeply again. The smell of horse manure, factory fumes, and the ever-present stockyards seemed tame after visiting the slums.

"It was wonderful to see you again, Violet," Louis said as he waited with us for our car. "I enjoyed working with you."

"Yes. I hope we meet again."

"Well, now that you mention it . . ." He paused, removing his spectacles to polish them. "I don't want you to feel pressured, Violet. I mean, your participation should be absolutely voluntary . . . but if you are able to play the piano for us next Thursday, we really could use your help." He wrapped the wires around his ears and gazed at me with his dark, intense eyes.

"All right. I'll come." I needed to shrug off more of the guilt that was blanketing me. Playing the piano sounded much easier than cutting up vegetables. And it wasn't likely to ruin my hands either.

"Wonderful," he said. "We'll meet in front of the school at one o'clock. I'll see you then." Our streetcar arrived, and Grandmother and I climbed aboard, waving good-bye. She sank onto the seat with a sigh.

"So. What did you think of the settlement house?"

"I never realized what a hard life those immigrant women have."

"My sister Matt has her way of helping women, and I have mine. But our work overlaps in places too. We're both working to change the laws so that women can earn higher wages and work shorter hours. We'd both like to improve working conditions so factories are cleaner and safer. And we're both trying to get new child labor laws passed—and enforced—so that children can get out of the factories and sweatshops and into schools."

"Their living conditions are terrible."

"Yes. And you can see why so many of the ramshackle wooden tenements like the one we visited today burned up like matchsticks in the Great Fire. Afterward, the poor people who'd lived in them had no place to go. They didn't have much to begin with, and then they lost it all. Many, many of the people who died in the fire were poor."

"Did my mother live in a tenement before the fire?"

Once again, my grandmother hesitated—as she always did when I asked a question about my mother.

"I honestly don't know where she lived, Violet Rose. I only know that wherever it was, her home burned to the ground. She lost everything—clothing, personal items, heirlooms—everything."

"Did she—"

"That's really all I can say about her, Violet."

I huffed in frustration. "Why won't you ever talk about her?"

Grandmother took my hand in both of hers and squeezed it gently. She had beautiful hands—strong and work worn and scented with flour and yeast. A week ago I would have described them as chapped and reddened from too much work. Today they looked beautiful to me.

"I can't talk about your mother because I promised your father that I wouldn't." She quickly changed the subject. "Since most immigrants work very hard for very little pay, it's an even greater tragedy when some of them waste it all on alcohol. That's why my work with the Temperance Union is so important. It goes hand-in-hand with the work we did today. I'll take you with me to the Union another day."

"I still don't understand why women like Irina don't leave their husbands if they beat them and spend all their money in saloons."

"Because they have no place to go. And if they did leave their husbands, who would care for their children while they worked? One of the needs that Miss Addams hopes to address is low-cost housing and day care for the children of working mothers."

It occurred to me that perhaps my mother had wanted to take me with her when she left home, but she'd had no place to live and no one to take care of me. I wished I could find her and ask her about it, but how could I find her if no one would talk about her?

Chapter

12

Grandmother and I returned home from our day at the settlement house to find Aunt Agnes sitting at our dining room table, drinking tea with Matt and Birdie.

"Sit down and join us, Florence," Aunt Matt commanded. "You never have time to visit with your own family anymore. You sit too, Violet."

"I believe I will," Grandmother said with a sigh. I could tell how weary she was by the way she lowered herself onto her chair. I sat down beside her as Aunt Birdie fetched each of us a clean teacup. It was the first time all four sisters and I had been together since I had arrived in Chicago nearly two weeks ago.

"I do hope you didn't wear Violet out this morning," Aunt Agnes said. "She has an important party to attend tomorrow night."

"There's no such thing as an *important* party, Agnes," Grandmother said.

"There certainly is! Isn't her future important to you? Marriage occupies the biggest portion of every woman's future."

"Who says?" Matt asked. No one answered her.

"Violet should have been making social calls with me this afternoon instead of running all around those appalling neighborhoods you visit." Aunt Agnes gestured broadly when she spoke, as if conscious of her many rings. She had elegant hands, in spite of the wrinkles, and her jewels glittered in the afternoon sunlight.

"Violet helped me work today. Didn't you, dear?" Grandmother said, patting my shoulder. I nodded lamely, feeling like a hypocrite. I knew how little I actually had accomplished. My tea was turning cold but I was afraid to reach for the cup, afraid that Aunt Agnes would notice my stained fingers.

"I could have used an extra pair of hands down at the Suffrage Association," Aunt Matt said. "The forty-fifth anniversary of the first Women's Rights Convention is coming up next month, and we need to get the information mailed out to our members. That convention has the potential to *greatly* improve Violet's future—and the future of *all* women."

"Nonsense!" Aunt Agnes said with a wave. "I happen to know that several very important young men are interested in our Violet. Marriage to one of them will make her future secure."

"Humph!" Aunt Matt grunted. "Her marriage is going to do more for *you* than it ever will for her—poor thing."

I wondered if Aunt Matt was right. Did I really want to be used as a prize to help increase my aunt's social standing? Meanwhile, I was supposed to be searching for my mother. That was the reason I had come to Chicago in the first place, yet I was no closer to my goal than the day I'd left Lockport.

"Poor thing indeed," Agnes sniffed. "She looks very peaked, Florence. I do hope she isn't getting ill. Heaven knows what sorts of diseases she might catch in that wretched neighborhood."

"She isn't ill," Grandmother said calmly. "She got up early this morning to go with me—that's all."

"And see how tired she looks? I do hope those bags beneath her eyes go away by tomorrow night."

"Oh, I do too," Aunt Matt added. "Get some rest, Violet. Otherwise you might fall asleep from boredom while discussing Mrs. Pullman's new spring hat."

"Don't be mean-spirited, Matilda. But speaking of fashion, Violet, I brought your new gown with me. Mrs. Riggs finished it. Be a dear and go try it on, will you? So I can see it? The Kents only invited young people to the party tomorrow night, so I won't be there to see you."

"Yes, I'd be happy to. Where is the dress, Aunt Agnes?"

"I believe Birdie hung it in your wardrobe."

I hurried upstairs, grateful to flee their discussion. But I wondered how the gown would look on top of the guilt overcoat I still wore. Irina's family probably could eat for a month on the money Agnes had spent. And while Mrs. Riggs had been sewing my new ivory brocade gown, frail eight-year-old girls had been forced to stitch men's trousers in dreary sweatshops for seven cents a dozen. How could I possibly enjoy myself in that dress, knowing the true cost?

Nevertheless, I slipped the gown over my head. The brocade felt like cool water against my skin. It swished magnificently when I walked. I never wanted to take it off.

"Lovely!" Agnes applauded when I descended the stairs. "You look beautiful, darling!"

"Oh, how nice," Aunt Birdie said.

"It's quite . . . revealing, isn't it?" Grandmother asked. She spread her hands across her own chest, forgetting that her dress buttoned clear to her neck. "What in the world will her father say?"

"Why don't you just put the poor girl on the auction block and sell her to the highest bidder?" Matt asked before huffing out to the kitchen with the empty teapot.

"Thank you for modeling it for me, dear," Agnes said, "but I'm afraid I have to run along now. What time shall I have my driver pick you up tomorrow night?"

"Um . . . that won't be necessary, Aunt Agnes. Nelson Kent has offered to escort me."

"Oh, Violet! You didn't accept his offer? The point of the party was to give you another opportunity to play the field."

"Yes, Violet. Why settle for *rich* when there might be someone even *richer*?" Aunt Matt asked as she returned for the remaining teacups.

"There's no call for sarcasm, Mattie," Grandmother said. "Violet knows there is more to life than material riches. Don't you, dear?"

"There's love," Birdie said in her dreamy voice.

"I'm disappointed that you accepted Nelson Kent's offer so soon," Agnes said. Her ability to ignore all of her sisters and stick to the subject impressed me.

"I'm sorry, Aunt Agnes. Nelson caught me off guard, and I agreed to let him escort me before I had a chance to think it through."

"Apology accepted. Besides, he would be an excellent match. You could do much worse. And you are getting up in years . . ."

"Fiddlesticks," Grandmother said. "Violet is only twenty."

"That means she'll soon be twenty-one, and you know what *that* means." Agnes' voice dropped to a whisper. "You wouldn't want her to become an *old maid*, would you?"

"I really don't think Nelson intends to propose on Saturday night," I told my aunt. "But if he does, I'll tell him I have to think about it."

"Good girl." She grabbed my hands and squeezed them. Then her mouth dropped open in horror. "My stars, Violet! What in the world have you done to your hands?"

"It's beet juice. I helped peel some of them today at the settlement house." I was afraid she would be furious with me, but she directed all of her wrath at my grandmother.

"Florence Howell Hayes! Don't you care at all if your granddaughter marries well? How could you make her slave all morning like a common servant? She should be commanding a household full of servants!"

"I didn't make her do anything, Agnes. She volunteered." Grandmother caressed Agnes' arm as if smoothing her ruffled feathers. "You should be praising her for doing something useful to help others. Besides, it gave Violet a chance to meet some wonderful young people her age who volunteer there. They're students at the Chicago Evangelistic Society."

Aunt Matt stopped stacking teacups and planted her hands on her hips. "Don't tell me, Florence! Are you trying to match Violet with one of those radical young ministers?"

"Those students are fine young men."

"Shame on both of you! After all of the things the pair of you have suffered, why would you want Violet to follow either of your examples? Agnes, do you really want that girl to have a life like yours? And you, Florence—you, of all people, should have the blinders off when it comes to marrying a minister!"

Her words made my skin tingle. I knew what she was referring to in Aunt Agnes' marriage, but what about my grandmother's? I held my breath, waiting for more information, but for a long moment no one spoke.

"It's true, I've had my share of sorrows," Grandmother finally said. "But my blessings have far outweighed them. I would be proud to have Violet follow my example when it comes to helping others."

"Not by peeling vegetables!" Agnes said. "My stars! The women to whom I've introduced Violet are very active in charity work. Potter Palmer and his wife are two of Mr. Moody's biggest supporters. So are Marshall Field and Gustavus Swift and the banker Lyman Gage . . . They've all given money to Mr. Moody's campaigns."

"Is that true?" I asked.

Grandmother nodded. "Yes, all of those men have been very generous."

"Their wives and my other society friends spend a good deal of time raising money for charity too," Agnes added.

"I know they do," Grandmother said. "And I appreciate your generosity, Agnes. But I enjoy working with people, getting involved with them and not simply tossing money their way. It's just the way I am. Lord knows your work and mine are both necessary."

"If Violet marries well she can influence her husband to support your work. So you see? We are working for the same cause."

"Why does Violet's happiness depend solely on whether or not she gets married?" Aunt Matt asked. "Or does misery love company? You want her to be as miserable as you are?"

"Don't be spiteful, Matt."

Aunt Birdie cleared her throat. "I have just one thing to say about all of this," she announced in her wispy voice. She paused dramatically, as if delivering the final word on the matter. "Make sure you marry for love, Violet."

I wondered about her advice. If I fell in love as deeply as Aunt Birdie had, I also would risk having my heart broken.

"I need to be going," Agnes said. "Violet, make sure you wear gloves tomorrow night so no one sees those wretched hands."

"I will. And thank you again, Aunt Agnes, for the beautiful dress."

"You are quite welcome, dear. *Au revoir*, everyone."

Chapter

13

Saturday, June 17, 1893

On Saturday night, Nelson Kent arrived in a splendid carriage, complete with a footman, to take me to his grandmother's party. I felt like Cinderella in my magnificent new gown, especially after laboring like a scullery maid the day before. If only I had a fairy godmother to wave her magic wand and fix my stained hands so I wouldn't need to wear gloves.

"You look beautiful, Violet," Nelson told me when we arrived at the party. "You are by far the loveliest woman here. I'm congratulating myself for having the foresight to claim you before anyone else had a chance." His eyes widened as he slipped my wrap from my shoulders. "Your dress is stunning!"

It was stunning, all right. Every man who gazed at the generous view of my assets looked as though he'd been stunned by a blow to the head. Men flocked to me like crows to a cornfield, but I noticed that very few of them looked me in the eye. Instead, their gaze seemed to stray twelve inches below my face. Nelson acted as the scarecrow, shooing them off as fast as they flew to me.

"Sorry, gentlemen," he said, linking my arm through his. "She's mine for the evening." He seemed to revel in his role as King of the Hill.

"Give us a chance, Nelson."

"Not tonight."

"We'd like to get to know Miss Hayes too."

"Then ask her out yourselves—some other time."

If Mrs. Riggs ever sewed another gown for me, I promised myself that I would choose my own pattern next time.

It wasn't only the men who noticed my apparel. "Your gown is exquisite," Haughty told me. Her dark brown eyes shone green with envy.

"Thank you, Hau—um . . . Hattie." I cleared my throat to make it seem like I had something caught there, but in truth I had nearly slipped and called her "Haughty" to her face. Nelson noticed and covered his mouth to hide his amusement.

"May I inquire where you had your dress made?" Naughty asked.

Competition for good dressmakers was always fierce—their names a closely-guarded secret. I couldn't allow the two Grant sisters to monopolize Mrs. Riggs' precious time.

"You'll need to ask my aunt for the woman's name," I said, avoiding an outright lie. "Aunt Agnes is the one who made all of the arrangements."

For the first hour or so, Nelson and I walked around, arms linked, conversing with his guests as we nibbled appetizers. I often felt excluded as they discussed people and past events that I knew nothing about.

"Everyone seems to know each other," I told Nelson as we moved from one group to the next.

"Yes, most of our families are longtime friends."

"Aunt Agnes told me that I was 'new blood.'"

"And very lovely blood, I might add. That's why they're swarming around you like mosquitoes. It's all I can do to swat them away."

Long before our hostess served dinner I'd grown bored. The girls spent all of their time flirting. And as I watched Haughty and Naughty working hard to be mysterious and coquettish, I felt relieved that I didn't have to play the field.

None of the men interested me, rich or not. They were the same phonies I'd danced with at the fund-raiser. They might have been nice underneath their facades, but no one gave me the opportunity to find out.

My trip to the settlement house had tainted this party for me. Everything we talked about now seemed unimportant and frivolous, the evening a shameless folly compared to the way that Louis Decker and his friends lived their lives. Nelson noticed that I had grown quiet.

"Will you excuse us?" he asked the group with whom we had been chatting. He pulled me aside and steered me out of the noisy parlor and into the hall.

"You look as tired of all this as I am, Violet. And we haven't even had dinner yet."

"Being nice is exhausting," I said.

"I've never heard it put quite that way, but you're right—this is hard work. Come on."

We crept out to the garden where Nelson and I had visited on the day we met, and stood side by side on the veranda, basking in the warm, starlit evening. We easily resumed the comfortable conversation we'd enjoyed at the fund-raiser a week ago.

"How have you been keeping busy since I saw you last?" he asked.

Did I dare tell him about the settlement house or my visit to Irina's tenement? "My grandmother and my aunts have kept me occupied, and I've seen a little more of the city since then."

"Have you been to the fair?"

"No, not yet."

"Good. I would like the honor of taking you for the first time. I'd love to see what you think of it. By the way, your hands must be sweating in those gloves. You can take them off, you know."

"No, I really can't. I'm afraid I've ruined my hands."

"Ruined them? Now I'm intrigued. Let me see." We laughed as Nelson began tugging playfully on one of my gloves.

"No, really . . . Aunt Agnes would have a fit!" But he managed to pull off one of them, and I finally relented. "Okay, but I'll only show you. And you can't tell anyone."

"It'll be our secret." He lifted my bare hand to the light that streamed from the mansion's windows. "What's all over them? Don't tell me you've murdered someone."

"It's beet juice. I volunteered to help my grandmother with her charity work, and she had me peeling beets. I peeled an onion too. I hope you aren't too shocked."

"I think it's sweet." He lifted my hand to his lips and kissed my fingers.

Nelson was the first man who had ever kissed me, and I was surprised by how warm and soft his lips felt against my skin. I wondered how his lips would feel against my own. But it was curiosity that I felt, not desire. Even so, it took me a moment to regain my balance.

"The . . . um . . . the place where my grandmother works seems like a different world compared to this one. I confess that I feel a little guilty for enjoying this life of luxury so much more."

Nelson's blasé smile vanished. "I know. There's a terrible gap between the rich and the poor. And there's an even larger gap socially. My father inherited our wealth from his father, and to be honest, he isn't as generous to the poor as some of the self-made men who've worked their way up from the bottom. Turlington Harvey, for instance."

"Who is he?"

"Chicago's lumber baron. The story goes that Mr. Harvey arrived in town with only a toolbox and a lucky penny. But he worked hard and eventually got rich rebuilding Chicago after the fire. Now he gives a great deal of money to charity."

"Do you ever feel guilty that we have so much and the immigrants in the tenements have so little?"

"I do." He was gazing back at the house, not at me. Light spilled from the windows, and we could see his servants preparing dinner in the kitchen. "I should probably get back," he said. "Do you mind?"

"Not at all. And by the way, I'm glad that I came to the party with you. This is a lot less work than coming unescorted and fighting off suitors."

He laughed and reached for the doorknob.

"Nelson, wait. I need to put my glove back on."

He still held it in his hand. He looked at me, and for a moment I thought he might kiss me. Then he smiled and held my glove open for me. I slid my hand into it and he offered me his arm.

I liked Nelson, but I still didn't observe the feverish symptoms of love in either of us. I longed for love and romance. Perhaps I had read too many of Ruth's novels, or maybe Aunt Birdie's unchanging refrain had influenced me, but I wanted to fall madly, crazily, head-over-heels in love. I couldn't stop thinking about her description of my parents: *"Their passion was ignited the night of the Great Fire, and the fervor of their love was as all-consuming as the flames. . . ."* Was I naïve to want the same thing?

Once again, I strolled around the party on Nelson's arm while he played the part of host. I was struck by how comfortable and natural he was with his role as the wealthy young heir to the Kent family fortune. He was very skilled at making polite conversation, pretending he was interested in everyone's stories, laughing at their jokes. One would never know that he considered it a chore.

And I was very comfortable with him. If he had proposed to me that evening I might have said yes, in spite of my promise to Aunt Agnes and in spite of the fact that I wasn't in love with him. Nelson Kent was a handsome, charming man. He had a wealthy family, a magnificent home, scores of servants—all of the things I had dreamed of having while studying in Madame Beauchamps' School for Young Ladies. Except for love, that is. But love had been the midnight musings of schoolgirls. Love had never been part of Madame Beauchamps' curriculum.

We finally moved into the enormous dining room and sat down at the dinner table, all twenty-four of us. Nelson cleverly swapped my place card with another so that I would be seated alongside him. The other women wore lovely gowns and had arranged their hair in elaborate styles, but I thought that the prettiest girl in the room was the young parlormaid, Katya, whom I'd met during my last visit.

She wore a long gray gabardine maid's uniform with a ruffled white apron and had tucked her wheat-colored hair beneath her white cap. Even without adornment, Katya resembled a Slavic princess, her natural beauty simple and unpretentious. I watched her remove our soup bowls when we finished the first course and saw that she had an inborn grace that hadn't come from walking around with a book on her head. Then I noticed that Nelson was watching her too.

"Your grandmother's servant is lovely."

"Yes . . . yes, she is." His voice sounded sad.

I recalled the suspicion I'd had the last time I'd visited, that Nelson and Katya were secretly in love, and for the first time all evening something intrigued me. I decided to pay close attention to them—as any good detective would do—and find out if my suspicions were correct or merely a figment of my imagination.

Each time Katya emerged through the servants' door, Nelson looked up at her—if only for a moment. He enjoyed the rear view just as much when she returned to the kitchen. For her part, Katya kept her eyes properly lowered as she served each guest—except for when she served someone directly across the table from Nelson. Each time, she couldn't seem to stop herself from briefly glancing up at him.

They clearly were watching one another, and their furtive game continued throughout the lengthy dinner. Then, for a single shocking moment, their eyes met. It happened as Katya reached to remove Nelson's plate. He turned and looked up at her, directly into her eyes. Their faces were inches apart, and the warmth of their mutual gaze could have melted the silverware.

"Thank you, Katya," he murmured.

That was unheard of! Servants were supposed to be ignored during dinner parties, treated as part of the furniture. Madame Beauchamps had lectured extensively on how to handle servants: *"One must treat them kindly but firmly. Never be overly friendly. You may call them by their first name, but they must refer to you as Miss or Madam. Eye contact is necessary only when being firm with them or when reprimanding them. Servants must always avert their eyes. Each of you must always, always, remember your place."*

Nelson and Katya both knew the rules. Clearly, I was not imagining a relationship.

After dinner we moved from the dining room to a small ballroom, where an orchestra had begun to play. With the lovely Katya out of sight, Nelson became my charming suitor once again.

"Would you like to dance, Violet?"

"Yes, thank you."

Nelson was a wonderful dancer. We were comfortable in each other's arms. As we waltzed around the dance floor for the next hour or so, I talked to him as easily as I had talked to Ruth Schultz.

"If you could choose," I asked, "which would you rather be: the captain of a pirate ship or the captain of a warship?" My question made him laugh out loud.

I happened to look up as Nelson laughed and spied Katya watching us. She had come into the ballroom presumably to collect the used punch glasses. But as Ruth's romance novels had phrased it: *Her love and her longing for him were written in her eyes.* Clearly, it broke her heart to see us together. She loved Nelson. I was certain of it. The question was, did he love her?

"That's a great question!" Nelson said when he stopped laughing. "I would have to say the captain of a warship." He swung me around, and Katya disappeared from view.

"A warship?" I repeated. "Now you have to tell me why."

"Well, let's see. . . . I love working in the business world, and it's very much like commanding a warship. It's all about taking charge, conquering new territory, building an empire. And also about accumulating wealth if you're the one who wins the war. And I like to win. Besides, some of the colonies I subjugate might be interesting places to visit."

"Have you traveled a lot?"

"Of course. It's expected. I've made the obligatory tour of the continent." He spoke casually, as if it was nothing special, yet I couldn't fault him. His sense of entitlement was part of him. He hadn't chosen to be born into wealth any more than Katya had chosen to be born an immigrant.

"I would love to hear about your travels. Tell me about the loveliest place you've ever visited."

"Let's see . . . There were so many, but I would have to say Italy. Especially Lake Como. It's a long, narrow lake surrounded by mountains and dotted with charming villages. You would love it."

"How do you know?"

"Well, for one thing, you would fit right in. You're as lovely as an Italian princess. The Mediterranean men would all flirt with you. I would love to take you there. You would be a fun traveling companion because you see things differently from other women.

"You view everything through fresh eyes. And you're very imaginative. That's obvious from the charming questions you ask. You aren't vain either. Most women I know are very self-focused. They want the whole world to look at them, and in the process they miss seeing the world."

The song ended and we sat down on a small loveseat to rest. I had enjoyed staying by Nelson's side all evening, but I didn't realize that people were getting the wrong impression of us until one of the young men I'd met last week came over to ask me to dance.

"Give someone else a chance, Nelson. We want to get to know Miss Hayes too."

Nelson turned him down. "Sorry. She's all mine."

"Oh, I see how it is. When's the wedding?" He stalked away.

"Does it worry you that people are talking about us?" I asked.

"Not in the least. I like you, Violet. In a few short hours, I've gotten to know you better than the girls I've known all my life. You're different from them. Don't you agree that we work well together?"

"Yes, I suppose."

I had to admit that I was content with him. Fair-haired Nelson was a prize by anyone's standards. But I suddenly had a disturbing thought. Was I merely a distraction? What if he had chosen me as a suitable woman who would keep his family from noticing his love for Katya?

"We enjoy each other's company," Nelson continued. "And we seem to enjoy the same things. You told me that you like this life of luxury, didn't you? I think we could be happy together."

Again, I had to admit he was right. Forgive me, but I loved this life—the fine food, the gracious home, the beautiful clothes. I never could live with the smells and distresses of the slums. But the weight of guilt that this confession caused me was as enormous as the gap between Irina's home and the one I stood in. I couldn't understand how people like my grandmother and Louis Decker could be so selfless. I never wanted to peel another onion as long as I lived. And if I did marry Nelson Kent, I could be as generous with my money as the other Chicago socialites were, couldn't I?

"What about love?" I asked Nelson.

"What about it? People in our social circle don't marry for love. There is usually an attraction, perhaps even fondness. But in most cases, marriages are all about family alliances and power and finding a wife who will be a social asset."

"Does that fondness ever turn into love?"

"Yes, it often does . . . Violet, it seems as though you become sad whenever you mention love. Tell me, did you have your heart broken?"

"No. I've never been in love. I was thinking of my parents. According to my aunt, my parents married for love. But something happened and now they're divorced. I wish I knew why."

"Come on, let's dance."

The music lifted both of our spirits until, once again, I saw Katya watching us. This time, I pointed her out to him.

"We're being watched." He followed my gaze and saw her. Their eyes met, and even from across the room I could sense the passion they shared. Then she quickly turned and hurried away. The song ended a moment later.

Nelson smiled at me and said, "Will you excuse me, Violet? I'll be right back."

I couldn't resist the impulse to follow him. He caught up with Katya in the front hall, and I ducked behind a door to listen. Eavesdropping was an unforgivable offense. It would destroy my friendship with Nelson if he caught me. But I needed to know the truth.

For a long moment neither of them spoke. I risked another peek around the doorframe and saw that they were kissing. But this was no mere kiss—this was two starving people encountering food for the first time in days! I ducked behind the door again as the heat rose to my cheeks.

"Katya, wait!" I heard Nelson call a moment later. "Don't go! I want to explain."

"No, Nelson. You do not need to explain. She is very beautiful, and you must go back to her."

"Violet is just a friend—"

"Please stop. This is too hard. For both of us."

"Listen, I'm doing this for us. We—"

"But I don't want you to. It isn't right. . . . Good-bye, Nelson."

I peeked around the corner in time to see Katya run through the swinging door and disappear into the servants' quarters. Nelson didn't follow her. Instead, he stood for a long moment, staring at the door that separated them. Then his head drooped, his shoulders sagged.

If this had been a scene from a novel, our literature teacher would have pointed out the symbolism of that door, how it represented the division between them: master and servant, rich and poor, gentleman and immigrant. They lived separate lives in separate spheres, with barriers between them that could never be crossed.

Then I slipped from the doorway and hurried back to the party to avoid being caught. I quickly grabbed a glass of punch and sat down in an empty chair to think.

I had been right. Katya and Nelson were in love. How else could I interpret what I had just seen and heard? But it was forbidden love, the most difficult kind. Poor Nelson.

A cynic might have insisted that he was a spoiled rich boy who probably was taking advantage of an innocent girl whom he had no intention of marrying. But I'd seen his reaction when Katya turned away from him, and I didn't think so. Might he even go so far as to marry me—and keep Katya as his mistress on the side? I was pondering the situation when I felt Nelson's warm hand on my shoulder.

"I'm sorry for running off, Violet. I needed to speak to one of the servants. Ah, I see you helped yourself to more punch. Can I get you anything else?"

"No, thank you."

"Would you dance with me, then?"

I let him take me into his arms. We danced as smoothly as before, but now I was very conscious of his hand resting on the small of my back and of his other hand holding mine. I no longer felt comfortable in his arms, knowing the pain I was causing Katya—and perhaps

Nelson as well. I needed to complete my detective work, so I decided
to ask him one more question.

"If you had to choose between living in poverty with your true
love, or living alone with wealth and success, which would you
choose?" This time he didn't laugh.

"I don't think I could choose," he said quietly. "I wouldn't know
how to live without money. But I couldn't live alone either." Then he
surprised me by asking, "Which would you choose, Violet?"

I thought for a moment and realized that I couldn't choose either.
"I would like to think that I'd choose true love," I said. "But I've seen
horrendous poverty, and I couldn't bear to live that way, even with a
man I loved. I think that the struggle to survive would quickly choke
out our love." I knew for the first time that it was true. Yet I couldn't
live the way Aunt Agnes did either, having money without love.

"I would be very unhappy living without love," I added, "no matter how much money I had. My Aunt Birdie keeps telling me to
make sure I marry for love, but I don't know what to think anymore. . . . Don't people ever find both—love and money?"

"As I said, that's not the way it's usually done in our social circle.
It's a sad indictment . . . but it's true."

"Do you think poor people marry for love?"

"Ah, I see we've come full circle. We're back to the differences
between rich and poor, aren't we? I'm afraid I don't know the answer
to that. I've never been poor—nor do I ever intend to be."

Nelson Kent had a soft heart. He wasn't just a handsome shell. I
wasn't in love with him, but I liked him. I considered him a good
friend. I wished I could help him solve his dilemma with Katya.

By the time the evening drew to a close, he looked tired and
strained. His grandmother announced that dessert and coffee were
being served, but I noticed that Katya wasn't among the servants who
waited on everyone. I watched Nelson make the effort to put his
mask back into place as he conversed with his guests, but I could tell
that he wished the party would end. I think we were both relieved
when it did.

Chapter

14

Monday, June 19, 1893

"V iolet! Come quick! You've received a letter!" Aunt Birdie's
voice was breathless with excitement.

It was Aunt Birdie's job to fetch the mail every day, and it broke
my heart to see how hopeful she became each time she heard letters
slide through the mail slot. She never stopped believing that she
would hear from Gilbert. I was tempted to hunt down some of his
old letters and mail them to her, one by one, to cheer her. But today,
the fact that I had received a letter seemed to cheer her as much as if
it were her own.

"It's from your beau, Silas McClure." She said his name with the
same glee that a child said "Santa Claus."

"He's not my beau, Aunt Birdie."

"Well, I think he would like to be." She handed me the envelope.
I stared at Silas' name on the return address.

"Well, open it up! See what he says!"

I broke the seal and pulled out his letter. Silas had used stationery from a hotel in Cleveland, Ohio. His chunky, schoolboy penmanship made me smile as I quickly skimmed the note.

"Well. . . ?" Aunt Birdie prompted.

"Mr. McClure is going to be in town this week."

"Oh, how nice."

"He would like to take me to the World's Fair on Tuesday."

"Tuesday? Why, that's tomorrow!"

"Yes. I know." He had also mentioned that he'd found a chaperone.

"Florence," Aunt Birdie sang, "Silas McClure is taking our Violet to the fair!"

"Do I know this gentleman?" Grandmother asked, hurrying out to the front hallway where we stood. "I'm responsible for her, you know."

"You met Mr. McClure at the train station," I said. "Remember? The day I arrived?"

"Oh yes. The gentleman who accompanied you from Lockport."

I didn't confirm or deny her assumption. She could think whatever she wanted to about him. Besides, if she was going to withhold information about my mother, why should I tell her about Silas?

"Did you notice what a nice smile Mr. McClure has?" Aunt Birdie asked.

"It's pretty hard not to notice it," I mumbled.

"And he has the most beautiful blue eyes too. They're the color of the sky on an autumn afternoon."

I looked at her in surprise. "An autumn afternoon? Why autumn? Aren't all blue skies the same?"

"Oh no, dear. Of course they aren't. Mr. McClure's eyes aren't summer blue—a summer sky is bleached from the heat. And they're not wintry blue either, when the cold air frosts the sky with silver. No, his eyes are the color of an autumn sky, warmed by the glorious leaves that have turned all those exciting colors."

I stared at her. She was exactly right. Silas McClure was warm and exciting at the same time. And he did have wonderful eyes.

"My Gilbert has blue eyes. Oh, I do hope the weather isn't too stormy in Virginia where he's fighting. I would hate to think of him tramping through the mud or shivering in the rain. Maybe I'll write him a letter to lift his spirits. See how much Mr. McClure's letter has lifted our Violet's spirits?"

I glanced in the mirror and caught myself smiling. And my cheeks were pink. "Excuse me," I mumbled as I raced up the stairs. At school we hadn't been allowed to race up the stairs—or to race anywhere for that matter. *"Slowly, girls. Slowly and gracefully. You must float when you walk."* Lately I seemed to be ignoring a lot of the things I'd learned.

I stuffed Silas' letter into my journal and shoved the journal beneath my mattress. Something about the unseemly Mr. McClure reminded me of the romance novels and true crime stories that Ruth and I had read, and we had kept those illicit books under the mattress too.

I didn't know why, but I had a hard time falling asleep that night. Was I excited about finally visiting the fair or nervous about going out with a man that none of my family members knew? A proper young lady sought her father's approval before courting someone. The young man's background would be thoroughly investigated to make certain that he wasn't a scoundrel. My grandmother could vouch for Louis Decker. Aunt Agnes knew Nelson Kent's family. Maude O'Neill had given Herman Beckett her support. But the only endorsement Silas McClure had was that Aunt Birdie liked his blue eyes. Was I behaving foolishly to trust him?

In truth, the lure of adventure far outweighed any fear I might have felt. I was tired of being a proper young lady, tired of all the social constraints that held me back and tied me down. I wanted the freedom that Aunt Matt's suffragettes had promised me, but I wanted it now. I finally fell asleep, anticipating a taste of that freedom in the morning.

My first thought upon awakening was of Silas McClure. What if he arrived in his baggy plaid salesman's suit and had his hair slicked with oil again? And what if someone from Nelson's social circle saw me with him at the fair? I never would be invited to another party. Aunt Agnes would disown me.

While it was true that Silas had looked presentable the last time he had called on me, I made up my mind to plead illness and stay home if his clothes and his hair were too embarrassing. My only reason for allowing him to escort me in the first place was so that he could take me to my mother's address.

When I opened the door he was grinning from ear-to-ear, as if he'd just won a thousand dollars—or maybe stolen it.

I breathed a sigh of relief. He obviously hadn't replenished his supply of Macassar oil yet, and his wavy brown hair looked clean and neat. So did his plain dark suit. He smelled faintly of shaving cream, and I noticed that he'd shaved so closely he had nicked himself in two spots. Was he nervous about seeing me—or too cheap to pay for a barber?

But he had come to the door alone.

"Good morning, Silas dear," Aunt Birdie said, hugging him like a long-lost friend. "It's wonderful to see you again."

"Great to see you too, Mrs. Casey."

"Where is our chaperone?" I asked in surprise.

"They wanted to wait outside."

"*They. . . ?*"

He gestured behind him, and I saw a woman in a long black dress standing by the curb with a short, bearded man in a straw hat. The woman was very tall and evidently very modest. In spite of the warm day, she wore a long-sleeved dress and a large black hat with a veil that covered her face. Her outfit was very much out of fashion unless she was in mourning. And if there had been a death in the family, why was she going to the fair?

"I figured if one chaperone was a good thing then two might be even better," Silas explained.

"Would they like to come in so you can introduce them properly?"

"No, they'd rather wait outside. I'll introduce everybody on the way there."

"Are they relatives of yours?" I asked. I turned to the hall mirror and fussed with my hatpin, stalling for time. From the moment I'd opened the door to him, my heart had begun beating like an African drum, and I was no longer sure I wanted to accompany him if he was going to have this effect on me.

"Nope. They're just friends of mine."

"Has she had a death in the family?" I whispered.

"I have no idea," he whispered back. "Are you ready?"

"I-I guess so . . . Maybe I should take my parasol . . . for the sun." It might also come in handy as a weapon if I needed to defend myself.

"Good-bye, you two," Aunt Birdie cheered. "Have fun!"

"I wager we will," Silas said. He offered me his arm and we walked down the front steps to where the chaperones waited. "These are my friends Josephine and Robert. And this is Violet Hayes, the lady I've been talking your ear off about."

"I'm pleased to meet you," I said, wondering if they had last names.

"Yeah."

"Likewise."

It was apparent that Josephine had never been to charm school.

"Did I exaggerate when I told you how pretty Violet is?" Silas asked, nudging Josephine in the ribs.

"She's lovely," Josephine said. "Let's get going." Her voice sounded hoarse, as if she had a cold. Perhaps she needed a dose of Dr. Dean's Blood Builder.

I couldn't get a very good look at Robert—he wore his hat down so low it nearly covered his eyes, and the rest of his face was hidden behind a bushy brown beard and exuberant mustache. But Josephine was very homely, and apparently quite hirsute—poor thing. I saw a fringe of dark hair poking out between her long sleeves and her gloves. She seemed very self-conscious about her appearance—and I would be too if I were as unpleasant looking as she was. Both chaperones kept their faces averted and their eyes lowered.

"Do you mind taking a streetcar?" Silas asked. "I can hail a cab if you want, but it might take a while to find one."

"I don't mind the streetcar if the others don't."

"They're fine with it."

I glanced over my shoulder. The two stayed several paces behind us as we walked to the streetcar stop. I wanted to be polite and include them in our conversation, but it was almost as if they were avoiding me. Maybe they had never played the role of chaperones before.

"It seems rude not to include them in our conversation, Mr. McClure. Should we slow down for them?"

"They're fine," Silas said. "They're as excited about going to the fair as I am."

I would have to take his word on faith because their grim expressions revealed little excitement. When they turned their backs on me and began whispering to each other as we waited for the streetcar, I saw no sense in worrying about being polite.

"By the way, will we be passing anywhere near LaSalle Street?" I asked Silas. This time I had remembered to bring my mother's address with me.

"LaSalle Street? Not really. Why?"

"There's someone I've been hoping to visit while I'm here in Chicago. Her address is on LaSalle Street."

"Oh, yeah, that's right. You showed it to me the day we arrived in town."

"Might it be possible to stop there on our way home?"

"Yeah, sure. We can arrange that." My heart leaped with excitement at the prospect. At last!

We rode the streetcar for several blocks—Silas and I sharing a seat, our chaperones sitting in the rear of the car—until we reached the south side elevated train station. The tracks were the oddest things I'd ever seen, suspended in the air above our heads on trestle-like bridges. We would have to climb a set of stairs in order to board them. I instinctively ducked as a train rumbled into the station and screeched to a halt overhead, blocking out the sun.

"What do you think?" Silas shouted, pointing up.

"Quite impressive," I shouted back. "I had heard that the city was building a set of train tracks up in the air, but I couldn't imagine such a thing."

"These are specially built to carry the crowds to the fair."

Another locomotive roared into the station as we climbed the stairs, and I had to grip my hat to keep it from blowing away in the wind. I felt the metal scaffolding shake beneath my feet.

"I hear they're planning to extend these elevated trains until they make a loop all around the city," Silas said. "Aren't they something?"

I didn't want to hurt his feelings, but I thought the steel framework was quite ugly. The trains did little to beautify the city and might better have been buried underground, as they were in other cities.

"It seems a little scary, doesn't it?" I shouted above the noise. "I mean, it's not every day that you see trains up in the air, above our heads."

"I think they're great! I get all pepped up, don't you? All that power and energy—it's contagious!"

"Yes." It must have been the excitement of the trains because my heart was banging like a factory in full swing. Our train arrived, and once again Josephine and Robert took seats well away from us when we boarded. "Have they ever chaperoned anyone before?" I asked.

"I don't know. Why?"

"Well, I suppose it's nice of them to give us privacy, but I feel rude for not including them in our conversation."

"They aren't very talkative."

I looked down at the streets below as the train propelled us through the air at breakneck speed, squealing into stations to pick up more passengers, then racing out again. In no time at all I caught my first glimpse of the fair up ahead. The day was magnificent without a cloud in the sky, and the white buildings and silvery water seemed to glow in the sunlight.

"Oh, it's wonderful!" I breathed.

"It's like a little piece of heaven just floated down to earth," Silas said when he saw my reaction. "You can see why they call it the White City."

"Beautiful doesn't seem descriptive enough."

"You should see it at night, all lit up with electric lights." I recalled Nelson Kent saying the same thing.

Silas paid my admission fee of fifty cents, but I thought it odd that our chaperones paid their own fare. As soon as we entered the gates, Josephine and Robert took the lead, walking briskly ahead of us as if they had an appointment to keep. Silas and I hurried to stay apace.

"That's the Transportation Building," he said, pointing to our left. "And that enormous one across the water is Manufactures and Liberal Arts. It has a walkway up on top, if you want to go up for a good view later on. And look—we can ride around the lagoon in a gondola."

"Oh, I would love to go for a gondola ride!" It was like a scene from a travel book with the gondolier in his brightly colored costume, propelling his passengers across the tranquil waters. The pristine white buildings in the background had arches and pillars and graceful statues. "This is amazing, Silas! It's like another world. I've always wanted to travel to faraway places."

"You name any country or state you want and they have a pavilion or a display here. You can see the world for only two bits—Japan, Egypt, Africa . . . They even have an Eskimo village with reindeer."

Silas' childlike excitement was contagious. I didn't know which way to look or where I wanted to go first. I wanted to see it all, but Josephine and Robert had raced so far ahead of us that Silas and I had to hurry down the path or risk losing them.

"Why are they in such a hurry?" I panted.

"Josephine wants to see the Woman's Pavilion."

"I do too. My Aunt Matilda has been singing its praises."

Silas and I finally paused to rest once we arrived in front of the stately pavilion. "That's the Wooded Isle in the middle of the lagoon," he told me. "And that's the Swedish Pavilion on the other side with the thatched towers. That castlelike one is the Fisheries Building. They have the most amazing aquariums inside, with the strangest and most beautiful underwater creatures you could ever imagine."

"Where did our chaperones go?" I asked, glancing around.

"I think they went inside already."

"Without us? Shouldn't we go in with them?"

"You don't really want to see the Woman's Pavilion, do you? It's boring, Violet. The Midway is a lot more fun."

"I don't know . . . um . . . I guess—"

"We can meet up with them later. Come on."

"Where are we going?"

"To the big wheel, of course! You said you wanted to ride Mr. Ferris' wonderful wheel, remember? I thought we'd go there first."

"Alone?"

"Look—there it is." He took my shoulders and swung me around, pointing into the distance.

"Wow!" The moment I saw the huge mechanical wheel poking into the sky I no longer cared about Josephine and Robert. We hurried toward the broad Midway Plaisance and plunged into the buzzing crowd of people.

"I guess we really don't need chaperones in a crowd this big," I said.

"I don't understand why you need them at all. It's almost the twentieth century, you know? All this fuss over manners and things—that's from the olden days, isn't it?"

I couldn't seem to compose a reply. "I . . . um . . . I guess the assumption is that women should be protected."

"From what? People say women are helpless, but I don't buy it. You strike me as a sensible, intelligent woman. I'll wager you're quite capable of taking care of yourself. In fact, you've been gripping that parasol like it's a weapon ever since we left home. I'd sure hate to come between you and that thing." I had to laugh at his words. I also eased my grip on the umbrella handle.

The wild, chaotic Midway seemed like an entirely different world from the symmetry and beauty of the White City. Even the crowds seemed different. These were boisterous, commonplace folk, unlike the more genteel crowd I'd seen strolling past the lagoons.

Here was another example of the many contrasts I'd encountered since coming to Chicago: Nelson Kent's luxurious life compared to Irina's desolate one. Louis Decker's passion for God versus the religious indifference I'd grown up with. The narrow roles I had assumed all women must play contrasted with the opportunities that Aunt Matt and her friends foresaw for women. And the strict manners and rules I'd learned from Madame Beauchamps, which couldn't compare with the delicious freedom I felt walking down the Midway with Silas McClure—without a chaperone.

Silas stood a head taller than me, and it was hard to hold on to his arm in the crowded streets. I lost my grip momentarily when someone jostled us, and Silas reached for my hand as naturally as if we were children. Once again, the moment his strong, warm palm touched mine, the sensation was like gripping the wrong end of a flat iron.

"I would hate to lose you in this mob," he said when he saw my reaction. He lifted our entwined hands slightly and said, "This is so we don't get separated."

It was highly improper—wasn't it? But hadn't I held Nelson Kent's hand when we'd danced together? What was the difference?

I quickly forgot about propriety as we passed all sorts of fascinating displays—the Libby Glass Works, a Colorado gold mine, a rustic log cabin, the Hagenbeck Animal Show, an Irish village, a Japanese bazaar. The accompanying smells of woodsmoke and animals and exotic spices entranced me.

"What are those drums?" I asked. I hoped it wasn't the sound of my heart pounding for all to hear.

"There's a Javanese village on the right. We can go there later, if you want." The comfortable way he said "we" both frightened and thrilled me.

"I wish I had the freedom to go places on my own and make my own decisions," I said. "I've had my father hovering over me all my life when I wasn't in school. And my school was very strict. They told us that rules and chaperones were there to protect women. But you're right—who says I need to be protected?"

"I'll wager those rules will be out-of-date in a few years."

"Do you think so? That's what my Aunt Matt thinks too. She's a suffragette. What do you think of women voting?"

"I don't know. Why do they want to vote?"

I tried to recall what Aunt Matt had told me. "They want to be able to elect people who will represent their interests—women's interests."

"That makes sense to me." Silas McClure seemed to have very modern views as far as women were concerned. I decided to probe further as we walked past a genuine Bedouin Arab with his camel.

"What if you were ill and the only physician available was a woman. Would you let her care for you?"

"Sure, why not? But I can't say as I've ever met a woman doctor. I'll wager there aren't too many of them, are there?"

"My aunt spoke as if there were at least a few."

We arrived at the base of the wheel, and it was even more amazing up close than from a distance. The intricate spokes were enormous and graceful—but they looked quite insufficient to bear the weight of dozens of passenger carriages the size of streetcars. I had to look up and up to see the very top of the wheel—as high as the clouds, or so it seemed to me. My knees trembled as Silas paid our fares and we joined the line of waiting passengers.

"That's the Algerian Village over there," he said. "Maybe we can come back and get something to eat there later. They have amazing food with flavors like you've never tasted before."

"I hear that people in foreign countries eat all manner of interesting things."

"Yeah, like monkey meat and alligator and water buffalo," he said excitedly.

"What's the most adventurous thing you've ever eaten?"

"Rattlesnake."

"You didn't! Where? Were you stranded in the desert for days and days with nothing to eat after bandits attacked your train, and you had to kill the snake with your bare hands and eat it raw?"

"No," Silas laughed, "but I think I'll tell your version of the story from now on. It was in a saloon in Texas cattle country. They served pretty decent food for a saloon, so when I saw rattlesnake on the menu I figured I had to try it."

"You're very adventurous, Silas. What did it taste like?"

"A little bit like chicken. Only chewier." The line moved forward as the group in front of us boarded the wheel. We would board next. I wondered if Silas could feel my hand trembling as he held it in his.

"I read somewhere that the wheel is 265 feet high and can carry a total of 2,160 passengers at a time," he said.

"How can you remember all that?"

"I'm pretty good with numbers and things."

Finally it was our turn to step into the enormous car. Silas quickly pulled me over to the front window. "So we'll have the best view," he said.

The wheel operator closed the door and bolted it shut.

"Hang on!" Silas said.

His warning came too late. The car lurched as it began to ascend, and I fell forward against him. His arms encircled me, and he held me against his chest for a moment until I adjusted to the motion and regained my balance. He smelled good, like the barbershop in Lockport that I used to visit with my father on Saturday mornings. Silas had strong arms and a rock-hard chest.

"You okay?" he asked.

"Yes. Thank you." I pulled away reluctantly. "I lost my footing for a moment."

I had danced with Nelson and other gentlemen, but never before had I been held so closely by any of them. Hugging a man felt wonderfully different from hugging a woman's pillow-soft body. The only man I could recall embracing was my father, who had an ample belly-cushion in front. I envied Aunt Birdie's simple freedom of embracing everyone. Madame B. would wag her finger at me, but I began to hope that the car would lurch again so I could fall back into Silas' arms.

He gently took my hand in his again on the long, slow ride to the top. "Isn't this something?" he breathed.

"It sure is!" I gripped his hand tightly in return. In fact, our hands might have been glued together.

I risked looking down as we climbed and had the peculiar sensation that my stomach was sinking toward my toes. I had never been up this high before—and certainly had never dangled from such a spindly structure before. The sensation was dizzying. We were hanging over empty air, suspended from the slowly turning wheel. I tried to take it all in at once, watching the intricate steel supports drifting past, then gazing down at the ground, then at the distant view of the fairgrounds and the lake and the smoky city on the horizon.

"Wow! This is frightening—but fun!"

"I knew you would like it."

"I wish I could fly!"

"I know what you mean. I want to go for a ride in a balloon someday. They have a tethered one here at the fair that you can go up in, but I doubt it's as exciting as a real balloon ride."

"Tell me about your family, Silas. Where did you grow up? Is your family as adventurous as you are?"

"I was raised on a farm in Ohio outside a town you probably never heard of. I'm the fourth of seven kids. I left home after high school for the excitement of the city and never looked back. I'd see the whole world if I could afford it."

I hadn't thought of Silas as a thief all morning, but I suddenly had an idea how I could find out if he was one.

"If you could choose, would you rather be the captain of a pirate ship or the captain of a warship?"

"A pirate ship. No question about it." Somehow I knew that would be his choice.

"You have to tell me why."

"Wars are so long and drawn out and pointless. Nobody really wins them, do they? I don't hate anyone badly enough to fight them in a war. Besides, the captain of a warship has to follow orders. But the captain of a pirate ship, now he's his own boss. That's the life for me. Sailing the seas, seeking adventure. Finding buried treasure . . ."

"But pirates are outlaws."

"I know," he said with a grin. "And they get to hijack sailing vessels and carry off gold doubloons and beautiful maidens."

"You must have read the same adventure stories that I did."

"Which ship would you choose, Violet?"

He was gazing into my eyes, and it was so romantic to be climbing above the fairgrounds with an exciting, adventurous man that I lost my train of thought altogether. It took me a moment to remember the question.

"Well . . . I don't think women get to be ship captains."

"But what if you could be one?"

"If I could? . . . I guess I would want to be the captain a pirate ship too."

"Why?"

"I've been taught to follow the rules all my life. It might be fun to see what it was like to break a few."

"You're the most interesting woman I've ever met."

My heart was booming like a bass drum. I turned away to look at the view and to remind myself why I had agreed to come with him. Silas was going to help me find my mother on the way home. Winning his affections had not been part of my plan.

"I love your questions, Violet. Ask me another one."

"All right . . ." It took me a moment to think of one. "If you had to choose between going blind and never seeing the face of your beloved again, or becoming permanently deaf, so that you could never hear music or a child's voice, which would you choose?"

"I'd choose to be deaf. I think I would miss seeing beautiful things more than hearing them. Besides, people don't really need to talk, do they? They can say so much more with their eyes . . . don't you think?"

I made the mistake of looking up into his eyes, which were as blue as the distant lake. I felt breathless, as if I were treading water, trying not to drown. I quickly turned away and looked back out at the lake.

"Is that a boat out there?" I asked, pointing.

"It looks like one. . . . But tell me how you would answer that question, Violet. Would you rather be blind or deaf?"

"The same as you, I think. The world is much too beautiful to miss. Just look at that view."

We had been stopping to let passengers on and off as we'd slowly ascended, but now the wheel paused at the very top, swaying slightly in the breeze. The sounds from the Midway had grown faint, and a hush seemed to fall over the other passengers in our car as we gazed down from the dizzying height. But the view was wasted on Silas McClure. He never took his eyes off me.

"We've stopped," I murmured.

"To tell you the truth," Silas said softly, "I hope we get stuck up here for a few days."

"Me too." I didn't want the ride to end either. But a moment later I felt the sinking sensation in my stomach as our car started down again.

"Ask me one more question, Violet."

I decided to ask the same one I'd asked Nelson Kent—the one neither of us had been able to answer.

"If you had to choose between being desperately poor but in love, or being enormously wealthy but alone, which would you choose?"

"I'd choose love. A thousand times over. Life wouldn't be worth living without it."

"But you would be poor, remember?"

"I don't care. People get along fine without money all the time. But money can't buy the happiness that love brings."

I thought of how sad Nelson had seemed after Katya had disappeared through the servants' door, and I wondered if Silas was right.

"You believe in love, then?" I asked.

"Absolutely! Don't you?"

"I don't know. I was told that my parents married for love, yet somehow it died. I don't know why. Now they're divorced."

"Gosh, I'm sorry to hear that."

"My Aunt Birdie was madly in love with her husband, but as you've probably guessed, he died in the war. Now she's so lost and lonely without him."

"I know it seems very sad. But I'll wager that if you asked her, she would gladly trade her house and all of her money to have him back."

"You're probably right."

"But you haven't answered the question, Violet. You and your grandmother and your aunts seem pretty well off. Would you give it all up for love?"

"I'm not sure. My grandmother does charity work among the immigrants, and she took me with her the other day. I saw the terrible living conditions in those tenements, and I'm afraid my love might wear thin if I had to live in a place like that and struggle every day just to get enough to eat."

"But you said that the other choice was to be rich but alone, right?"

"I know. And I wouldn't like that either."

"Have you ever been in love, Violet?"

"No."

"Then maybe it's not fair to try to answer that question until you've experienced it."

Something about the way he was smiling made me wonder. "Have you been in love, Mr. McClure?"

"Yes, Miss Hayes. I have felt myself falling in love—just once. That's why I know I'd give up everything else for it."

He was gazing at me as if I was the one! I couldn't breathe. He was like a magician, dangling a shining object in front of me—back and forth—until I was hypnotized by him.

Suddenly the car lurched as it came to a halt at the bottom. This time I stumbled backward, away from him instead of into his arms, and my good sense returned. Silas McClure was a snake charmer, a salesman, and he'd been performing his trade on me. That's what thieves and con artists like him did, feeding their phony lines to weak-willed women and spinning their charms. He was obviously a master at this trade and I had nearly fallen for it. Fortunately the ride ended so I could come to reality.

"Wasn't that wonderful?" Silas asked. "I could ride all day."

"Yes, me too." I needed to let go of his hand and break the spell completely, so I slowly slid my hand from his and took his elbow again. I kept a safe distance between us as we walked.

"What shall we see now?" Silas asked. "You want to see the Street in Cairo, or the African dancers, or—"

"I think we had better find Josephine and Robert first."

"They're okay."

"I'm sure they are, Silas, but if someone were to see us walking together without a chaperone, it might ruin my reputation." I felt scared, not of him but of the way I had reacted to him. I was being drawn to him—and he was thoroughly unsuitable!

"Okay. Sure. We can go look for them." At least he was cheerful about it.

As we neared the main steps to the Woman's Pavilion, Josephine suddenly materialized out of the shadows. One moment no one had been there, and the next—there she stood, as if she had been hiding in the bushes, watching for us. She glanced all around nervously as we approached, then hurried forward and took Silas' other arm, steering us away from the building.

"We gotta go," she said.

"Wait, wait. What's the hurry?" Silas asked.

"I can't say in front of . . ." Josephine nodded toward me.

"Will you excuse us for a moment, Violet?" He pulled Josephine aside to talk. Their voices were so soft I could hear only snatches of their conversation.

"What happened?"

I heard Josephine say the words *caught* and *money*. My stomach began to sink as it had when riding the wheel.

"Can't you take care of things?" Silas asked. His voice rose in anger and so did Josephine's.

"Don't be stupid. I gotta leave right now and you gotta come with me."

Silas exhaled, then turned back toward me and linked my arm through his. "I'm sorry to end our day in a rush, Violet, but I'm afraid we have to go."

All three of us started walking briskly back toward the elevated train station. It was the first time I'd ever seen Silas without a smile on his face.

"But we just got here. And what about Robert? We're not going to leave him here, are we?"

They answered simultaneously: "He got tied up," from Silas. "He has business to take care of," from Josephine. They couldn't leave the fair quickly enough. Could what I suspected really be true? Were Silas and his friends truly thieves?

When we reached the station, Josephine scanned the platform as if searching for someone while Silas purchased our tickets. He offered me a seat on the bench while we waited for the next train to arrive, but he didn't sit. He paced in front of me, and Josephine paced a short distance away. Their eyes roved the station like searchlights.

Silas barely spoke on the ride home except to say, "I'm sorry, Violet." He had forgotten all about taking me to the address on LaSalle Street, and when I saw his worried expression, I didn't dare bring it up. Once again, I'd been thwarted in my search for my mother.

"This wasn't at all how I wanted our day to end," he said when we finally reached my front door. "Can you ever forgive me?"

"Of course. I enjoyed riding the wheel. . . ."

"Yeah. Me too."

"But I don't understand why—"

"I'm so sorry, Violet. I have to run."

He left me standing at the door and jogged down the block to the streetcar stop where we'd left Josephine. He didn't look back. I felt as though I'd been tossed from a train like a sack of mail. I was fighting tears of disappointment and frustration when Aunt Birdie greeted me in the front hallway with a hug.

"Back so soon? Did you have a nice time, dear? Why didn't you invite him in?"

I couldn't reply. How could I explain something that I didn't understand myself?

"You're crying, Violet. What happened?"

"Nothing. Our chaperones were . . . were called away. So we had to come home."

"Oh, what a shame. I would be disappointed too if I couldn't spend the day with my beau."

I started to protest that Silas wasn't my beau, then stopped. The real reason I was upset, I told myself, was because I still hadn't found my mother.

Wasn't it?

Chapter

15

Wednesday, June 21, 1893

W ould you like to come with me to the settlement house?" my grandmother asked the following morning. "I think Louis Decker will be there. And we won't be cooking this time."

"Maybe another day. I'm supposed to play the piano for Louis tomorrow, and I really need to practice." I also needed a break from all of my would-be suitors after my unsettling day with Silas McClure.

I sat down at the keyboard and was warming up with a few scales when I remembered Aunt Agnes. If she found me at home today, she would want me to go calling with her. Maybe I should feign illness. Aunt Agnes was determined to find me a husband, and she was firing her Cupid's arrows at Nelson Kent.

I couldn't erase the image of him and Katya kissing. It had been like a scene from a romance novel. What would it be like to be kissed with such passion? Nelson had told her, *"Violet is just a friend . . . I'm doing this for us. . . ."* Doing what? Was Nelson using me?

I pounded out another set of scales on the piano. When I looked up, Aunt Matt stood in the parlor doorway with her hat, gloves, and parasol.

"I'm leaving now to work at the Suffrage Association."

I swiveled around on the piano stool and stood. Aunt Matt was the one person who wouldn't pressure me to find a husband.

"May I come with you?" I asked.

She looked surprised. "Certainly."

"Um . . . you're not marching today, are you?"

"No, not today. Why?"

"I-I need to know which shoes to wear." In truth, I had no desire to get arrested and end up in a jail cell alongside Silas and his thieving pals, Robert and Josephine—or whatever their real names were.

"We're not marching today; we're stuffing envelopes," Aunt Matt explained while I fetched my hat and gloves. "Next month is our anniversary rally. We need to spread the word so we'll get a good turnout."

"Yes, of course." I nodded as if I was as concerned with the turnout as she was, but as we headed toward the streetcar stop, I began formulating a scheme of my own.

"Aunt Matt? I noticed that we passed LaSalle Street the last time I went to the association with you, and I was wondering . . . Do you think we could make a stop on our way there? There's someone I've been meaning to visit who lives on LaSalle Street." I held my breath, hoping she wouldn't ask for a name.

"It will have to be on our way home, after our work is finished. They're expecting me at headquarters at ten-thirty sharp."

"Yes, I understand. That will be fine. On the way home, then."

My heart raced with excitement. Finally, I would see my mother. I bit my lip to keep from grinning foolishly and told myself to calm down. I had all morning to plan what I would say to her. In the meantime, I didn't want Aunt Matt to learn my true intentions.

"What will the rally be about?" I asked her.

"This July marks the forty-fifth anniversary of the first Women's Rights Convention in America. That was when Elizabeth Cady Stanton, Lucretia Mott, and the other women drew up our Declaration of Sentiments and Resolutions."

"Is that when the Suffrage Association got started?" A streetcar rounded our corner as I asked the question, the horses' hooves clomping noisily on the cobblestone street. Aunt Matt waited until the vehicle stopped and we'd taken our seats before answering.

"One of our organization's founders, Lucretia Mott, was a Quaker minister. They allow women to preach, you know. The Quakers also believe in equal education for men and women. Lucretia met another one of our leaders, Elizabeth Cady Stanton, at the World Anti-Slavery Convention in London, England. Elizabeth and her husband had traveled to England on their honeymoon just to attend the convention."

I nodded and began sliding down in my seat, already sorry that I had asked. I had forgotten how loudly Aunt Matt lectured—and how openly the other passengers stared at us.

"Several of the delegates arriving from America were women," she continued. "But they—along with Elizabeth and Lucretia—were forbidden to take part in the meetings with the men. Can you imagine traveling all that way and then not being allowed to participate? Simply because they were women? Instead, all of the women, even the duly elected delegates, were forced to sit in a separate gallery."

"That's terrible." My voice sounded like a whisper compared to hers.

"Of course they were outraged. Mr. Stanton was entirely sympathetic and supportive, but most husbands aren't, you know. That's when the two women decided to work together for women's rights here in America. They held the first convention in 1848."

"That seems like a long time ago."

"You're right, Violet. Progress has been much too slow."

My mind drifted back to my conversation with Silas yesterday.

He'd seemed sure that in the new century many of the restrictions on women, such as chaperones, would be considered outmoded. "How long until women have the same rights as men?" I asked.

"Well, even though victories have been few, we are making progress nonetheless. Three years ago, Wyoming became the first state to grant women the right to vote. Colorado will follow suit this year. We're focusing on voting rights because then we'll be in a position to influence lawmakers to make other changes."

"Is that why men don't want women to vote? Because we'll change things?"

"Yes, that's part of the reason. It's also because they would have to acknowledge the fact that women are capable of thinking for themselves. They would have to do away with the belief that a woman needs her father or her husband to make decisions for her."

"I want that freedom now, Aunt Matt. I wish I didn't need a chaperone, and that I could go wherever I wanted and do whatever I wanted instead of what my father wants me to do. Aunt Agnes said he sent me here to find a husband."

"And he probably told Agnes to keep you well away from me. . . . Here, this is where we get off," she said, rising from her seat. She set off down the street, walking at an even brisker pace than usual. Evidently our conversation had her up in arms.

"I understand why you don't want me to marry a rich husband," I said, puffing to keep up, "but how can I support myself if I don't get married?"

"Someday it will be different. Someday women will be able to earn a decent living, and we won't be dependent on our husbands or fathers. I'm not against marriage, Violet. It's the idea of marrying someone just for his money that seems wrong. There should be qualities in the man that draw you to make the commitment to him besides his money."

"Do you believe in love, Aunt Matt?"

She paused before replying. Too late, I remembered Aunt Birdie telling me that Aunt Matt had once been in love.

"It's better to marry someone for love than for his money," she finally said.

We reached the association headquarters and went inside. Aunt Matt introduced me to the president.

"It's so nice to meet you, Violet. We are very grateful for your help."

"I'm glad that I could come."

She and the other ladies seemed like gentle, intelligent women, not militant radicals or men-haters. We sat around a huge worktable with stacks of letters and envelopes piled in front of us. It was mindless work, folding letters and stuffing them into envelopes and licking them shut. I enjoyed it more than peeling vegetables at the settlement house though. Better to have a dry tongue and a few paper cuts than hands stained with beet juice—not that the state of my hands mattered much. I didn't plan on holding hands with Nelson anytime soon, nor with the devout Louis Decker—and never again with Silas McClure.

The women chatted while they worked. I wasn't paying too much attention until one of them said, "By the way, ladies, did you hear that there was another robbery at the Woman's Pavilion yesterday?"

I stopped licking. My entire body began to tingle as if I were being slowly submerged in boiling water.

"I didn't see anything in this morning's paper about it," Aunt Matt said. "What happened?"

"You know how the lady managers have their cookbooks for sale? Well, a pair of thieves came into the building, and one of them grabbed the money box when no one was looking."

My cheeks must have bloomed like hothouse roses as the heat rose to my face. I hoped no one would notice.

"That's the third robbery we've had, isn't it?"

"No, it's the fifth! And the worst one yet. In all of the other incidents, the women had things stolen from their purses. This time they snatched an entire strongbox full of cash. There were two of them, working together."

I stopped breathing. The Great Fire couldn't have burned hotter than I did.

"That's dreadful!" all the ladies agreed. "How frightening."

"They figure that the thieves must have been watching the sales booth for some time, because they knew exactly what they were doing. One of them distracted the clerk while the other one grabbed the money box. But what they didn't know was that we've hired the Pinkertons. They were guarding the pavilion at the time of the robbery, and they came running to the rescue as soon as the theft occurred. They caught one of the thieves—the one with the cash box, fortunately—but the other thief slipped away."

The room began to spin. I had to grip the edge of the table to keep from sliding out of my chair. I was involved with a gang of thieves! Silas McClure and his friends truly were thieves—and I had helped them escape! Did that make me an accomplice?

"Have they had thefts in any of the other pavilions?" someone asked.

"A few, I think. But not nearly as many as ours. We're presumed to be an easy target because we're 'helpless' women."

"I guess we showed them! We were clever enough to hire our own guards, weren't we?"

"Yes, but it's very costly to have Pinkerton's men there all the time."

"Where were the police? Doesn't the fair have security people?"

"They have the Columbian guards, but have you seen them? They're all young pups in their twenties with no experience doing police work. They can barely help lost children find their parents, let alone deal with professional thieves."

"What's this country coming to when one must hire private investigators?"

"W-were the thieves men or women?" I asked when I finally could speak.

"I don't know. I've never heard of women thieves, have you? But I suppose it's possible. Why?"

"No reason. But since it's the Woman's Pavilion, I just wondered . . ."

I suddenly recalled how oddly Josephine had behaved and how strange she had looked with her homely face and hairy arms. I added all of the clues together: her tall frame and unfashionable clothes, her hoarse voice and lack of manners. Of course! She had been a man disguised as a woman! I had been stupid not to figure it out the moment I met her. Silas McClure had intentionally deceived me.

I heard my aunt talking with the other women, but their voices grew softer and softer, drowned out by the rushing sound in my ears. The worktable slid out of focus. I felt as dizzy as I had when riding the giant wheel. I closed my eyes to make the dizziness stop, and the next thing I knew, Aunt Matt was calling my name.

"Violet. . . ? Violet! Are you all right?" She gripped my shoulders and gave me a little shake. "What's wrong? You look as though you're about to faint."

"She's as white as those envelopes."

"Is her corset too tight? Maybe she should unlace it."

"I-I don't feel well," I murmured. But it had nothing to do with my corset.

"It's my fault," Aunt Matt said. "I should have waited for you to eat some breakfast."

"Take her into the privy, Matilda, so she can unlace her corset."

"Corsets should be outlawed. It's a crime that young girls have to torture themselves simply for the sake of attracting a man."

"I-it's not my corset," I said. I didn't think I could stand, let alone walk to the privy. Someone brought me a glass of water, and I took a long drink.

"There. Feeling better?"

"Yes. Thank you. I guess I got dry after licking all those envelopes and stamps."

"If women ran the world, envelopes wouldn't need to be licked," Aunt Matt declared. "Stamps either."

I felt like one of the main characters in a *True Crime* story or Ruth's *Illustrated Police News*. If Pinkerton's men had captured all four of us yesterday, my picture might have been on the cover of it!

"I should take you home."

"I think it might be better if I stayed seated, Aunt Matt. I'll be all right. I want to help finish the envelopes."

"You've been burning the candle at both ends, haven't you, young lady? Rising at dawn to run all over the slums with Florence and going to parties with Agnes until all hours of the night? And weren't you at the fair yesterday?"

"Y-yes. I was."

Should I tell the authorities what I knew? But I really didn't know anything at all about "Josephine" or how to find him. No wonder Silas hadn't told me his last name. I had Silas' business card with his post office box information. I could give that to the authorities.

"What did you think of the fair, Violet? Did you see the Woman's Pavilion?"

"Just from the outside. I-I didn't go in."

"Good. I'd like to show it to you," Aunt Matt said. "They sponsor wonderful lectures by prominent women on all manner of subjects. We'll go some afternoon when the mailing is finished."

I wasn't sure I wanted to return to the scene of the crime, so to speak, but I smiled and said, "I would like that."

The conversation switched to other topics, and the opportunity to report what I knew about the robbery passed. I felt relieved. I really didn't want the police to arrest Silas. After all, he was with me at the time of the robbery. He wasn't responsible for his friends' actions, was he? But I made up my mind to have nothing more to do with Mr. McClure.

"Let me give you and your niece a ride home, Matilda," someone offered when we'd finished our morning's work. "She still looks pale to me."

I started to protest, but Aunt Matt overruled me. "Yes, thank you, Emily. We accept. That's very kind of you." I clenched my fists in frustration and disappointment. I couldn't impose upon Aunt Matt's friend by asking her to stop at LaSalle Street to visit my mother.

By the time we arrived home, I'd recovered from my shock and no longer felt faint. My heart was beating normally again—until Aunt Birdie greeted me at the door with an envelope.

"Violet! You've received *another* letter."

"W-who is it from?"

"Someone named"—she read the return address—"Herman Beckett."

"Oh no." I closed my eyes in dismay. I had forgotten all about him.

"Who is he, dear?" Aunt Birdie asked.

"A gentleman I know from back home in Lockport. Mr. Beckett courted me a few times before I came here."

"Oh, how nice."

I ripped open the envelope without benefit of an opener, guessing what it might say. Herman's printing was so small and neat it might have been made on a typing machine. The somber black ink nearly bled through the page. I scanned it quickly, wincing at every sentence.

"You have such a long face, Violet. I do hope it isn't bad news," Aunt Birdie said. "Is your young man fighting the Rebels?"

"No, Mr. Beckett isn't fighting. He's coming to call on me this weekend. He wants me to go to the fair with him and his sister."

"Don't you care to go with him?"

I not only didn't care to go with Herman Beckett, I didn't care if I ever returned to the fair.

"No," I sighed, "but I already promised him that I would go. My father gave Herman permission to court me. He likes Herman."

And so did Maude O'Neill, which was reason enough for me to hate him. But Herman was also my best source of information on Maude and my best hope of proving that she had murdered her first husband. If I wanted to stop Father's wedding, I had better not eliminate Herman from my life just yet.

"I suppose I'll go with him," I said.

"Oh, how nice."

That night I tried to sort out my thoughts by writing in my diary. I felt so confused. Suitors seemed to be piling up like cordwood in the three short weeks I'd lived in Chicago. I doodled on the page as I contemplated my gentlemen callers.

Nelson Kent was first and foremost. I did love his splendid life—most of the time—the food and the dancing, if not the incessant pretending. But I suspected that he was really in love with Katya, and that he was using me to gain his father's fortune. His actions might be deceitful, but they were no worse than making me an accomplice in a theft ring.

Stop thinking about Silas McClure!

Louis Decker lived a world away from Nelson Kent. Louis was doing something worthwhile with his life, helping the poor and needy. But I had no desire to join him in that work if it involved slaving in a kitchen, regardless of how worthwhile it might be. I had promised to help Louis tomorrow, and I should have stayed home today and practiced the piano. Then I never would have discovered what a no-good dirty-rotten scoundrel Silas McClure really was. At least Louis Decker was honest and upright and law-abiding, unlike . . .

I pushed Silas from my thoughts a second time.

And now Herman Beckett would reenter my life, arriving this weekend to take me to the fair. Maybe he would behave differently while on a holiday in the city. Maybe he would be more relaxed, less somber. I would have to take care not to play my "choosing" game with him. Herman didn't have a playful, imaginative bone in his body. He had become quite upset when I'd asked him if he'd rather be a horse or a carriage. Silas, on the other hand, had loved my questions. *"Ask me another one, Violet . . ."*

"Stop it!" I said aloud.

Silas McClure was part of a gang of thieves. Yet I liked him the best—stupid me. He was the easiest one to talk to, with no pretending—if you didn't count pretending to be respectable when he was really a rogue. Or pretending that "Josephine" was a woman. But Silas was fun. He made my heart race and my cheeks turn pink. He had actually eaten rattlesnake. . . .

"Stop it!" I would have nothing more to do with Silas McClure, even if he did love my questions.

I quickly flipped to the next page in my diary. I didn't have to decide tonight who I would marry, did I? I refused to worry about Aunt Agnes' warning that my beauty was fading or that I would be an old maid by the age of twenty-one. I had mysteries to solve. After all, that was the reason I had come to Chicago in the first place.

I wrote *Mysteries to Solve* on the top of the page. I had arrived in town with two of them and had made no progress at all in solving either one.

1. Why did Mother leave us? Where is she?
2. Did Maude O'Neill murder her first husband? How can I stop the wedding?

Instead, I had accumulated even more mysteries:

3. Why did Father change from being one of Mr. Moody's Yoke-fellows to being indifferent about religion?
4. Why are Grandmother and Father estranged? What were the "sorrows" she mentioned in her life with my grandfather? Why won't Father let her talk about my mother?
5. Was Aunt Matt's fiancé, Robert Tucker, really a thief, or was

Aunt Birdie simply rambling? Did Mr. Tucker get caught? Is
he in prison?

Once again, my mind drifted back to thoughts of the thieving
rogue Silas McClure. I quickly dismissed them.

6. Does Nelson Kent really love Katya, or is he using her? Is he
   using me?
7. And speaking of being used—is Silas McClure using me, or
   does he truly have feelings for me? And if he does care for me,
   then why didn't he tell his thieving friends to get lost so that
   we could stay at the fair?

I drew a line through the last question, crossing it off my list as
the answer occurred to me: Silas and I couldn't stay at the fair without a chaperone.

My mind felt like a tangle of briars. The more I struggled to
unsnarl things, the more ensnared I became. And those briars had
thorns.

I turned off the lamp and pulled the pillow over my head. I could
hear a horse trotting down the street outside my window, and I
wished it could be my imaginary fair-haired lieutenant coming to rescue me. When the sound of horse hooves faded and the silence
returned, I heard Aunt Birdie's feathery voice whispering in my
mind.

"Make certain you marry for love, dear."

Chapter

16

Thursday, June 22, 1893

Grandmother and I waited for Louis Decker outside the Chicago Evangelistic Society's stern brick building on Thursday afternoon. It was near her church, which was on the corner of Chicago Avenue and LaSalle—that tantalizing street. I checked the house numbers while we waited and saw that we were many blocks north of my mother's address. Would I ever have a chance to search for her?

The door to the Evangelistic Society opened, and a group of young men surged through it, their voices loud with excitement. I thought one of them might be Louis—they were so much like him in their intensity and passion—but he wasn't among them. They politely tipped their hats to Grandmother and me and continued on their way, their conversation sprinkled with references to books of the Bible like powdered sugar on a pancake: "In Corinthians it says . . . Yes, but in Ephesians . . . What about Paul's letter to the Galatians?"

"I think it's wonderful that you're willing to help Mr. Moody's campaign this way, Violet."

I turned my attention back to my grandmother. "I hope Louis isn't disappointed in me. I'm not a very accomplished pianist."

"I'm sure you'll do fine." Why did everyone seem to have more confidence in my musical ability than I did?

"What does the Chicago Evangelization Society do?" I asked, gesturing to the building behind us. "Did they build this place just for the fair?"

"No, it's a school, dear, where they train people to do mission work. The students are just ordinary men and women from all walks of life who will eventually spread out to evangelize the city and the nation. It used to be called the May Institute because classes met only one month a year—in May. But the school became a year-round institution nearly four years ago."

"So Louis Decker is a student here?"

"Mmm-hmm. And now that the World's Exposition is here in town, it's the perfect opportunity for him and the others to reach people from all over the world."

The sun disappeared behind a cloud, and it seemed as if someone had snuffed out the gaslights. I glanced up and saw dark, heavy clouds erasing the blue sky like words from a chalkboard.

"Where did those clouds come from?" I asked. "The sun was shining when we left home." Grandmother looked up at the sky and winced.

"The weather is so changeable here in Chicago. I do hope this storm blows over."

"Do you think Louis will cancel his plans if it rains?" I hoped so. In my mind, this was certain to be more of an ordeal than an adventure.

"Oh, I doubt that he would do that. We probably should have brought our umbrellas."

Wagons and horsecars had been coming and going along the

street as we talked, but a large open carriage, pulled by two horses, suddenly drew to a halt in front of us. I was surprised to see Louis Decker driving it. The carriage had a canopy for shade and was designed for passengers. A flatbed freight wagon carrying a small wooden shipping crate drew to a halt behind it.

"Violet! You came!" Louis leaped down from the seat and fastened the reins to the hitching post. "Thanks for bringing her, Mrs. Hayes. Are you ladies ready to go?"

"Yes, I've been looking forward to it all week," Grandmother replied. I said nothing. My apprehension had far outweighed my enthusiasm this past week.

"My friends Curtis and Jack are coming too," Louis said. "They should be here any minute. Do you mind waiting?"

"I don't mind," I told him. "Maybe you can explain what you'd like me to do in the meantime."

"We're going to drive these Gospel Wagons around and advertise some of the services Mr. Moody will be holding this weekend. I've got a stack of free tickets to give away too. We always start with some music to draw people's attention. That'll be your job, Violet, making the music."

"What will I use for a piano?"

"It's right there." He pointed to the freight wagon. The crate was about three feet high and four feet wide, much too small to hold a piano. "It's a traveling organ," he explained.

"Inside that box?"

"No, the box *is* the organ. Watch this." He climbed onto the wagon and undid the latches, folding back the top to reveal a small five-octave keyboard.

"That's amazing!"

With the top of the crate folded back, the inside of the lid became the front of the box, facing the audience. It had a Bible verse painted on it:

God so LOVED the world that HE GAVE His
Only begotten
Son that WHOSOEVER BELIEVETH in Him shall not
Perish but HAVE
Everlasting
Life

"See? It spells GOSPEL," Louis said. "And that verse is the heart of the good news we're sharing. Gospel means 'good news.' It's what the angel at Bethlehem came to announce when Christ was born. 'Behold, I bring you good tidings of great joy, which shall be to all people. For unto you is born . . . a Savior, which is Christ the Lord.'"

My grandmother ran her fingers down the letters that spelled GOSPEL. "This is very clever," she said.

Louis introduced us to Richard, the wagon driver, who was also a student. While Louis was closing the packing crate, his friends Curtis and Jack bounded out of the building, their faces alive with excitement. All of these young men oozed so much passion and fervor that I couldn't help wondering where it all came from. I compared their lively faces to the bored, aloof expressions that Nelson and his friends always displayed, and decided that if Louis could have bottled up his enthusiasm and sold it as an elixir like Dr. Dean's Blood Builder, he could have made a fortune. Herman Beckett from back home in Lockport could have used a dose or two as well.

Jack and Curtis unhitched the reins and took over the driver's seat. Louis helped Grandmother and me into the back of the carriage, then sat down alongside me.

"Here's Ira Sankey's songbook," he said, handing me a hymnal. Several more were stacked beneath the seat. "I'm sorry I didn't get this music to you sooner, but I believe you'll find that the songs are very simple to play."

I leafed through the book as the carriage began to move and saw that he was right. Most of the key signatures were simple, without too many sharps and flats. I began to feel a bit more confident—

while remaining mindful of my disgraceful performance the last time I had worked with Louis.

"Where are we going?" I asked.

"Mr. Moody divided the city into districts with a church head-quarters in each one. We're going to our assigned district so we can let everyone know about this weekend's services."

"So we're like those barkers who come to town before the circus arrives and try to drum up business?" I had hoped to elicit a smile from Louis, but he nodded earnestly.

"Yes, that's exactly what we're like. Except there are several shows to choose from. Our evangelistic teams hold as many as 125 services on a single Sunday, all over the city."

I heard the first few plops of rain hitting the carriage roof as we plodded along. I stuck my hand out the open side and drew it back, sprinkled with raindrops.

"It's starting to rain," I said, hoping we could turn back. Neither Louis nor my grandmother seemed to hear me.

"Mr. Moody isn't afraid to venture into the more disreputable areas of Chicago," my grandmother told me. "He even held a service in the Haymarket Theater."

"Where is that?"

"It might as well be hell itself," Louis said. "The Haymarket is surrounded by saloons and . . . well, I'm sure you don't want to know what else." He blushed so deeply that I knew exactly what he meant. *Bawdy houses.*

"Is that where we're going?" Now I really wanted to turn back.

"I would never ask you to venture there, Miss Hayes. Even though the Lord has promised that His angels will surround us."

"I'm surprised that Mr. Moody—and the Lord—don't distance themselves from such places."

"No, no. It's just the opposite. Jesus said it's the sick people who need a physician, not the healthy ones. Mr. Moody certainly doesn't approve of such places, but that's exactly where the Gospel is needed.

People matter the most to God. This campaign is all about finding people, regardless of their situation in life, and letting them know that God loves them. And not just the poor and the downtrodden, but even pickpockets and thieves and other criminals."

I knew a few criminals who needed a dose of religion.

"My sister Matilda showed me one of Mr. Moody's newspaper advertisements this morning," Grandmother said. "His service was listed right alongside Buffalo Bill's Wild West Show."

"That's because the people who frequent those amusements are the very people we're trying to reach," Louis said.

The neighborhoods rapidly deteriorated as we clopped along at a steady rate. Even if I had been blindfolded, I would have recognized the slums by their smell. To make matters worse, our carriage seemed to lack a proper set of springs, and we bounced and jostled unmercifully in the rutted, unpaved streets. Then I smelled something truly horrific and saw a dead horse rotting in the street, covered with flies and maggots.

"Oh! That's awful!" I fumbled for a handkerchief to cover my nose and mouth. I wanted to jump off and run home.

"The city is supposed to collect the garbage regularly," Grandmother said, "but as you can see—and smell—they tend to skip the poorer neighborhoods. And I'm sure you can also tell that not all of these tenements have been connected to the city's sewer system yet."

"I can't do this. . . ." I mumbled into my handkerchief. No one seemed to hear me. Nor did they seem to hear the rain plopping on the carriage roof, faster and faster, like popping corn.

"The crowds are coming to Chicago in record numbers this summer," Louis said, "from all around the world."

"This fair is a God-given opportunity to win souls," Grandmother agreed.

"Mr. Moody has been traveling all over the world for the past twenty-five years, and now the world is traveling right to his doorstep. This will be one of his greatest evangelistic campaigns ever."

The carriage slowed to a halt when we came upon two boys, no more than ten or eleven years old, fist-fighting in the middle of the rubbish-strewn street. One boy's face was already bloodied. A dozen more youths surrounded them, cheering them on and blocking our path.

"Look at those poor little souls," my grandmother said. Louis and Curtis jumped from our carriage and waded into the melee.

"Boys, listen—" Louis began. Within seconds, the kids scattered and vanished. He returned to the carriage, shaking his head in despair as our ride resumed.

"God loves them so much, and He longs to gather them in His arms as His children, and they don't even know it. These kids live such hard lives with so many needs, but their greatest need is for a loving Savior. I get overwhelmed when I see them . . . and I feel such a sense of urgency that I can scarcely sit still."

I couldn't sit still either, but it was because I wanted to jump off this rump-sprung carriage seat and run toward fresh air. What was wrong with me? Why couldn't I get past my own discomfort and see these people the way Louis did?

At the end of the block, we turned onto a wider thoroughfare lined with market stalls and jammed with people. The rain was falling steadily now. A few of the pedestrians had umbrellas, but most of them seemed oblivious to the rain as they went about buying and selling. Perhaps this was the only way they could take a weekly bath.

Several saloons competed for business along the street, and I saw a billboard advertising a burlesque show. Customers didn't need to read English in order to understand exactly what sort of risqué entertainment the show promised. I knew better than to stare, but I couldn't help myself. We had been as sheltered as nuns at Madame Beauchamps' School, and here was the real world.

"This is a great place to stop," Louis told the driver. Our carriage drew to a halt and the three men scrambled out of the wagon. Within moments, Curtis and Jack had drawn a small crowd while

Louis unlatched the crate containing the keyboard. He beckoned to
me to come and perform. It was last thing in the world I wanted
to do.

I had performed recitals at school for my classmates, and I had
occasionally entertained family friends in our parlor after dinner. But
I had never dreamed of playing in front of a burlesque theater on a
rainy, stench-filled street to an audience of immigrants, vagabonds,
vagrants, and criminals. I turned to my grandmother for help. She
handed me a hymnal.

"Go on, dear. You don't need to be nervous. You'll do just fine." I
climbed down from the protection of the covered carriage and into
the rain. Louis helped me get seated on the open wagon.

"You have to pump the organ with your feet," he informed me.

"What should I play?"

"It doesn't matter—anything." When I just stared dumbly at him,
he took the songbook from me and propped it open on the music
stand. "Here—how about this one."

Thankfully, the audience made too much noise to hear my first
fumbling attempts to play. But once I got the hang of pumping and
playing simultaneously, the mob eventually quieted down to listen.
They seemed very appreciative—applauding and whistling and
shouting for more. I didn't want to play more. Rain poured from the
sky, and I was getting quite wet.

Louis, Jack, Curtis, and Richard worked their way through the
crowd as I played, passing out tickets and, presumably, God's love.
Eventually, they grabbed hymnals and stood on the running boards
to sing along on a few of the hymns in the style of a barbershop
quartet.

One of their songs told the story of a shepherd who left his flock
of ninety-nine sheep to search for his one lost lamb. The shepherd
braved the dangers of a stormy night and towering cliffs, refusing to
abandon his search until he had found his lamb. By the time they
sang the last line, "Rejoice, for the Lord brings back His own," I

could barely read the notes through my tears. They blended with the rain that was now dripping from my drenched hat brim.

I knew they were singing about Jesus, the Good Shepherd, but they made Him sound like a hero from *True Romances*. My favorite stories had always been the ones where the hero risked his life to rescue the damsel in distress. He would overcome terrible dangers as he searched for her, and he always arrived in the nick of time when all hope seemed lost. I had come to Chicago to search for my mother, but I wondered if she or anyone else would ever love me enough to search for me the way that shepherd had.

"One last hymn, please, Violet," Louis said. "How about page 186?" His glasses were slick with rain, and he took them off to dry them on his vest. As usual, his efforts did little good; his vest was as wet as his spectacles were. He still hadn't seemed to notice that it was raining.

I was soaked and miserable, but this was the last song. Then I could go home. And that was what the song was about. "'Come home ... come home,'" the lyrics said. "'Ye who are weary, come home.'"

"Come home, my friends," Louis told the crowd when the song ended. "Come home and let the love of Jesus Christ wash you clean. That's all for today. See you at the rally."

"That's all"—the very words I longed to hear. I jumped down from the wagon without waiting for anyone's help and hurried toward the covered carriage. But in my haste to get out of the rain I forgot to watch where I was going and stepped into a deep puddle, immersing my foot up to my ankle in muddy water. It was such a shock that I lost my footing altogether and went down on my *derriere* with a splash.

I yelped in outrage. The streets weren't paved, of course, and the rain had turned the dirt into mud. It was mixed with horse manure, and the overflow from outhouses, and who knew what else—and I had landed in it!

I scrambled to my feet, fighting tears. At least my humiliating tumble had been hidden from Louis and the others by the carriage. They were still looking the other way. If I could reach the carriage and sit down before they turned around, they might not notice my muddy backside.

I stood, took one hurried step—and slipped on the slimy muck again! This time I fell forward. I reached out to stop my fall and landed on my hands and knees in the mire. I heard giggles. Glancing up, I saw four small children laughing at my predicament. I pulled my hands out of the mud, but there was nothing to wipe them on except the sides of my skirt. Now the others were certain to notice my disarray.

I stood once again, took a tentative step—and fell for a third time. The giggles turned to outright laughter.

"Violet?" Louis called. I heard him splashing to my rescue and felt the splatter from his shoes peppering my face. "Are you okay?" It would have been wrong to lie to a man of God, so I didn't reply. I let him take my arm and help me into the carriage—at last.

"Violet—what happened?" my grandmother asked.

"I slipped," I said with as much dignity as I could muster. "Can we go home now?" *Quickly, before I burst into tears.*

I thought I remembered a verse in the Bible about pride coming before a fall. If so, I was guilty. I had taken great pride in my faultless posture, my ability to walk gracefully with a book on my head as I'd paraded into fancy drawing rooms with Aunt Agnes. I had reveled in everyone's admiring stares as I had promenaded on Nelson's arm with my new silk gown swishing, my feet clad in dainty slippers. Yes, I had indeed fallen far.

At last the carriage began to move. I would never take sweet-smelling air or paved streets for granted again.

"I love that last song," Grandmother said as we rolled toward home. "It's about the Prodigal Son coming home, isn't it?"

Louis nodded. "The Prodigal Son is Mr. Moody's favorite sermon theme for this campaign. The city is filled with people who've moved here from their small towns and farms. And like the prodigal, they often take up lives of sin, falling for all the worldly temptations that the city offers—saloons, theaters, lusts of all sorts, including the lust for money. That's why Jesus' message of the prodigal son is so important. People can come home to the God of their youth, the God many of them left behind in their hometown churches."

"I think many of the immigrants can relate to that story too," my grandmother added. "They're far from their families and homelands, struggling to make a living. They hoped for a better life in America and have found only disappointment. Jesus, who was born into poverty, understands their plight."

"I've heard Mr. Moody preach on the prodigal many times, and I believe it is his most stirring sermon subject. Every time he preaches, dozens of people come forward to be saved."

As I listened to their excited chatter, I couldn't help thinking of Silas McClure. He had left his home on the farm and taken up with thieves. Maybe if he heard Mr. Moody preach he would give up his thieving ways.

"Could I have one of those tickets?" I asked Louis. "I know someone who might be interested in coming."

"Sure!" He pulled a wad of them from his pocket and fanned them out in his hand. "How many do you want?"

"Could you spare three?" Maybe Silas would share them with "Josephine" and Robert. I would mail them to him, anonymously of course, to the post-office box listed on his card. I had no intention of speaking to Silas McClure ever again.

"You did a wonderful job today, Violet."

"Thank you." Louis didn't say a word about my soaked, muddy clothes and dripping hat. He was either very polite or very oblivious to how disheveled I looked. My guess was oblivious.

"I hope you'll work with me again."

I gave him my well-rehearsed enigmatic smile in reply. I was trying not to weep. I never wanted to visit one of these wretched neighborhoods again for as long as I lived. I knew squeamishness was a poor excuse for refusing to serve the Lord, but I couldn't help it. Given a choice, I would sooner marry a wealthy, adulterous husband and contribute financially to Mr. Moody's campaigns than do this again.

"We work well together, don't you think?" Louis asked. I recalled Nelson Kent asking the same thing. Eager, sincere Louis Decker was dripping wet and awaiting my reply. I had to say something.

"It's refreshing to find an area of work where men and women can labor side by side," I replied. Aunt Matt would have been proud of me.

"You're right," Louis said. "The Scriptures tell us that in Christ there is neither male nor female, slave nor free man. The Lord's work couldn't proceed without women like you and your grandmother and all of the others—especially at the settlement house. And that reminds me . . . would you two ladies allow me to escort you to Folk Night down at the settlement house next week?"

"Oh, that's very sweet of you, Louis," Grandmother said. "We would love to go. You'll have a wonderful time, Violet."

"What is Folk Night?" I practically grunted the words. At the moment, I didn't want to go anywhere except home.

"It's the night when Miss Addams invites her neighbors and their families to share some of their ethnic customs and culture with everyone," Louis explained. "There's usually good music and folk dancing and sometimes food. I believe her Bohemian neighbors will have their turn next week, right?"

My grandmother nodded. "Folk Night lets people take pride in their heritage," she said. "Sometimes the poor need a sense of dignity much more than they need charity. We've had German songfests, Irish dancing, and wonderful Italian cooking."

"I'll pick you up at your home," Louis said, "so you ladies won't have to venture out alone after dark."

"That's so kind of you, Louis. Violet and I would appreciate that." Grandmother gazed at him in admiration. I couldn't recall agreeing to go.

The rain stopped, of course, by the time we arrived back at the Evangelistic Society. Louis' friends all climbed out, and he took the carriage reins again to drive Grandmother and me home. The sun shone through the thinning clouds, mocking me as we halted in front of the house.

"Thanks again, Violet," he said as he helped me down from my seat. "I'll see you next week." He smiled at me as if he hadn't even noticed that I looked like a drowned rat.

I hurried into the house, avoiding my reflection in the hall mirror. I was wet and muddy and miserable.

"You take off those wet clothes, dear, so we can soak the mud out of them. Birdie and I will fill the bathtub for you and make you some hot tea."

I plodded upstairs and stripped off my muddy dress. The remains of my hat went straight into the trash. I pulled all the pins out of my dripping hair, then burst into tears when I finally saw my filth-smeared reflection in the mirror. I didn't recognize myself. This certainly wasn't the princess who had floated into the ballroom on Nelson Kent's arm. And if Madame Beauchamps saw me now, she would revoke my diploma.

By the time I finished crying and went downstairs in my robe, Grandmother had filled the copper tub with warm water. She had set it up in the kitchen behind a folding screen. I stepped into the bath gratefully and took the hot cup of tea she offered me.

"You and Louis Decker work so beautifully together, don't you think?"

"Mmm." If I said anything else I might start crying again.

"He is such a fine young man, isn't he?"

"Yes. Very nice."

And that was the problem—he was nice and I wasn't. Any pro-

longed niceness on my part was nothing but an act. I always grew
weary of being nice after a few hours. I was certainly not nice unless
I had to be, and I could never be nice for an entire lifetime. Being
nice was exhausting. It implied conformity, and conformity had been
a lifelong trial for me. It went against my nature—which is why I'd
grown so weary of pretending at Aunt Agnes' parties. I was beginning to understand Aunt Matt's claim that all women were actresses.
But could I ever act nice enough to marry a minister?

*"You of all people should have the blinders off when it comes to
marrying a minister,"* Aunt Matt had told my grandmother. I wondered what she had meant. My grandmother had pulled out a kitchen
chair to sip a cup of tea with me. I decided to probe.

"Did my grandfather go into the streets and preach like Louis
and Mr. Moody are doing?"

She shook her head. "He preached to his own little flock in his
church in Lockport. He often railed against the evils of city life and
would never have ventured to Chicago to preach the way Dwight
Moody does."

"I don't remember Grandfather very well. To tell you the truth, I
was a little afraid of him. He always looked angry."

"In some ways he was angry. He didn't preach about the love and
grace of God very often, choosing to emphasize our need for obedi-
ence to Christ's commands instead."

"Wasn't one of those commands to love our neighbor?"

"That one often slipped his notice." She smiled faintly. "All in all,
I think he was very disappointed with his life. When he died, my life
changed completely. I had to leave Lockport and move in with Matt
and Birdie to make room in the parsonage for the new minister."

"Why didn't you take care of us?"

"Your father didn't want me to."

"Why not?"

"I can't answer that. You'll have to ask him."

"You *can't* answer it, or you *won't?*" I asked angrily.

My grandmother smiled sadly. "I made a promise to your father that I would let him answer all of your questions. I'm so sorry, dear."

I handed her my empty cup and grabbed a bar of soap to scrub the mud off my face. I waited for my temper to cool before asking, "Is my father like the Prodigal Son?"

"I'm not sure what you mean."

"You told me he worked as a Yokefellow, and that he went into saloons and tried to convert people. He certainly doesn't do things like that anymore. What happened?"

She seemed very reluctant to reply. I was surprised when she did.

"There was a time in your father's life when he nearly became a preacher. But he found out, just in time, that he was doing it for the wrong reasons. It's never right to serve God out of guilt or in order to please someone else. Your grandfather wanted a son who would follow in his footsteps. He didn't understand that being a minister wasn't your father's calling."

"What do you mean—it wasn't his 'calling'? Going calling is what I do with Aunt Agnes, with our calling cards."

Grandmother smiled. "Your calling comes from God. It's what He would like you to do with your life. He calls some people to be evangelists and ministers, but most of us are called to serve Him in other ways. I believe my calling is to serve the poor in His name. But regardless of what God's plans for us are, He always gives us a choice. We can go our own way and do something else with our life if we choose to. God won't force us."

"How do I know what my calling is? Will I really hear Him calling? Like a voice in the dark?"

"No, although it would be a good deal simpler if He did call us that way. He'll ask you to do something that uses your unique gifts and interests."

"Like playing the piano? Is it my calling to play piano for Louis? Because if it is, God is going to have to do something about the stench, and the mud, and the dead horses, and—" My tears started to fall again, and I couldn't finish. Grandmother handed me her handkerchief to wipe my eyes.

"I'm wet all over, Grandma," I said, smiling at the irony. "It's useless to dry a few tears."

"Yes, I suppose so. . . . But listen, Violet, ministering to the poor may not be your calling. God has a reason for creating each of us as individuals, with no two people alike. He has a unique place for you in His kingdom. Look how different my three sisters and I are—and we all have different callings. We would be wrong to judge each other or to expect each other to do the same work."

I swished my hands through the water as I pondered her words. "At school, we were all taught to be alike. Madame Beauchamps wanted us to act the same and talk the same—we were even supposed to smile the same and walk the same. She told us that society has standards of decorum and proper manners, and we were taught to conform to them. We weren't supposed to stand out. We were punished if we did."

"I think that's very wrong, Violet. I agree that manners help keep our society civilized, but we're still individuals. Even twins aren't exactly alike."

I thought of all the "pea-pod" partners I had danced with at Aunt Agnes' parties, and how boringly alike they were. I'd been drawn to Nelson because he was different. He could conform as readily as the rest of them when he had to, but he behaved differently with me.

"Madame Beauchamps taught me how to be a proper young lady, but sometimes I don't want to be so prim and . . . and *boring*. It isn't the real me. I used to rebel—quietly—against some of the rules at school. I stayed in bed late and read books after lights-out with my friend Ruth, books that Madame B. would never approve of. A lot of the time I lived in my imagination. So how do I know if I'm still rebelling or if this is the way God made me? How can I tell the difference?"

"You be exactly who God created you to be," she said fervently, "and don't let anyone tell you otherwise. And whatever you do, don't make choices in life just to please somebody else. The only One you ever need to please is God."

"But how will I know what my calling is?"

"Do you ever pray, Violet?"

"Yes, on Sunday mornings . . . and before I go to sleep. . . ." I gave a guilty shrug.

"From now on when you pray, ask God to show you what He wants you to do."

As I sank down into the tub to scrub my hair, I pictured Louis standing in front of the crowd in the rain shouting, *Come home and let the love of Jesus Christ wash you clean.*

I knew then that even though Silas McClure and his friends might need to be washed clean, I was in no position to point a finger at them. When I went upstairs to my bedroom to get dressed, I tore up the rally tickets and threw them away.

Chapter

17

Saturday, June 24, 1893

I was upstairs still getting ready when Herman Beckett arrived on Saturday morning to escort me to the World's Fair. Aunt Birdie answered the door.

"Oh, Florence! Come quick!" I heard her cry out. "Someone died! The undertaker is here!"

I reached the top of the stairs in time to hear Herman say, "I'm here for Violet."

"Oh no! Not Violet!" Aunt Birdie moaned. "She was perfectly fine at dinner last night. How could she pass away so quickly?"

"Wait! I'm not dead, Aunt Birdie!" I thundered down the stairs as gracelessly as a six-year-old.

"Oh, thank goodness." She pulled me into her arms and hugged me tightly. I could feel her heart pounding. When she released me, she turned to Herman. "It seems that your services will not be needed after all, young man. Violet is perfectly fine. Good day." She closed the door in his face.

"Aunt Birdie, wait! Mr. Beckett is here to take me to the fair."

"Why in the world would you want to go to the fair with an undertaker?"

"Herman isn't an undertaker," I said, opening the door to him again.

"Well, he certainly looks like one. It just goes to show that you can't judge a book by its cover, Violet. Remember how you thought that other gentleman caller of yours was a thief? But see? Our silver tray is still here." She held it up for me to see.

"Have there been other gentlemen callers?" Herman asked in a worried voice.

"Please come in, Mr. Beckett," I said, ignoring his question. "I'm sorry for all the confusion."

Herman stepped aside and gestured for our chaperone to enter first. "I'd like you to meet my sister, Mary Crane," he said. She was dressed entirely in black and wore such a gloomy expression on her face, I could see how Aunt Birdie might have mistaken her and Herman for undertakers. The small picnic basket that she carried on her arm offered the only hint that we were out for a day of fun.

"Mary lives in Riverside with her husband and two children," Herman explained.

"Oh, will your family be joining us as well?"

"No. They won't."

Herman offered no explanation for the missing family, so I didn't pry—although my imagination quickly supplied several reasons. Maybe she had chained them in the cellar for a few hours so she could have a day of fun without them. Or maybe they were horribly disfigured and she was ashamed to have them be seen in public. Maybe they were feral children who ate raw meat and howled at the moon, or maybe . . .

I noticed Aunt Birdie hovering in the hallway behind me, and I introduced her. She nodded curtly in reply. Herman Beckett and his sister were the first visitors we'd had that Birdie hadn't greeted with one of her famous hugs. I could understand why.

"Would you care for a cold drink before we leave?" I asked.

"Thank you, but no. We have a lot to see today, and I think we should get going."

I had dreaded returning to the fair and being reminded of my unsettling visit with Silas McClure, but seeing the fair with Herman Beckett turned out to be a completely different experience. Herman had purchased *Claxton's Guidebook to the World's Columbian Exposition* and he followed it as religiously as Louis Decker followed the Scriptures. He opened to the first page as we rode the streetcar to the fairgrounds and gave us a taste of what was ahead.

"It says here that the fair offers 'the assembled achievements and products from the mind and hand of mankind, such as never before presented to mortal vision.'"

"My word," his sister murmured. She was evidently too over-whelmed to say more. I said nothing. It was going to be a very long day.

We got off the streetcar at the fair's 57th Street entrance and stood in line for our tickets. Herman showed me the guidebook's map as we waited. "This red line shows the recommended route we should take. It's the best way to experience the fair. We'll start here," he said, tracing the line with his finger, "and gradually make our way around from the north end of the fairgrounds to the south. The rec-ommended pavilions and exhibits are highlighted."

"Why see what the author wants you to see, Herman? Why not decide what you're interested in and skip the rest?"

Herman's dark brows met in the middle as he frowned. They reminded me of two wooly caterpillars kissing. "The author made a thorough study of the fair. I'm sure that the advice he gives is very sound. The grounds cover 633 acres, Violet, and there are more than sixty-five thousand exhibits. It would be impossible to see it all in one day. The guidebook has rated the best attractions as 'interesting,' 'very interesting,' or 'remarkably interesting.'"

"Does he recommend that we ride Mr. Ferris' wheel?"

"Certainly not! The wheel is on the Midway." Herman made *Midway* sound like a dirty word.

"What's wrong with the Midway?" My question caused his eyebrows to kiss once again.

"Those amusements cater to the lowest sort of person. I have no interest at all in seeing bawdy attractions."

Herman's sister leaned close to whisper in my ear as we walked through the entrance gates. "Some of the Midway exhibits are very vulgar. One of them features hootchy-kootchy dancers who are indecently clothed! And those women make the most obscene gyrations! Many of the primitive Africans on display are scantily clad as well."

"Oh, I see." I decided not to mention that I had already visited the pagan Midway and had found it "remarkably interesting." But then, a thief like Silas McClure was exactly the low sort of person Herman had referred to.

We strolled around the northern section of the fairgrounds for a while, passing dozens of state pavilions and exhibits. In the center stood a magnificent building with enormous statues of women serving as support pillars. "That looks *remarkably* interesting," I said. "What's inside that building?"

"It's the Palace of Fine Art." Herman said *art* with the same horrified tone that he'd used for the Midway.

"What's wrong with art?"

Mary cupped her hand around my ear again and whispered, "They have *nudes*." I stifled a sigh.

Viewed from the outside, the state pavilions were all very different from each other and seemed very interesting to me, but the only building that Mr. Claxton's guidebook allowed us to enter was the Illinois State Pavilion.

"Why would we waste time here?" I asked. "We live in Illinois. We can see the real thing every day."

Herman stared at me, oblivious to the irony. "The pavilion offers a chance to learn something new about our state. The guidebook says it will be 'very interesting.'"

I dutifully wandered through the Illinois building, longing to see exotic displays that were truly very interesting. I didn't find General Grant's memorabilia interesting in the least, nor the Women's Corn Kitchen featuring one hundred different ways to prepare Illinois' favorite agricultural product—corn. I couldn't imagine that the pavilion had earned even an "interesting" rating, let alone "very interesting." I decided to start my own rating system: "boring," "exceedingly boring," and "I'm-falling-asleep boring." In the "exceedingly boring" category was a huge mosaic of a prairie farmyard, complete with cattle and horses, made entirely out of seeds and grains. Herman stood before it awestruck.

"Look, Mary! Even the frame is made from ears of corn."

"My word," she murmured. I stifled a yawn.

We walked around the fairgrounds all morning, following the approved path as if it would lead us to buried treasure. As Herman narrated the highlights for us, I learned that he was very fond of statistics.

"Did you know that the fair has more than sixty-one acres of lagoons and waterways, and over three miles of intertwining canals?"

"My word . . ." his sister replied breathlessly. I wasn't sure if it was from wonder or the brisk pace Herman set.

Whenever he began a sentence with "Did you know. . . ?" I braced myself for another batch of statistics, invariably followed by another awestruck, "My word . . ." from his sister.

"Did you know," he asked as we viewed the enormous Manufactures and Liberal Arts Building, "that you're looking at the largest building in the world? The fair is comprised of fourteen Great Buildings and more than two hundred others—at a cost of twenty-eight million dollars."

"My word . . ."

"Did you know," he asked as we approached the Electricity

Building, "that each of that building's ten spires is one-hundred-seventy-feet high? The fair uses more than one hundred twenty thousand incandescent lights and seven thousand arc lights."

"My word . . ."

"Did you know," he asked as we viewed the Horticulture Building, "that this building houses the world's largest collection of horticultural products? The gardens feature a half a million pansies and one hundred thousand roses."

"My word . . ."

We spent a considerable amount of time in the glass-domed Horticultural Building, viewing an endless number of plants and flowers. It earned my highest rating for boring. I longed to see something truly exciting.

"Does the guidebook recommend any foreign pavilions?" I finally asked.

"A few, but I'm not sure we'll have time for any of them."

I decided that I would never suffer from insomnia again if I married Herman Beckett. Nelson Kent, on the other hand, might not be faithful to me, but he would take me to Italy and Paris.

"Do you ever feel the urge to see the world, Herman?"

"Not really. If one can't find contentment at home, one is unlikely to find it anywhere else."

Could that be true? Did the fact that I had been discontented living in Lockport mean that I was doomed to a life of discontent? If so, I may as well marry Nelson and be discontented but rich.

Shortly before noon we at last viewed something that was "remarkably interesting." The Fisheries Building featured ten aquariums displaying beautiful, fascinating worlds that I never knew existed beneath the seas. I got so carried away that I found myself asking Herman, "If you could choose to live on another planet or to live under the sea, which would you choose?"

"I wouldn't want either," he replied. "I'm content where I am." His sister nodded.

"Suppose you *had* to choose?" My impatience and frustration must have shown; perhaps in the way I stomped my foot. Herman turned from the aquarium to gaze at me with a look of concern.

"I don't understand why the question is so important to you, Violet."

I didn't know either. I couldn't stop thinking of Silas and how much fun he'd had answering my questions.

On the way out we passed a statue that reminded me of Cupid, and I found myself asking, "Do you believe in love?"

"What do you mean?"

"You know—falling in love, love at first sight, true love, everlasting love. Or do you think it's only found in fairy tales?"

Herman's face turned the color of beet juice. "Honestly, Violet. Does it matter what I think?"

"I would like to know."

"Well, then, I would have to say I believe love exists—although I would be highly suspicious of love at first sight. I believe love is something that grows over time as two people get to know each other."

He whipped open his guidebook and gave it all of his attention, cutting off all further discussion of love. "Let's see, now. . . . What's next?"

"How about a gondola ride on the lagoon?" We were standing alongside one of the many canals, and the boats looked as graceful as swans as they glided over the water. The gondoliers in their colorful costumes added to the illusion of adventure and romance.

"The lines are too long. The guidebook says we would waste too much time waiting. Besides, the admission fee is rather expensive."

But Herman did consent to eat our picnic lunch on the grass alongside the lagoon so we could watch the gondoliers poling more fortunate fairgoers across the water. Mary unpacked her picnic basket and passed around the ham sandwiches she had made.

"What do you want in life, Herman?" I asked. It must have been the Grecian-style buildings with their multitude of pillars that had made me so philosophical.

"I would prefer a simple life with a peaceful home in a quiet town like Lockport," he replied. "I couldn't stand to live in a big city like Chicago with all of this noise and dirt and rushing around."

"Wouldn't you like to travel and see new places?"

"As I said, I believe that we are happiest when we learn to be content at home. We should want nothing more than the life God has given us. Why try to be something we're not?"

Contentment. I didn't have it. In truth, it sounded boring—like the last stage one reaches before falling asleep. House cats were content, and they slept all day.

"I would like to have a happy home," Herman continued. "A refuge I could return to after a day's work."

"What about fun?"

"Well, I enjoy boating in Dellwood Park in the summertime . . . skating in the winter . . . attending church on Sunday. I would like to have children and a family. . . ."

"A family," I repeated. I was suddenly reminded of my father and Murderous Maude. "Speaking of families, have you heard that my father plans to marry Maude O'Neill?"

"Yes. They seem very content."

I tried not to roll my eyes. "I understand you know Maude O'Neill quite well. Tell me, was she content with her first husband?"

"I'd rather not say."

He didn't have to; his face said it all. He not only was blushing, his wooly-caterpillar-eyebrows were kissing as voraciously as Nelson and Katya had. Mary rummaged through the picnic basket as if searching for her ticket out of this conversation.

I suddenly recalled something that I'd learned from Ruth's detective novels: *Sometimes it's not what people say that's important, it's what they don't say.* If Maude and her husband had been happy, why not say so? *"Mr. O'Neill was a wonderful man. They were so happy. She was devastated when he died.*" Herman's silence spoke volumes.

"Why won't you tell me, Herman?"

"It isn't right to gossip." He started to rise, but I gripped his arm, stopping him.

"It isn't gossip. She's going to marry my father. She will be my . . . my stepmother." I winced as I said the word. How I hated it. "Listen, I know that my father's first marriage ended unhappily, so I'd like to know if he'll find happiness the second time around."

"I'm not in a position to say." He broke free and stood, then offered me a hand up as well.

This detective business was very hard work. I had read about reluctant witnesses in Ruth's *True Crime Stories*, and now I had encountered one. I decided to try a different approach, hoping that my feminine charm would do the trick. I linked my arm through his as we started walking and mustered all of my feminine weapons: my coy, flirtatious voice; my enigmatic smile; my fluttering eyelashes. I gazed up at him adoringly.

"Listen, Herman, just tell me one thing: do you think Maude loves my father or is she still pining for her first husband?"

"I hardly think she is pining for him! He—" Herman stopped, horrified that he had said so much. "I never meant to gossip."

"I know. I don't think telling someone the truth is in the same category as gossip."

"Maude O'Neill is a wonderful woman," he said, showing more passion than I had ever seen from him. "She deserves a happy life with a good man like your father."

"How did she and my father meet? As you know, I've been away at school for the past three years."

"They've known each other for several years. Mr. O'Neill worked for your father at one time."

His words horrified me. What if Maude and my father had fallen in love before Mr. O'Neill's death? What if I continued to probe and discovered that Father was Maude's accomplice in the murder?

"You'll be home for their wedding, I assume?" Herman asked.

"Huh?"

"When are you coming back to Lockport?"

I wanted to shout, *"Never!"*

"I-I'm not sure," I said instead. Perhaps I should stop my investigation. But how else could I prevent Father's marriage?

I pondered my dilemma for the next hour or so as we journeyed through the fairgrounds. None of the exhibits fascinated me as much as the aquariums had. And many of them, like the display of every type of paper money the government had ever issued, were astoundingly boring. But when we came upon a replica of the Liberty Bell made entirely out of oranges, it was such a ludicrous sight that I had to cover my mouth to keep from laughing out loud. I glanced at Herman to see his reaction and caught him staring at the bell with a look of wonder on his face.

"Isn't that a marvel?" he asked. "It even has the famous crack!"

"My word . . ." Mary breathed.

A giggle that I could no longer suppress sputtered out. Once unleashed, my hilarity bubbled forth until I was laughing out loud.

"Violet? What's so funny?" Herman asked.

"That bell! I think it's the most ridiculous thing I've ever seen!"

"Excuse me?"

"Aren't there better things to do with a couple of crates of oranges? I mean, why not pass them out to the poor children instead of gluing them into the shape of a bell?" Now I sounded like Louis Decker. Herman gazed at me as if I'd spoken blasphemy.

"Sometimes I don't understand you at all, Violet," he said, slowly shaking his head.

"They're oranges, for goodness' sake," I said, still unable to control my laughter. "What do oranges have to do with the Liberty Bell? The founding fathers didn't win our freedom by lobbing oranges at the British, did they?"

"Maybe we should move on." People were staring at us—or more specifically, at me—and I could see that my laughter embarrassed Herman. I couldn't seem to stop.

"Did George Washington cross the Delaware on a raft of orange crates?" I asked. "Did Thomas Jefferson toast the signing of the Declaration of Independence with a glass of orange juice? Did Patrick Henry say, 'Give me oranges or give me death'?"

"I really think we should move on." Herman marched me from the building as if dragging me to the headmistress' office by my ear. Mary scurried behind us with her head lowered.

I was still wiping tears from my eyes when we emerged from the building into the sunlight. Herman paused for a moment to bury his nose in the guidebook, searching for the next marvel on his list, when all of a sudden I saw Silas McClure walking straight toward me. At least I thought it was Silas.

He was dressed like a British lord in a suit that was as finely cut and tailored as Nelson Kent's suits were. He had grown a mustache and a neat goatee since the last time I'd seen him, and he wore a fedora on his carefully barbered head. He even carried a silver-topped cane.

"Mr. McClure?" I said as he approached.

He didn't turn his head at the sound of his name, but continued to stroll straight down the pathway. A moment later he vanished into the crowd. Could I have been mistaken? Did Silas have a twin brother? And if so, was he a thief too? If so, he was a much more successful thief, judging by his clothing.

"Who was that?" Herman asked.

How in the world could I explain Silas McClure? *"Oh, just a thief I met on the train to Chicago. I helped him and his pals pull off a robbery the last time I visited the fair."*

"No one," I sighed. "He resembled someone I know, but I guess it wasn't him." Yet the stranger had the same effect on me that Silas always had. My heart was chugging like an engine at full steam. I had to change the subject.

"I hear there's a walkway on the top of the Manufactures and Liberal Arts building that offers a marvelous view. Does your guidebook recommend it by any chance?"

"It costs extra."

I might have known.

The aroma of exotic food and spices rose to my nostrils in tantalizing fashion from dozens of pavilions we passed. We didn't sample anything. The only food item Herman purchased was water from the Hygeia Water stand, and he complained about that.

"I think it's outrageous to charge money for a drink of water! Water should be free. Just look—there's a Great Lake full of water, right over there. What will they charge us for next? Are they going to make us pay for soil? Or for air?"

"My word . . ." Mary said.

I kept my mouth shut.

By late afternoon, I was relieved to learn that the guidebook scheduled a stop at the comfort station. I went inside with Herman's sister, and as soon as she had me alone she unleashed a sales pitch on behalf of her brother that rivaled Silas McClure's pitch for Dr. Dean's Blood Builder.

"My brother is a fine young man—hardworking, sensible, modest, and upright. Unlike a lot of other men, he has no vices. . . ." And so on, and so forth. I could have added that he also had no sense of adventure, no sense of humor, and no imagination, but Mary barely paused for breath. When her sales pitch ended, she began to interrogate me.

"Do you have a lot of other suitors, Violet?"

"Well, no . . . not a lot . . ."

"How many? Are they seriously courting you?"

"I've only been in Chicago for three weeks. It's pretty hard to form a serious relationship in—"

"Listen." Her face was close to mine as she pleaded with me, begging with the same fervor that Louis might use when asking sinners to repent. "I beg you to be fair to my brother. Don't toy with him. Some girls do that, you know. They make a game out of winning a man's heart just so they can break it. Herman deserves your honesty, Violet. And your loyalty and trust."

"I won't lead him on."

"Thank you."

I had to admit that Herman did exhibit sterling character. And he was neither devastatingly poor nor exorbitantly rich. Maybe Herman would be a compromise between Louis' world of smells and sorrow and Nelson's life of pretentious pretending. Maybe it was my calling to settle down in Lockport and raise a peck of children and hire a housekeeper like Mrs. Hutchins to peel my onions.

Later, as we passed a souvenir stand, I asked Herman if we could stop. "I would like to purchase a packet of postcards with photographs of the fair." The photo on top—the one that had lured me—was of Mr. Ferris' wheel. For a moment I thought Herman might have to check his guidebook to see if the stop was authorized, but he not only stopped, he even paid for the postcards.

"Thank you. This will be a nice reminder of my visit to the fair." I didn't mention which visit.

There were hundreds of interesting exhibits besides the Palace of Fine Art and the enticing Midway that we never had a chance to see. If Herman's guidebook didn't recommend it, we didn't see it. Would he go through life this way, following someone else's agenda and living by the book? I briefly considered launching into a motivational speech: *What about spontaneity? What about fun? Why not ride life's Ferris wheels once in a while?*

Yet I knew that his sister was right. Herman was a good man, kind, thoughtful, well-mannered. He was hardworking; he didn't love money; he wanted a family. In fact, Herman was very much like my father—which led to another thought: If I was like my mother, perhaps boredom was the reason she eventually left him.

We stayed to watch the fireworks display before returning home.

I arrived at Grandmother's door thoroughly exhausted. My feet ached from walking all day, but my head ached even more from holding back all of the outrageous thoughts that had bubbled up in my imagination throughout the day. I had longed to say so much more but couldn't, especially after the Liberty Bell incident.

"When are you coming home to Lockport?" Herman asked as we said good-night in my grandmother's foyer. Once again, I wanted to reply, *"Never!"*

"To tell you the truth, I haven't thought much about Lockport. I'm still enjoying my visit to Chicago very much."

"If I may say so, Violet, I hope you will come home soon." He fumbled for my hand and took it into his sweating one, squeezing it limply before releasing it again.

"Thank you, Herman," I managed to say. "And thanks for an . . . interesting day."

Chapter

18

I happened to be standing in the front hallway on Monday morning when the mailman pushed several letters through our mail slot. The one on top was addressed to me.

It was from Silas McClure.

I dropped the other letters onto the floor and ran upstairs to read it in the privacy of my room. I didn't find his chunky, schoolboy penmanship at all endearing this time. I opened the envelope to find that the stationery he'd used came from a hotel in Chicago. He had put another Dr. Dean's Blood Builder card in the letter, along with a commemorative coin from the Exposition.

Dear Violet,

Please accept my deepest apologies for ending our visit to the fair so abruptly. There were hundreds of things that I wanted to see and do together, and I'm still sulking because we didn't get a chance to do any of them. I never would have asked Robert and Josephine to be our chaperones if I had known they would leave us in the lurch like that. Do you think you can ever forgive me?

*I had a great time with you, even though our day was cut short.
I can still see the look on your face when we rode the wheel together.
I enjoyed every minute that I spent with you, as few as they were.*

*I'll wager that I'm probably asking too much to expect you to accom-
pany me again, but I sure would love a second chance if you can find it
in your heart to give me one. I'll be in town at this hotel for the next
few weeks, so if you're willing to give me that second chance, please write
me a note. You can send it in care of this hotel, or to my post-office box.
You'll find the number on my card, which I'm enclosing.*

*I'll understand if you still feel shortchanged. To tell you the truth,
I feel shortchanged myself. Drat those useless chaperones! I'll find better ones next time. I promise.*

Yours very truly,
Silas McClure

The coin was an Exposition souvenir. I turned it over in my hand
and a tear rolled down my cheek when I saw the image of Mr. Ferris'
wheel on the back. I could still remember what it felt like to hold
Silas' hand. And to land in his arms when the wheel lurched the first
time. Nor could I forget the way he had looked at me when we
halted at the top of the wheel.

"Stop it!" I told myself.

Silas was a thieving elixir salesman. He had been trained to be a
smooth talker. I could not—would not—have anything more to do
with a thief. Or the friend of a thief. It could only lead to enormous
heartache.

I wiped away another tear and shoved the letter under my mattress. I refused to answer it. I was on my way out of the room with
the coin in my pocket when I remembered the well-dressed gentleman I had seen at the fair. Had that been Silas? If so, why had he
been dressed that way?

The only explanation that made sense was that he had been wearing a disguise. He could have been posing as a wealthy gentleman in

A P R O P E R   P U R S U I T

order to rob other wealthy gentlemen. I faced the truth that Silas McClure was probably a pickpocket as well as a thief.

I pulled the commemorative coin out of my pocket as if it might set my skirt on fire and laid it on the hall table beside the packet of postcards that Herman had bought for me.

On Tuesday, I decided to go calling with Aunt Agnes. After my muddy afternoon with Louis and my boring tour of the fairgrounds with Herman, I needed a dose of beauty. I had missed the luxurious homes, the gorgeous dresses, the elegant atmosphere—and the cucumber sandwiches. One of the women on whom we called was Nelson's grandmother.

"Where have you been, Violet? I was so afraid you'd left Chicago for good. And without even saying good-bye."

"I would never do that, Mrs. Kent."

"My Nelson would never forgive you if you did. He is so very fond of you." She took my hand in both of hers and added, "I probably shouldn't have told you that. Nelson would be peeved with me for tattling on him. But I've never heard him talk about the other girls the way he raves about you."

We sat in the afternoon room and sipped tea. Everything was lovely but—I hated to admit it—boring. I entertained myself by watching the serving girls flitting in and out with our tea and finger sandwiches, hoping to glimpse the stunning Katya. But when the luncheon ended and the maids cleared away our tea things, I still hadn't seen her. I decided to discreetly ask one of the other servers about her.

"Excuse me, but I haven't seen Katya today. Is it her day off?"

"She no longer works for the Kents, Miss." The maid's cool voice revealed her unwillingness to say more.

I was instantly intrigued. "What happened to her?"

"They hired Sadie in her place."

"Did Katya quit or was she fired?"

"I couldn't say, miss. Will you excuse me, please?"

If someone had seen Katya kissing Nelson the way I had, I could

understand why she would be sent away. Far, far away. I pictured her
in an igloo in Lapland, shivering with the Eskimos.

Aunt Agnes and I were preparing to leave when Nelson saun-
tered in.

"Violet! It's wonderful to see you." There was warmth in his voice
as he squeezed my hands, but he might have been greeting anyone.
"Listen, I'm glad I caught you. I've been invited to a string of gala
affairs at the Columbian Exposition fairgrounds. Might you be able to
accompany me to some of them? I would like to show you the fair."

"Violet would love to go. Wouldn't you, dear?" Aunt Agnes replied.
"You'll enjoy it, I'm sure. The fair is a marvelous, marvelous place."

She and Mrs. Kent gushed on and on, never giving me a chance
to reply. Nelson and everyone else simply assumed that I would go.

"Will you be using a guidebook?" I asked him, remembering my
visit with Herman Beckett.

"A guidebook? What for?" He appeared amused.

"To see the fair."

"I don't need a guidebook," he said, laughing.

"Then yes, I would love to go."

"Good. I have tickets for a concert in Choral Hall on Thursday
evening. Afterward there is a private party I've been invited to attend
in one of the other pavilions."

"That sounds nice." I could wear my new gown again. I could
listen to beautiful music, enjoy sumptuous food—and pleasing smells.

"I'll pick you up a little before seven."

When I returned home, Aunt Matt stopped me in the front hallway. "Don't make any plans for Wednesday afternoon, Violet. I'm
taking you to see the Woman's Pavilion."

And she did.

We got off the streetcar at the 59th Street entrance and walked a
dozen yards to the pavilion. The Midway was directly behind us, and
I peeked over my shoulder at the wheel, towering above the fair.
Then I gave Aunt Matt my full attention.

"First of all, you need to know about this building. It was designed by a woman architect in the Italian Renaissance style. The Board of Lady Managers launched a nationwide search for a woman architect and received twelve submissions. All of the women were under the age of twenty-five, by the way. The winner, Sophia Hayden, was around your age, Violet—twenty-one—and had recently graduated from the Massachusetts Institute of Technology."

I couldn't comprehend it. A girl my age? And she knew how to design a building? I stared at the pavilion for a moment as I tried to take it all in—the lagoon in front, the prolific flowers in the hanging gardens, the graceful staircase to the terrace, the triple-arched entrance. Designed by a woman my age.

"It truly is beautiful, Aunt Matt."

"Keep in mind as we go inside that it was also decorated entirely by women. And The Board of Lady Managers, which is composed of members from every state and territory in the U.S., are in full charge of it all. This is unprecedented, Violet. Women have never been given control of a pavilion at such a huge, important exposition as this."

The first displays we viewed were a model hospital and a model kindergarten. I glanced around as we walked through the exhibits, hoping to see the famous Pinkerton guards, standing in uniform at all of the strategic places. I wanted to ask one of them how much it would cost to find my mother. But I saw very few men, and none in a guard uniform.

"Where are the Pinkerton guards?" I asked Aunt Matt.

"You can't see them—that's the whole point. They purposely blend in so the thieves don't know they're being observed." She pulled her father's gold watch and chain out of her purse and glanced at the time. "We can see the rest of the building after the speech. Come on."

"A speech? What's it about?" I asked as we marched to the lecture hall.

"I believe a woman physician is going to present her research on women's health."

The lecture hall was packed, and we had to take seats in the front row. One of the Lady Managers introduced the physician, and I had to cover my mouth to disguise my amusement. Instead of a proper dress, the good doctor wore a baggy tunic and an enormous pair of bloomers. They looked like the pantaloons women wore beneath their skirts—but without the skirt!

"Ladies," she began, "I'm well aware that the majority of you are, at this very moment, trapped in the confines of a whalebone corset. But you might be shocked to learn that, according to my research, your tightly laced corsets are responsible for more than fifty feminine ailments."

She proceeded to enumerate them, one by one, but my mind began to wander after "heart palpitations, difficulty breathing, and light-headedness." The symptoms sounded suspiciously like a romance novel's description of love. Could it be that thousands of women had married their husbands in the mistaken belief that they were in love, when all along their corsets had been too tight? How disappointing to watch their love mysteriously vanish once their corsets were unlaced. I made up my mind that if I ever felt love's symptoms, I would loosen my corset immediately before accepting a proposal of marriage.

I turned my attention back to the speaker and learned that she not only advocated tossing out our whalebone corsets, but expected us to replace all of our leisure dresses with bloomers.

"Someday, dresses for women will be a thing of the past," she insisted. She bounced around the stage as she talked as if she had taken an overdose of Dr. Dean's Blood Builder, her baggy bloomers flopping like a clown suit. "Women will experience more comfort, better health, and more freedom of movement when they switch to wearing bloomers. Once you try them, every one of you will want to wear them. We'll see bloomers on trains, in the parks, and in every public place. Freedom, ladies! Bloomers mean freedom!"

I had to work hard to stifle my giggles. I was probably the only woman in the audience who thought the lecture—and the doctor's bloomers—were hilarious.

The applause that followed her speech seemed a bit tentative to me. As much as Aunt Matt and her friends might yearn for freedom, I don't think they could picture themselves in bloomers. Nor could I. Admittedly, corsets were uncomfortable. But the unrestrained female form, especially on some of the plumpest dowagers, might yield more freedom than the world was prepared to see.

Aunt Matt and I continued our tour of the Woman's Pavilion after the lecture, and it truly was awe-inspiring. The Women's Christian Temperance Union and Susan B. Anthony's suffragettes both had booths. The sky-lit gallery housed every type of artistic endeavor I could imagine: paintings, sculpture, needlework, pottery. The pavilion overflowed with women's accomplishments in science, health care, literature, education, and exploration. The variety of inventions was staggering—everything from washing machines and surgical bandages to egg beaters and frying pans. All created by women.

"I had no idea that women were doing so many things," I said.

"Yes. While it's still an unfortunate fact that men dominate our culture, we would like our pavilion to show that creativity and inventiveness aren't limited to men. Have you read the novel *Jane Eyre*?"

"Yes, of course."

"We have a copy of it on display written by Charlotte Bronte's own hand. I can also show you an original copy of the law that allowed women to argue cases before the Supreme Court for the first time. This pavilion is going to further women's causes far into the twentieth century."

"Where did the Lady Managers ever find all these things?"

"We sent invitations to women around the world, and even asked queens and princesses for their help. Women in every state and nation gathered together to search for their most outstanding accomplishments in every field. An all-women jury judged the entries and selected the winners."

"I am truly amazed, Aunt Matt."

"Good. But don't stop there, Violet. As you look at all of these achievements, think of what you might accomplish someday."

"Me? It never occurred to me to do anything. I mean . . . no one ever told me that women could do these things."

"That's why I wanted to bring you here. No one ever encouraged me either. But I hope you will begin to dream of more for your life than sipping tea or marrying a wealthy husband."

"This pavilion is like . . . like a celebration!"

"You're absolutely right. That's exactly what this pavilion is—a celebration of women's abilities and talents. The world can no longer dismiss us. You will have so many more opportunities in life than I ever did. Take your time choosing, Violet."

I gazed around at the variety of displays and remembered my grandmother's words about being unique: *You be exactly who God created you to be, and don't let anyone tell you otherwise.* Where did I fit in? Could I really do something as amazing as all of these women had?

Later, Aunt Matt stopped at a booth that sold silk scarves handmade by women in India. "Pick one," she said, "and I'll buy it for you. I want you to remember your visit."

I came out of the building inspired to accomplish great things. But as we walked back to the streetcar stop, it seemed that everywhere I looked I saw men and women together—strolling the fairgrounds arm in arm; pushing children in baby carriages; sitting beside each other on the streetcar. I realized that in spite of all the wonderful things I'd seen in the Woman's Pavilion, I still longed to fall in love.

More than anything, I wanted to know what it felt like to be kissed the way I'd seen Nelson kissing Katya. I didn't want to spend my life all alone, even if I could accomplish great things.

Did I really have to choose one or the other? Why couldn't I have both?

Chapter

19

Thursday, June 29, 1893

On Thursday evening, Nelson Kent and I boarded the whale-back steamship *Columbus* in Chicago's harbor and sailed to the fairgrounds. A large group of pea pods and their dates joined us, including Haughty and Naughty. The Grant sisters greeted me like long-lost friends.

"What a fine-looking couple you two make," Haughty said, looking us over.

"Don't we?" Nelson replied. He treated me very possessively, as if letting the others know he had staked his claim. We conversed politely with everyone for a few minutes, then Nelson steered me away.

"I've had enough of them," he said. "It takes forty-five minutes to get there, and I want to enjoy the cruise with you."

"I am enjoying it already." We stood at the rail and watched as the ship steamed along the shoreline. Homes and factories, shipyards and church steeples slipped past us. Soon the fair's domed buildings came into view, its towers and turrets topped with colorful flags and streamers. A little daylight remained in the warm June evening, and the setting sun leaked streams of vivid colors across the western sky.

"What do you think of your first view of the fair?" Nelson asked. I didn't have the heart to tell him that I had seen it three times already.

"It's beautiful from this vantage point. It looks like a magical city with the white buildings all lit up with electric lights."

"It's like something from a storybook, isn't it?"

Indeed, it resembled a scene from an entirely different world, and I couldn't resist asking Nelson the question, "If you could choose between living on another planet or living beneath the sea, which would you choose?"

"I can't imagine either place being more lovely than our own planet."

We got off the ship at the end of the pier, and Nelson paid our ten-cent fares to ride on the "people mover." The moving sidewalk had chairs to sit on, as it transported us all the way down the pier to the fairgrounds. We got off in front of the Peristyle, a long hallway of massive columns that made me think we had arrived in ancient Greece. Nelson took my arm as we walked beneath the arch, and then we paused to admire the scene. The Court of Honor lay ahead of us with a view of the Grand Basin, the Statue of the Republic, and MacMonnies Fountain.

"This is so beautiful, Nelson!"

"And it's only the beginning."

He stopped at a souvenir stand on the way to the concert hall and bought me a beautiful ivory fan with a picture of Columbus on it. "In case it's warm in the theater," he said.

We stopped again to admire the statues of Handel and Bach in front of Choral Hall and the portraits of famous musicians and composers that decorated the building's facade. We found our seats inside, and when the music began, I closed my eyes and lost myself

in the magnificent sound. This was a world away from the Gospel
Wagon's wheezing organ and muddy streets. We might have been on
a different planet altogether instead of the same city.

We went outside for air during intermission. Nelson grabbed
my hand. "Come on, we have a few minutes. I want you to see the
Electricity Building all lit up at night."

We hurried past a pavilion that looked as though the Moors had
built it, with an arched doorway painted in vivid reds and gold.

"What's inside that building?" I asked.

"I wish I had time to show it to you. It's the Transportation
Building, and it's amazing, Violet. Every means of transportation
you can imagine is inside from the smallest wagon to the largest
locomotive."

"It sounds interesting." In fact, it must have been "remarkably
interesting" since it hadn't been on Herman Beckett's list.

"There are so many new inventions and ideas at this exposition,"
Nelson said. "You can really get a glimpse of what the future is going
to be like. Someday all of the streetcars will run without horses. And
everyone will ride around in their own horseless carriage too."

"How will a carriage get anywhere without horses?"

"They will all have miniature steam engines to power them. And
man is going to figure out how to fly like the birds one of these days
too. The modern age is just ahead of us. If only I could convince my
father to invest in that future."

A statue of Ben Franklin stood guard in front of the Electricity
Building. I had never seen so many electric lights in one place.

"I wish I had time to show you Thomas Edison's displays. He has
some amazing new inventions. There is a machine that makes
music—or rather, reproduces the sound of music from an orchestra
or choir. Can you imagine what it will be like to have a music
machine in your own home? We'll be able to hear a concert like the
one we heard tonight whenever we want to."

"It will put a lot of musicians out of a job." I happened to glance behind me at the Wooded Island and saw thousands of tiny lights twinkling in the dark like fireflies. "Oh, look, Nelson! It's like a fairy-land!"

"Come on, let's go." He took my arm, leading me toward the island.

"What about the concert?"

"This is more fun, isn't it? Besides, I'm pretty sure there's a path that will take us across the island and back to Choral Hall again."

I linked my arm through his and we hurried across the footbridge and onto the island. I was so entranced by the trees and the lagoon and the twinkling fairy lamps that several minutes passed before I realized that Nelson and I were alone.

"We don't have a chaperone!" I said, skidding to a stop.

"It doesn't matter, Violet. You're safe with me."

It annoyed me that America was entering an era of inventions and innovations, yet I still had to live by an old-fashioned set of rules. I was tired of them.

"I want to be a modern woman," I told Nelson, "and go wherever I'd like with whomever I'd like. I can't even get on a streetcar and go downtown without someone to accompany me. I wish I didn't need a chaperone."

"They're for your protection, Violet. Believe me, there are plenty of unsavory rogues and thieves out there who would like nothing bet-ter than to take advantage of a pretty young woman like you."

Silas McClure, for one.

"Speaking of change," I said, swiftly changing the subject, "would you support a woman's right to vote?"

"I don't know . . . I haven't given it much thought."

"My aunt Matt reads the newspaper every day, and she believes that women not only should be allowed to vote, but that a woman can do any job that a man can do."

"Surely not manual labor like building railroads and working in coal mines. Why would a woman want to do that kind of work?

Besides, aren't there jobs that only women can do—such as having children? Only a woman can nurture a child properly."

We slowed our pace, enjoying the evening as we strolled down the winding pathway past hundreds of fairy lamps. Neither of us was paying much attention to where we were going.

"I sometimes wonder what it would be like to be able to make my own decisions," I said, "the way men do. Jane Addams defies convention with her work among the immigrants. Aunt Matt defies tradition too."

"But money is a big factor in both instances. If you can support yourself, you can do anything you want. Didn't your aunt inherit her father's estate? And Jane Addams inherited money too, I believe. That's how she started her work."

"I guess you're right. And I'm not likely to inherit any money. My father is comfortable but not wealthy. When he remarries everything will go to his new family. There's not much chance that I could inherit enough to be independent."

"There is another way to inherit money and be independent."

I looked up at Nelson. "There is?"

"Yes, you could marry into it."

I halted in the middle of the path and a group of people walking behind us nearly ran into us.

When I didn't respond, Nelson continued. "Some wealthy, modern-minded men—such as myself—are willing to give their wives a great deal of independence. My wife would have enough money to do whatever she pleased."

"That sounds so . . . so devious—to marry someone for money."

"Women do it all the time," Nelson said with a shrug. "So do men."

"Men do? What do you mean?" We started walking again.

"Well, if a man who is without financial means marries a woman from a wealthy family, all of her property and assets become his. It works in a man's favor to marry well, just as it does for women."

I understood what Nelson meant, but it didn't seem right. "Aunt Agnes told me that your father won't let you get ahead in his business until you settle down and get married. Is that true?"

"Yes, it's true."

"May I ask you a question . . . ? Is that why you're courting me?"

"Would you think less of me if I told you it was? I mean, aren't you and the other young ladies—Haughty and Naughty and all the rest—doing exactly the same thing? Isn't it your goal to marry the richest man?"

"I suppose so. I just don't like the sound of it."

"Hey, we were having fun until the subject of money came up. Can't we simply enjoy this evening?"

We stopped in a clearing and watched the colored floodlights sweep across the sky, lighting up the distant buildings and domes and fountains. I felt as though I had stepped into a storybook.

"This is a beautiful place, Nelson. Thank you for bringing me here at night." He took my chin in his hand and lifted my face toward his. He was about to kiss me. And I was about to let him— until I remembered Katya. I quickly turned away.

"We should probably get back."

"Violet, wait." He captured my arm. "I understand that you have other suitors, but tell me—how can I win you away from them?"

I knew that I couldn't explain the true reason for my hesitation, because it had been wrong to spy on him and Katya. I decided to tell a story instead.

"Years ago, Gilbert Casey fell madly in love with my great-aunt Bertha. He easily obtained her father's permission to marry her, but that wasn't enough for Gilbert. He wanted Bertha to fall in love with him—really and truly in love. And so he set about to win her heart."

"You're quite the romantic, Violet Hayes. Always bringing up the subject of love." He lifted my hand to his lips and kissed it. "But at least I know, now, what it will take."

"We'd better get back," I said again. And quickly too—before my curiosity won the battle with my good sense and I allowed him to take me into his arms and kiss me the way he had kissed Katya.

When we finally got back to the Choral Hall, all of Nelson's friends were standing around outside. "There you are," one of the pea pods said. "We wondered what happened to you two."

"I can guess what you've been doing," Haughty said.

"You would be wrong," Nelson told her. "Our excursion has been entirely aboveboard, I assure you. Miss Hayes is a very proper lady." He offered me his arm and we started walking, along with the whole group, away from the music hall.

"Is the concert over? Where are we going?"

"We've been invited to a private party in one of the other pavilions."

I never did learn the name of the building. The party took place in a rented hall, away from the exhibits and displays. The lavishly decorated room resembled a European casino, complete with a roulette wheel, dice games, playing cards, and other games of chance. I thought they were merely elaborate props until I saw the stacks of real money being exchanged for multi-colored chips. Waiters circulated with trays of appetizers and drinks. Judging by the raucous laughter and loud voices, the drinks were alcoholic.

Nelson took a wad of bills from his wallet and exchanged them for a little tray of chips. He chose a game of dice, and I could see right away that he wasn't gambling for fun. His intent was to win. But the longer he played, the more money he lost, and as his pile of chips dwindled away, he began to grow angry.

"Let's leave, Nelson. This isn't fun anymore." I rubbed his arm to soothe him, but he shrugged me away.

"Not until I win my money back."

"Do you think that's a good idea? You might lose even more."

He turned on me with surprising anger. "You know, women aren't the only ones who lack the freedom to make their own decisions. But if I can accumulate enough money on my own, I'll be able to do whatever I want with it. I'm going to be a self-made man, Violet, like

Turlington Harvey and Marshall Field and all the rest of them."

"By gambling? Didn't you tell me that the lumber baron, what's-his-name, worked his way to the top through hard work? Mr. McCormick invented his machine and Mr. Field built his store, and—"

"What difference does it make how I get it?" He turned back to his dice game.

"That looks like a lot of money," I said as he placed his last few chips on the board. "Why risk it all? Why not just work for your father?"

"It will take too long."

"Too long for what?" But I thought I knew. He could break free from his father's control and marry Katya if he had his own money.

"Too long for my father to trust me," he said. "I want to make my own investments and get in on some of the new inventions from Mr. Edison and the others. New modes of transportation. Father won't try any of them."

"Well, I don't know anything about investments, but it's hardly a good idea to win your father's trust by gambling away all your money."

Nelson seemed to have a moment of sudden clarity. "I suppose you're right. I'm sorry for yelling, Violet."

I sighed with relief. Surely Nelson would scoop up his remaining chips and leave—but he didn't.

"One more throw. Kiss the dice for me, would you, Violet?" He held them up to my lips and I reluctantly gave them a peck. I held my breath as he rolled the dice—and won!

"We can't leave now," Nelson said. He was back in the game with all of the fervor and excitement of Louis Decker and his friends at an evangelistic rally. Every time he made me kiss the dice, he won.

"You're my good-luck charm!" He grinned and gave me a quick hug.

I had to admit that winning was exciting. The Grant sisters and all of the pea pods gathered around to cheer us on. With each roll of the dice, my heart pounded a little faster, and the tension and excitement grew greater and greater—along with the risk. I couldn't help jumping up and down each time Nelson won. We cheered louder as the pile of chips in front of Nelson grew into a large mound. We were on a winning streak! I hadn't felt this alive since Ruth Schultz and I decided to sneak out of the dormitory after curfew.

An hour after I had first kissed his dice, Nelson had won all of his money back along with a little more. He would have continued to play, but the fairgrounds were closing down for the night.

"Too bad we have to go," he said. "Just when we were winning too."

He traded in his chips and stood counting his money as the casino lights dimmed. One of the blackjack dealers offered to escort Nelson and me to the ship for our protection. I thought of Silas' thieving friends roaming the fairgrounds and told Nelson he should accept.

"I would feel much safer," I told him. "People have been robbed here at the fair, you know."

"You're my lucky charm," he told me again as we boarded the ship. "We make a great team, don't we?"

Chapter

20

Friday, June 30, 1893

I managed to forget all about Louis Decker and Folk Night at the settlement house until Friday afternoon. By then, my grandmother was so excited about our evening out that I didn't have the heart to hurt her feelings by staying home. I decided to douse a handkerchief with perfume and carry it in my pocket so I would have a way to defend myself against the putrid smells. I also wore my least favorite dress and oldest pair of shoes.

Louis looked thoroughly bathed, combed, tucked, and spit-shined when he arrived at the house to escort Grandmother and me. Only his spectacles remained smudged, as usual. He really was a nice-looking man when he was all cleaned up. Not as classically handsome as Nelson, perhaps—and certainly not as well dressed—but attractive, nonetheless.

The evening began with a dinner held in the dining room where we had served the soup. Thankfully, the delicious aroma of roasting meat overwhelmed the stench of the neighborhood, and I could relax and tuck my perfumed handkerchief into my pocket. Scores of Bohemian people crowded inside the room, some in their colorful, traditional clothes, but most in much humbler attire. I felt a pang of guilt for enjoying the finer things in life that Nelson could offer. I should like Louis Decker. I should gladly choose him and a life of meaning and purpose and good values. Nelson enjoyed gambling—and I had helped him win. I had joined in. First I'd helped a thief and now a gambler. What was wrong with me?

Grandmother sat with a group of her friends, leaving Louis and me alone—if you can call sitting with hundreds of other people alone. Louis was a very quiet man when he wasn't preaching, and he didn't seem to know how to begin a conversation or keep it going. I did all the work of keeping the tennis ball in the air as plates of roast pork, potatoes, vegetables, and several other things I didn't recognize circulated around our table.

"Have you been to the World's Fair, Louis?"

"Not yet. I've been too busy working with our evangelism team."

"Are you planning to go this summer?"

"Only if the Lord leads me, and if it fits His purposes."

"You wouldn't consider going just for fun?" He looked up at me as if he had never heard of the word. At least I think he was looking at me. His glasses were so smudged I didn't understand how he could see anything at all, including the plate in front of him.

One of the platters that circulated around our table was piled with slices of a mysterious-looking meat. It had a strange, gelatinous consistency and resembled what you might get if you made a gelatin dessert out of random pieces of leftover meat.

"What is this?" I asked.

"I can't pronounce the Bohemian name, but it's similar to what we call head cheese."

"I've never heard of head cheese. What's in it besides cheese?"

"It isn't really cheese. They take the animal's head with all of the unused parts such as the brain, the tongue, and so forth, and boil it together to make a sort of sausage out of it. It's quite delicious."

I quickly passed the plate to the next person. As much as I longed to be as adventurous as Silas McClure, who had eaten rattlesnake, I lacked the stomach for it. And I did not care to sample any body parts from an animal's head. I nibbled a bit of the roast pork and dumplings but was afraid to fill up, remembering the smelly ride home. What I did eat, however, was delicious. Louis had a voracious appetite and devoured everything in sight.

"What is the most adventuresome thing you've ever eaten?" I asked him.

"What do you mean?"

"I once met a person who'd eaten rattlesnake meat. Would you try it?"

"Only if I had a very good reason to." I had hoped to make him laugh, but I was beginning to realize that Louis Decker didn't laugh much. He wasn't as gloomy and boring as Herman was—Louis would become quite animated when he preached or sang. But I had the feeling that he would never laugh unless God instructed him to.

"Suppose you became a missionary and the natives you were trying to convert served you something disgusting, like alligator eyeballs. Would you eat them?"

"That's different. I would do anything for the sake of the Gospel."

Yes, I was quite certain he would. I watched him swipe his bread across his plate to sop up the gravy and asked, "Have you always lived in Chicago?"

"No. Like Mr. Moody, I came to Chicago to get rich. Mr. Moody was a shoe salesman at one time, and his goal in life was to make a lot of money. But then the Lord changed his life and he gave up chasing wealth to serve God. That's basically my story too."

"Where do you see yourself living and working after you finish school?"

"Wherever God sends me."

For dessert we had little cookies with fruit in the middle of them, and there was something about the sight of them, or maybe the flavor, that seemed familiar to me. The Bohemian women pronounced them "ko-latch-key."

"I've eaten cookies like these before," I told Louis. "I can't recall when or where."

Everyone relaxed while we waited for the folk dancing to begin, and some of the smaller children chased each other around the tables, giggling. The sound of their laughter was as lovely as the music I had heard with Nelson Kent. I remembered Herman Beckett saying that he wanted a family, and Grandmother had told me that Louis was wonderful with the children. Yet I suspected that if I asked Louis if he envisioned children in his future, his reply would be something like, "Whatever God plans for me."

"Tell me about your family, Louis."

"My father owns a bakery in Milwaukee. We're just an ordinary family—three sisters, two brothers. I came to Chicago to make my mark in life, and I was doing very well in the business world until I saw the light of Christ. I'm like the man Jesus healed: I once was blind, but now I see." Louis always managed to talk more about God than about himself. I decided to change my tactics.

"If you had to choose between being struck blind and never being able to see the face of your beloved again, or becoming permanently deaf and being denied the sound of music and of a child's laughter, which would you choose?"

"I believe that we're responsible for our own behavior, but the choices you're talking about come from God. Not a hair can fall from our heads unless it's His will. The disciples once asked Jesus about a man born blind and wanted to know who had sinned to cause that tragedy. Jesus said that the man had been born blind in order that God would be glorified. And so, whether deaf or blind, I pray that my life would bring Him glory."

Of the many times I had asked that question, I had never heard an answer quite like Louis'. I decided to ask another one.

"If you had to choose between being rich but disfigured, or poor but handsome, which would you choose?"

"The Bible says, 'Give me neither poverty nor riches; feed me with food convenient for me: Lest I be full, and deny thee and say, Who is the Lord? or lest I be poor and steal, and take the name of my God in vain.' . . . That's from Proverbs."

The moment he mentioned stealing, I thought of Silas McClure. And wealth reminded me of Nelson Kent.

"Is money bad? Should wealthy people give it all away?"

"No, money itself isn't bad. The Bible says that it's the *love* of money that's the root of all evil."

I nodded, pretending to understand what he was talking about. I had never met anyone who talked about the Bible as much as Louis did. He made me ashamed of my shallowness. So I pretended to understand.

Once again, I thought of Aunt Matt's contention that every married woman was an actress. I was beginning to think she was right—and also that all the unmarried women, like myself, were continually auditioning to become actresses. Ever since coming to Chicago I seemed to be playacting. I had to smile enigmatically at Aunt Agnes' parties. I had to pretend not to be bored when I was with Herman Beckett. And now I had to pretend to be nice with Louis Decker. In fact, the only person I had been myself with was Silas McClure—and he was a thief! What did that say about me?

"Do you think it's possible for people to change?" I asked, still thinking of Silas.

"Not on their own. Only God can transform people. But when the Son sets you free, you are free indeed."

"What about real criminals? Have you ever known a hardened criminal, such as a thief or a con man, to change his way of life after hearing Mr. Moody preach?"

"Sure, I've heard plenty of stories where that's happened. And of course there's the example of the thief who was crucified beside Christ. After the thief repented, Jesus told him, 'Today shalt thou be with me in paradise.'"

Talking to Louis Decker was like conversing with Moses or one of the Apostles. I wondered what he had been like before he'd started studying the Bible.

The sound of musical instruments warming up began to drift into the restaurant as we talked—a clarinet, an accordion, a couple of violins, a bass fiddle—and soon a little orchestra began to play outside in the street. The musicians were quite good. Everyone spilled outside to listen and to watch the dancers perform in their colorful, embroidered dresses. As I watched, the same feeling of familiarity that I'd had with the cookies suddenly returned. This dance was somehow familiar to me.

"I've heard this music before," I told Louis. "I can't recall where."

"It certainly is lively," he said, clapping in tune.

For the next dance, the women all produced colorful scarves and waved them joyfully in the air as they whirled in time to the music. That's when it all came back to me: the bright colors, the dancing, the joy—my mother used to twirl a colorful scarf the same way and sing in another language as we danced around the room together. My heart pounded with excitement as the memory returned. It had been a long time ago. I had been very small. And Mother had been very beautiful.

Later, the band played a slow tune, and tears filled my eyes as the immigrants linked arms to sing along. I had no idea what the words meant, but I know that my mother used to sing the same song to me as a lullaby. She would sit on my bed stroking my hair, singing to me until I fell asleep. A tear rolled down my cheek as the song ended.

"That was beautiful, wasn't it?" Louis asked. I nodded. I didn't reveal the real reason for my tears.

By the time the evening ended and people began to leave, many of the smaller children had grown tired and overly excited. I heard a little girl crying, "I don't want to go," and I couldn't blame her. She would have to leave the warm companionship and laughter and music to go home to a bleak tenement building. The child's mother scooped her up in her arms.

"Come to Mama, *ho-cheech-ka*," she murmured. For a moment, the street in front of me seemed to tilt. I had to grip Louis' arm to keep from stumbling as another memory stirred. That was what my mother used to call me. She would hug me as tightly as Aunt Birdie always did and whisper the word tenderly, just as that mother had: *ho-cheech-ka*.

"Are you all right, Violet?"

"No . . . I mean . . . I think my mother might have been Bohemian."

"Why don't you ask her?"

"She . . . she left when I was nine years old. I don't know where she is."

"I'm sorry."

I knew I had discovered an important clue to my mother's past, and like the little girl, I didn't want to go home. I wanted to stay and talk to these people and see what other memories of my mother might spring to life. But the evening had drawn to a close and everyone was leaving.

I felt too emotional to converse much on the way home, so I listened as Louis and my grandmother talked. She had much more in common with him than I did. They spoke the same language, sprinkled with Bible verses and references to God as if He were an old friend.

"Thank you for a nice evening," I told Louis at our front door.

"I hope to see you again soon, Violet."

The moment the door closed, I turned to my grandmother. "May I ask you just one question about my mother?"

"You may ask. I can't promise I'll be able to answer it."

"The songs tonight reminded me of her." My voice trembled with emotion. "She used to sing tunes like that to me. And then I heard a mother call her child *ho-cheech-ka*, and that was what Mother used to call me. Was she a Bohemian immigrant?"

"I believe that her family might have been from that region of Europe, yes."

"So she was poor, like those people, before she married my father?"

"I never saw her house, Violet, and I never met her family."

"Please tell me *something*," I begged as my tears spilled over. "Anything! What does it matter now, since my parents are divorced and Father is going to marry Maude O'Neill?"

Grandmother saw my tears and hugged me close. Then she led me into the kitchen and sat me down at the table while she fixed a pot of tea.

"Your parents met on the night of the Great Fire, as you know. Your father rescued her." I wanted to ask how, but I was afraid to interrupt. "Your mother lost everything she owned. Our church in Lockport took in many of the homeless families—and there were so many of them. More than one hundred thousand people here in Chicago lost everything in the fire. Your father brought your mother home to our church in Lockport. When they fell in love and were married, she didn't return to Chicago. There was nothing to go back for, she said."

"They really loved each other?"

"Yes, at one time, they really did."

"What happened?"

Grandmother shook her head. She wouldn't answer.

"Aunt Birdie keeps telling me that I should marry for love, but that's what my parents did, and look what happened to them. I need to know why their love ended and why my mother left."

"Have you asked your father that question?"

"He told me that she hated her life in Lockport, hated being tied down."

"He would know much more about it than I do."

"But why was she so unhappy? Please tell me *something*!"

Grandmother reached across the table and took my hand in hers. "Violet, I don't know all the details of your parents' lives, but I do know there were huge differences between them. And once Angeline married John, she had new expectations placed on her as his wife. He is a prominent man in the community, as you know."

My grandmother gave my hand a squeeze, then released it. I watched her take a sip of tea and tried to picture my father when he had been young and in love. I couldn't do it. It was like trying to imagine Herman Beckett as Shakespeare's Romeo.

My grandmother set her teacup down and said, "Your mother came from Chicago and your father from tiny little Lockport. Maybe she missed the excitement of the city once in a while. Maybe she missed her own family too."

"I understand what you're saying, but that doesn't explain why she left *me*. Didn't she love *me*?"

Tears filled my eyes again. Grandmother stood and hurried to my side, smoothing back my hair and kissing my forehead. She had tears in her eyes as well.

"She loved you very, very much, Violet Rose. I know that to be true."

"Then why did she leave me? Do you know why?"

Grandmother bent and drew me into her arms, holding me tightly. "I'm sorry, Violet Rose. You need to ask your father that question."

Chapter

21

Saturday, July 1, 1893

I stayed in bed the next morning until long past breakfast. If I kept the pillow over my head to drown out all of the other noises, I could recall the music from the night before and imagine the dancers whirling. I wanted to hang on to the wispy memories of my mother for as long as possible.

It was Saturday, and my grandmother and aunts were at home, but I didn't want to face any of them. They all had such high hopes for me, which I had encouraged by accompanying them on their various pursuits. But I felt very confused. I didn't know what I wanted to do with my life. So I remained in bed.

It was close to noon when I heard Aunt Agnes' silvery voice gilding our front hallway. "*Bonjour*, darlings! How is everyone?"

I made up my mind that I would plead illness rather than endure any social calls with her today. Even so, it was rude of me to remain in bed when she had come to call. I got dressed and went downstairs. All four of the Howell sisters sat in the parlor.

"*Bonjour*, Violet dear. Good news! Nelson simply *raves* about you. His grandmother is *so* pleased. So is his father, by the way. Did you enjoy the concert at the fair the other night? And how was the party afterward?"

I didn't know what to say. Grandmother seemed to be waiting for my reply too. They would be shocked to learn about the gambling. I was still trying to formulate a response when someone knocked on the front door.

"I'll get it," Aunt Birdie sang. She fluttered out to the hallway, and a moment later I heard her say, "Why, it's Johnny!"

I jumped up and hurried to the foyer—and there stood my father on the other side of Aunt Birdie's embrace.

"What are you doing here?" I asked.

"I came for you," he replied, as if stating the obvious. "I'm going to accompany you home and help with your trunk."

"Oh, how nice," Aunt Birdie said.

"Home?" I shouted, forgetting to be ladylike. "I just got here!"

"Violet, you've been here for a month."

"Today is the first day of July," Aunt Birdie said helpfully.

"But I'm not ready to go home!"

Father looked perplexed. "You told me that you wanted to see the World's Columbian Exposition. You've seen it, haven't you?"

"Yes, but—"

"Violet has seen it four times. Isn't that right, dear?" Aunt Birdie gestured to all the souvenirs I had collected, which for some reason had ended up on the hall table: the Ferris wheel coin from Silas McClure, the picture postcards from Herman Beckett, the silk scarf from Aunt Matt, and the beautiful ivory fan with Columbus' portrait on it from Nelson Kent.

"Four times?" Father repeated. "Then you should be more than ready to come home."

"Shall I help you pack?" Aunt Birdie asked.

"I don't want to go home!" I sounded like one of the petulant children at the settlement house last night.

Aunt Matt marched into the foyer. "Lunch is ready," she declared. "Let's sit down and eat like civilized people. It's nothing fancy, Agnes, only vegetable soup, but you're welcome to join us."

"I believe I will," Agnes said. "John and I need to talk "

We all trooped into the dining room and sat down. Aunt Matt filled our soup bowls and Grandmother prayed. The room felt tense as everyone passed the rolls and butter around the table. I stared at my soup, unable to eat.

"I spoke with Herman Beckett," my father began. "He holds you in very high regard, Violet, and is eager for your return. Maude says that he is serious about your courtship. She thinks you should marry him."

"We hardly know each other!"

"That's why he's eager for your return, so he can court you in earnest. He seemed very pleased when I told him that I was coming to fetch you this weekend."

"Maude just wants to marry me off so she'll be rid of me."

"That's very unkind, Violet. Maude has your best interests at heart."

"Wait a minute, John," Aunt Agnes said. "Who is this suitor you're discussing?"

"He's a young man from Lockport. He works as a shipping clerk."

"He's a bore," I mumbled.

"John, dear, never mind some yokel from Lockport. I've found a much better match for our Violet. His father is the business tycoon Howard Kent. His family is swimming in old money. And Nelson's grandmother insists that he has grown very fond of our Violet. She hinted that he might be ready to propose soon."

I nearly choked on a mouthful of lemonade. I coughed a few times, then managed to say, "I like Nelson, but I'm hardly ready to marry him."

"For goodness' sakes, why not?" Agnes asked. "Nelson is eager to settle down and take his place in his father's firm. It's a wonderful opportunity."

"Yes, for Nelson."

"I don't know why you're being so contrary," Agnes said, "but you had better come to your senses before it's too late. Things are going so well with him, and he's a wonderful catch. John, perhaps you could speak with Nelson's father while you're here in the city. I could arrange a luncheon or something so you could meet the Kent family."

"It does sound promising," Father said.

I got my grandmother's attention across the table and pleaded silently with her for help.

"Louis Decker admires our Violet a great deal too," she said, jumping in. I lowered my head in despair. That wasn't at all what I'd wanted from her. "If Louis knew you were in town, John, I'm sure he would want to ask permission to court Violet as well."

"Who is this Louis Decker?" Agnes asked. "Is he any relation to Homer and Nettie Decker on Prairie Avenue?"

"I doubt it," Grandmother said. "But I think John should meet Louis in person, rather than hear about him or his family secondhand from me."

"He must be a religious zealot," my father muttered. "I'm not interested in meeting one of those. I wouldn't let my daughter marry one either." He turned to face me again. "If you aren't interested in this Kent fellow, then I want you to come home. Herman Beckett would make an excellent husband. He comes from a very good family."

"What about love?" I asked. "Shouldn't two people love each other before they marry?"

My father made a face. "Don't be naïve, Violet. There is plenty of time for love to grow once a commitment has been made."

Aunt Matt dropped her soup spoon with a clatter. I thought she had shown remarkable restraint by keeping quiet for as long as she had. "This is nearly the twentieth century, John, not the fourteenth! Arranged marriages are a thing of the past. Violet is a sensible young woman. Shouldn't she be allowed to choose for herself?"

"Violet, dear," Aunt Birdie said, "make certain you marry for love."

Her words gave me an idea. "Do you love Maude?" I asked my father.

"We aren't discussing Maude; we're discussing you. I'm responsible for you. Your future is much too important for you to ruin by making a bad choice."

"Aunt Birdie, help me! Please!" I begged, tugging on her sleeve. "Tell my father how important love is."

Aunt Birdie picked up her spoon and tapped it against her water glass to command everyone's attention. "I think Violet should marry that nice gentleman with the wonderful smile. He's *madly* in love with her."

"Oh no." I covered my face with both hands.

"Which gentleman is that?" Father asked.

"I think Birdie means the man who accompanied Violet on the train from Lockport," Grandmother said.

This was getting worse and worse. If Father learned about Silas McClure, he would never trust my judgment again. I cringed, waiting for Father to angrily declare that no one had accompanied me from Lockport, but Aunt Birdie spoke first.

"I don't recall his name, but he gave us his card. I'll go get it." She rose from the table and headed out to the hall to fetch the silver tray. Thank goodness I had hidden all of Silas' cards inside my diary. How would I ever explain why I foolishly had gone to the fair with a thief who sold Dr. Dean's Blood Builder?

"Don't mind her," I said after Aunt Birdie had left the room. I waited until my father took another slurp of his soup and asked, "What if I'm not ready to marry?"

"Why wouldn't you be ready? You've finished school, you'll be twenty-one next April. What else would you do with yourself?"

"Women are doing all sorts of things. I saw some of their accomplishments when I visited the Woman's Pavilion with Aunt Matt."

"I might have known." He gave Aunt Matt a dark look. I turned to her next, silently pleading for help.

"John knows my opinion on the matter," she said. "Violet doesn't need to marry at all in order to lead a fulfilling life. But if she does choose to marry, it should be to whomever she wants, whenever she wants. And it should be to someone who loves her and appreciates her for herself, not for what *he* stands to gain from the marriage."

"I disagree," Father said. "I think parents are in a much better position than their children are to see the good qualities in a spouse and make a sound choice. Parents have the maturity and experience that young people lack."

"Why, John Jacob Hayes!" Grandmother said. "I'm surprised you would say that, considering your own experience."

"My own experience serves to prove my point. I believe I have made a much better choice for my second marriage now that I'm a mature adult. You'll see that immediately when you meet Maude O'Neill. And that's another reason why you need to come home, Violet. Maude would like to spend some time with you and get to know you a little better since we're going to become a family in a few months."

My stomach seethed in protest. My soup lay untouched. If only I could find my mother and remind Father of the power of true love.

"And it's because of my own experience that I've decided to choose for my daughter as well," Father continued. "I want Violet to avoid repeating the mistakes I've made. Marriages work better if people are from a similar background, a similar social class." I knew he was talking about my mother.

I realized that I didn't have a pattern for a happy marriage. Father was divorced, Aunt Matt was a spinster, Aunt Agnes' husband had affairs, and even Grandmother had admitted that her marriage hadn't been ideal. Aunt Birdie claimed to be happily married, but Uncle Gilbert was dead. Besides, Birdie seemed to tap-dance around reality a great deal of the time.

"I want to know what went wrong between you and Mother," I said boldly.

"I've already explained it to you, and I'm not going to repeat myself." He stuffed a roll into his mouth to avoid saying more.

I refused to give up. "You said she was bored, that she hated living in Lockport and being tied down. That's exactly how I feel! I don't want to settle down in Lockport either, and be bored to death by Herman Beckett."

"Violet is so much like her mother, isn't she?" Aunt Birdie asked as she glided back into the dining room with the empty silver platter.

Her question was met with a long, spine-tingling silence. It was as if she had lit the fuse on a stick of dynamite, and everyone in the room was holding his or her breath, waiting for it to explode. I broke the silence.

"Am I like her, Aunt Birdie? In what way?"

Father cleared his throat, interrupting before she could reply. He held up the empty breadbasket. "Are there any more rolls, Aunt Bertha? I would like another one."

"I'll go and see," she said with a smile.

"You told me that you find Nelson Kent interesting," Aunt Agnes said. "Think of what a wonderful life you could have with him."

Yes, if I was willing to share him with Katya. I had to do something, fast, but I was too panic-stricken to figure out a plan. I had come to Chicago with two goals and had accomplished neither. Now it was time to return home. Why hadn't I figured out a way to find my mother and to stop Father's marriage? Why had I wasted time running around the city with worthless suitors? If I didn't find my mother soon, I would have to marry whomever my father chose.

"It's my life, isn't it?" I blurted. "I don't trust you to choose for me, Father. I hate Maude. Besides, you lied to me all these years about my mother." I knew I sounded childish, but I was desperate.

"I kept the truth from you for your own good. I was protecting you. You can be very impulsive and prone to theatrics, Violet. That's why I want to see you safely married to a good husband who will provide you with a comfortable life."

"Can't you give Violet a little more time with us, John?" Grandmother asked. "July has just begun."

I saw him glance briefly at Aunt Matt. She saw it too.

"He's afraid I'll be a bad influence on you, Violet."

"But if she spends more time with Nelson Kent," Aunt Agnes said, "I'm certain he'll propose."

"Do you want to continue seeing this Kent fellow?" Father asked.

"Yes," I said, gulping. I wasn't ready to marry Nelson, but courting him would buy me some more time.

Father paused for a long time while he thought it over. "All right," he said with a huge sigh. "I suppose you can stay."

"Oh, how nice," Aunt Birdie said.

"Will you be spending the weekend with us, John?" my grandmother asked. "I can make up an extra bed . . ."

"No, I think I'll catch the train home tonight." He pulled out his pocket watch, stared at it for a moment, then snapped it closed again. "Maude will be expecting me this evening. But I'll be back in two weeks, Violet, do you understand? You seem to have no shortage of interested suitors from which to choose. Just don't prolong this, or I'll be forced to make the decision for you."

Chapter

22

I couldn't sleep that night. I needed to know which man I was destined to marry. My only recourse was to perform the Midnight Stairway Ritual.

Ruth Schultz and I had tried the ritual at school with mixed results. According to tradition, if a woman wanted to see the face of her future husband she had to dress all in white, let down her hair, and wait until just before the stroke of midnight. Then, with an uplifted candle in her right hand and a mirror in her left, she had to walk slowly down the stairs, backward, all the way to the cellar. When she reached the final step and the clock struck twelve, her future husband's face would appear in the mirror.

Ruth tried it first and swore that she saw a handsome man's face. "He was someone I didn't know," she'd said, "But I'll recognize him the moment I see him again."

Ruth and I had only one mirror and one candle so I had to wait until the second night for my turn. The ritual had to be performed at the stroke of midnight. Besides, it was easier to walk backward down the stairs with someone helping you. Otherwise, you risked falling down the stairs and breaking your neck and never finding your one true love. No one wanted to marry a cripple.

But when my turn came the second night, a jealous classmate who had gotten wind of what Ruth and I were doing snitched on us. The headmistress caught us and punished us for being out of bed after curfew. The fact that we had "endangered the dormitory" with a lit candle had prolonged our imprisonment. I never did see my future husband's face. Now, in desperation, I decided to try the midnight ritual without Ruth's help.

I borrowed a candle from the silver candelabra on the buffet in the dining room and a box of matches from the kitchen drawer. I didn't have a hand mirror, so I decided to use Aunt Birdie's silver tray. It was shiny enough for me to see my reflection, and besides, it wouldn't break if I fell down the stairs. My luck had been pretty bad lately, so I couldn't risk seven more years of it.

I let down my hair, dressed in my white muslin slip, lit the candle, and crept from my bedroom as midnight approached. My stomach felt as knotted as one of my knitting projects as I stood at the top of the stairs and waited for the case clock in the hallway to begin chiming the hour.

Bong!

The first stroke startled me as it reverberated through the silent house. I quickly recovered and started carefully down the steps, walking backward.

Bong! . . . Bong! . . .

I reached the front foyer and grabbed the silver tray from the hall table.

Bong! . . . Bong! . . . Bong! . . .

I could hear Aunt Matt snoring as I crept backward down the hall past her door. The clock was still chiming as I reached behind me to open the cellar door and start down.

Bong! . . .

My foot touched the last step at the stroke of twelve, and I held up the mirror, waiting for the face of my husband to appear. Instead, a shadowy figure suddenly materialized in front of me at the top of the stairs.

I gasped in fright. I couldn't seem to scream. My mind told me to run, but I didn't know what dangers loomed in the murky blackness behind me. Besides, the only part of me that could move was my heart, which was trying to escape from my chest.

Suddenly a trembling voice called out, "Give me back my silver tray you dirty, rotten thief!"

Aunt Birdie.

My knees gave way and I sank to the cellar floor in relief. Aunt Birdie slowly descended the stairs, brandishing an umbrella like a club. I finally found my voice.

"Aunt Birdie, wait! It's me! Violet!"

She halted, her eyes wide with surprise. "Violet Rose Hayes! Why in the world are you stealing my silver tray?"

"I'm not stealing it. I'm . . . I'm using it to see my husband's face." But the stroke of midnight had long since passed, and his face was lost to me.

Aunt Birdie sat down on the stairs and laid the umbrella in her lap. When my heart finally slowed again, I explained what I had been doing.

"I should have tried the wedding cake method," I said when I'd finished my story.

"Wedding cake?"

"It's another test Ruth told me about. You're supposed to put a slice of wedding cake under your pillow before you go to sleep. She says you'll dream about the man you'll marry that night."

"Oh, how nice."

"But I haven't been to any weddings, Aunt Birdie, and I don't intend to wait for my father's. I have to find my one true love and stop Father from marrying Maude—and I'm running out of time."

"I've never heard of either of those methods for discovering who you'll marry, dear, but I do know one method that works every time."

"Really? What do I have to do?"

"You place two walnuts on the stove, one for your suitor and one for yourself. If your suitor's walnut cracks or jumps, it means he will be unfaithful to you. If it blazes and burns, it means that he loves you. And if his and yours burst into flames at the same time it means you will marry him."

I scrambled to my feet. "I'm going to try it."

"Oh, how nice."

We went upstairs to the kitchen. The fire in the stove was out since it was summertime, but we shoved in a few sticks of kindling along with one of Aunt Matt's newspapers, all crumpled up. I blew on the wood to stoke the flames while Aunt Birdie fetched a bag of walnuts from the pantry.

"I have more than one suitor," I told her. "Will it still work if I test all three?"

"Let's try it and see." She pulled a chair over to the stove and sat down to watch.

"The first one is for me," I said, placing one walnut on the stove. "And this one is for Nelson Kent." I felt the heat from the growing fire as I put the second walnut in place. "The third is for Louis Decker . . . and this fourth one is for Herman Beckett."

"Don't forget that other gentleman." Aunt Birdie handed me another walnut.

"Which other gentleman?" But I knew very well whom she meant.

"You know, that man with the autumn blue eyes and beautiful smile."

"He's not even in the contest, Aunt Birdie." She looked so sad with her lips in a pout and her head tilted to one side that I relented. What could it hurt? Besides, she already had taken Silas McClure's walnut away from me and laid it on the stove.

"Fine. That one is for Silas McClure," I said.

I pulled up another chair and we sat watching for several long minutes. I fully expected Nelson Kent's walnut to crack and jump, proving that he would be unfaithful. Louis Decker's and Herman Beckett's might blaze and burn, revealing that they loved me, but I kept a close eye on my own, hoping it wouldn't burn along with one of theirs and indicate that we would marry. The suspense mounted as the fire roared and the flames grew hotter. I fidgeted nervously. Suddenly Aunt Birdie jumped up, moved behind my chair, and covered my eyes with her hands.

"Wait! What are you doing? I can't see."

"I know you can't," she said sweetly. "So now the question is, which beau are you hoping for?"

I saw the logic in her method.

"Is . . . is that how you discover the answer?"

"It isn't magic. Your heart knows which man is the right one for you. Tell me what your heart sees."

I was still in the dark with my eyes covered, but I thought I was beginning to see. "I would have a meaningful life doing good deeds if I married Louis, and he would consider me his partner in every way. But I don't think I could stand being poor or working with poor people. I know that makes me seem shallow, but I can't help it. I can't do what he does for the rest of my life. He works in such terrible places. Besides, Louis' passion is for God, not me."

"So he isn't the one."

"No, I don't think so. And Nelson would give me a wonderful life with servants and gowns and fine food. I know he would let me donate money to help the poor and everything. But is that enough for a lifetime together? He doesn't love me, Aunt Birdie. Nelson and I are good friends, but I think he's in love with someone else. He looks at her with love in his eyes, and I saw them kissing." I suddenly felt warm, remembering their impassioned kiss—but the heat might have been coming from the stove. "Do you think love could grow after we were married?"

"Every fire needs a spark in order to kindle a flame," she said. I had to admit that the spark between Nelson and me just wasn't there.

"Herman Beckett would be a compromise, neither rich nor poor. He seems to care for me, and he wants a home and a family. He could offer me a life that is safe and stable—but he's so *boring*! My mother was discontented living in Lockport. What if I'll be too?"

"Is he that young fellow who works for the undertaker?"

"Um . . . yes." It was late at night, and I didn't have the patience to explain Herman Beckett to her.

"Well, he's *out*! You can't spend the rest of your life with an undertaker, Violet. They're such dreary people. I despise undertakers."

"Then I guess you can take your hands away now." She didn't uncover my eyes.

"Aren't you forgetting the other fellow?"

"No, Silas McClure is a thief. He's out of the question." I imagined his walnut rolling into the flames, proving that he would spend eternity in hell with all of the other thieves and criminals.

"I think you know which husband you want—don't you, dear?"

"None of them."

"Well, then. That says it all, doesn't it?"

She finally uncovered my eyes. The walnuts all sat on the stove, exactly where I had placed them. The newspaper and kindling wood had nearly burned up, and the fire was going out. I opened the stove lid and pushed all of the nuts into the dying flames.

"Let's go to bed," I said with a sigh.

As I walked up the stairs, I wondered which would be the worst fate: to live with a husband who didn't love you, like Aunt Agnes did; to marry a man whose passion was directed toward God, like my grandmother had; or to be like Aunt Matt and never marry at all. But when Aunt Birdie hugged me good-night at the top of the stairs,

I suddenly knew the answer: The worst fate of all was to lose the man you truly loved the way Aunt Birdie had.

I blew out the candle and climbed into bed, burying my face in my pillow. I couldn't hold back the flood of tears any longer. That's when I admitted the truth to myself for the first time: before Aunt Birdie had covered my eyes, I had been hoping that Silas McClure's walnut would burst into flames at the same moment as mine. I could have fallen in love with him if he hadn't turned out to be a thief. But now Silas was dead to me, just as Gilbert was dead to Aunt Birdie.

Then I had another thought. Like Aunt Birdie, my father also had lost the love of his life when my mother left him. Maybe that was why he didn't want me to marry for love. Maybe he wanted to spare me the same heartache he'd experienced.

I wanted to live happily ever after, but I was beginning to believe that true love existed only in romance novels.

Chapter

23

Monday, July 3, 1893

I was desperate. My father had granted me only two more weeks in Chicago, and I couldn't waste another day. I rose early Monday morning determined to take action, any action—yet I hadn't decided what it would be. I found my grandmother in the kitchen flipping pancakes.

"You're up early, Violet Rose. Are you going to the settlement house with me?" She set a plate in front of me and turned back to the stove, humming a hymn.

"Sorry. Maybe another day."

"We could use some help down at the Suffrage Association," Aunt Matt said. She lowered her newspaper long enough to slice into her morning grapefruit. The pungent aroma filled the kitchen.

"Next time," I told her. "I promise."

"Are you going out with Agnes, dear?"

"No," I told my grandmother, "not today."

As soon as Aunt Birdie and I were alone, I yanked the drawer full of photographs out of the secretary and sat down on the sofa to look through them. Most of them were of Aunt Birdie and her sisters and their families. But I stopped when I found one that looked like a younger version of my father. Alongside him posed another young man who looked remarkably like him.

"Is this my father?" I asked Aunt Birdie, who was hovering nearby.

"Yes, that's Johnny. Wasn't he a handsome devil when he was young?" She sank onto the sofa beside me.

"Who is this man with him? A cousin?"

"No—you know. That's his brother, Philip, of course."

"Wait a minute. My father doesn't have a brother."

"Well, he certainly does. Philip and Johnny are two years apart and as loyal as twins."

I held the photo closer, studying it. "No one ever told me he had a brother. I never knew he even existed. Why doesn't anyone talk about him? Where is he?"

Aunt Birdie's wistful smile faded. "He's away at war, just like Gilbert," she said sadly.

Oh no. What Pandora's box had I opened *now*?

"I believe Florence got a letter from him not too long ago. I'll go look for it." She started to rise from the sofa.

"No, that's okay. I'll read the letter later. Let's finish looking at these photos."

The last thing I wanted to do was remind Aunt Birdie of the truth about her beloved Gilbert. But why hadn't anyone ever mentioned Philip? Here was one more secret that my family had kept from me. I tossed the photo of my mysterious uncle onto the pile and went on to the next one. And the next, and the next. When I reached the bottom of the drawer, I exhaled in frustration.

"Why aren't there any photos of my mother?"

"I don't know . . . Do you think someone could have stolen them?"

"Or else destroyed them." I decided to try a different approach. "You said the other day that I was a lot like her. Can you tell me what you meant by that?"

"She was a pretty little thing, just like you. And very imaginative. A free spirit."

I stuffed all the photos back into the drawer, upset that the search had proven fruitless. Trying to pry information from my family was a waste of time. Why not just get on the streetcar and ride down to LaSalle Street and find my mother myself? As Silas had pointed out, we were entering the twentieth century. Women should have more freedom to go places alone. I could find her address on my own, couldn't I?

Yet as I remained seated on the sofa, I realized that it wasn't the fear of the journey or the lack of a chaperone that made me hesitate. I finally came face-to-face with the truth that I had been avoiding for the past month: I was afraid to find my mother. Afraid of what I would discover about her. Afraid to learn that she didn't love me. Afraid that she would reject me all over again.

I now had to weigh those fears against the reality of my father's ultimatum. If something didn't change in the next two weeks, he was going to arrange for me to marry Herman Beckett or Nelson Kent. And my father would marry Murderous Maude O'Neill. Homely and Horrid would become my siblings. The time had come to lay aside my fears and summon some courage.

"Aunt Birdie, how would you like to go for a ride downtown with me?" I didn't quite have the courage to make the journey alone.

"Okay," she said, rising from the sofa. "Where shall we go?"

"To LaSalle Street. To find my mother."

"Oh, how nice."

Unlike her two sisters, Aunt Birdie did not walk briskly and purposefully. A stroll to the streetcar stop with her resembled a leisurely waltz in the moonlight. But Birdie was a cheerful companion and didn't lecture at the top of her voice on the ride downtown. I linked arms with her after we disembarked onto crowded LaSalle Street, feeling as though I was holding on to a balloon that might float away on the breeze if I loosened my grasp.

I located a house number on the nearest building, then turned in circles for a few moments like a blindfolded three-year-old until I got my bearings. When I'd figured out which direction to walk, we finally set off to the south. I noticed that odd and even house numbers were on opposite sides of the street, so we crossed at the first intersection to the west side of LaSalle.

We were getting very close. My feet longed to run as quickly as my racing heart, but Aunt Birdie drifted slowly beside me like a sailboat on a calm day. She smiled at perfect strangers and greeted any man in a uniform—policeman, bellhop, doorman, streetcar driver. She probably would have hugged them all if I had relaxed my grip on her arm.

And there it was—my mother's building. Except that it wasn't an apartment building at all, but a squat three-story office building wedged between two much larger ones. A sign dangling above the door advertised a dancing school.

"This can't be it!"

"Why not, dear?"

"I don't see any apartments."

Nevertheless, I towed Aunt Birdie into the miniature lobby and read the directory. The first-floor offices belonged to an engineering firm, the second floor to the dancing school, and the third to a law firm.

"Oh no," I groaned. "This must be the lawyer's office that my mother used for her divorce."

"Well, then. That says it all, doesn't it?"

I refused to give up. We trudged up the stairs to the third floor and met an unsmiling clerk guarding the portal to the shabby office suite behind him.

"May I help you?"

I struck a dignified yet flirtatious pose, hoping to penetrate his officiousness with my dignity and his male instincts with my feminine charms.

"Oh, I surely hope so, Mister . . ." I spotted the nameplate on his desk. "Mister Morgan. You see, my name is Violet Rose Hayes, and I'm trying to locate one of your clients, Mrs. John Hayes—who happens to be my mother. Her first name is Angeline. This address was listed on my parents' divorce papers. Would you happen to have the address of her residence?"

"We can't divulge our clients' personal information." His cold voice and lack of interest felt like a slap. It didn't require much for me to summon tears.

"Oh, please . . . you must help me! She's my mother. She left home when I was nine, and I haven't seen her in eleven years."

Mr. Morgan might have been carved from stone. "That's unimportant."

"Unimportant! I've traveled all the way from Lockport by train, and it's vitally important that I get in touch with her immediately!"

"Our clients' confidentiality is also vitally important."

I took a deep breath to calm myself. My feminine charms obviously weren't working. Grumpy Mr. Morgan showed more interest in the papers he was shuffling around on his desk than in me.

"Suppose . . . suppose I wrote her a message? Could you forward it to her?"

"We are not a courier service."

"I realize that, but what if . . . What if I paid to become one of your clients, and then you could give—"

"Our firm only consults on legal matters."

I grabbed Aunt Birdie's arm and stormed away. As soon as we were out of his sight on the stairwell landing, I started to cry. Aunt Birdie offered me her handkerchief and a hug.

"There, there . . ."

"I need to find my mother, Aunt Birdie!"

"Well, then, we'll just have to keep looking, won't we?"

We went outside and started to walk again. I was too upset to care which street we were on or which direction we were going. We had stopped at an intersection and were waiting for the traffic to clear, when Aunt Birdie suddenly pointed to a group of men standing in front of the Municipal Court Building across the street.

"Oh, look. Isn't that the young man with the lovely blue eyes who came to call on you? What was his name?"

"Silas McClure . . ." I breathed. He was unmistakable, even from this distance. I whirled around so quickly to walk the other way that Aunt Birdie broke free. Before I could stop her, she waved her arms like a drowning victim and called to him.

"Yoo hoo! Mr. McClure!"

"Hey there!" he shouted when he saw her. He waved in return, then left the other men and hurried across the street, weaving expertly between horses and wagons and carriages. "Miss Hayes! And Mrs. Casey. Hey, it's great to see you!" Aunt Birdie greeted him with an enormous hug.

My pulse began to race, and I didn't want it to, but Silas' face had lit up like the White City at night when he saw me. It was so seldom that someone looked that pleased to see me. Nelson greeted me coolly, Louis was cordial, and gloomy Herman might have been comatose. I told my heart to slow down, reminding myself that Silas was a thief and a criminal—he had just come out of the courthouse, hadn't he? But the element of danger only made my heart beat faster.

"What brings you ladies down here?"

"Violet is looking for her mother," Aunt Birdie said. "Have you seen her?"

He blinked. Then I saw understanding dawn in his eyes.

"Hey, that's right! On the day we arrived in Chicago you asked me to take you to LaSalle Street, and then—" He halted. His blinding smile disappeared. "I am really, really sorry, Violet. I was supposed to bring you here after the fair, wasn't I? I really let you down that day."

"It doesn't matter," I said, sniffing away my tears. "The address turned out to be a lawyer's office. They're the ones who drew up my mother's divorce papers, but they won't tell me where she lives."

"Your mother loved the theater," Aunt Birdie said. "That's probably where she went. Why don't we look there?"

I grabbed Birdie's arm in time to stop her from leaving. "I don't think she went to the theater, Aunt Birdie. She's been gone for eleven years."

"And there are dozens of theaters in Chicago," Silas added.

"Well, there was a wonderful production of *Romeo and Juliet*. She would enjoy that. She and Johnny were just like them—star-crossed lovers."

"Gosh, I can't tell you how bad I feel for letting you down," Silas said. "I'd like to make it up to you, Violet, and help out. If you give me your mother's name, maybe I can help you find her."

"How? I don't even have an address."

"I've . . . uh . . . I've got ways."

I imagined him using the seedy underworld of thieves and pickpockets, whispering her name from one den of criminals to the next. I knew Silas was a thief, yet I didn't feel at all afraid of him. Besides, as far as finding my mother was concerned, I was at a dead end and facing my father's deadline. How could it hurt to tell him? I needed all the help I could get.

"If I give you her name and you do find her, will you promise not to say anything to her until I've had a chance to talk to her? I don't want to frighten her off."

"How could he frighten her, dear?" Aunt Birdie asked. "He wouldn't hurt a fly. Would you, Mr. McClure?"

"A mosquito, maybe," he said, winking at her, "but never a fly. Listen, Violet, don't worry about a thing. Tell me her name and I'll see what I can do for you."

He reached into an inner pocket of his jacket to pull out a wad of folded paper and a stubby pencil. But as he did, I noticed a large bulge in another inside pocket and saw something metallic poking out.

Was that a gun?

I had never seen a pistol up close before, but from the brief glimpse I caught before he buttoned his suit coat closed, I feared that's what it was. My heart started thudding so loudly that Silas' friends probably could hear it across the street. Now I *was* afraid of him! I opened my mouth but nothing came out.

"Her name is Angeline," Aunt Birdie said. "Angeline Hayes."

"An-ge-line . . ." he repeated as he scribbled it down. "Anything else you can tell me that might help?"

"She was a pretty little thing," Aunt Birdie added. "Just like Violet. And she loved the theater."

"I think . . . I think she might be Bohemian," I finally managed to say. Desperation had won the battle over fear. "I-I heard some Bohemian folk music the other night, and the language and the songs and everything sounded very familiar to me. I don't remember much about my mother, but I remember that she sometimes sang in a different language."

He finished writing everything down and refolded the paper. I held my breath, waiting for him to open his jacket again, but he shoved the paper and pencil into an outside pocket.

"Okay then, Violet. I'll see what I can do."

"Can you hurry, please? I have less than two weeks to search for her."

"Two weeks? And then what happens?"

"Then my father is going to make me go home to Lockport."

"Hey, McClure. Come on," one of the men called from across the street. "Court is back in session." I tried to get a look at their faces and see if I recognized "Josephine" or Robert, but the men had already turned away.

"Sorry, but I gotta run." He squeezed my arm. "I'll let you know as soon as I find out something, okay?" He gave me a long, lingering look, like he was memorizing my face. His candelabra grin had returned. "It was great seeing you ladies again. Bye."

I watched as he dodged around the traffic again and bounced up the courthouse steps. He turned and waved before disappearing inside. I couldn't seem to move. There was something terribly wrong with my heart. It was out of rhythm and pounding wildly. *It's because of the gun,* I told myself. *He has a gun!*

Aunt Birdie tapped me on the shoulder, breaking the spell. "He's in love with you," she said.

"No. Th-that's impossible. He's . . . he's completely unsuitable!"

"Your cheeks aren't pink this time, dear, they're bright red."

I covered my cheeks with my hands and felt the warmth. Aunt Birdie cocked her head to one side and smiled at me.

"Make sure you marry for love, dear."

Chapter

24

B y the time Aunt Birdie and I arrived home, I had finally stopped shaking from my encounter with gun-toting Silas McClure. But I battled tears of bitter disappointment because I hadn't found my mother. I wished I'd gone to LaSalle Street four weeks ago instead of wasting all this time. Now less than two weeks remained in which to find her, and my best hope of doing so was with the help of a thieving elixir salesman. I wanted to push past Aunt Birdie and run upstairs to my room and weep.

"It looks like you got another letter," Aunt Birdie said. She had stopped in front of me to scoop up the mail that lay waiting for us on the foyer floor.

"From whom?" I asked wearily.

"It says, 'Mrs. Charles Crane' on the return address. 'Riverside, Illinois.'"

It took me a moment to realize it was from Herman Beckett's

sister—whom I had dubbed Misery Mary. I took the letter from
Aunt Birdie and ripped it open.

Dear Miss Hayes,

    *I am writing to invite you to a family picnic on July the fourth
here at our home in Riverside. Herman will be coming by train from
Lockport along with our mother, so you will have the opportunity to
become better acquainted with our family. I know this is short notice,
but I do hope you will be able to attend. Herman and my husband,
Ernest, will call for you around ten o'clock in the morning. I look
forward to seeing you again.*

                Sincerely,
                Mary Crane

"Is it from one of your beaus?" Aunt Birdie asked.

"From his sister. She invited me to her Fourth of July picnic."

"Oh, how nice. And tomorrow is the Fourth."

"It is? Oh no," I moaned. "That means there won't be time to
write back and send my regrets."

"Don't you want to go, dear? I do love Fourth of July picnics with
the parades and the fireworks and everything. Don't you? And everyone is so patriotic now that our country is at war."

"It's just that I can't afford to waste another day, Aunt Birdie. I
need to find my mother before the two weeks are up, and I have no
idea where to look."

"Well, you could always ask Philip. He would know where
she is."

Philip? My father's missing brother? A strange, tingling sensation
rippled through me—the kind I used to get when one of the detectives in *True Crime Stories* unearthed an important clue.

"Did my Uncle Philip know my mother?"

"Well, I'm sure he did."

I hesitated before asking the next question. "Where . . . um . . .
where can I find Philip?"

"Well, he's . . . I mean . . . Oh, that's right. Philip is off fighting in the war like my Gilbert. He . . . they . . ."

Her gray eyes clouded over with tears. She looked down at the pile of mail she was holding and her frail hands trembled as she leafed through the letters again.

"I can't imagine why Gilbert hasn't written. He must be so warm down in Virginia this time of year—the poor dear. Those uniforms are ever so hot. And the Virginia Peninsula is such a muggy, buggy place. And it looks like Philip hasn't written either. . . ."

She dropped two letters as she shuffled clumsily through the mail. I picked them up, then gently took the rest of them out of her hands and laid them on the hall table.

"Let's go make some lemonade and you can tell me all about my Uncle Philip, okay? What's he like?"

"Full of life," she said with a smile. "But headstrong. He and his father are always butting heads, you know. Isaac didn't want his boys to fight, but as soon as Philip turned eighteen, he ran away to enlist. Is that a letter from him?" she asked, pointing to the invitation from Mary that I still held.

"No. I've been invited to a picnic tomorrow."

I decided not to ask any more questions about Philip. I feared that he also had perished in the war, and I worried that my probing would hurt Aunt Birdie. We made lemonade and a light lunch. Afterward, I went upstairs to my room to devise a new plan.

I couldn't afford to waste time crying helpless tears of disappointment. My future was at stake. My father seemed determined to marry me to Herman or to Nelson. I had been taught to be well mannered and compliant, trusting that men were more knowledgeable than women and better able to make choices for me. But that was before I'd seen for myself what women could accomplish; before I'd visited the Woman's Pavilion and the suffrage headquarters and seen the work that my grandmother and Jane Addams did.

Yes, I needed to take matters into my own hands. My two goals would now become three: find my mother, stop Father's marriage, and—did I dare believe it?—decide my own future.

I had no idea what that future might be, but I knew that I did not want to marry Herman Beckett. Tomorrow I would make certain that he saw a side of me that he would find unacceptable. But first, I would use the picnic as an opportunity to glean more information from Herman's mother about Murderous Maude O'Neill. I needed something so damning it would prevent my father from marrying her.

While rummaging through my wardrobe in search of something to wear to the picnic, I came upon an idea that was pure genius. I had found the outfit that Madame Beauchamps made all of us girls wear for physical exercise classes at school. It consisted of a baggy pair of light blue pantaloons with elastic around the ankles and a tunic-style blouse with short, puffy sleeves and a sailor collar. It even had a navy blue sailor tie. I had tossed the exercise outfit into my trunk on a whim, and now I was glad that I had. Herman would be so scandalized to see a woman wearing bloomers that he would probably cancel the picnic as well as the courtship. Yes, my idea was ingenious. Ruth Schultz would have been proud of me.

When the time came the next day to button on my bloomers, I nearly lost my nerve. In truth, I felt naked without my usual layers of petticoats and skirts. I couldn't imagine all women everywhere throwing away their skirts and dressing in pants someday, in spite of the lady doctor's predictions. Fortunately, the Fourth of July had dawned cloudy and gloomy. I drew courage from the fact that we weren't likely to be viewing parades on public thoroughfares or picnicking in a city park in such weather.

In the end, the hideous prospect of becoming Mrs. Herman Beckett strengthened my resolve. I climbed into my bloomers and stood at my bedroom window to wait for Herman. For my plan to work, I needed to watch for his arrival and make a quick escape from the house. I couldn't let my grandmother see me dressed that way, or she would never let me out of the door.

As soon as Herman's carriage drew to a halt out front, I raced downstairs to make my escape—and nearly collided with my grandmother, who was in the foyer pinning on her hat.

"Violet Rose Hayes! What in the world. . . ?"

"Herman's here, I'm going to be late, bye," I said breathlessly.

"Wait a minute!" she said, snagging my arm. "Where are you going? You can't go outdoors that way! You aren't dressed!"

"Yes, I am. These are called bloomers." I twirled around in the hallway to demonstrate my freedom of movement. "All the girls at Madame Beauchamps' school were required to purchase a pair. And according to a very distinguished female doctor, it is much better for a woman's health to wear bloomers in place of a stifling corset."

"Where did you hear such a thing?"

"I heard the doctor speak at the Woman's Pavilion."

"Matilda!" I had never heard Grandmother raise her voice, let alone yell so loudly. "Come out here right now!"

Aunt Matt's bedroom door burst open. "What? What's the matter?" She had a look of startled fear in her eyes, as if the Great Fire had just been rekindled.

"Look what you've done!" Grandmother said, pointing to me. Someone knocked on the door.

"That's Herman Beckett," I said sweetly. I turned to open it, but Grandmother blocked my path.

"Oh no, you don't. I'll answer it. You go straight up those stairs, young lady, and put on some clothes."

"What's wrong with her clothes?" Aunt Matt asked. She had folded her arms across her chest, ready to do battle. "Those are called bloomers, Florence, in case you don't know. Many of our suffragettes are already wearing them. And I dare say that all women will wear them someday."

"They're indecent! She looks like she's in her undergarments."

"Don't be absurd. She's covered all the way to her ankles."

I heard Herman Beckett knock again, louder this time. Aunt Birdie glided into the hallway.

"Isn't someone going to answer the door?"

"In a minute, Birdie." Grandmother held out her arms to bar the way as if guarding against my escape.

"What's the difference between a baggy pair of bloomers and a long skirt?" Aunt Matt demanded.

"Well . . . well, for one thing," Grandmother stammered, "everyone can tell that Violet has a derriere! And legs!"

"Of course she has legs. And I'm sure people are just as aware of that fact when she's wearing a skirt."

"No, Matilda. Her backside is much more . . . more *apparent* . . . in bloomers."

"Violet, dear," Birdie asked, "why are you wearing your underwear?"

"See what I mean?" Grandmother asked. Herman knocked a third time.

"Someone better answer that," I told my grandmother.

"Go on, Violet," Aunt Matt said. "You go and have a nice time at your picnic. And good for you!" She applauded quietly.

"Matilda!"

I ducked beneath Grandmother's arm and opened the door. I had taken a daring step, but if Herman and his mother reacted the way my grandmother had, the courtship would be called off before noon.

Herman's eyes boggled when he saw me. He never had been overly talkative, but my bloomers turned him into a stone mute. I took his arm, chattering enough for both of us as we walked down the front steps to the waiting carriage. Misery Mary's husband, Ernest, would be driving us to Riverside. He caught himself staring at me, then carefully averted his eyes from my shocking costume, staring at my toes as Herman introduced us.

"Violet—Ernest. . . . Ernest—Violet," Herman said curtly.

"How do you do, Ernest? It's so nice to meet you. I'm so sorry

you were unable to join us for our day at the fair, but it's kind of you
to invite me to your holiday picnic."

"Um. Yes."

I climbed into the back of the carriage and sat cozily by Herman's
side as I continued my monologue.

"How have you been, Herman? Do you have the holiday off from
work? Too bad the weather is so gloomy. It's not a very nice day for
a picnic, is it? Do you think it will rain? How far is it to Riverside?
Will the ride take long?"

His mouth opened and closed in response to each of my questions, but nothing came out. His caterpillar brows had crawled halfway to his hairline in surprise and seemed to be trying to hide in his
hair. He slowly blinked after each of my questions, as if hoping he
would open his eyes and discover, to his great relief, that he had been
having a nightmare.

It seemed to take forever to ride the nine miles to Riverside. In
Herman's muted condition, our conversation resembled a one-
woman tennis match in which I was required to lob the ball over the
net, then run over to the opposite court to retrieve it. I reached our
destination verbally exhausted.

The Crane home was a sprawling, three-story residence with a
turret and a wide front porch adorned with wooden gingerbread. It
was in a lovely neighborhood of winding streets and stately homes
near the Des Plaines River. The grassy front yard would have made
a splendid spot for a picnic, but the damp day and misty rain would
drive us inside.

Our carriage pulled beneath a covered entryway on the side of
the house where Herman's mother and sister awaited our arrival. I
watched their faces transform as I stepped from the carriage. I had
seen expressions like theirs before in a crowd that had witnessed a
spectacular buggy crash in which horses and wagon wheels and
bloodied victims had become hopelessly entangled.

Mrs. Beckett stuttered incoherently in a brave effort to be polite.

Misery Mary couldn't seem to look at me, as if I had arrived stark-naked. Her two daughters, four-year-old Emily and six-year-old Priscilla, stared and stared and stared, their eyes frozen open, unblinking. I expected one of them to declare *"The Emperor has no clothes!"*

When I finally realized that Herman's family was too well mannered to comment on my attire, I took the first step. "What do you think of my bloomers? They're all the rage in Paris this season."

"My word . . ."

"According to all the fashion experts they are *de rigeuer* for leisure events such as boating or bicycling—and very appropriate for picnics." I held the material out to the sides as if I were about to curtsy, then twirled around like a ballerina to demonstrate my freedom of movement. The silent pause that followed was big enough to drive a streetcar through.

"They . . . they are . . . interesting," Mary managed to say. "If you'll excuse me, I'll fetch us something to drink."

"I'll help you," Herman's mother added. They scurried from the room, herding the two little girls ahead of them as if shielding them from an appalling sight. Herman led me into the front parlor, where we sat opposite one another on the overstuffed furniture.

"Your nieces are lovely girls. Too bad they couldn't have accompanied us to the exposition."

"Mary feared it would be too much excitement for them."

I nodded, trying not to giggle. The gigantic bell made from oranges might have kept them awake all night.

"Is there a parade today?" I asked.

"A small one. Riverside isn't a very large town."

"Oh, good. I do love parades." But when Mary returned with our beverages, she and Herman had a quick, whispered consultation.

"We've decided not to watch the parade after all," she told me. "The day is much too damp. It wouldn't be good for the girls. I would hate for them to catch a fever."

"Will we be picnicking in a park, perhaps?" I asked.

Mary shook her head vigorously. "No. Here at home. Inside."

They were embarrassed to be seen with me. Good. My plan was already working.

We ate our picnic lunch at precisely two o'clock, seated around the dining room table. With my future at stake, I made up my mind to ignore all of Madame Beauchamps' diligent instructions and do the opposite of everything I'd ever learned about table manners. I started eating before the hostess sat down. I didn't use my napkin, much less place it on my lap. I reached across the table for my food instead of asking someone to pass the serving dishes. I ate Mary's fried chicken with my fingers, when the proper way was with a knife and fork. I buttered the entire dinner roll instead of breaking it into small pieces. I slurped my iced tea. I didn't have quite enough nerve to belch when I'd finished eating, but I considered it.

Not one of the Becketts or Cranes uttered a word about my behavior. In fact, Herman's family was so quiet and reserved that I could hear the silverware scraping across the plates while we ate.

Afterward I joined Herman's mother outside on the front porch, determined to use all of my detective skills to learn the truth about her good friend Murderous Maude. I was quite certain that my courtship with Herman was about to end today, so this might be my very last chance to interrogate Mrs. Beckett.

"I understand that you and Mur—um . . . Maude O'Neill are good friends."

"Yes, she is such a sweet person. You'll love her."

I doubted that. I leaned closer, as if we were conspirators.

"Listen, I know the truth about her first husband," I bluffed. A detective in one of Ruth's novels had used this method with excellent results. He had pretended to know the truth, then waited for a response. If it worked, Mrs. Beckett would either say, "I don't know what you're talking about," or else confess that Maude had murdered him, believing that I already knew the truth. I waited, holding my breath. Mrs. Beckett glanced all around, as if expecting eavesdroppers.

"You know the truth?" she finally asked in a hushed voice.

"Yes. About his death." She stared at me, as if waiting for an explanation. "Mrs. O'Neill is marrying my father, after all. And of course I'm holding her secret in strictest confidence. But you must agree that I had a right to know everything since Maude is going to be my . . . s-stepmother." I almost choked on the word.

Mrs. Beckett nodded and glanced all around again. "Maude was very courageous throughout the ordeal."

"Of course."

"It happens more often than people know . . ." Her voice dropped to a whisper again. "Behind closed doors."

It happens often? Was she talking about women murdering their husbands? I stumbled to find an appropriate response.

"Y-yes. I-I'm sure that's . . . true."

"Your father was such an enormous help; bless his soul. I don't know how many times he traveled to Chicago to the Jolly Roger. He said he wanted to do it for his brother's sake."

The Jolly Roger? For his brother's sake? Was my uncle a pirate? Blast my secretive family!

"Y-you mean my father's brother, Philip?"

"Yes, I believe that was his name. Still, it was kind of your father to help Maude."

Yikes! My father had helped Maude?

Fortunately, my hours of practice at school holding an enigmatic smile in place kept my mouth from dropping open in horror and shock. How could my father do such a thing?

"Now that Lloyd O'Neill is gone, Maude's life has been blessedly peaceful," Herman's mother continued. "And it's good that the truth was never revealed. . . . For the children's sake," she added in a whisper.

Ah-ha! She practically had admitted it was murder!

"Much better to have it ruled an unfortunate accident," she said, "instead of . . . well, you know, Miss Hayes."

I nodded mutely, realizing that I faced a troublesome dilemma. How could I expose Maude as a murderer if my father had helped her?

Herman chose that opportune moment to join us on the porch. "Would you care for a game of croquet on the back lawn, Violet? It's no longer raining, as you can see, and the grass has dried out."

"That would be lovely," I said, struggling to regain my composure. "Would you excuse us, Mrs. Beckett?"

I was badly shaken by what I had learned, and I used my mallet to vent my emotions. I played cutthroat croquet. It was very unfeminine of me to be so competitive, but I was trying to absorb the fact that my father might be an accomplice to murder. At the same time, I had to be mindful of my plan to discourage Herman from courting me. I was prepared to swing from the trees and howl at the moon to accomplish that goal.

Herman played croquet very slowly and patiently, helping his two little nieces, who were playing with us. None of them was prepared for my ruthlessness. Priscilla pouted when I whacked her ball into the shrubbery, yards and yards from the nearest wicket. Emily ran into the house, crying, when I sent her ball rolling down the driveway. My bloomers gave me an amazing degree of freedom as I attacked my opponents' balls.

"Aren't you being a little hard on the children?" Herman asked. "After all, it's only a game."

"The world is a cutthroat place, Herman. I don't believe it is wise to raise one's children in a sheltered environment." I sent his ball bouncing behind the tool shed and won the game. Afterward, I decided to shock him further with one of my grisliest questions.

"If you could choose, Herman, would you rather perish in an appalling cataclysm such as a mine explosion or a train wreck and die amid twisted iron and tons of rock, listening to the screams of trapped and suffering humanity—or would you prefer to linger at home in your bed from a long, agonizing illness, your helpless body growing weaker, your every breath a painful gasp?"

"It's quite distasteful to discuss death, Violet."

"I know that. But it's a game, Herman. The point is to think about what you would do if faced with two impossible choices. So which would you choose?"

"I really don't know."

I sighed and gave up. Herman Beckett was never going to play. But with any luck, I had shocked him right out of my life today.

Later, under the cover of darkness, we ventured out to the public park to watch the fireworks. Most of the rockets had gotten damp and they fizzled dismally. I couldn't wait to return home. The day had seemed twenty-four years long, but when it finally ended, Herman stopped me on our front doorstep before bidding me good-night.

"Violet, there is something I need to say to you."

Here it comes. It's good-bye forever to stuffy Herman Beckett.

"I believe that you are the wife for me."

"W-what? But—"

"No, let me finish. I understand from your father that you have other suitors, but I want you to know that I intend to continue my courtship in all earnestness and sincerity once you return to Lockport, with the hope of winning you. I wanted you to get a glimpse today of the simple contentment we could share if you married me."

I almost blurted *"You still want me—in bloomers?"* But I didn't. His speech reminded me of my Uncle Gilbert's touching pursuit of Aunt Birdie, except that Herman hadn't mentioned love.

"To be honest, Violet, I have worried in the past that you were out of my reach. You attended such a fancy school, where you learned proper manners and how to speak French and all the rest. My mother didn't think you could be content with an ordinary family like ours. But today I saw a different side of you. You aren't pretentious or high-class at all. Now I'm more certain than ever that we could be happy together."

"Your mother approves of me?"

"She thinks you're vivacious. She said you would be a good balance for me in that regard. And I must say I believe she is right. You're an unusual woman, Violet. I find you . . . *exciting!*" His eyes met mine, and even in the dark I could see an uncharacteristic gleam in them. "The way you whacked those croquet balls! My word! And you looked so attractive in those . . . in your . . . in that attire!"

Now I was the one who was mute. My plan had backfired! Why hadn't these stupid bloomers come with a warning? *Caution: Stodgy men may find this garment attractive. Bloomers have been known to precipitate a proposal of marriage!*

"You don't need to answer me tonight, Violet. I know that you'll be coming home in less than two weeks' time. It will seem like an eternity to me, but I'll wait. Until then . . ." He gripped both of my hands in his and gave them a determined squeeze. "Good night."

Good grief!

I fled up the steps and into the house. Grandmother met me in the foyer as if she had been standing there since I'd left. She heaved a weighty sigh.

"Violet Rose. I have been sick at heart all day, just knowing that you've been running around in public dressed that way."

"I'm sorry. I didn't mean to upset you—"

"Believe me, if I had been strong enough to bar your way I would have. Your father—"

"My father wants me to marry Herman Beckett, and I don't want to. Wearing bloomers was part of my plan to discourage him—but it backfired! It seems I've enflamed his passions. He thinks I'm exciting."

"I shouldn't wonder. You could awaken a dead man in that outfit with your backside so . . . so . . . prominent. If your father hears that

I allowed you out of this house in bloomers, he'll never speak to me again."

"I'll tell him it wasn't your fault. You tried to stop me, but—"

"Oh, Violet! Thank goodness you're home!" She pulled me into her arms for a fervent hug. I hugged her in return.

"Do you think there is really such a thing as true love?" I asked.

She drew back to gaze at me. She seemed taken aback by my question. "Of course there is."

"Do you know anyone besides Aunt Birdie who has ever found it?"

She closed her eyes and exhaled. "You are more than I can handle, Violet Rose. No wonder your father wants to see you safely married."

Chapter

25

Wednesday, July 5, 1893

W hen a deliveryman brought a dozen red roses to our door the next morning, I feared they were from Herman. Why hadn't Madame Beauchamps ever taught us that bloomers unlocked the door to romance? I would at least have expected *True Romance Stories* to have mentioned it. I tore open the attached card with dread.

> *Roses for my Violet—*
> *Will you attend a gala dinner with me at the fairgrounds tonight? I promise to woo you with a romantic gondola ride in the moonlight.*
>
> > *Yours,*
> > *Nelson*

I sighed with relief.

"From your beau?" Aunt Birdie asked. I could only nod. I felt as though I had stepped onto the pages of one of Ruth's romance novels. A proposal of marriage one day, roses and moonlit boat rides the next.

"Gilbert charmed his way into my heart with flowers too," Aunt Birdie said.

"Nelson Kent is going to take me on a gondola ride in the moonlight," I said, showing her the card.

"Oh, how nice. Will you be going out in your underwear again?"

My smile vanished. "No. That turned out to be a huge mistake."

"Well, then. That says it all, doesn't it?"

As I carried the flowers into the kitchen to look for a vase, I suddenly remembered Katya and the impassioned kiss I had witnessed. How could he kiss her that way, then turn around and woo me? Nelson Kent obviously was deceiving one of us. I had the sinking feeling that it was me.

Nevertheless, the roses were beautiful. I bent to inhale their rich, velvety scent, and the aroma brought another memory to mind. My mother had smelled like roses. I closed my eyes and inhaled again, remembering how she would give me her handkerchief, sweetened with her scent, to sleep with at night.

Where was she? How could I find her? If only there was something I could do instead of waiting for Silas McClure and his unsavory friends to locate her.

I debated all day whether or not I should accompany Nelson to the gala dinner. In the end I decided to go. But I made up my mind to learn the truth about Katya before I allowed him to pursue me any further.

Nelson and I sailed to the fair by steamship once again. It was crowded with all of the regular members of his social circle, including his grandmother and my Aunt Agnes. I saw the two ladies whispering like thieves as Nelson and I stood side by side at the ship's rail, gazing at the distant silhouette of Chicago. Tonight the harbor resembled an overstuffed pincushion with dozens of ships' masts poking into the sky. They brought to mind the intriguing clue that Herman's mother had let slip yesterday: *My father traveled to Chicago . . . to the Jolly Roger . . . for his brother's sake.*

"Have you ever heard of a ship named the *Jolly Roger?*" I asked Nelson.

"Is this one of your amusing questions?" he asked, smiling. "I think we already discussed the fact that I'd rather be the captain of a warship than a pirate ship, didn't we?"

"No, I'm serious. Someone mentioned that my father used to come to Chicago to the Jolly Roger. I thought it sounded like a pirate ship."

"Or a saloon. There aren't many pirate ships in Chicago these days, but there are plenty of saloons—" He must have noticed the surprise on my face because he quickly added, "But I'm sure your father wouldn't frequent a saloon. Perhaps it's a restaurant?"

Little did Nelson know that my father had indeed frequented saloons when he'd worked with Mr. Moody's Yokefellows. Maybe I had found another important piece of the puzzle.

"How would one go about finding an establishment by that name?" I asked.

"I don't know. I'm sure the city must keep records of all the businesses and so forth. Maybe in the city administration building?"

I gazed into the distance, trying to add up all the clues—and trying not to think about the fact that my mild-mannered father may have been an accomplice to murder. Nelson took my chin in his fingers and turned my head to face him.

"You're a million miles away, sweet Violet."

"I'm sorry."

"I'm trying to romance you. Aren't you the lady who craves romance?"

"Yes, I know. And I forgot to thank you for the flowers. They were beautiful, Nelson."

"I sent them to remind you of the first day we met. Remember our stroll through my grandmother's flower garden?"

"Of course. How could I forget?"

What game was he playing, making sweet talk and gazing into my eyes? I needed to find out if he was still in love with Katya before I succumbed to his considerable charms. Though she no longer worked for the Kents, it didn't mean that Nelson no longer loved her. Maybe he had hidden her away somewhere as his mistress, like my Uncle Henry hid his mistresses. I had to figure out a way to bring Katya into our conversation.

"I remember our first meeting very well," I said. "Your grandmother sent that beautiful young serving girl to fetch you, and I had no idea what to expect or what you would look like. I was very pleasantly surprised, by the way, when I met you." I smiled flirtatiously.

Nelson glowed at my compliment. "I was surprised too."

"I also recall how lovely that little serving girl was. What was her name? . . . Katy? . . . No, it was foreign sounding . . . Katya! That was it. Katya always serves the tea when I come to visit with my Aunt Agnes, and I love watching her. Such natural grace and poise. But come to think of it, I didn't see her the last time I called. Some clumsy oaf of a girl served us instead. She dripped tea all over my shoes."

"I'll have her fired."

"No, don't do that. Just make sure Katya serves us the next time."

His smile vanished. "She no longer works for us." I found it very revealing that Nelson knew exactly who I was talking about. And that she was gone.

"What happened to her?"

"Servants come and go all the time, Violet." He waved as if dismissing the topic, but his cool, blasé facade had slipped from its usual place. "It's the housekeeper's job to keep track of them, not mine."

So Katya really was gone. Maybe the affair between them had fizzled. Maybe that was why he had decided to pursue me in earnest.

We arrived at the fair and rode the moving sidewalk once again to the Peristyle. I fell into step with all of the other partygoers when I got off, but Nelson drew me to a halt.

"Wait. You need to stop and look at this magnificent view. Can you even imagine a more perfect spot for romance?" Once again, sparkling lights lit up the lagoon and water splashed from the fountains. Electric lights twinkled from the whitewashed pavilions and reflected off the water like diamonds.

"I feel like a princess in a fairy tale," I murmured.

"And it's just the beginning."

We dined on quail and truffles in the garden restaurant on the rooftop of the Woman's Pavilion. Our hosts had rented the entire dining room, along with a thirty-piece orchestra so we could dance afterward. The scent of flowers filled the air and stars shone in the night sky as I waltzed in Nelson's arms. The evening was designed to make any woman fall in love.

"Do you have any idea how fortunate you are?" Aunt Agnes whispered when Nelson left to replenish my punch cup. "There isn't a woman in this city who wouldn't give her right arm to marry a young man like him."

"Yes. I know." But I wasn't in love.

The moon had risen above the horizon when Nelson took me for a gondola ride on the lagoon. Colored searchlights and fireworks blazed above our heads as we glided gently across the water. Nelson pulled me close on the seat beside him.

"A beautiful night . . . for a beautiful woman," he murmured. "Who could ask for more?"

He bent his face toward mine, and I was certain he was going to kiss me. Instead, he pressed his warm cheek against mine and said, "If you marry me, you can have this life from now on."

I pulled away and looked up at him in surprise. "Are you proposing?"

"Isn't this the most romantic place in all of Chicago for a marriage proposal? Must I do something more? I was certain you told me that romance was the way to win your heart."

"It is, but . . . it's just that we haven't known each other very long."

"That's what engagements are for. Listen, I understand that your father is coming back to Chicago for you soon, and I plan to ask him for your hand to make it official. We can be engaged for as long as you like—but I hope it isn't for too long. I'm dying to kiss you, Violet."

I couldn't seem to reply. But I wasn't considering his proposal; I was analyzing my symptoms. My pulse seemed disappointingly normal, my palms were dry, I could draw great, hearty breaths, and I didn't feel the least bit shivery or feverish. A handsome, charming, wealthy man had just proposed to me and . . . nothing! Even with my corset tightly laced! Maybe there was something wrong with me.

"I'll give you anything your heart desires," Nelson said. "Beautiful gowns, jewels, the finest home, dozens of servants . . ."

Servants. Katya suddenly materialized in the boat with us. Nelson hadn't hesitated to kiss her before their engagement. If I hadn't spied on them that night, I might be accepting his proposal this very minute.

"And I promise to give you independence as well," he said.

"Independence? What do you mean?"

"What you do with your free time will be entirely up to you, Violet. For instance, Potter Palmer's wife is the director of the Woman's Pavilion. Mrs. McCormick works for several charities. You could do whatever you wish."

"Suppose I decided to march with the women's suffrage movement—in bloomers?"

"Well . . ." His smile wavered slightly before returning to its place. "As long as you don't disgrace me by getting arrested, I suppose that would be okay."

He hadn't declared his love. Should I ask him if he loved me? Would I believe him if he said that he did? He had dismissed love as unnecessary when I'd mentioned it before. But if he didn't love me, why was he working so hard to woo me? Was it for money and a position in his father's business?

I shook myself. What was wrong with me that I was questioning Nelson's motives? The heroine of every romance novel I'd ever read would have gladly lived happily ever after with someone like him—especially if he wooed her with roses and moonlit gondola rides.

Our gondolier returned us to the dock, and Nelson and I returned to the party. I wondered if he'd noticed that I hadn't answered his proposal.

He waited on my every whim, charmed me with his wit, and held me close as we waltzed to the glorious music. I saw his grandmother and Aunt Agnes watching us, smiling in approval.

"My friends and I are going to the private casino again tonight," he said when it was time for us to leave. "I'm hoping you'll come with me and be my good luck charm again."

"I-I'd rather not. I really don't like gambling, and besides, I got terribly carried away the last time." I continued walking as we came out of the pavilion, following my aunt and all of the others as we headed toward the pier.

"Please?" he begged. "I'm not ready to call it a night yet."

"It scares me to think that you could lose all your money."

"But I'll win if you're with me. Please stay."

I shook my head. "I don't want to spoil your evening, Nelson, but I would like to go home. Why don't you go with your friends, and I'll ride home with my aunt Agnes?"

"You won't feel like I'm deserting you?"

"Not at all. It was a wonderfully romantic evening. I'll remember it for the rest of my life. Thank you so much." I stood on tiptoe and quickly kissed his cheek. "Good night."

The kiss was a test, of sorts. I had hoped that my heart would send off a few fireworks, but nothing happened. Nor did anything happen when Nelson lifted my fingers to his lips and kissed them.

"Good night, my beautiful Violet."

I followed the others to the pier and boarded the steamship back to the city. Aunt Agnes pulled me into a quiet corner and sat me down as soon as we left the dock.

"My stars, Violet, why did you leave Nelson? Did something go wrong between you two? It looked like things were going so well."

"They were . . . I mean, they are going well. Nelson asked me to marry him."

"That's wonderful! So why are you sitting here with the face of doom, twisting your gloves into a knot?"

I dropped my gloves onto my lap and sighed. "I don't know . . ."

"You didn't refuse him, did you?"

"No . . ."

"Well!" She exhaled. "Thank goodness for good sense! Do you want to tell me what's wrong, then?"

"Nelson never said that he loved me. I know you don't think love matters, but I-I want to fall in love. And I want to be loved."

"And you're too impatient to wait for it to grow?" She caressed my cheek with her sparkly fingers.

"What if it doesn't, Aunt Agnes?"

"Listen, it's probably no secret that Henry and I weren't in love when we married. But over time, living together, raising our sons, our love grew to become very deep."

"It did?" I remembered my uncle's mistresses. "How long did it take? And when did you know?"

"I found out on the night of the Great Fire," she said matter-of-factly. "Sometimes it takes a tragedy such as that one to make us realize how we really feel about someone."

I immediately thought of my parents, falling in love during the fire. I wanted to hear everything that Aunt Agnes knew about that night. I perched on the edge of my chair and leaned toward her.

"Were you living here in the city during the fire?"

She nodded. "Henry and I had a Terrace Row townhouse, right on Michigan Avenue and Congress Streets. Michigan Avenue used to be on the lakefront, you know, but after the fire they dumped all of the rubble into the lake and created Grant Park and a new shoreline. But anyway, that's where we lived."

"Grandmother said that my parents met that night."

"She would know more about that than I would. Henry and I were sound asleep when our son Michael woke us up at around two o'clock in the morning. He was the only one of our children still living at home at the time.

"'I think the city is on fire,' he said. 'You'd better get dressed.'

"All the alarm bells were ringing, and the great courthouse bell was tolling like it was doomsday. Henry opened the bedroom curtains, and the sky to the southwest of us was an eerie shade of orange. It made the lake across the street glow like molten lava. The wind howled around the eaves like a hurricane and rattled the panes. I thought I had awakened in hell itself.

"Henry decided to go out and see where the fire was and in which direction it was spreading. He had important papers and ledgers and things that needed to be rescued if the fire was spreading toward his downtown office. He told me not to worry, but I got dressed and proceeded to pack, just in case.

"It's so hard to choose which things are important and which ones aren't when it comes to fleeing for your life. I didn't really believe that the fire would spread all the way to the lake. It seemed to be across the river. But I decided to take precautions.

"Henry was gone for a very long time. He came back with a cartload of documents and descriptions of the inconceivable damage he'd seen—the courthouse was burning, as was the main post office and several grand hotels, including one that Henry owned. The fire seemed to be spreading out of control, heading toward his office building and all of the others on LaSalle Street. I couldn't imagine it. But I could see how badly shaken Henry was. He described the panic in the streets, all the frightened people running in every direction, carrying their belongings—the silliest and saddest things: an oil painting, a birdcage, a chair. Others dragged screaming children by the hand as burning cinders rained down from the sky. I asked Henry if we needed to evacuate.

"'No,' he assured me, 'the fire seems to be heading in the other direction for now. I believe you'll be safe here.' But he took Michael and they went back to retrieve more things from his office.

"The servants and I continued to pack everything of value, and we piled it all in the foyer. Every time I looked out the window, the sky seemed brighter with flames. I could hear the wind howling and whipping ashes and cinders against the panes as if we were in a sandstorm.

"Hours passed. I became sick with worry for Henry and Michael's safety. I could see that the fire was moving closer and closer, and I feared we would soon lose our home. I decided to haul our belongings out of the house and across the little parkway that was on the other side of Michigan Avenue to the beach. Our neighbors were all doing the same thing. It proved extremely difficult. All manner of vehicles and panic-stricken people jammed the avenue, trying to escape the flames.

"The servants helped me save a great deal of our furnishings and household goods and valuables. We rescued most of Henry's books. Our eyes burned and watered and stung from the smoke, and our faces turned black with soot.

"Believe it or not, there were unscrupulous men who took advantage of the disaster to help themselves to our personal effects through the open door. One neighbor had an entire wagon full of his salvaged goods driven away by a stranger, never to be seen again. I found a thief in Henry's dressing room, helping himself to his clothing and cigars. He laughed at my outrage and said, 'Go ahead and holler for the police, lady.'

"We continued to work, trying to empty the house, while fear for my husband and son grew with every passing hour. The approaching flames seemed to ride through the sky in the clouds. It would have been beautiful if it hadn't been so horrifying. And the noise! I could hear rumblings and explosions as buildings crumbled in the distance. And always, the roar of the flames and the sound of screaming.

"When the heat became too strong and we'd carried the last load that we dared to the beach, I sat down on my pile of belongings and watched my home burn. The flames leaped to the roof, then spread down through the interior, hollowing it out and devouring everything inside until only a blackened shell remained. Everyone on the beach was weeping, but I felt little sorrow for my home compared to the terror I felt for Henry and our son. They had been away for too long. I wept for them, not our home.

"That was when I knew how very deeply I loved Henry—when I was faced with the prospect of losing him. We weren't in love when we married, of course. But we'd lived together all those years, raised our family, built a life with one another—and I couldn't bear the thought of living without him.

"Meanwhile, Henry and Michael had been forced to take a wild, circuitous route back home in order to avoid the flames and the mobs of fleeing people. One of the drawbridges they'd tried to cross had to be raised just as they reached it in order to allow several ships to get out of harm's way. Henry walked for miles and miles and made it home in time to see the rear wall of our townhouse topple to the ground. He had been terrified for my safety as well and had been trying desperately to escape the fire's relentless path and return home for me. All the while, he'd had to fight the current of humanity fleeing in the opposite direction.

"When we were finally reunited, we stood on the lakeshore clinging to one another for a very long time. Henry's face was black and tear streaked, his clothing stank of smoke, his entire body trembled from all of the horrors he'd witnessed. But he held me tightly and whispered, 'I love you, Agnes.'"

My aunt Agnes paused as her voice choked. She wiped away the tears that had rolled down her cheeks. Her story had moved me deeply, and I couldn't speak. I took her hand in mine.

"Henry and I lost our home, several other properties, and his brand-new office building. But we had each other, and that was all that mattered.

"Love will grow, Violet. It comes from mutual respect and from building a life together, one day at a time. Romance is fine when you're young, but you can't always trust the emotions that seem so strong in the beginning. Those feelings often fade, and you wake up one morning to find you have nothing in common with each other. Marriage is about maturity and creating a future together. It's not about romance."

I nodded, thinking about my parents.

"Yes, Henry's family was wealthy when I married him. But I helped him prosper and gain stature in Chicago. I played hostess for his business and social contacts. I volunteered in countless charitable causes to help build his good name. We are Mr. and Mrs. Henry Paine, and that's so much more important than fleeting feelings of romance."

She met my gaze for a long moment; then her voice grew very soft. "I know that Henry loves me. His dalliances don't mean anything, Violet. They allow him to believe that he is still young and indestructible. I'm the one who shares his name and his home—and his life."

I nodded, too moved by her confession to speak.

"Nelson Kent is a fine young man from a lovely family. In many ways, he is still young and unformed. You could be the woman behind the man. With your grace and intelligence and wit, you could help him make a name for himself and find his rightful place in this city. Every man needs a good woman to believe in him. And in time, love and affection will follow."

I thought of Nelson's passion for new inventions. I could encourage him, cheer him on, and be his source of inspiration. As my aunt had said, Nelson could make a name for himself and find his place in life.

But what about my name and my place? I would no longer be known as Violet but as Mrs. Nelson Kent. If I joined my life to his, would I find myself—or become swallowed up in him and lost?

I still wasn't sure if I wanted to accept Nelson's proposal. But if my father forced me to choose, I would rather marry Nelson Kent than Herman Beckett.

Chapter

26

Thursday, July 6, 1893

Only three days had passed since Silas McClure had offered to help me find my mother, but it seemed like three weeks. As my father's deadline neared, I thought I understood how Aunt Agnes had felt on the night of the Great Fire, watching disaster creep closer and closer and being helpless to stop it. It should have been a relief to know that I had an alternative to marrying Herman Beckett, but it wasn't. I didn't love Nelson Kent, and the idea of marrying him for his money made me feel very shallow, even if I believed that love would grow over time.

I had to do something. It was already Thursday morning. Since my efforts to find my mother had reached a dead end, I would renew my efforts to stop Father's wedding. I needed to learn the truth about Mr. O'Neill's death, and that meant following the clue that Herman's mother had given me: the Jolly Roger.

I waited until my grandmother and Aunt Matt were both gone,

then I approached Aunt Birdie, who was rubbing furniture polish onto our dining room table.

"Would you like to take a little trip downtown with me?" I gently took the polishing cloth from her and handed Birdie her straw hat.

"All right. Where shall we go? To the theater?"

"Well . . . maybe another day. I need to visit the city administration building today."

Nelson Kent thought that I might be able to locate the Jolly Roger by asking for information there. I had no idea where that building was, but I had graduated from charm school—it was my only natural resource—so I would spread my charm liberally until I found the place. I towed Aunt Birdie to the streetcar stop on the corner and boarded the first car that arrived. I greeted the driver in my sweetly charming voice.

"Good morning, I wonder if you could help me? Do you know where the city administration building is?"

"Not exactly, miss. But if I were you, I'd get off downtown at State or LaSalle or maybe Michigan Avenue. From there, I'm sure you can find a patrolman to help you."

It sounded like a good plan. But Aunt Birdie and I wandered up and down LaSalle for quite a while before locating a patrolman. When we tried to follow his directions, we got lost and had to consult a second patrolman. He sent us in the wrong direction entirely. But the third patrolman was very young and obliging; he walked us right to the door of the administration building.

"Good luck to you, Miss." He held open the door for us and tipped his hat.

By that time Aunt Birdie was so weary she seemed to be dragging a ball and chain from each ankle. I felt guilty for using her this way, but I couldn't run around alone in the city. We wandered through the building, asking for information, and eventually found the department of records. I had learned my lesson after trying to pry information from my mother's lawyer. I would have to use deceit if I wanted to get anywhere in the detective business.

An apathetic-looking clerk with a handlebar mustache met us at the information counter. His eyelids drooped at half-mast as if I'd awakened him from a long nap. Even my dazzling smile didn't seem to move him.

"May I help you?" he asked wearily.

"Yes. I plan to open a restaurant—"

"Oh, how nice!" Aunt Birdie interrupted. "I didn't even know you could cook, Violet."

I patted her hand and continued. "I was told that I could come here to learn if another business is already in possession of the name I've chosen."

His bored expression remained firmly in place. "What is the name?"

"The Jolly Roger."

His drooping eyelids narrowed in suspicion, as if I were playing a prank. "The Jolly Roger?"

I nodded.

"That says it all, doesn't it?" Aunt Birdie asked.

The clerk eyed the two of us as if we had recently escaped from an asylum. "One moment."

"What a lovely surprise," Aunt Birdie said as the clerk trudged away. "A restaurant! I had no idea you possessed culinary aspirations. And to think I knew you when."

The man returned with a large ledger book and set it on the counter between us while he paged through the alphabetical entries. He either was paid by the hour or he was quite unfamiliar with the alphabet, because his search took a very long time.

"You're out of luck, miss," he finally grunted. "There's already an establishment named the Jolly Roger."

"Oh, dear. I'm so disappointed," I said, masking my excitement. "How do they spell it? Perhaps if I varied the name a bit . . ." He turned the ledger around so I could read it. I not only saw the address on Bishop Street but the name of the proprietor as well: Lloyd O'Neill. My mouth dropped open in surprise. He was Murderous Maude's first husband!

I was so shocked that I took Aunt Birdie's arm and left the office without thanking the clerk. I wanted to hail a cab and go to the Jolly Roger right away, but I had no idea where Bishop Street was or how to get there. What if it was in a disreputable part of town?

I was looking all around for the helpful young patrolman when Aunt Birdie said, "Can we go home, dear? I must make lunch for Florence, and besides, my bunions are killing me."

"My grandmother is coming home for lunch? I thought she was going to be gone all day."

"No, she and Matt said they both would be home by lunchtime."

"Then I guess we'd better go." I didn't want my grandmother to know that I had been out searching for my mother.

I felt as though I had the ball and chain on my ankle as I dragged Aunt Birdie home. Once again I was bitterly disappointed, but at least I had made some progress in my search. I not only knew where the Jolly Roger was located, but I'd discovered a connection to Murderous Maude.

We arrived home the same time as my Aunt Matt. "Where have you two been?" she asked.

I answered before Aunt Birdie could. "I had an errand to run, and I thought Aunt Birdie could use some fresh air. Exercise is good for women, you know."

"Well, I came home to see if you wanted to accompany me this afternoon. We're marching on a factory in the garment district."

Marching on a factory? I had no idea what she was talking about and no desire at all to find out. But Aunt Matt knew her way around the city pretty well. She probably could tell me where Bishop Street was and therefore the Jolly Roger. At the very least, I could ask her about my mysterious Uncle Philip.

"I would love to go with you. How does one march on a factory?"

"Let's have lunch first, and I'll explain on the way there."

"We should let Violet prepare lunch," Aunt Birdie said. "She's opening a restaurant." Fortunately for me, Birdie's sisters were in the habit of ignoring most of the things she said.

"By the way, Aunt Matt," I said as we sat in the kitchen, "I never thanked you for supporting my decision to wear bloomers the other day."

"You're welcome. You looked ridiculous in them, but it was the principle that mattered."

"Oh. Well, thanks anyway."

Having heard the word "march," I chose the largest, widest-brimmed hat that I owned, hoping to hide beneath it. As usual, Aunt Matt's thundering lecture began as soon as we boarded the crowded streetcar.

"This has been a landmark year for legislation that protects women and children," she began. "Our lawmakers down in Springfield just passed the Illinois Factory Act. It bans labor for all children under the age of fourteen and regulates work for children between the ages of fourteen and sixteen. The law also forbids garment-making in the tenements. Work must be done in a factory with certain safety guidelines in place. And the law states that women and minors can't be made to work more than eight hours a day. In other words, factory owners will no longer be allowed to exploit women and children in order to boost their profits."

"That sounds like a very good law."

"It is indeed. Some of us have lobbied very hard to get it passed. Unfortunately, there are factory owners who simply ignore it. We've been gathering the names and locations of the most offensive places so that we can stage demonstrations and read them the law."

"That sounds . . . confrontational."

"It is."

I suddenly felt very reckless and brave. My father might force me to move back to Lockport and settle down next week, but at least I would have an adventurous story to tell my children at bedtime.

Aunt Matt and I rode a very long way and changed streetcars three times before meeting up with the other women who were marching with us. Quite a mob of us showed up. The neighborhood near the river where we gathered stank of fish. It was every bit as ugly and unpleasant as the area near the settlement house, but since none of the other women covered their noses, I decided not to cover mine. I hoped that the women we'd come to rescue appreciated our sacrifice.

No one carried signs this time, so I had nothing to hide behind except my floppy hat. I decided that it didn't matter. I felt proud to be making a difference in the world. We lined up in the middle of the street a few blocks from the factory and began to march toward it. Several women had brought pots and pans, which they banged together as we chanted, "Unfair to women and children! Unfair to women and children!"

People came out of saloons and tenements to see what was going on. Pedestrians turned to watch. Little children skipped alongside of us. As we neared the river, dockworkers stopped loading their ships to stare. One group of men pointed and laughed and called us unrepeatable names.

"Get out of the road!" an ice vendor yelled. "My ice is melting!" He and several other deliverymen grew irate because our march blocked the street. It was such fun. I wished Ruth Schultz were with me.

"If all of these factories are breaking the law," I asked Aunt Matt, "shouldn't the police be raiding them instead of us?"

"Of course they should. But the police have been known to take a bribe to look the other way instead of enforcing the law. Or else they plead ignorance. In the end, it's usually up to women like us to protect other women and children."

The door to the low-slung brick factory stood open on this sweltering July day, and we poured inside as if storming a castle. The interior was so dark and dingy that I could hardly see where I was going at first. The dusty, lint-filled air made me sneeze. I heard the clatter of hundreds of sewing machines before I saw them—row after row of them, stretching into the dim workshop, with a woman bent over each one, sewing as if in a race against time.

As my eyes grew accustomed to the light, I realized that most of the seamstresses were teenaged girls, younger than I was. Each had a towering pile of clothing pieces by her side, waiting to be stitched. Small children scurried around between the rows, carrying more bundles of cloth. The workers glanced up when we entered, then quickly resumed sewing. A man I assumed to be the factory manager hurried over to us.

"Hey, now, see here! What's going on? You're trespassing on private property!" The woman who had led our march launched into a heated debate with him, enumerating the details of the new Illinois Factory Act.

Meanwhile, the other women in our group quickly fanned out in every direction, weaving up and down the rows, informing the workers of their rights. I followed my Aunt Matt.

"A new law has been passed, and this factory is violating it," she announced in her commanding voice. "You no longer have to work more than eight hours a day. You have the right to refuse to work longer. The owner must provide safe working conditions." And so on.

Three men, who I assumed were foremen, started running up and down the aisles trying to round up the marauding marchers like so many stray cats.

"You're trespassing! Get off our property."

"Go ahead and summon the police," Aunt Matt told one of them. "They'll arrest you for being in violation of the Illinois Factory Act."

It turned into quite a circus. In fact, it would have been comical if it hadn't been so exhilarating. Through it all, the teenaged girls kept right on sewing as if their lives depended on it. Maybe they did.

Eventually, everyone grew tired of the chase. Aunt Matt and I marched from the factory with the other women, cheering in victory. Sweat rolled down Matt's stern, flushed face as I fell into step beside her. Then I remembered my grandmother's friend Irina.

"Um . . . Aunt Matt? What about all the women with little children who work at home? How will they make a living from now on if it's against the law to work in the tenements?"

"Those women are being taken advantage of at the moment, and they don't even know it." We were parading back down the street in triumph, and Aunt Matt and I had to shout in order to be heard above the sound of cheering and banging pots. "The point of the law is to make factory owners hire those women to work decent hours for a fair wage in a safe environment, instead of paying them mere pennies for hours and hours of labor at home. Children shouldn't be working at all. If women ran the world, all of the children would be in school where they belong. Education is the only way that the working poor will ever get ahead in this world. If factories paid their mothers a fair wage, indigent children could attend school."

"When I visited the tenements with my grandmother, it seemed like there were thousands of children—most of them working. And the women seemed little better than slaves."

"I know. And it's very difficult to change the status quo, especially if you're a woman. Without the right to vote, women in our society are powerless. They are forced to work for slave wages in poor working conditions, or else get married and have too many children. The prettier women can make money in bawdy houses, I suppose. Mind you, I don't condemn women who make that choice. But I would like to give them a better alternative."

"Thank you for taking me today," I said when we reached our first streetcar stop. "I found it very invigorating to do something worthwhile."

"We'll be marching to other factories in the coming weeks if you want to join me again."

"I'd love to—but I'll only be in Chicago for another week, remember? My father is taking me home. And I don't want to go."

We sat on the streetcar in companionable silence, heading toward home again. The more I thought about returning to Lockport without finding my mother, the more anxious I became.

"Aunt Matt, will you talk to my father? Will you help me convince him to let me stay?"

"I would be happy to, but I'm sorry to say that he's not likely to listen to me. He thinks I'm a bad influence on you."

"No, you've been a wonderful influence, Aunt Matt. I've learned so much from you." I waited until we'd disembarked from the first car and boarded the second before saying, "I've had two marriage proposals this week. One from Nelson Kent and one from Herman Beckett."

"You don't sound very pleased."

"I'm not in love with either of them. But Father wants me to get married, and I'm afraid that if I don't choose one of them he'll decide for me."

Aunt Matt's fists seemed to clench a little tighter. "Someday fathers won't have that kind of power over their daughters."

"I wish 'someday' would come soon. . . . Can I tell you a secret, Aunt Matt? The truth is that I came to Chicago to find my mother. Father told me she was ill all these years, and when I finally learned that she wasn't, I decided to find her and ask her if I could live with her. I've been trying to learn more about my parents and their past, and one of the clues I discovered is this address." I pulled the paper from my pocket and showed it to her. "Do you know where Bishop Street is? Would you be willing to take me there?"

"If it's where I think it is, it's out of the question. That's not a very nice part of town, Violet." She handed the paper back to me and said, "What makes you think your mother is at this address?"

"I don't know whether she is or not, but someone told me that my father used to go there. It's connected with Uncle Philip, somehow.

And Aunt Birdie said that Philip knew my mother."

"You've lost me, Violet."

"I didn't even know I had an Uncle Philip until Aunt Birdie showed me his picture a few days ago. Why doesn't anyone ever talk about him?"

"It's Florence's place to tell you about Philip, not mine."

"But I want to know—"

"I won't talk about him, Violet. But I will tell you that Birdie imagines things. Philip has nothing to do with finding your mother."

I groaned in frustration. "Don't you understand? If I don't solve this mystery I'll have to choose a husband."

"I honestly don't believe that your father would force you to marry against your will. You don't have to marry at all, you know."

"I know. But I want to find out what it's like to fall in love, and to be kissed. No one has ever kissed me, Aunt Matt, and it looks so . . . so wonderful." I drew a breath for courage and decided to take a chance. "Aunt Birdie also told me that you were engaged once. Do you mind if I ask why you broke it off?"

Aunt Matt was quiet for so long that I was afraid I had offended her—or else hurt her feelings. According to Birdie, Aunt Matt had loved her beau deeply.

"I didn't marry Robert," she finally said, "because he didn't love me." She was speaking very quietly for once. "When he asked me to marry him, he had ulterior motives."

I waited for her to say more, but she didn't. After we'd boarded the last streetcar, I decided to probe again.

"Aunt Birdie said that your beau turned out to be a thief." I hadn't thought about Silas McClure all morning, but he suddenly sprang to life in my mind with his bright, candelabra grin.

"A thief?" Matt repeated. "I'm not sure what she meant."

"Well, what did happen to him?"

"My sister Agnes threw an engagement party for us," she said with a sigh. "Everything was going well until Robert and a friend went outside to smoke cigars. They were gone for quite a while, so I went outside to find him. That's when I accidentally overheard him talking." Aunt Matt was usually so stern and abrupt, but now her voice grew soft with emotion.

"I heard him saying unkind things about . . . about my physical appearance. He and his friend were laughing at me because . . . because I had been foolish enough to fall in love with him. He told his friend that he didn't love me. He had been lying to me when he'd said that he did. I don't think he even liked me. His friend asked Robert why he'd proposed to me, and he said it was because my father was going to die soon, and I would inherit the house and all of Father's estate. By law, a woman's inheritance transferred to her husband the moment they were married."

I didn't know what to say. No wonder Aunt Matt distrusted men. "Aunt Birdie was right when she called him a thief," I finally murmured.

"Yes. I suppose she was." Her voice quavered with emotion— even after all these years.

I was no longer sure that I wanted to fall in love if it hurt this much. Aunt Birdie was still devastated after losing Gilbert. My father had become emotional when he'd talked about my mother. And now I'd learned that Aunt Matt still felt the pain of rejection after all these years. Romance novels never warned about this side of love—the not-so-happily-ever-after part.

"Now, Violet," she said, clearing her throat. "I don't want to sound critical, but is what Robert Tucker planned to do so different from what Agnes did, marrying Henry Paine for money and social privilege? Would it be so very different from your choosing a husband you didn't love for no other reason than because he's wealthy?"

Ouch!

"But . . . but there are a lot of women like me who have no way of supporting ourselves. We have to marry a man who can support us."

"He doesn't have to be wealthy, does he? Any decent, honest, hard-working man can support you. The point I'm trying to make is that everyone—man or woman—should marry because they are in love, not for what they stand to gain. And I hope that you'll do the same."

"Do you believe in love?" I asked after we stepped off the streetcar near home.

"Yes, of course," she said sternly. "The problem is, most of us are selfish. And so we often choose a mate for selfish reasons. That's my advice as far as your two proposals are concerned. Don't marry either man for selfish reasons. And make sure they aren't marrying you for selfish reasons either."

I now had one week. And two marriage proposals.

I had to find my mother.

Chapter

27

That evening the house felt so warm and stuffy, even with all of the windows open, that I could scarcely breathe. Part of it might have been panic. My life seemed headed on a course that I couldn't control.

My bedroom was especially hot, so I went outside after supper and sat on the front steps, hoping to find a cool breeze—and a plan. I needed to make sense of the various clues I had been given and find a way to solve all the mysteries I'd unearthed. Maybe they would lead to my mother.

Daylight was fading and the lamplighter was making his way along our street, lighting the gas lamps, when I saw Silas McClure striding toward our house from the streetcar stop. I recognized him by his smooth, boneless stride. When I'd seen him on the train that first day I had described his movements as slippery, but I viewed Silas differently now that he no longer oiled his hair and wore his cheesy suit. His athletic stride was smooth and panther-like, and he carried himself as if every muscle was so well greased he could break into a run at a moment's notice. No doubt he needed to stay fit in order to make quick getaways.

He saw me as he approached and waved. I sprang to my feet, longing to run to him and ask if he'd found my mother. But I noticed that his grin wasn't as bright as usual, and I feared bad news.

"Good evening, Violet." He swept off his hat, revealing clean, wavy hair.

"Good evening, Silas. Do you have news of my mother?"

He exhaled. "I'm sorry to say that I've had no luck, so far. I haven't been able to locate anyone by the name of Angeline Hayes here in the city."

I slapped my fists against my thighs in frustration. For the first time I began to wonder if she still lived in Chicago. Perhaps she had come to the city only to sign the divorce papers. Silas must have seen my reaction, or perhaps the tears that filled my eyes, because he quickly said, "I'm not giving up, yet, Violet. I have another idea."

"Would you care to come inside?"

"Actually, it's such a nice evening I'd rather sit out here, if you don't mind."

"All right." I sat down again, moving over to make room for him on the steps beside me. His face looked freshly shaved, and he smelled as though he had lavished a great deal of aftershave on himself. I wondered if his efforts were for my sake. Might he propose marriage to me too? The steps were not very wide, and I felt his shoulders brush against mine when he sat down.

"How did you know where to look for my mother?"

"I know a lot of people in this city who get around . . . if you know what I mean." He gently nudged my ribs for emphasis. "I have my ways. "

"I would love to hear about them. Solving mysteries fascinates me. I used to read *True Crime Stories* and *The Illustrated Police News*."

"That's pretty unusual reading material for a proper young lady like yourself. I'm surprised you'd go for that sort of thing."

"One of my favorite books was Allan Pinkerton's biography."

"Is that right?"

I tried to read his expression, but his face was turned away, and I couldn't see his features in the fading twilight. "Have you heard of Mr. Pinkerton's detective agency, Silas?"

"Who hasn't? I'll wager they're the best crime-fighters in the country. But back to your mother . . ."

His reluctance to discuss Mr. Pinkerton seemed highly suspicious and should have served as a warning to me to have nothing more to do with him. No doubt Pinkerton's men were hot on Silas' trail at this very moment. They were famous for tracking down notorious criminals. But I needed Silas' help.

"Yes? What about my mother?"

"Sometimes women take back their maiden names after they're divorced. I just thought that your mother might have done the same thing. Do you know what her maiden name was?"

"I have it written down. It's upstairs. Shall I go get it?"

"It might help."

He stood, offering me his hand to help me up. A jolt passed from his hand to mine as I gripped it, traveling up my arm and giving me the same sensation I'd once had after accidentally striking my funny bone. I raced upstairs, my arm tingling, and dug out my journal from beneath my mattress. Thank goodness I'd had the good sense to copy down my mother's full name from her signature on the divorce papers along with the now-worthless address. I ripped out a blank page and copied her full name on it then carried the paper down to Silas.

"Her maiden name was Cepak. Angeline Cepak."

"Good. That might help. But keep in mind . . ." He hesitated.

"What? Please tell me."

"She might have remarried. That might be why we haven't found an Angeline Hayes. And in that case we won't find an Angeline Cepak either."

I sat down on the steps again and motioned for Silas to sit beside me. His shoulder seemed to press closer to mine this time, as if the stairs had mysteriously shrunk while I was gone.

"You seem very knowledgeable about this sort of thing, Mr. McClure." I was fishing for more information, perhaps even a confession. I wanted to know the truth about Silas and his mysterious friends.

"I have friends who know a lot about the goings-on in Chicago."

Thieves and murderers, no doubt. I suddenly remembered my second goal: to stop father's wedding.

"Would any of your friends know how to investigate a murder?"

"A murder?"

"I read about an intriguing case in my hometown, where a man fell down the cellar stairs and died. There are some people"—I didn't mention that it was me—"who suspect that he may have been murdered. Do you have any idea how someone would go about proving that?"

"Wow, you really are into crime-fighting, aren't you?"

"I find it fascinating, don't you?"

He shrugged. "I like a good mystery now and then."

"You seem to have friends in the world of crime, so I just wondered if you might know how the police would go about proving that a suspicious death was murder and not an accident."

"Well, I once read a real good book about solving crimes called *The Adventures of Sherlock Holmes*."

"I love that book!"

"You do? Where in the world did you run into it?"

"A friend at school had a copy. It was fascinating."

"Then maybe you recall that Sherlock Holmes always looked for two things: motive and opportunity. First of all, did the suspected killer have a reason for wanting the victim to die—that's motive. And second, did he have a way to do it—access to the crime scene or to the weapon that was used. The knife or the poison or the gun, for instance. Or maybe they knew about one of the victim's weaknesses—he couldn't swim or he needed a certain medicine—and therefore had opportunity."

"I know she was at the scene of the crime when it happened."

"She? Your suspect is a woman?" I nodded. "Then I'll wager that it's highly unlikely that she's a murderer. The vast majority of convicted murderers are men."

A shiver of horror rocked through me. It couldn't be my father! I didn't want to believe it of him.

"After all, how many women's prisons do you know of?" Silas continued. "Most women are much too delicate and sensitive to do such a grisly thing."

"You don't know Murderous Maude. She—"

"Murderous Maude?" he asked with a wide grin. "Is that her alias? Is she on a wanted poster somewhere?"

"No, that's what I call her. Anyway, she was home at the time of her husband's death. He supposedly fell down the cellar stairs, but isn't it possible that she pushed him?"

"What about motive? Why would she push him?"

"She wanted his money, I suppose?"

"Not good enough. Too hard to prove unless he was exceptionally wealthy. Was he?"

"No," I admitted. "They have two small children, and—"

"Children? See, that's why I don't believe she did it. If she kills her husband and goes to prison, who's going to look after her kids? Women think about these things, and it keeps them from committing murder."

What Silas said made sense. Yet Herman's mother had seemed to imply that women murdered their husbands more often than people realized. Perhaps I should raise that possibility.

"A close family friend dropped a hint about suspicious things going on behind closed doors."

"You mean husbands who beat their wives?"

"W-what?"

"I'm sorry. I probably have no business talking about this stuff with a lady of your sensitivities and all."

"I'm the one who raised the subject, Mr. McClure. I would like to know the truth."

"Okay. But usually when I hear people talking about what goes on 'behind closed doors,' they're talking about men who get drunk regularly and beat their wives and kids. It happens more often than people realize in the poorer parts of town—and especially in the tenements."

I remembered my grandmother's friend Irina—her bruised face and broken leg.

"If I were one of these women, I'd leave my husband," I said.

"Well, once again, wives usually stay because of their kids. From what I understand, it's very hard for a woman to get by on her own, especially if she has children. Some women stay because they're religious, and the church believes that marriage is sacred. And most of these husbands keep promising to change, and their wives keep hoping that they will."

"What if Murderous Maude pushed her husband down the stairs because he was a drunkard who beat her? Would the police still charge her with murder?"

"They might look the other way and rule it self-defense . . . unless there were other circumstances."

"What do you mean?"

"Well, suppose the police found out that she was—how can I say this delicately?—stepping out with another man while her husband was alive. Now *that* would be motive. It proves that she wanted her freedom so she could marry someone else."

His words horrified me. The deeper I dug, the more I seemed to implicate my father! I didn't want him to go to jail. He wouldn't hurt a flea. All I wanted to do was stop his marriage to Maude. Silas must have seen my shocked expression.

"Sorry. I didn't mean to embarrass you with such indelicate stuff. Maybe we should change the subject."

I shook my head. I had to uncover the truth. "Have you ever heard of a place called the Jolly Roger?"

"No, can't say that I have."

"It's on Bishop Street. Do you know where that is?"

"I have no idea."

"Could you ask around? Maybe one of your friends has heard of it or knows where Bishop Street is. It might be connected to finding my mother."

"Sure. I could try."

He pulled out a pencil and scribbled *Bishop Street* and *Jolly Roger* beneath my mother's maiden name. He had to lean even closer to me as he tucked the paper and pencil back into his pocket.

We both fell silent for a few moments as crickets chirped in the bushes. My mind raced with thoughts of murder and mayhem and my mother, but Silas' thoughts had obviously drifted elsewhere.

"Did I mention how pretty you look tonight, Violet?"

"I don't believe so—but thank you."

"And isn't it a beautiful night? Look at those fireflies winking like stars. And that moon!"

Silas might have been talking about the moon, but he wasn't gazing at it. He had shifted around until he was looking right at me with the same dreamy expression that Aunt Birdie always wore on her face. My heart started thumping like a three-wheeled carriage. I needed to distract him—fast!

"H-how did your trial turn out?"

"My what?"

"You were at the courthouse when we met downtown on Monday, remember? Your friend called to you and said that court was back in session."

"Oh, that. It wasn't my case. It was . . . I mean, I was there with . . . I can't explain it."

"Guilty or innocent?"

"Huh? Oh the, uh, thief was found guilty. Sentenced to three years."

"Was he your friend?"

"No, the thief wasn't my friend. I mean . . ." He exhaled. "I don't want to waste time talking about this stuff. I came here to ask if you would please consider going to the fair with me again. I promise I'll find a better chaperone this time. I'd like to make it up to you, Violet. And there's so much more to see."

That was true. I'd seen the fair's elegant side with Nelson and the boring side with Herman and the educational side with Aunt Matt. It would be fun to explore some of the exotic foreign pavilions and of course the Midway. And if I went with Silas—

But no. Silas was hypnotizing me again, dangling adventure and excitement in front of my eyes, hoping I would fall under his spell. I shook myself.

"I'm afraid I don't have time to return to the fair. My father is coming to take me home to Lockport one week from tomorrow, and—"

"One week?"

"Yes. So you see, Mr. McClure, I have to find my mother. Right now the Jolly Roger on Bishop Street is the only clue that I have. It's connected to my Uncle Philip somehow, and Aunt Birdie says Philip might know where my mother is. I'm prepared to go there myself, even though my aunt Matt said it's probably not in a nice part of town, but—"

"I'll take you. I'll find out where Bishop Street is and I'll take you there."

"You will?" I breathed an enormous sigh of relief. I would be safe with Silas. He carried a gun.

"Would I still need to find a chaperone?" he asked.

"Not this time. I'll provide one." I would sooner drag poor Aunt Birdie along than go out with another one of Silas' chaperones.

"Suppose I took some time off on Monday afternoon?" Silas said. "Would that work for you?"

"That would be wonderful!"

"I'll try to find out where Bishop Street is in the meantime. And if I may make a suggestion, Violet—don't dress too nicely."

"You want me to wear a disguise?"

Silas laughed out loud. "No, I was thinking that I would hate to be robbed."

"Oh. I see." I was disappointed. I had liked the idea of traveling incognito.

"I guess I'd better go," he said, rising to his feet. "But one more question: If we do find your mother before next Saturday, then will you go to the fair with me?"

I gave him my famous enigmatic smile. "Perhaps."

As I was writing in my diary later that night, I realized how much fun it had been to piece together clues and discuss crimes with Silas. Of all the things I had done since coming to Chicago, tonight's conversation had made me feel more alive and invigorated than I'd felt since . . . since . . . riding Mr. Ferris' wheel—with Silas.

What in the world was wrong with me?

Chapter

28

Friday, July 7, 1893

Silas McClure had given me an idea when he'd asked for my mother's maiden name. The women who had danced at the settlement house on Folk Night had all been Bohemian like my mother. Perhaps one of them knew her or had heard of her family. I needed to go back and talk with them. I would ask for my mother by her maiden name. Somebody might have heard of her. I made up my mind to get out of bed early for once, overcome my loathing for horrific smells, and go to work with my grandmother.

"Are you going to the settlement house today?" I asked her on Friday morning. She was bustling around the kitchen making breakfast, but she stopped to stare at me in surprise, a frying pan in her hand.

"Why, Violet Rose. You're up very early this morning. Would you like some eggs? They're fresh."

"No, thank you." I couldn't risk returning to that neighborhood with a full stomach. "But I would like to go with you today, if that's okay."

"I thought you didn't like working at the settlement house?"

"I have a hard time with the stench. But Father is coming for me next week, and . . . and so I would like to go with you." I was deliberately vague about my reasons. It was hard to lie to a woman who was as kind and good as my grandmother was. Even so, I couldn't risk telling her about my search for my mother. I didn't know how she would react.

I wouldn't have believed it possible for the neighborhood to smell any worse than it had the last time I'd visited, but it did. The first week of July had been scorching, and all of the decaying, molding, putrefying odors had intensified tenfold. From the looks of things, the garbage hadn't been collected since the last time I'd visited either. I nearly swooned the moment I stepped off the streetcar. I clutched my perfumed hankie to my nose, longing to run to Miss Addams' house for refuge.

"Let's go inside the main house," my grandmother said, "and see if we can find a job for you in there. The soup kitchen will be much too hot today."

I pushed open the heavy front door and rushed inside like a sprinter reaching the finish line. I could hear the chant of children's voices in the distance. The massive beauty of the home's woodwork struck me once again, each window and door framed with ropy carving that resembled thick braids. How did the immigrants handle such loveliness when their own lives were so stark?

"Would you like to work with the kindergarten children today?" my grandmother asked. "I believe I hear them in the parlor."

"Where will you be working?"

"I'll go wherever I'm needed, dear."

"I guess I could try it."

"Good. Then if it's okay with you," my grandmother said, "I'll leave you here and see if Magda needs help in the soup kitchen."

"Yes, of course. I'll see you later."

I found the children in the parlor, sitting on the floor in a circle while their teacher read a book to them. Louis Decker sat cross-legged on the floor with them. The children were very young, no more than five or six years old, but they looked more like shrunken old people to me than children. The hard life they'd endured was deeply etched on each somber, careworn face. Every one of them looked hungry.

I couldn't do this job either. I couldn't get involved with these little ones and let them into my heart, knowing that some of them would die of polio or typhus or dysentery before the year ended. How did gentle, kindhearted women like my grandmother and Miss Addams ever cope?

I stood in the doorway and leaned against the jamb to watch. The teacher held up a picture book with drawings of farm animals. She pronounced the name of each one carefully—cow, pig, goose—and then the children repeated it after her. My heart nearly broke. She may as well have been showing them unicorns and fire-breathing dragons. The only farm animals they were likely to see would be hanging in the window at the butcher shop.

When the teacher closed the book, Louis Decker glanced up and saw me. He scrambled to his feet. "Miss Hayes! It's so nice to see you!"

"I-I've come to help."

"That's wonderful!" He introduced me to the teacher, Miss Dow. "Violet plays the piano beautifully," he told her. "Maybe the children would like to hear a song?"

"Yes, please, Miss Hayes. I'm sure they would enjoy that."

It was the very least I could do. I made my way over to the small spinet piano in the corner and rifled through the sheet music that lay on top of it. I found a few pieces that I could sight-read and pounded my way through them, then finished with a lively etude that I had memorized for a recital at school. The children applauded my efforts.

The sound of their tiny, clapping hands brought tears to my eyes. I stood and bowed.

"Thank you."

For the next hour or so I assisted Louis with the children as Miss Dow led them in a variety of educational chores: learning to tie a bow, learning their left hand from their right, recognizing shapes such as triangles and squares. Each time I helped a child I would ask, "What's your name?" Most replied with only a first name. "And can you tell me your family name?" I would ask. None of their nearly incomprehensible replies sounded like Cepak.

Eventually, it was time to take the children outside to play. I had no desire to leave my stenchless sanctuary, so I remained indoors. I wandered into Miss Addams' library and greeted a woman who seemed to be working there.

"Do a lot of people in the community borrow books from you?" I asked.

"Quite a few. Especially the ones who are trying to learn English. But our neighbors work very hard, you see, and don't have much time for reading and other leisure pursuits." I spotted what appeared to be a list of names lying on the round wooden table where she was seated.

"You probably see a variety of ethnic names, working here," I said. "I find foreign names fascinating. May I?" I gestured to the list.

"Those are some of our regular borrowers," she told me. I read through the list twice. There was no one named Cepak.

I browsed around the library for a few more minutes, pretending to show an interest in the book titles and in the artwork on the walls. The sound of childish squeals and laughter drifted through the open windows along with the muted odors of the neighborhood and Louis' booming bass voice.

I explored more of the house and found a friendly, middle-aged woman named Miss McPhee working in a cramped office. I took out my verbal tennis racket and engaged her in a conversation about Folk Night.

"I especially enjoyed watching the Bohemian ladies dance," I told her when we'd chatted for a while. "I would love to meet some of them. Might you know their names or where they live?"

"I know, generally speaking, where they live. The area between Halsted and the river is made up mostly of Italian immigrants. To the south on 12th Street you'll find the Germans. Those side streets are where the Poles and Russians live. Still farther south is where you'll find the Bohemians."

"That's very interesting."

"And if you're looking for the Irish, they're mostly north of us."

"Thank you."

A few minutes later, Louis returned with the children. He was as sweaty and red-faced as they were. "It's lunchtime, Violet. Want to help me feed this gang?"

The children gobbled down their meal as if it might be their last. I nibbled on a slice of bread, balancing my need for sustenance with the necessity of walking to the streetcar stop. When the school day ended, Louis invited me to walk to Irina's tenement house with him.

"This is Irina's daughter, Nessa," he said. The little girl gripping his hand had wispy blond hair and pale blue eyes. "Irina still can't get around very well, so I've offered to pick up Nessa in the morning and walk her home whenever I can." I recalled my real goal and drew a deep breath—perhaps my last comfortable one—for courage.

"Sure. I'll go with you." I reached for her other hand. "How old are you, Nessa?" She lowered her chin and stared at the floorboards.

"She doesn't say much," Louis whispered.

We stepped outside. The afternoon had grown oppressively hot, and the sun was a glaring fireball in the hazy sky. I wished I had brought my parasol, even if it would have looked out of place in a slum.

"Do you know many of these neighborhood people's last names?"

I asked. I couldn't afford to waste time easing my question into the conversation.

"Some of them. Why?"

"I'm mainly interested in the Bohemian ones who danced last week. Do you know if anyone has the family name of Cepak?"

"It doesn't sound familiar. I'm sorry."

"Is Irina a Bohemian?"

"No, she's Polish." I would have huffed in frustration, but I couldn't risk inhaling that deeply.

When we reached her tenement, the area around the water faucet was littered once again with a variety of pots and containers. This time, the child patiently filling them was a small girl.

Nessa raced up the stairs ahead of us and into her apartment. When I reached the door, she was hugging her mother's skirts. I felt a pang of longing as I watched Irina caress her daughter's feathery hair. My mother's hands had been beautiful and graceful with long, tapered fingers. The nannies that Father hired had taken care of all my needs, but none of them had held me and loved me the way that my mother had.

"Tank you. Tank you," Irina said, "for bringing my Nessa."

Louis took a moment to bow his head with Irina and pray for her and her family. I watched, moved by his compassion and faith. When he finished I felt Nessa tugging on my skirt. I bent my head toward hers. "Yes?"

"I am five," she whispered.

"That's the very best age to be," I whispered back. If I could have hidden her in my trunk and taken her back to Lockport with me, I would have.

"Irina looked much better than the last time I saw her," I said as we descended the tenement stairs. "I hope her leg is healing well."

"It seems to be . . . until the next time."

"Do you think her husband will beat her again?"

"Undoubtedly." Louis' gentle face tightened with anger. "So many immigrant men feel frustrated and disappointed with the hard lives they find in America. The only way they know to drown their sorrow is at the saloon. They're good men, for the most part, until Demon Liquor takes over their life. It causes them to lose control and take out their frustration on their families."

His words reminded me of what Silas had said. Was it possible that Maude O'Neill's husband had done the same? It made sense, especially if the Jolly Roger turned out to be a saloon. If Lloyd O'Neill had beaten Maude, she might be very glad he was dead. But did that prove she had killed him? I remembered how Irina had looked the last time I had visited: the bruises, the terror in her eyes. And the shame. Her husband deserved to go to jail.

"Isn't it against the law for a man to beat his wife?" I asked.

"Of course it is. But the law isn't always enforced. There's an attitude that a man's wife is his property, and what a man does inside his own home is his business. Only the Gospel can change people and break the power of alcohol. That's why it's so important to preach Christ's love in these neighborhoods."

Would I blame Irina if she pushed her husband down the stairs? But even if it turned out that Maude had pushed Lloyd O'Neill in self-defense, I still didn't want my father to marry her, no matter how much O'Neill may have deserved it.

As I walked, I wondered where my Uncle Philip fit into the picture. He seemed to be connected to Maude and her husband. Herman's mother had mentioned something about the war. But was Uncle Philip connected to my mother? I had to solve this!

"I need to talk to some of the Bohemian women who danced the other night," I told Louis. "Is that possible?"

He stopped walking. He touched my elbow to stop me as well. "Slow down, Violet. It's much too hot to keep up this pace."

"I'm sorry. . . . But could you take me to visit some of those women? Miss McPhee in the office says that many of them live south of 12th Street."

"May I ask why?" When I hesitated, he said, "I can see that this is really important to you, Violet, and I want you to know that you can confide in me. I promise I won't betray your trust."

"I don't want my grandmother to know, but I'm trying to find my mother."

"I see." He gestured to Miss Addams' front porch a dozen yards away. "Let's sit down and talk, okay?"

"My mother left home when I was nine," I said when we'd reached the shady front steps. "She abandoned my father and me."

"That must have been very hard for you."

"I didn't know she was abandoning me at the time. My father told me that she went away because she was sick. It was easy to believe. She had become so sad before she left. It was like she was in a boat that was slowly drifting away from me on the tide. I kept begging her to be happy again, to dance with me—but she wouldn't. I felt so lonely after she left. I missed her hugs. She gave the best hugs. . . ." I couldn't continue.

Louis gently patted my shoulder, the way I'd seen him soothe Irina. "I'm so sorry," he murmured, handing me his handkerchief. He was easy to talk to, kind and sympathetic. I found myself opening up to him, sharing things I'd never talked about before.

"When I was Nessa's age, my mother was a lively, vibrant woman who sang to me at night and danced the way those Bohemian women danced. She smelled wonderful, like roses. She would tell me stories— marvelous, magical adventures with flying horses and talking cats. She made up tales about a princess who battled evil sorcerers and monstrous dragons and finally married a handsome prince. She was like the sun to me, full of brilliant light and warmth. But then her light began to dim. Our house seemed to grow darker and colder as time went on. When she left, our house was always shadowy and cold, no matter how many lamps or fires we lit. I kept believing that if my mother was sick, she would get better and come home again. But she never did."

Louis had removed his glasses while I was speaking. I looked up into his moist, gentle eyes and said, "I need to find her, Louis. Won't you please help me?"

"Of course. What can I do?"

"Could you take me around the neighborhood so I can talk to the other Bohemian immigrants? My mother's maiden name was Cepak. Maybe someone knows her, or knows where I can find her family."

"I would be happy to."

"Can we go today?" I sprang to my feet.

"I'm sorry," he said, rising slowly. "I promised to help out at a rally this afternoon, but maybe you can meet me here next week sometime?"

"I'll only be in Chicago one more week—"

"One week?"

"Yes. Then I have to go home."

"Meet me here on Monday, then."

"Tuesday would be better," I said, remembering my plans to go with Silas to Bishop Street.

"Violet . . ." Louis cleared his throat and shuffled his feet, as if struggling to say something important. "Violet, I feel as though I've known you much longer than one month. I know this is sudden, and that we haven't spent a great deal of time together, but your grandmother told me so much about you that I feel as though I met you long before I actually did. And . . . and she is such a devout woman of God that I feel that you . . . you're obviously a wonderful woman too, Violet. I would feel diminished if you walked out of my life forever next week. I want so much for you to be part of what I do."

"You mean—work with you on Mr. Moody's campaign?"

His face reddened as he stared at his feet. "Well, yes . . . Well, not exactly." He had been fiddling nervously with his glasses and finally dropped them onto the grass. "What I meant," he said as he scooped them up, "was that . . . I mean, I had in mind the possibility of . . . of marriage. In the future, of course."

Three proposals in one week. I couldn't reply.

"I'll be finished with my studies at the end of the summer," he continued, "and there is a church here in Chicago that is considering me for their pastor—" He halted, perhaps stopped by the look of surprise and dismay that was probably on my face. "I'm sorry. I can see that I'm pushing you too fast. Is there some way you could stay longer than a week? We could spend more time working together and see if we wanted to have a future together. July has just begun. We have Mr. Moody's summer campaign ahead of us, and you could play the piano for me."

"I want to stay, Louis. It's my father who is making me leave. I have a suitor back home in Lockport—but I don't want to marry him," I added quickly when I saw Louis' expression.

"That's good news for me. Suppose I spoke with your father and asked for permission to court you?"

I hesitated, recalling my father's mumbled words about religious zealots. "You could ask him."

I wasn't sure I wanted the life Louis was offering me, but courting him meant I could stay in Chicago longer. And that meant more time to find my mother. I knew it was wrong to use Louis for selfish reasons the way Aunt Matt had warned. But wasn't Louis using me to play the piano? I felt so mixed up! Would I ever unravel the mysteries of love?

My grandmother noticed how perturbed I was on the long ride home. "What's wrong, Violet? I can see that you're not yourself today. In fact, you haven't been yourself all week."

"It's been quite a week, that's for certain." I sighed and slouched lower in my seat. Madame Beauchamps had called girls who slouched "jellyfish" and made us balance a book on our head for a full hour as punishment. But Madame Beauchamps never had a week like the one I'd had.

"Herman Beckett proposed to me on Tuesday," I told my grandmother.

"Is he the gentleman from Lockport that your father wants you to marry?"

"Yes. Then Nelson Kent proposed to me on Wednesday night. He's Aunt Agnes' choice."

"You have had a busy week."

"That's not all. Louis just proposed to me this afternoon."

"That's wonderful!" She clapped her hands. Then her shoulders sagged. "It seems I'm happier about it than you are. Are you trying to decide which proposal to accept?"

"I don't want to accept any of them right now. I'm not ready to get married. And even if I was ready, none of the three ever said that he loved me. Father is the one who's in a hurry for me to marry. I'm so afraid he's going to choose for me, and he favors Herman Beckett. Herman is so boring! Nelson Kent could give me a comfortable life, but he . . . And now Louis . . ."

"Louis is a fine young man, Violet. You would have a very fulfilling life with him, serving God. And plenty of excitement too, I would think."

"May I ask you a question, Grandmother?" After a slight hesitation, I continued. "Aunt Matt said something about having the blinders off when it comes to marrying a minister. What did she mean?"

Grandmother gazed into the distance. Her eyes looked sorrowful to me. "Being a minister is not like having a job with regular working hours. Louis will be gone a lot, tending to the needs of his flock. His passion is first and foremost for God, and that's a good thing. When you serve your husband, you'll always know that you are serving God and helping Louis to do the same."

Her words reminded me of what Aunt Agnes had said about supporting and encouraging Nelson in his work.

"Of course, there are unfair pressures on the pastor's family—people who expect them to be perfect," Grandmother continued. "That's not always a good thing. And pastors often make the mistake of putting their congregation's needs ahead of their family's needs.

There will be times of sorrow. But also times of great joy."

"Did you and my grandfather love each other?"

"People didn't talk much about love back when I was a young woman. My father had four daughters, much to his sorrow. He wanted to find decent, honest husbands for each of us. Isaac was a good man. He chose me because of my devotion to the Lord. Love does grow, in time, as you make a life together and raise a family."

Again, I was reminded of what Aunt Agnes had said. I wanted to ask my grandmother about Uncle Philip, but I was afraid that I would have to explain how I had heard of him in the first place. I didn't want her to know that I was digging into my family's past and searching for my mother.

"Did my father fight in the war?" I asked instead. She seemed surprised by the sudden change in topics.

"He had just turned eighteen and was old enough to be drafted when the war ended—thank heaven." She took my hand in hers. "Violet, what is it that you really want in life?"

I thought for a moment, then said, "I want to be loved. I don't want to spend my life all alone like Aunt Matt. I want to find someone who loves me for myself, just the way I am, not for what he'll gain by marrying me. Is that too much to ask?"

"Not in the least." She slid her arm around my shoulders and gave me a hug. "I know someone who loves you that way right now."

I sat up in surprise. "You do? Who?"

"God."

"He doesn't count."

"Of course He counts! I know you're facing some very important choices in your life. And that you're trying to understand all the new things you've experienced this summer. You're trying to figure out how they fit with the experiences you grew up with and what you learned at school. Ideally, you will be able to bring everything together—and find God's purpose for your life in the process. He allows tragedies such as losing your mother in order to shape us into better people. It's not His will that we suffer, but He can bring good from it if you'll allow Him to."

"I can't see any good in it. And now I feel like I'm trapped. Father is going to choose a husband for me if I don't make up my mind."

"When my husband died, I couldn't see any good in it either. I didn't know which way to turn. But all the loose ends came together when I sought God. I pray that you'll do the same. And that you won't marry for the wrong reasons."

"Will you talk to Father for me?"

"Yes, of course I'll talk to him. I'll tell him that I disagree with him, and that I think you should wait a little longer before getting married. But talking is all I can do, Violet. You are his daughter."

"What would you do if you were me?"

"I would pray."

Chapter

29

Monday, July 10, 1893

I fretted all weekend about my trip with Silas on Monday to the Jolly Roger on Bishop Street. I wanted to dress nicely and look my very best in case this rabbit trail led to my mother, but I remembered Silas' advice about wearing plain clothes so that we wouldn't get robbed. I was pacing the floor, wearing a bare spot in the bedroom carpet, when Silas finally arrived on Monday afternoon.

"Any news about my mother?" I asked as I thundered down the stairs. He was in the front hallway, returning Aunt Birdie's hug.

"No, sorry. I've been asking around, but I haven't found anyone named Angeline Cepak. I'm still looking though."

"Thank you. I appreciate your help." I exhaled and took Aunt Birdie's arm. "Come on, Aunt Birdie. We're going out this afternoon with Mr. McClure."

"Oh, how nice. You know, Violet, out of all your beaus, he is my favorite. Too bad his walnut didn't burn up with yours." She beamed at Silas and he grinned in return. I couldn't speak. I felt my cheeks grow warm.

"And out of all of Violet's aunts," he said, "you're my favorite." He offered her his arm and led her outside. "I borrowed a horse and a runabout," he said, gesturing toward the street. "To make things easier on you ladies."

I looked where he was pointing and saw a skinny, swaybacked horse tethered to our hitching post. The horse looked so weary with its head drooping to the ground that I feared it would keel over and die before Silas could untie it. It was harnessed to a rickety runabout that was in even worse condition than the horse. I didn't think either one could make it to the end of the block, let alone to Bishop Street.

I watched Silas help Aunt Birdie onto the rump-sprung seat and wanted to ask if he had resurrected the rig from the garbage dump. Silas offered me his electrified hand so I could climb onboard, then he untied the reins and settled onto the carriage seat between us. He made a clucking sound and jiggled the reins. The horse started off, meandering down the street as if sleepwalking. I tapped my foot impatiently.

"I do believe we could get there faster on foot," I finally said.

"You might be right. But this rig does have one advantage for where we're going."

"Oh? What's that?"

"It's not likely to be stolen while we're inside."

I couldn't help smiling. "I'll be more worried that the horse will die of old age while we're inside."

Silas laughed out loud. He had a wonderful laugh.

I cleared my throat. "So. I gather that you found out where Bishop Street is?"

"I got directions. Do you think your mother might be there?"

"I'm not sure, but here's what I do know: Aunt Birdie said that my Uncle Philip would know where my mother is. Someone else told me that my father used to come to Chicago to the Jolly Roger for his brother Philip's sake. So I thought perhaps I would find my uncle there, and I could ask him about my mother." I didn't mention that my Aunt Matt had said Philip had nothing to do with my mother.

"That makes sense, I guess," Silas said with a shrug.

"But here is where it gets mysterious—when I checked the records at the city administration building, I found out that the proprietor of the Jolly Roger is listed as Lloyd O'Neill."

"Who is he?"

"He's the man who I believe was murdered."

"The guy whose wife pushed him down the cellar stairs?"

I nodded. "If O'Neill owned a saloon," I continued, "perhaps he really was a drunkard who beat his wife."

"That makes sense."

I couldn't tell if Silas was taking me seriously or not, because he hadn't stopped grinning since Aunt Birdie let him through our door. I had to admit that when I added up all the clues—my mysterious uncle, my missing mother, the murdered alcoholic, and the ridiculous name Jolly Roger—the story did sound like a corny plot from a dime novel.

The horse trudged slowly through the city streets as if on its way to the glue factory. We finally reached a neighborhood that was very much like the one where I'd played the piano for Louis. Saloons and burlesque theaters crowded both sides of the street, and there might have been bawdy houses too, but I wasn't brave enough to look for them. I didn't look up at all until I heard Silas say, "Whoa." The runabout rattled to a stop in front of a tawdry-looking saloon.

"I think this is it," Silas said.

My body began to tremble as if I had caught a chill. "H-how do you know?"

He pointed to the sign hanging above the door: *Jolly Roger*. Aunt Birdie had been silent throughout our journey, but she suddenly piped up.

"I certainly hope this isn't your new restaurant, Violet. I wouldn't step one foot inside that place."

"She's right," Silas said. "A classy woman like you should think twice about going in a dump like that."

I drew a breath for courage—or as deep of a breath as I dared, considering my odiferous surroundings. "It's broad daylight," I said. "And I have you for protection." I could see his inside pocket sagging with the weight of something heavy. He had his gun.

"So what's your plan?" Silas asked.

"I brought along a photograph of my Uncle Philip. I thought I would show it around and ask if anyone knows him."

"That's a great idea, Violet. Let's go." He climbed down to tether the horse, then offered Aunt Birdie his hand.

"I don't think I care to eat here," she said. "This isn't a very nice place at all. We need to find a different restaurant."

I hated taking her inside the saloon against her will, but I couldn't leave her alone in the carriage either. She seemed to dig in her heels as I dragged her reluctantly through the open saloon door.

"You want me to do the talking?" Silas whispered.

"No. I appreciate your help, Silas, but I need to take charge of my life. I can do this."

I had learned to be brave this summer, going to neighborhoods like this with Louis, visiting tenements with my grandmother, confronting abusive factory owners with Aunt Matt. I'd received an entirely new education in a few short weeks, learning things that Madame Beauchamps never dreamed of putting in her curriculum.

The Jolly Roger was as dark as a mausoleum inside. I saw a lump in a corner booth that might have been a sack of rags or a customer—it was hard to tell in the grimy light. No one sat at the bar, thankfully, but a distasteful-looking man with entirely too much facial hair stood behind it, wiping a beer mug with a gray rag.

"Good afternoon," I began in a quivering voice. "My name is Violet Rose Hayes, and I'm looking for information."

"You the police?" he asked, glancing at Silas.

"Hardly!" I blurted.

"Then give me five good reasons why I should talk to you."

I couldn't reply. I was unable to think of a single one, let alone five. Silas slipped his hand inside his jacket, and for a horrible moment I feared he was reaching for his gun. But when his hand came out it held a folded five-dollar bill. He slid it smoothly across the bar and beneath the man's fingers. It disappeared into the bartender's pocket.

"Those are very good reasons," he said. "What do you want?"

"I'll have a cup of tea, please," Aunt Birdie replied. She had seated herself on one of the wooden barstools. "And some scones, if you have them."

The man bellowed with laughter. "That's rich, lady! I can probably fix you some Irish coffee but no tea."

"Well, I don't care for coffee. Let's go someplace else, Violet." She slid off the stool and turned toward the door.

"We'll leave in a minute, Aunt Birdie, I promise. I just need to ask this man some questions first."

Silas linked his arm through Aunt Birdie's and hung on to her as if she were made of smoke and might blow away. I turned back to the bartender.

"I understand that this establishment is owned by Mr. Lloyd O'Neill?"

"You understand wrong. O'Neill sold it to me more than ten years ago."

"Oh. I see."

"O'Neill got married and moved to some little one-horse town— Lemont or LaGrange or Lockport . . ."

"Yes, Lockport."

"Why're you asking me if you already know?" He picked up his greasy rag and swiped it across the top of the bar.

"There are still a lot of things I don't know," I replied. "I'm trying to locate a friend of Mr. O'Neill's named Philip Hayes."

"Never heard of him."

Silas bent close to me. "Show him the picture," he whispered. I pulled out the photograph of my father and his brother and laid it on the bar, facing the man.

"I don't remember this guy," he said, pointing to Philip, "but I certainly remember this one." He pointed to my father. "He was a real troublemaker. Tried to break up the act, if you know what I mean. After O'Neill sold this place to me, he would show up every couple of months, begging to buy it back. This guy in the picture would show up soon after and insist that O'Neill come home to Lockport and be respectable. Got him all screwed up with religion, telling him to quit Demon Rum and so on. Had the poor guy on and off the wagon more times than a deliveryman. I gotta admit that O'Neill was good for business, with his leg and all. He could really tell a story, and all his buddies from the war would come in to hear them."

"What do you mean, with his leg. . . ?"

"Lloyd O'Neill has a peg leg. Made out of wood. That's why he called this joint the Jolly Roger in the first place. Thought it fit in with the whole pirate theme, if you know what I mean."

"Was he a pirate?"

"No, lady. There aren't any pirates in Chicago." He gave the bar another swipe. "O'Neill lost his leg in the war. Used to brag that he got hit while saving some other fellow's life. Don't know if that's true or just drunken swagger."

"Was the man he saved named Philip Hayes?" I asked.

"No idea. I'd tell you to ask O'Neill yourself but I heard he died. Can't say if it's true, but I haven't seen him in more than a year."

"Was O'Neill ever involved with a woman? She would have been Bohemian. Very pretty. Dark-haired."

"Don't know nothing about a woman," he replied, shaking his head. "But if she's as pretty as you are, I'd give her a job. I could use a good-looking barmaid, if you're interested. And I've got another business going on upstairs, if—"

"She's not interested!" Silas yelled. "Come on, Violet. I think it's time for us to leave. Unless you want to ask him something else."

"I-I can't think of anything else."

"Thanks for your help," Silas said.

The sunlight seemed blinding when we stepped into the street again.

"Well!" Aunt Birdie huffed. "That says it all, doesn't it?"

My knees shook so badly that I couldn't negotiate the carriage step. Silas had to put his hands on my waist and lift me onto the seat. It would have been very dramatic and appropriate to gallop away, leaving the Jolly Roger behind in a cloud of dust, but the horse wasn't up to the challenge. Neither, I suspected, was the runabout.

I couldn't speak for several long minutes for fear I would burst into tears. Silas seemed to understand my silence and didn't say anything either, until we finally reached a more pleasant neighborhood.

"Do you mind telling me what you gathered from all that?" Silas said, "Or is it none of my business?"

"No, I don't mind. I'm grateful that you came with us." I paused to swallow the lump in my throat and wipe a tear.

"I'd really like to help you find your mother, Violet. I sure hated seeing a classy lady like you in place like that. I think you were very courageous for venturing there—foolish, perhaps, but courageous just the same."

"I knew you could protect us, seeing as you carry a gun and—"

"A gun?" he asked in surprise. I clapped my hand over my mouth. How had I let it slip out?

"I saw it in your pocket the other day when we met on LaSalle Street," I explained. "And if I'm not mistaken, it's in your pocket today too."

"You mean this?" I shrank back as he reached inside his jacket. He pulled out something and laid it on my lap.

"It's . . . it's a harmonica! I feel so foolish."

"No, you made an honest mistake. I'll wager most people would agree that a mouth organ is an unusual thing to carry around."

"Good thing we weren't in any danger," I said, exhaling.

"Well, if we had been, I could have played a jig for the rogues before they robbed us." Silas scooped up the harmonica and played a few bars of "Yankee Doodle." I couldn't help laughing.

"You're lucky nobody stole it from you in that neighborhood."

He shrugged, as if money wasn't an issue. I wondered if Silas had stolen the harmonica to begin with.

"Well, thanks again for taking me."

"I admire you a great deal, Violet. You were amazingly brave in there. Now, do you want to explain to me what that was all about?"

"I'm trying to find my mother."

"I know that."

"All I have are a bunch of clues, and I'm trying to connect them. I've read hundreds of detective stories—but this is so much harder. My family is so secretive. All I know is that my father used to travel to Chicago to the Jolly Roger for his brother Philip's sake. I'm guessing that O'Neill saved Philip's life during the war, which is why my father tried to help him. Even if O'Neill was a drunkard who may have beat his wife, my father probably brought him home to Lockport for Philip's sake."

"That sure makes a great story. Too bad there's no way to find out if it's true. Is this Philip guy missing too? Where is he?"

"I don't know."

"Philip is away, fighting in the war," Aunt Birdie said. "My husband, Gilbert, is fighting too. He's quite determined to help free all of the slaves." Silas smiled at her and patted her hand.

"You know," Silas said, "if this O'Neill had only one leg, I can see where he might have taken a tumble down the cellar stairs— especially if he was drunk. Cellar steps are usually pretty narrow and steep. Maybe his wife didn't murder him after all."

"Oh. I see what you mean." I didn't know whether to be happy about that conclusion or not. It meant that my father was innocent, but it also meant that Maude was too. I would have to find another way to stop their marriage.

"How does your mother tie into all of this?" Silas asked.

"I guess she doesn't," I admitted. "Aunt Birdie told me that Philip knew her, so I thought—"

"Philip loved the theater too," Aunt Birdie said.

"Are you sure my mother didn't go to the theater with my father?" I asked.

"Certainly not! Your father is dead set against theaters and saloons and all those other worldly amusements. Just like his father is."

"I hate to be the one to suggest this," Silas said carefully, "but is it possible that your mother and Philip . . . you know . . . that we'll find them in the same place when we finally find them?"

I gasped. "You think they ran off together?"

He shrugged. "It happens."

"No . . . no, I-I can't believe that!"

Silas laid his hand on my arm. "Hey, I'm sorry. I didn't mean to upset you. It was a wild thought. . . . It's just that they're both missing and . . . Just forget I brought it up, okay?"

But it explained why no one would discuss either one of them. I didn't want to believe something so scandalous could happen in my family, that one brother would steal the other brother's wife. Most of all, I didn't want to believe that my mother would choose to leave me behind in order to run away with my uncle. I preferred to believe what Aunt Matt had told me: *Philip has nothing to do with finding your mother.*

I was quiet for the remainder of the ride home, thinking about my parents and everything I had learned. I wished I had never raised the ugly suspicion that my father and Maude had killed Lloyd O'Neill. I wished I had never heard of Uncle Philip. I had been much better off believing that my mother had left me because she was ill.

If only my father had lied to me at Maude O'Neill's house. If only he had told me that my mother was dead.

C h a p t e r

30

T u e s d a y ,   J u l y   1 1 ,   1 8 9 3

Violet Rose? You're up early again," my grandmother said when I appeared at breakfast the next day.

"I'm meeting Louis down at the settlement house this morning."

"He's such a fine young man. And already like a son to me." She looked so pleased and so hopeful. I felt guilty for misleading her. But maybe I would fall madly in love with Louis as he gallantly helped me search for my mother. Things like that happened sometimes in romance novels.

Louis had arrived at the settlement house even earlier than I had, and he'd begun asking questions to find out which of the Bohemian women would be our best source of information. Everyone at the settlement house adored Louis, and I saw how indispensable he was. Miss Dow wanted him to help with the kindergarten children again. Magda said he was needed in the kitchen. Miss McPhee had a list of repairs she hoped he could attend to. If only I liked him as much as they did.

"Another day," he told them all. "I promised Miss Hayes I would help her. Are you ready?" he asked me. I nodded, dreading the walk outside.

"Is it far? Where are we going?"

"I have the address of the woman who helped organize all the food and the dancing on Folk Night. She's sort of the matriarch of the Bohemian community. I'm told that she knows all of the families."

We walked several blocks south, then wove through a warren of back alleys and side streets to a cluster of tenement buildings similar to Irina's. The four-story brick structures were built right up against each other in the shape of a U, with a bleak patch of dirt for a courtyard. More brick tenements towered across the alley and stretched down the block, until there was no way that fresh air or a cooling breeze could penetrate the apartments.

Children swarmed all over the place, tussling in the dirt, leaning from open windows, playing on the landings and on the open-backed wooden stairs that led up the outside of the structure to each floor. The children reminded me of myself at that age, with their dusky skin and dark curly hair, but I glimpsed sorrow and hopelessness in their expressions in spite of their playful laughter. I recalled Louis saying that for many of these people, the reality of life in America had not lived up to their dreams.

Back home in Lockport, children like Horrid and Homely could spend the hot summer days playing in Dellwood Park, where there were trees and grass and a refreshing breeze from the canal.

"The woman we're looking for lives up on the fourth floor," Louis said, pointing to the rickety wooden stairs. "Are you ready to climb?"

I could feel the steps wobbling and the handrail shaking as I began to ascend. The stairs were so steep—and there were so many of them—that I had to stop for breath on every landing, even though I was in a hurry to escape the neighborhood's horrid smells. The door to the Bohemian woman's apartment stood open, and she and her children recognized Louis immediately.

"Is good to see you, Louis. Come in, come in. You are always so kind to help all the people. So kind." She motioned us inside. The apartment was clean but cramped and crammed with too many beds. A very old woman with skin like crumpled paper sat in a wooden chair by the window.

"Thank you," Louis said. "Do you know Mrs. Hayes who works in the soup kitchen with me, ma'am?"

"Yes, yes, of course. She is a kind woman."

"This is her granddaughter, Violet Hayes. She wants to ask you some questions about the Bohemian community, if you don't mind."

"Yes, yes, I try to answer. But you must sit down, please." She pulled out two splintery chairs from beneath the kitchen table. "Let me fix you something," she said, opening a crude wooden cupboard beside the stove.

"We really don't need anything," I said. "You don't have to—"

"Yes, yes, you are my guests. It is important to give you . . . how do you say it? To make you at home." She removed a greasy, cheesecloth-wrapped lump and set in on a cutting board.

"I'm really not hungry—" I began, but Louis elbowed me.

"It's rude to refuse," he whispered. "These people have so little, and they are honoring us by offering it."

She unwrapped the cloth to reveal a jiggling lump of headcheese, just like the one they had served us on Folk Night. Our hostess sliced off two sizeable pieces, carefully transferring them to two mis-matched plates, then set them in front of us. My stomach flipped like a pancake. I was certain that my portion contained an eyeball.

"Excuse, please, while I get water for tea." She lifted a kettle from the stove and disappeared through the door.

"I don't think I can eat this," I whispered to Louis. "Can't we tell her I'm allergic?"

He looked horrified. "We can't *lie*, Violet."

The meat was every bit as slimy and gelatinous as the dish they'd served on Folk Night, with varying-sized chunks of things imbedded in it. My choosing game had sprung to life. I was living one of my questions: *If you had to choose between eating something disgusting in order to find your mother, or refusing to eat it and never seeing her again, which would you choose?* The next time Ruth Schultz asked about the most disgusting thing I'd ever eaten, I would win the prize.

I reminded myself that I had eaten snails at Madame Beauchamps'. This was no worse, was it? I could always just gulp it down without chewing or tasting it. But in retrospect, the slippery garlic butter had helped expedite the snail's passage down my throat. Garlic can disguise the most obnoxious of flavors.

I decided against gulping down the headcheese. If I finished it too quickly my hostess might offer me more. She returned with the kettle of water and proceeded to brew tea for us. The finished concoction smelled and tasted as though she had used a clump of weeds from alongside the road instead of real tea leaves.

"I'm trying to find my mother," I began, swallowing the first tiny nibble of meat. "She was Bohemian, I believe. Her maiden name was Cepak. Angeline Cepak. Do you know any other families in this neighborhood by that name?"

"No, I cannot think of any. But I have heard this family name in the old country. Is not so unusual there."

I swallowed a second bite along with my disappointment. "Do you know of any other places in the city where other Bohemian families live? Or do you know someone else I might ask?"

"No, I know only the families around here. I am sorry."

"How long ago did you immigrate to Chicago? Were you here during the Great Fire?"

"No, we are coming here nine years ago. I am sorry I am not helping you find your mother. I wish I could. When did you lose her?"

"Eleven years ago." I ate a third bite and chased it down with a sip of tea. Both tasted terrible.

I had to think! What other clues had I gathered about my mother? Aunt Birdie kept mentioning that she'd loved the theater—but my aunt often got her stories mixed up. Was it possible that my mother *worked* in the theater as an actress instead of merely attending the shows? I knew she had loved to dance. I took a chance. I had nothing to lose.

"Have you heard of anyone named Cepak who worked in the theater? An actress, maybe? Or a dancer?"

"No, I don't think so. . . ."

All of a sudden the little old grandmother in the corner began talking a mile a minute in another language. She pointed to me and gestured with her twig-like hands as she talked.

"What is she saying?" I asked.

"My husband's mother says there are Cepaks in the old country who are married with gypsies. They are thieves." She turned to her mother-in-law and said loudly, "They cannot be her family. She is nice girl." The old woman babbled even louder, waving her arms.

"What did she say? Please tell me."

"She said in America the gypsies perform in the shows. But it cannot be the family you look for. The shows are . . . how do you say? . . . Not so nice." She lowered her gaze, brushing crumbs off the table.

I knew that the old woman was talking about burlesque shows, not the legitimate theater or even vaudeville. The thought made me feel ill. But then, I already felt queasy from the headcheese and bitter tea. I choked down the last bite of meat and stood.

"Thank you so much for your help," I said. "We need to be going." I wondered if I should offer to pay her for the information the way Silas McClure had paid the bartender.

Louis took my arm to help me down the steep flight of stairs. My head reeled from the heat and from this new information.

"I'm sorry we didn't learn more, Violet. Is there someplace else you want to go?"

"No—back to the settlement house, I guess. I'm all out of ideas."

When we reached the main street, I suddenly heard a terrible squealing sound, like a child being tortured. We rounded the corner and Louis halted abruptly.

"Violet, wait!" He tried to hold me back and block my view but his warning came too late. In the middle of the filthy, littered alley, someone was butchering a pig. The man had hoisted the animal up on a scaffold by its rear legs, and he proceeded to slit the pig's throat, right before my eyes. The screeching halted abruptly. The amount of blood that gushed out was unbelievable. I bent over by the side of the road and vomited.

"Violet? Are you okay?" Louis asked, squatting beside me.

"Yes," I lied. I wanted him to go away. Being sick was bad enough, but I was horrified to have him see me this way. I tried to stand up and walk and felt my gorge rise again. I turned away and threw up a second time.

Louis offered me his handkerchief. His kindness and sympathy only added to my humiliation. Every time I was with Louis something degrading seemed to happen. First I had encountered the horrid onions and beets, then the drenching rain and mud, now this. This humiliation was by far the worst.

"I need to go home."

Louis let me lean on his arm as I staggered back to the settlement house. Someone brought me a cool cloth to wash my face. Louis brought me a glass of water.

"I'm sorry for forcing you to eat," he said.

"No, it wasn't your fault. It was the sight of . . . you know."

"I think you should go home."

Home. I would have to go home to Lockport in four more days. I couldn't stop my tears. Could my mother's family really be involved in those horrible shows? Visiting the Jolly Roger had been bad enough, but going to a burlesque theater to search for her would be much, much worse. Nevertheless, I had to do it.

"I need to find my mother, Louis. I need to find the family of gypsies named Cepak who are involved in the theater."

"But the woman said—"

"I know. You don't have to help me anymore. But you've been to some of those neighborhoods—if you have any advice . . ."

"I don't know what to tell you. Mr. Moody sometimes rents theaters for his rallies, but not those places. He's holding a rally on Thursday, in fact, but it's in a respectable theater—"

"Maybe we could talk to the theater manager and ask if he has heard of the name? Or maybe one of the other actors at the theater has heard of her."

He looked very dubious, but he said, "I guess it's worth a try."

"Thank you."

I heard a babble of excited voices in the front hall. The house seemed to be filling with young women my age.

"What's going on?" I asked Louis.

"I think they're registering new girls for the Jane Club. Miss Addams started a boardinghouse for single women using several of her vacant bedrooms. Many of these girls don't have families in the city, and they need a safe place to live that won't use up all of their meager wages."

I nodded, thinking of all the vacant bedrooms in our house in Lockport.

"We should go find your grandmother and tell her you're not well," Louis said. "You need to go home."

My stomach rolled at the thought of venturing outside. "Would you mind if I stayed here while you fetched her? The smells in the street . . ."

"Sure. I'll be right back."

The sound of laughter and babbling voices grew louder as the girls spilled into the other rooms from the front hall. One of them looked very familiar to me. It took me a moment to realize that it was Katya. She looked bedraggled without her crisp maid's uniform and starched white apron. Her skirt was patched and threadbare, her shoes scuffed and worn. My strength had returned, so I stood and made my way toward her, calling her name.

"Katya . . . Katya . . ."

Her eyes widened when she saw me. She whirled around and hurried away, plowing a path through the crowd and out of the house.

"Katya, wait!" I called. "Come back!"

Why was she running from me? I braved the terrible odors outdoors and chased her down crowded Halsted Street, weaving between the other pedestrians. Katya was very fast, and I was still feeling light-headed after being sick, but I kept running. I caught up with her at the corner when she encountered too much traffic to risk crossing the street.

"Don't run, Katya. I'm your friend!" Both of us were breathing hard, and I could taste the terrible odors as well as smell them. "What's wrong? Why did you run?" When she didn't reply, I said, "Listen, I know that you're in love with Nelson—and that's okay with me."

"No, please . . ." I saw her surprise and fear. She had no idea what I would do with that knowledge.

"It's okay. I won't tell anyone."

"But you are the woman Nelson is going to marry."

Now it was my turn to be surprised.

"How do you know that? He only proposed to me a week ago. And that was after you left the Kents. Besides, I haven't agreed to marry him."

Tears filled her eyes. "But he must marry you or he will have nothing."

"Listen, can we go back to the settlement house and talk this over? I want to help you."

"Why? Why will you help me?"

"For Nelson's sake. He's my friend."

"I do not understand."

I took a chance and told her the truth. "I saw you with him. I saw the way he looks at you and the way you look at him. Nelson is in love with you, not me. And I saw him kissing you."

Her hands flew to her face. "Oh no. He will get into trouble. . . ."

"I'm not going to tell anyone. Listen, I came to the settlement house to help women like you, not harm them. Let's go back and talk, okay?"

"You won't tell anyone—about Nelson and me?"

"No. I promise."

We walked back to the house and pushed our way through the crowd of girls. I led Katya into the library and sat down to talk with her at a table in the corner. She seemed very nervous, glancing all around as if she might get into trouble. She spoke so softly I had to strain to hear her above the noise.

"Tell me what happened. Why did you stop working for Mrs. Kent?"

"Because Nelson must forget about me. It is too hard for him, seeing me every day. He was so unhappy. So I quit."

"You mean, nothing happened? No one caught you two together?"

"No. No one knows about us. I leave because I love him." Tears flooded her eyes.

"I don't understand. Why would you leave if you loved him?"

"Nelson loves me too. He tells me over and over. He says he will find a way for us to be together, a way for us to get money. But I know that he is better without me. His family will be very angry about me. They will never want him to marry me. They will throw Nelson out of the family if he does, and he will have nothing. He is better with someone like you. I love him so much . . . and I want him to be happy."

I stared at Katya in amazement as she wiped her tears. Her love was genuine, self-sacrificing. She loved Nelson so much that she was willing to give up her own happiness for his. I envied her. And I wanted to help her.

My mind raced with plans. I could loan her some of my gowns and teach her everything I knew about proper manners. Nelson could break away from his father's business, and they could start a new life together on their own. There had to be a way to make this work.

"Listen, if you and Nelson love each other, then you should be together. I want to help you. Will you trust me?" She nodded slowly, as if afraid to hope. "Where are you staying? How can I contact you again?"

"Miss Addams is very kind to rent me a room here."

"Good. I'll be in touch with you after I talk to Nelson."

"Thank you." Katya stood and hurried away just as my grandmother walked into the library, her face creased with worry.

"Violet Rose! You're as white as a ghost. Louis told me you were ill." She felt my brow for a fever as she smoothed my tangled hair off my face.

"I'm feeling better now."

"I'm taking you home."

We walked to the main street, and for once my grandmother hailed a cab instead of waiting for the streetcar. I was grateful. I couldn't leave that stinking neighborhood quickly enough. When we had traveled a short way, my grandmother sighed and said, "Violet, dear, I know you've been looking for your mother."

"Did Louis tell you?"

She shook her head. "I've been trying to find her too."

"My mother? You've been searching for my mother? For how long?"

"Since coming to Chicago. It was one of the reasons I came here after Isaac died. And one of the reasons I started working down here at the settlement house. Hundreds of Bohemian people live in this area, so I decided to start here and do the same thing you're doing.

But I've had no luck, Violet, in all these years. I haven't found anyone who knows her or her family."

"What were you going to do if you found her?"

"Ask her to come home to you and your father."

I closed my eyes in disappointment and defeat. I wasn't going to find my mother. Grandmother had been searching for seven years and I had only three more days.

"While I was trying to find Angeline," Grandmother said, "I met so many women like her who needed my help. That's how I started working with the poor. So you see, something good can come from our sorrows and disappointments if we give them to God. And when I heard that D. L. Moody was preaching in theaters all over the city, I volunteered to help him too. I still hoped to find your mother—but I also hoped that other women like Angeline would have a chance to hear the Gospel."

I wondered if my grandmother realized that she had dropped a valuable hint. Once again, I pretended that I knew more than I did, hoping she would offer new information.

"You mean other actresses like my mother?"

"Yes. I'm sorry I couldn't find her for you, Violet, but I tried."

I was familiar enough with the neighborhoods by now to know that we were halfway home. I had to keep Grandmother talking and unravel more of the mysteries before we arrived.

"Did my mother run away with Uncle Philip?" I asked.

She drew a startled breath. "With Philip? Who has been talking to you about Philip?"

"Aunt Birdie showed me a picture of him and my father. She said he was away at war. I never even knew I had an uncle. Why won't anyone talk about him? Where is he?"

She turned away, gazing out of the window as if reluctant to answer. I continued talking.

"I came to the conclusion that Uncle Philip must have run away with my mother since nobody will talk about either one of them, and—"

"No, Violet," she said, shaking her head. "No. That isn't what happened." I waited for more, but she was quiet for a very long time. I was about to ask another question when she finally spoke. "No one talks about Philip because it's too painful—for your father as well as for me." Again, I waited.

"Your grandfather tried to control everything his sons did and said and thought. He forgot that God was in charge of the world, not him. He meant well, but he was much too strict. I didn't go against him, I'm sorry to admit, and we did a great deal of harm to our sons. Isaac wanted Philip and John to become ministers, like him. I got caught up in it, and I wished them to be preachers too. But that choice wasn't up to us.

"One day Philip had enough. There were too many rules in our household and not nearly enough love. Too much law and not enough grace. When Isaac tried to discipline Philip, he rebelled and left home. He had just turned eighteen, so he went off to war. He was nearly killed at Cold Harbor, but a good friend saved his life."

"Was his name Lloyd O'Neill?"

She nodded. "Philip returned home from the war filled with bitterness and resentment. He was angry with God. He had seen too much suffering and bloodshed to ever believe in God's mercy. He lived the reprobate life of a prodigal. The only thing that he and your mother had in common was that Philip was also involved in the theater."

"Are . . . are you still searching for Philip too?"

"No," she said quietly. "Philip died more than twenty years ago."

I leaned my head against her shoulder. "I'm so sorry."

"I know. No one talks about Philip," she said, wiping a tear, "because it hurts too much. None of us ever had a chance to reconcile with him."

"It must have been very hard . . . but at least you know why Philip left home and where he went. No one will tell me why my mother left me."

"Violet," she said with a sigh, "you know that I promised your father I wouldn't talk about her."

"Isn't there anything you can tell me?"

She sighed again. "Try to imagine a woman like Irina or one of the other women we met in these tenements. . . . Imagine her suddenly moving to your house in Lockport and having Mrs. Hutchins to cook and clean for her and a nanny to help take care of her children. Can you see what enormous changes she would face?"

"I guess so."

"Suppose Irina had to attend dinners and social functions in Lockport, and she didn't know anything about fine manners or social customs. Think of all the years of training you've had in school about proper etiquette. How would a woman like Irina ever learn those things? And do you think that the women in Agnes' crowd, for example, would ever accept Irina into their social circle?"

"No. They would make her life miserable."

I suddenly thought of Katya. She would never fit into Nelson's world or be accepted by his family and friends, even if I dressed her in my finest gown. If she were to rise from mere servant to lady of the house, Haughty and Naughty and their crowd would have nothing to do with her. Neither would Nelson's family. Could true love conquer all of those obstacles? It hadn't in my parents' case. And Nelson Kent was much wealthier than my father was.

"Can you understand the enormous strain on your mother?" my grandmother asked.

"Yes. I think I can. . . . Thank you." I had gained a little more understanding of my mother, even if I hadn't found her.

Then I recalled offering to help Katya live "happily ever after" with Nelson. I hadn't known what I was getting myself into.

Chapter

31

Wednesday, July 12, 1893

I needed to talk to Nelson. With only three days remaining until my father arrived, it looked as though I wasn't going to find my mother. But if I could help Nelson and Katya find the happiness that had eluded my parents, then at least I would have accomplished something this summer.

"I need to make social calls with Aunt Agnes this afternoon," I told my grandmother on Wednesday morning. She was bustling around the kitchen stove, trying to kindle a fire to brew coffee.

"What time is she coming for you?"

"That's the problem; Aunt Agnes doesn't know that I want to go with her. I'll have to call on her first."

Grandmother turned to face me, still holding a piece of firewood in her hand. "How can you do that? You can't go out alone."

"I think it's time that I did go out on my own, don't you? I can't lean on other people for the rest of my life. Aunt Agnes doesn't live very far, and I know the way. You and Aunt Matt travel all over the city by yourselves. I can too."

She studied me for a long time, a look of sorrow and concern on her face. "You've grown up a lot this summer, Violet."

"Yes, I know. But I needed to grow up."

Grandmother turned back to the stove, shoving the wood inside and closing the cast-iron lid. "I want you to hire a cab, then. I don't want you getting lost on the streetcars."

When I arrived at Aunt Agnes' home, she was surprised and pleased to see me. "Of course you can go calling with me, Violet; that's a wonderful idea. The other ladies have been so disappointed that they haven't seen much of you lately, and—"

"Can we pay a visit to Nelson's grandmother?"

"Certainly. She is more eager than anyone to get to know you better."

Her words were an unwelcome reminder that Nelson had indeed proposed to me—in spite of the fact that he loved another woman. I couldn't imagine what he was thinking or why he would do such a deceitful thing, but I intended to find out.

"We're all thrilled about the engagement, Violet. Just thrilled!"

Her words horrified me. "Y-you didn't tell anyone else about it, did you? Our engagement isn't even official."

"Now, Violet. Nelson's grandmother and I are very good friends."

"I know, but please don't say anything to the other women. Nelson should be the one who makes the announcement, don't you think?"

I could tell by her pursed lips and woeful frown that she was disappointed. She would have loved to stand on the tallest building in Chicago and announce the good news. I couldn't break her heart by telling her that I thought Nelson was using me or that I wasn't going to marry him.

"Well, it will be very difficult to remain quiet about something this momentous, Violet, but I shall respect your wishes. Just tell Nelson not to wait too long."

Making social calls that afternoon seemed almost as boring and tedious as spending an afternoon with Herman Beckett, but I made up my mind to get through it and leave a note for Nelson. For the first time, I found it difficult to paste on a phony smile and pretend that I enjoyed this life of social politics and gossip. I felt awkward making inane conversation with Nelson's grandmother and the other women as we sipped our tea and nibbled dainties.

I knew Aunt Agnes had told Mrs. Kent about Nelson's proposal because she gazed at me the entire afternoon as if it were her birthday and I was a chocolate cake. Meanwhile, I couldn't seem to forget that my father would arrive on Saturday to haul me back to Lockport and into Herman Beckett's stiff, black-suited arms. I felt like an actress— like my mother. I was still trying to adjust to that truth.

"Might I leave a message for Nelson to call on me?" I asked when the afternoon mercifully ended. Mrs. Kent beamed with delight.

"Why, Nelson is here, Violet. Shall I have one of the servants fetch him?"

I was prepared to confront him angrily, telling him that I knew the truth about his love for Katya and demanding an explanation for his marriage proposal—until I saw how terrible he looked. He hadn't shaved. His clothes looked as though he had worn them for days. His golden hair stood on end. Deep worry lines etched his handsome face, making him appear several years older. He hurried me outside to the garden, away from the scrutiny of the other women.

"What's wrong, Nelson? You look unwell."

"I lost it all, Violet. Everything!"

I wondered if he meant Katya. If so, I knew where he could find her. "What did you lose?"

"My luck was terrible the other night. I didn't have you for my good-luck charm and I lost everything!"

"Oh, money," I mumbled. "I might have known. Look, I'm sorry, but I was afraid that would happen. That's why I didn't want to come with you the other night."

"You don't understand. I borrowed the money from my father's business. I was supposed to deposit it in the bank but I . . . I diverted it. And now I've lost it all. I stayed home from work today so I could figure out what to do. It wasn't hard to play at being sick because I am sick. I have to pay the money back before he finds out, but I can't because I'm broke!"

I sank down on a stone bench in the garden to ponder this news, but Nelson couldn't seem to sit. Nor could he stand still. He paced in front of me, running his hands through his hair—which explained why it stood on end.

"If I could just scrape a couple of hundred dollars together, I could go back to the fairgrounds on Friday night and win it all back before my father finds out."

"Or you could lose even more," I pointed out.

"I don't know what to do."

"What about a bank loan?"

"Every banker in the city knows my father. Besides, I have no credit and nothing for collateral. I've heard there are loan sharks I could go to, but they charge high interest rates. It wouldn't matter, though, because I can win it all back on Friday night. . . ." He seemed to be talking more to himself than to me. I decided to confront him after all.

"You were gambling because of Katya, weren't you?"

His pacing stopped abruptly. "What did you say?" I didn't think it was possible for Nelson to look more unwell, but he did.

"I know about her, Nelson. Whenever I was at your house I watched the way you gazed at each other from across the room and saw how you followed each other with your eyes. I also saw you kissing her."

"It's not what you think, Violet."

"What do I think?"

"That it was a seduction. The rich, spoiled son seducing the innocent immigrant girl. It happens all the time in our circle and usually ends with paternity suits and payoffs and covered-up scandals. But this isn't like that. I haven't touched Katya—well, aside from a few stolen kisses. I love her. But she left. She quit. And I have no idea how to find her."

"I know where she is."

He grabbed my shoulders, gripping them tightly. "Where? Tell me, Violet. I have to see her."

"Why? What are you going to do when you find her?"

"I-I don't know . . ." He released me and his head sagged as he started pacing again. "Remember when you asked me whether I would choose true love with poverty or wealth and success without love? I'm living that dilemma, Violet. I love Katya . . . but I'm too much of a coward to give all this up." He gestured to his grand-mother's mansion behind me.

"And where do I fit in?"

"You came to Chicago to marry a rich husband, so I thought that . . . Oh, never mind," he said, waving his arms. "It doesn't mat-ter. I couldn't make up my mind what to do about Katya, and so she left, and I don't know where she went. She said it was better this way. We could never marry."

"Why not?"

"Don't you see? It's not just the money—it's my family. Their hold over me is very powerful. I have three sisters. I'm the only son. My father is counting on me to take over his business, but if I choose Katya, I'd have to turn my back and walk away from them forever."

"I understand," I said quietly. "But I talked to Katya, and do you know what she told me? She said she left you because she loves you. What a thought! She was willing to give up what she loved the most in the world—you—so that you could be happy and have all of this. That sounds like genuine love on her part, doesn't it? So the question is, would you be willing to do the same for her? To give up every-thing—even your family—in order to be with her?"

Nelson sank down on the bench beside me as if he had suddenly run out of strength. "I don't know," he said, shaking his head. "I don't know."

"There is a way out of your dilemma. You could make your own fortune. You're certainly smart enough. Isn't your love for Katya motivation enough? You told me all those other rags-to-riches stories about Mr. Fields and Mr. Harvey. Didn't you say you wanted to invest in some of the modern inventions you saw at the fair, like Mr. Edison's music-making machine?"

"Yes, but I have no capital to start my own business. That's why I started gambling. If I make my own wealth, I can marry whomever I want."

"Where do I fit into this picture? You asked me to marry you, remember?"

"It was never my intention to hurt you, Violet. You wanted a rich husband and I wanted Katya. I thought we could both get what we wanted."

"So I was supposed to share you? That isn't fair to me or to her."

"I wasn't thinking clearly. I was desperate. As long as my father thought I was settling down and was about to be married, he would give me access to his money. So I borrowed some, hoping to gamble with it and win more. You seemed reluctant to get married right away, unlike all of the other girls I know, so I hoped we could delay the wedding long enough for me to make my own money."

"You never intended to marry me?"

"I thought about it. I'm ashamed to say that I thought about marrying you and having Katya for my mistress. But I couldn't go through with it. Besides, Katya kept telling me that it was wrong to deceive you. I like you, Violet. That's why the only solution was to win my own fortune."

"But you lost."

"Yes. And unless I can get a loan, I'm going to be in enormous trouble. I've been trying to locate a loan shark, but I don't know anyone in the world of crime."

I felt sorry for him. And sorrier still for Katya. But after discovering some of the truth about my mother, I wanted to help them, for her sake.

"I might know someone who could help you."

"You do? How on earth do you—?"

"Don't ask. Mr. McClure is an . . . an acquaintance. I don't know him very well, but he seems to have a lot of connections in the criminal world. He might know how you can contact a loan shark."

"I'm starting to think that it's true what they say—that money is the root of all evil."

"Actually, a preacher friend told me that money itself isn't evil. It's the love of money that's at the root of all evil." I was about to ask him if he loved Katya more than he loved money when he interrupted.

"Listen, how can we contact this acquaintance of yours?"

"He's staying at a hotel here in the city. We can probably reach him there."

"How? When?"

"Let me think . . ." I had learned a lot during these past six weeks about detective work and stealth and getting around town. Before I arrived in Chicago it would have taken me hours or even days to figure out what to do. Now I was able to quickly concoct a plan.

"We'll tell my aunt that you want to escort me home. She'll agree because she's very eager for us to get together. We can go to Mr. McClure's hotel on the way—even though it's actually out of our way—and we'll leave him a note asking him to contact you."

We proceeded with my plan. Mrs. Kent and Aunt Agnes were indeed very obliging, imagining that we were in love and longing to spend every moment together. I borrowed paper and a pen to compose the note we would leave for Silas while Nelson returned to his room to attend to his appearance. He called for his grandmother's carriage and driver, and we set off downtown.

I had imagined Silas' hotel to be a shabby flea-bitten place, but the modest establishment had a quiet, understated elegance—and wasn't at all what I expected from an elixir salesman. I glanced around at the bright Turkish carpets, the gleaming brass fixtures and fresh flower arrangements, and wondered if Silas was staying here in order to rob the other hotel patrons. Nelson and I strode up to the front desk together, and I handed the clerk the envelope.

"Good afternoon. Would you please give this note to Mr. McClure when he returns?"

"Mr. McClure returned just a few minutes ago, miss, if you'd like to give it to him yourself. I just gave him his room key. Shall I send a bellboy upstairs for him?"

"Yes, thank you."

I gave the bellboy one of my calling cards and sat down in the lobby with Nelson to wait. I was remarkably calm compared to Nelson, who rapped his fingers on the armrest of his chair as if auditioning to be a drummer at the Javanese Village. I had a view of the elevator doors and I watched as they opened and Silas stepped out. To say that he looked pleased to see me would have been an understatement.

"Violet! What are you—?" He never had a chance to finish.

Nelson leaped from his chair and thrust out his hand to introduce himself. "Good afternoon. I'm Nelson Kent. I understand that you are acquainted with my fiancée, Miss Hayes?" Silas' customary grin vanished. He looked as though Nelson had punched him in the stomach. He glanced at me as if to ask if it was true, but I looked away.

"Yes . . . Miss Hayes and I are acquainted," Silas finally said.

"Look, I'll get right to the point. I need a loan, and for reasons that I'd rather not explain, I can't go to a bank. It would be a short-term loan, but I'd need the money by Friday night. Can you put me in touch with someone?"

"Possibly. Why don't you sit down, Mr. Kent?" He gestured to the chair beside mine and then sat down across from us on the sofa. "I'll be blunt, Mr. Kent. Most men of your obvious wealth don't go around asking for loans unless they're in trouble. I'll wager it's a gambling problem—am I right?"

"It's none of your business. Can you arrange a loan or not?"

"I'll need a few details about the casino first."

Nelson's gray pallor returned. He looked even worse than when I had arrived at his house. He ran his hands through his hair and leaned forward in his chair, staring at the floor as if he might need to vomit.

"Go ahead and tell him," I urged. "What do you have to lose?"

Nelson exhaled. "It's a private game in a rented hall at the World's Fair. By invitation only."

"Hmm. I heard rumors that there was a game going on there. . . . Let me guess—at first you lost, but then your luck changed and you won back all the money you'd lost and a little bit more. But it was closing time."

"That's right," I said. "How did you know?"

"That's the scam, Miss Hayes. The dealers can spot someone who's desperate a mile away. They'll let you win a little money so you'll come back another night and play for even bigger stakes. I gotta tell you, Mr. Kent—you'd be a fool to gamble away any more money at that place if it isn't legitimate."

"Look, I don't need a lecture," Nelson said. "Can you help me get a loan or not? I'll take my chances on winning. I have to."

"I'll tell you what." Silas leaned forward, his manner surprisingly sympathetic. "I have a friend who knows a thing or two about rigged games and weighted dice and marked cards. We'll meet you at this place, and he can check it out for you before you lose any more money."

"I told you it's private. Invitation only."

"Just get us in, okay? If my friend says they're not scamming, then we'll talk about a loan. Why throw away more of your money—not to mention a loan shark's—at high interest rates? Can you get us in?"

Nelson hesitated.

"I think you'd better take his advice," I told him. "What if you borrow money and lose it?"

"Okay, fine," Nelson said. "Just bring the money with you. And wear a tuxedo, if you can get one. The game is for high rollers only."

We all agreed. Nelson would pick me up on Friday night, and we would meet Silas and his friend at the fair.

"Tell me where I can find Katya," Nelson said as soon as we climbed back into his carriage.

"I think you need to decide a few things first. Don't lead her on, Nelson, if you have no intention of marrying her. It isn't fair to her. And you need to figure out how your marriage is going to work since you come from such different backgrounds. Katya doesn't know all the social rules that you take for granted. She would never survive the scrutiny of your grandmother and her friends. They would never accept her. And what are you going to do about Katya's family? Are you going to ask her to give them up along with all of her traditions? Would you be comfortable with her family, visiting their home, eating their food?"

"I told you, I don't know what to do. How do I separate my duty and loyalty to my family from my right to live my own life?"

"I'm sure your family only wants what's best for you. They're thinking of all the problems you would face if you made a bad choice."

As soon as the words were out of my mouth, I recalled my father saying something very similar to me. He wanted to prevent me from making a huge mistake and being hurt, as he had been.

"Why is it any of their business whom I marry?" Nelson asked.

I started to reply when I suddenly thought of Murderous Maude. I had been intent on preventing Father from marrying her, but was it any of my business whom he married? If I didn't want my father to choose a partner for me, what right did I have to choose one for him?

"If you decide to marry her, Nelson, I'll help you. I can teach Katya proper manners and social customs and things like that. It's all an act anyway, isn't it? But you'll have to be prepared to make it through life on your own, without any money from your father—and not from gambling either. So how badly do you want her?"

"I love her, Violet."

I believed him.

And I envied him.

As soon as I arrived home, I wrote a letter to Katya, inviting her to come home with my grandmother on Friday afternoon. I assured her that she could trust me. I asked Grandmother to deliver the message to Katya when she went to the settlement house tomorrow morning.

As for my own problems, I was nearly out of time.

Chapter

32

Thursday, July 13, 1893

I had agreed to meet Louis in the theater district on Thursday afternoon. Mr. Moody was holding a rally there, and I wanted to ask the theater manager for advice on finding my mother. Once again, I wasn't quite courageous enough to venture downtown alone to an unknown part of Chicago, so I dragged Aunt Birdie along as my companion. Louis was waiting in front of the theater with our tickets, pacing nervously and checking his pocket watch as hundreds of people streamed past him into the auditorium.

"I'm sorry I'm late," I told him. "I stopped to read all of the show bills we passed, hoping to see my mother's name on one of them, but I didn't see it."

"That's okay, but we'd better hurry." I introduced Louis to Aunt Birdie as we shuffled into the lobby with the crowd.

"I'm afraid we won't have much time to talk to the theater manager," Louis said. "The rally is about to begin, and I have responsibilities backstage."

"I understand. I just need to ask him a few questions. It shouldn't take long."

"And after Mr. Moody preaches, it'll be my job to pray with the people who come forward for the altar call."

"Okay." I had no idea what he was talking about.

"Just wait in your seats after the rally ends, and I'll find you," he promised.

"Oh, how nice!" Aunt Birdie said when we walked into the ornately decorated theater. I thought it was an outrageously elegant setting for a religious rally, with gilded woodwork, an elaborately painted ceiling, and maroon velvet seats, but I kept my thoughts to myself.

"Are we seeing one of Mr. Shakespeare's plays?" Aunt Birdie asked.

"It isn't a play, Aunt Birdie. We're here for a church service."

"Well, that's odd."

"Yes ... well ..." I didn't quite understand it myself, so how could I explain it to her?

Louis found our two seats along one of the aisles in the rapidly filling hall, and I left Aunt Birdie there while we hurried away to talk to the theater manager. My hair grew faster than she moved, and I didn't have the time or the patience to tow her any farther.

The backstage area resembled an anthill, with people darting around chaotically, shouting last-minute orders about lighting and curtains. Choir members milled around as they tried to find their places and their music. The male soloist sounded like Marley's ghost as he warmed up, moaning his way up and down the scale with eerie-sounding "Ohhs" and "Ooohs."

We found the theater manager sitting behind a desk in his tiny office, calmly reading a newspaper. "How can I help you?" he asked after Louis introduced me.

"I'm trying to find my mother. She's an actress. Her name is Angeline Hayes, but she might also go by the name Angeline

Cepak." I had written down the names for him on a piece of paper, and I handed it to him.

"Sorry. Never heard of her. Do you know which show she's in?"

"No, I'm not even sure she's in a show at the moment, just that she's an actress."

He tossed the paper onto his cluttered desktop. "Look, we've got people running all around town thinking they want to act. Most of them never end up in the business at all."

"Well, if she is in the business, then someone must know her, right? How would I go about finding her? Is there a list of actresses somewhere?"

"I don't know of any list." He must have seen my disappointment—or perhaps the tears that filled my eyes, threatening to spill over—because his manner suddenly softened. "Look, Miss Hayes. If I were you I'd hang a notice in all the places where they're holding auditions. Maybe she'll see it. Or maybe another actor who knows her will see it. And it wouldn't hurt to offer a reward. There're plenty of actors on the lookout for their next dollar."

"I see. Well, thank you for your help." I turned to Louis as soon as we left the office. "I don't have time to post notices in every theater. There must be dozens of them. My father is coming the day after tomorrow. And I don't have any money for a reward either."

"I guess it just wasn't the Lord's will that you find her," Louis said. "I'm sorry, Violet."

"Hey, Louis," someone shouted. "Come on, we need you."

"I have to go, Violet. Can you find your way back to your seat all right? I'll meet you there afterward and take you home."

I was deep in thought as I wandered back out to the auditorium, wondering how I could hang posters in at least a few of Chicago's theaters before my father arrived on Saturday. I could list my grandmother's name and address as the person to contact. Hadn't she told me that she was searching for my mother too?

By now, nearly everyone in the audience had found their places.

I hurried up the aisle before the lights dimmed—and found two empty seats. Aunt Birdie was gone.

Panic gripped me as I quickly scanned the theater. I couldn't breathe. Why had I left her alone? What was I thinking? Several hundred people filled the huge auditorium. Hundreds more filled the balcony. How would I ever find her? I turned to the people in the row behind mine.

"Excuse me. D-did you see my aunt? She's an older woman ... w-with her hair in a bun and a dreamy smile on her face. I left her sitting right here."

"I saw her get up," the woman said. "I think she went that way." She pointed behind her toward the rear auditorium doors.

Oh, God, help me! I prayed as I raced up the aisle. "Aunt Birdie!" I called. "Aunt Birdie, where are you?"

People turned to stare at me, scowling at my rudeness. I didn't bother to beg their pardon. My voice grew louder and louder as my panic escalated. I knew I looked foolish running in useless circles, shouting her name, but I didn't care. I had to find my aunt. One of the ushers hurried over to me as the house lights dimmed.

"Miss, you have to stop shouting and take your seat. The program is about to begin."

"Please help me. I lost my aunt! She's an older woman with a gray dress and she wears her hair in a bun—and I have to find her!"

"Have you tried the lobby? Or the ladies' room?"

The ushers closed the auditorium doors behind me as I raced out to the lobby, calling her name. She wasn't there. One usher pointed to the ladies' room and I ran inside, my voice echoing in the empty space.

"Aunt Birdie? Aunt Birdie, are you in here?"

She wasn't. I could no longer hold back my tears as I ran out to the lobby again. That's when I began to bargain with God.

Please ... I'll stop looking for my mother. I'll gladly welcome Maude and her children into our family ... I'll even marry Louis Decker, if that's what you want. Anything! Just please, please, help me find Aunt Birdie.

I could hear the muffled sound of applause inside the auditorium. Across the lobby from me, the doors to the street stood open. I ran outside, praying that she hadn't walked in front of a streetcar.

"Aunt Birdie!"

Pedestrians crowded the sidewalk, calmly going about their affairs, oblivious to my distress, while traffic streamed in both directions on the bustling thoroughfare.

"Aunt Birdie!"

Madame Beauchamps would have been horrified to hear me shouting like a fishmonger on a busy Chicago street, but I didn't care. How could I ever face my grandmother? How could I tell her that I'd lost her sister?

Please, God!

That's when I noticed a commotion down the block in the middle of the street. Traffic had halted, and people were craning their necks to see what was going on. I ran out into the middle of it all, certain that a team of horses had trampled poor Aunt Birdie. I pleaded with God to spare her life.

And there she was in the middle of the road, hugging a policeman who had been directing traffic.

"Ma'am . . . ma'am . . ." he pleaded as he tried to pry off her arms. "You have to let go of me, ma'am. You're obstructing traffic." I wept with relief as I ran to her.

"Your family must be so glad to see you safely home from the war," I heard Aunt Birdie say. "My husband, Gilbert, is fighting in Virginia to help free the slaves. Is that where you were fighting?"

"Ma'am, I don't know what you're talking about, but you have to let go of me."

"Aunt Birdie!" I called. "Thank God I found you!" She released the policeman to give me a hug. I had never been so happy to feel her arms around me. "I'm so sorry for the disturbance," I told the policeman.

"Next time, lock the asylum door," he replied. I wanted to upbraid him for his unkind remark, but we had caused enough trouble.

"Come on, we need to go back to our seats, Aunt Birdie. The program is starting."

"I thought that soldier was Gilbert at first," she explained as I pulled her out of the road. "He bears a remarkable resemblance, don't you think?"

"Yes," I told her, but in truth, I couldn't have said what the policeman had looked like. My knees were so weak from fright that I could barely walk. I dragged her back to the theater and through the lobby doors.

"I haven't seen this many soldiers since the war began," she said, gesturing to all of the ushers. They smiled and nodded at us.

"Glad you found her, miss," one of them said. "I'll escort you to your seat."

"Is this one of Shakespeare's plays?" Aunt Birdie asked loudly as we walked down the aisle. "I do love *Romeo and Juliet.*"

"Shh . . . It's a church service," I whispered as I helped her sit down.

"Well, it certainly doesn't look like a church!"

I collapsed into my seat beside her, but it was a long time before my pulse returned to normal. What if I hadn't found her? I shuddered at the thought and vowed never to involve her in my adventures again.

The choir sang several songs, as did the soloist I had heard warming up backstage. I was oblivious to all of it as I sat thanking God and waiting for my panic to subside. I remembered all the vows I had made during the crisis and wondered if God would hold me to them. I had promised to stop searching for my mother and to accept Father's marriage to Maude. And I had promised to marry Louis Decker. I deeply regretted making that last vow now that Aunt Birdie was safe.

When I finally drew my thoughts back to the stage, a woman was playing a solo on the grand piano. She was wonderful. I glanced around the packed theater and knew I could never perform that way, no matter how simple the music was. I would die of stage fright before I ever played a single note. Surely that wasn't my calling, was it?

At last, Dwight L. Moody rose to stand behind the podium in the center of the stage. He was a sturdy-looking man with a wide forehead and an impressive beard. A deep stillness fell over the auditorium as he began to speak.

"We have for our subject today the Prodigal Son. Perhaps there is not any portion in Scripture as familiar as this fifteenth chapter of Luke. This young man was like thousands in our cities today who want to get away from home and do as they please. So the boy came to his father and said, 'Give me my portion and let me go.'

"He left home and went into that far country and got into all kinds of vice. He went to the theater every night and to the billiard hall and the drinking saloon. It does not take long for a young man to go to ruin when he gets in among thieves and harlots; that is about the quickest way down to hell."

Mr. Moody paused and stared out over the audience for a moment. I had heard the story of the Prodigal Son before in my church in Lockport, but this time it moved me deeply. I thought of how my Uncle Philip had left home to patronize saloons, and how my father had joined Mr. Moody's Yokefellows to search for him. I thought of my grandmother's long years of waiting for Philip to return, her heart breaking. My mother was a prodigal too, turning her back on her home and her family to pursue a stage career in Chicago. She must have broken my father's heart as he waited for her to return.

"At last the Prodigal's money was gone," Mr. Moody continued, "and he joined himself to a citizen of that country to feed swine. Now just for a moment think what that young man lost. He lost his home;

you may live in a gilded palace, but if God is not there, it is no home. He lost his food; he would have fed on the husks that the swine did eat. You can never get any food for the soul in the devil's country. Then he lost his testimony. No one believed him when he said he was a wealthy man's son.

"But there is one thing he did not lose. If there is a poor prodigal here tonight, there is one thing you have not lost. That young man never lost his father's love. When he came to himself and said, 'I will arise and go to my father,' that was the turning point in his life. If you are willing to admit your sin, and confess that you have wandered far from God, He is willing to receive you. I say to every sinner in Chicago, I do not care how vile you are in the sight of your fellowmen, the Lord Jesus loves you still."

When Mr. Moody paused again, I remembered what Grandmother had said about her husband—he had preached too much law and not enough love. Love was what my Uncle Philip had longed for, and what I longed for too. I had traveled to Chicago to search for my mother, desperate to know if she loved me. And I had wanted a beau who would offer me all of the love and romance I had craved when reading Ruth's novels. I wanted to find someone who loved me for myself, just the way I was, and God already loved me that way, right now.

"I can see the prodigal's father up there on the roof of his house," Mr. Moody continued, "watching for his boy. How his heart has ached for him! Then one day he sees that boy coming back. The father runs and leaps for joy. It is the only time God is seen running, just to meet a poor sinner. What joy there was in that home!

"No other subject in the Bible takes hold of me with as great force as the wandering sinner. The first thing I remember as a young boy was the sudden death of my father. The next thing was that my eldest brother left home and became a wanderer. How my mother mourned for her boy—waiting day by day and month by month for his return! Night after night she watched and wept and prayed. Our friends gave him up, but Mother had faith that she would see him again.

"Then one day in the middle of summer, a stranger approached the house. When my mother saw the great tears trickling down his cheeks, she cried, 'It's my boy, my dear, dear boy!'

"My brother stood in the doorway and said, 'Mother, I will never cross the threshold until you say you forgive me.' Do you think he had to stay there long? Oh, no! Her arms were soon around him, and she wept upon his shoulder, as did the father of the Prodigal Son.

"Oh, my friends, come home tonight. God's heart is aching for you. I do not care what your past life has been like—God is ready and willing to forgive you. There is no father in Chicago who has as much love in his heart as God has for you.

"You can leave the pigpens and the gutters of this world and come home to Him. Give every area of your life to Him, and He will show you how He wants you to live. Offer yourself to Him, and you can know His will. Rich people can serve Him, poor people, men and women, old and young alike. There is a place for you in the Father's house that only you can fill. And you begin to find it right here, when you give your life to Jesus."

I felt like cheering. Again, I recalled my grandmother's words: *"Violet, you be exactly who God created you to be, and don't let anyone tell you otherwise."*

"I'm going to ask you to come forward in a moment," Mr. Moody told us, "so you can come home to Jesus. And you'll never know if this may be your last chance to accept His invitation. I preached on the night of the Great Chicago Fire, but when I heard the alarm bells ringing, I dismissed the congregation without offering this invitation. That night some three hundred people lost their lives. Perhaps one of them had been about to surrender to Jesus—but I didn't offer him the chance.

"After the fire, I vowed never to preach another sermon without inviting people to come to Christ. This is your invitation. Come now.

The Father's arms are open wide, waiting for you to come home."

I longed to go forward. Mr. Moody's sermon was the most compelling one I'd ever heard. Louis and several of his friends moved into place in front of the stage and I knew that's what he'd meant when he'd said he would pray with people afterward. But I remained in my seat. I couldn't leave Aunt Birdie alone, and she would be too confused if I tugged her forward with me. Instead, I closed my eyes and prayed silently.

Okay, I'm yours. Whatever you want me to do, God, I'll do it. I know you have my best interests at heart, just like my father does when he tries to make plans for me. You know even better than he does what I should do with my life. I want to offer it to you now.

As people streamed forward, the choir sang the song about the shepherd searching for his lost lamb. My tears slowly fell. God loved me! It seemed so amazing. God felt as anxious and determined to find me as I had been to find poor, lost Aunt Birdie. He would search for me to bring me home to himself just as diligently as I was searching for my mother. He would search as hard as Grandmother had searched for her, as hard as Father had searched for his brother in all of Chicago's saloons. God loved me that much.

I remained in my seat as the service ended and the lights came on and people began to leave. And as strange and untrue as it might sound, I felt loved for the first time since my mother left me. I still didn't know what my future would be, yet I felt certain that if I came home to my Heavenly Father, then I could face anything in life.

I would put as much effort into learning about Him as I had into learning all of Madame Beauchamps' rules of etiquette. I would discover my "calling," as my grandmother referred to it. I would serve God the way He wanted me to.

Chapter

33

I was still sitting in my seat in the theater, still feeling God's love, when Louis came up the aisle to find me. I became aware of my surroundings again and saw the crowds filing slowly out of the auditorium and heard the rumble of excited voices.

"That was wonderful," I told him. "Thank you for inviting me."

"I'm so glad you came today, Violet. You have no idea how much it means to me—and to our future."

I remembered my rash promise to marry Louis Decker. Was that really God's will for me? I understood now why Louis didn't need love and romance; he had God's love. So why was he so eager to court me? He had never professed his love, yet he seemed to be in a big hurry to marry me, in spite of the fact that we hardly knew each other. Did he love me or didn't he?

"I'm working at another rally this weekend," Louis said. "We could go together and work side by side. You could play the piano and—"

"May I ask you a question?"

"Of course."

"You seem so busy with school and your volunteer work at the settlement house and with Mr. Moody's campaign. Why are you courting me right now? I would think that courtship would be the least of your concerns."

"Actually, it's very high on my list. There is a church here in Chicago where I would very much like to minister after I graduate, but the board is reluctant to hire a bachelor. They would prefer a pastor who is a settled family man with a wife, especially a wife who will be a partner with him in the ministry."

I stared at him in surprise. "So you won't be considered for the job unless you're married?"

"They'll give preference to a married applicant."

The news that Louis was using me to secure a job stunned me. But to be fair, hadn't I been using Louis too? I had asked him to take me to the Bohemian woman's tenement. And I had come to the rally today because Louis had promised to help me search for my mother.

"Which reminds me, Violet, what time is your father coming on Saturday? I would very much like to meet him and ask his permission to court you. Then I can tell the church board truthfully that I'm courting someone."

"Why me, Louis? Is the fact that I play the piano an asset?"

"Yes, a huge one. But it's not only that. You would be surprised how difficult it is to find a woman who is willing to marry a minister. When I learned that you came from a minister's family, I knew you would understand what's involved. I have the highest regard for your grandmother. She is such a wonderful woman."

I had to look away, alarmed by what Louis was saying. He hadn't mentioned any of my own qualities or why he had been drawn to me. The real me, Violet Rose Hayes, didn't seem to matter at all when he'd made his choice. And he still hadn't mentioned love.

My thoughts raced in every direction as I tried to digest Louis' words. Once again, I wasn't paying attention to Aunt Birdie. She turned to Louis and poked her finger in his chest.

"Why aren't you fighting in the war, young man?"

"I don't understand. Which war are you referring to?"

"The War Between the States, of course."

Aunt Birdie had her back to me, and I began waving my arms and shaking my head, signaling to Louis not to reply. He didn't get it.

"I think you're confused, Mrs. Casey. The war—" He stopped when I grabbed his arm.

"Louis, could I talk to you, please?"

"Just a minute, Violet." He held up his hand. "Mrs. Casey, that war is long over with."

"Louis, stop!" I shoved myself between them, but I was too late. Aunt Birdie had already heard him.

"It is? The war is finally over? Oh, that's wonderful! Did you hear what he said, Violet? The war is over!"

"Come on, Aunt Birdie. I think we should be going now." I took her arm and managed to drag her away from him, moving as quickly as I could make her go.

"Why didn't you tell me it was over, Violet? Matilda reads the newspaper every day and she never said a word about it either. And you would think that Gilbert would write immediately to tell me the good news."

"Maybe you'll get a letter today. Let's go home and see." I was trying to rush her out of the theater, but the crowd was still too thick. People stood talking in the aisles and in the lobby, and we could barely move.

I didn't realize that Louis had followed us until Aunt Birdie turned around and said, "Did we win the war, young man? Did we set the slaves free?"

"Yes, the North won and the slaves are free. But the War Between the States ended in 1865, Mrs. Casey, and this is—"

"Louis, no!" I was too late.

"—the year 1893. The war ended twenty-eight years ago."

"Oh, but that can't be true!" Aunt Birdie said. "If the war ended that long ago, then what has become of my husband?"

There was a terrible silence that no words could fill.

"Please, let's go home, Aunt Birdie," I begged.

"Maybe that soldier would know," she said, pointing.

"He isn't a soldier. He's a theater usher. We need to go home."

"Is your husband deceased?" Louis asked. I punched his arm. Again, I was too late.

"Deceased?" Aunt Birdie repeated. "Deceased? My Gilbert didn't come home . . . he went . . . he's in . . ."

The look of pain that suddenly filled her eyes broke my heart. I knew it was my fault for dragging her away from the refuge of her home, but I took it out on Louis.

"Couldn't you have just shut up?"

"I don't understand what's going on, Violet."

"That horrible undertaker came to my house!" Birdie cried. "He was dressed all in black . . . and he said . . . he said that Gilbert was *dead!*" I pulled Aunt Birdie into my arms and hugged her tightly as she finally grasped the truth. Her grief was heartrending.

"He's gone . . . he's gone! Oh, my Gilbert, my love—he's gone forever!"

"I'm sorry, Aunt Birdie. I'm so sorry." I wept along with her. Her beloved husband was dead, leaving a hole that nothing else had ever filled.

I remembered the day that I'd learned my mother was gone. I had wandered into her bedroom searching for her and found the bed neatly made. The room was still rich with the scent of roses, but her clothes and shoes were no longer in the wardrobe. Father sat down on the bed with me and told me Mother was sick—that she had gone away to get better. I remembered the aching emptiness I felt, the deep sorrow, the loss. He had lied to me, and I finally understood why.

"Why did you have to tell her the truth?" I asked Louis.

"Because it's wrong to lie. Satan is the father of lies."

"Well, sometimes it's better not to know. Sometimes it's better to say the kind and loving thing, instead of the brutal truth."

Louis seemed at a loss to know what to do. He tried to offer me his handkerchief, but I shook my head. I didn't dare release my arms from around Aunt Birdie, fearing that she would fall to pieces like a broken vase.

"Did her husband know Christ?" Louis asked. "Do you think he's in heaven?"

"Stop talking, Louis!" His insensitivity infuriated me. I knew that I could never marry Louis Decker. "Why did you have to tell her?"

"I'm sorry, Violet. I didn't know. . . . What can I do?"

"Go flag down a carriage so I can take her home."

"I can drive you—"

"No! I don't want you to. Just get us a cab. I'll meet you out front in a few minutes." He hurried away.

Aunt Birdie wept as if she never would stop. I rocked her in my arms, murmuring "Shh, shh . . ." I couldn't say *"It'll be all right"* because I knew that it never would be. We were the objects of many rude stares and odd looks, but I didn't care. Several choir members and people from Mr. Moody's team tried to approach us, obviously concerned, but I waved them away. It was my fault for dragging her with me on my useless quest. The best thing I could do for her was to take her home.

By the time we reached the door to the street, Louis had a hired cab waiting. Aunt Birdie and I climbed in. We wept all the way home.

The truth hurt. Love sometimes brought a great deal of pain with it. These were the hard lessons I had learned this summer. In the past I had often tried to escape the grown-up world of sorrow through my imagination, dreaming that a handsome young lieutenant would ride to my rescue, or that a great impresario would discover my musical talents and whisk me away. I had envisioned knights in shining armor and happily-ever-after scenes to escape from rules or boredom or pain, including a vision of my mother walking through our front door, whole and well again. But now I knew that a lifetime of escape led to a life like Aunt Birdie's.

My imagination was a gift, but I had to live in the real world. My eyes had been opened this summer to poverty and crime and abuse, and I needed to use my imagination—not to escape, but to help people like Irina and Katya; to make my own contribution, as the women in the Woman's Pavilion had done. I couldn't do it in the same way that Jane Addams and my grandmother and Aunt Matt were, but I would find my own way in my own time.

Aunt Birdie was still mourning when our carriage halted in front of our house. I saw someone sitting on our front steps and couldn't believe my eyes. It was Silas McClure. He leaped up and hurried over to the carriage to help Aunt Birdie climb down while I paid the driver.

"What are you doing here?" I asked. "We're not going to the fair until tomorrow night."

"I know. I came by to show you something."

"Well, this isn't a good time. Aunt Birdie has suffered a terrible shock."

"What happened?"

"My Gilbert is dead!" she moaned. She moved into Silas' open arms. He closed his eyes as he held her, rocking her gently in sympathy.

"I'm so sorry to hear that, Mrs. Casey. So sorry."

"Come into the house, Silas," I said after a moment. I couldn't have her weeping on the front steps for the entire world to see, and she was still clinging to Silas.

He led Aunt Birdie into the parlor and sat beside her on the sofa. She gazed around as if she had never seen this room before—then started crying all over again.

"Gilbert . . . Oh, my love, my Gilbert! What will I do without him? How can I go on?"

I had no idea how to console her. I could only cry along with her.

"The undertaker came and brought Gilbert home to me in a wooden box!"

Silas took her limp hands in his. "That wasn't him in the casket,

Mrs. Casey. Gilbert is alive and in heaven with the Lord, where he'll live forever. He's waiting there, waiting for the resurrection of the dead. Jesus rose from the dead on Easter—and that means all of His followers will live again one day. Gilbert is waiting for you."

His words astonished me. How could a thief like Silas suddenly start talking like a preacher? He must have astonished Aunt Birdie too, because she stopped crying and looked up at him in surprise.

"Yes . . ." she murmured. "That's what Gilbert promised me the day that he left. He promised that we would be together again—if not here on earth, then in paradise."

"Mrs. Casey, tell me again why Gilbert went away to war."

She drew a shuddering breath, as if for strength. "He wanted to end slavery. He worked so hard to abolish it—going to meetings, writing articles. For years and years. We both were involved. He saw me for the first time at a meeting of the Chicago Abolition Society . . . and he fell in love with me."

"He died a hero, you know. The slaves are all free. Millions of men, women, and children—and they'll never have to suffer as slaves again. Your husband did what he could to help make this country a better place."

"So their freedom was worth dying for?"

"Absolutely, Mrs. Casey. And he's still here with you, you know. We never lose our loved ones, because we always carry them in our heart. When we love someone as much as you loved him, we're changed. We become better people. That's how our loved ones always remain with us. We're different because of them."

"Have you lost a loved one too?" she asked.

"My mother—God rest her soul. But I remember all the things she taught me and the sacrifices she made to raise me—and I carry her here, in my heart."

"Gilbert used to help runaway slaves escape to Canada. He would risk going to prison himself just so they could be free. I used to be such a fearful person, but he taught me to be brave."

"And he would want you to be brave now, wouldn't he? As long as you remember his love, he will always be with you."

"But I can't hold him in my arms. I miss his arms . . ."

"I know, I know. That's why God gives us friends to hold." Silas drew Aunt Birdie into his arms and let her cry. I watched in amazement, aware that I never would have been able to console her the way he was doing.

"Did he send letters to you, Mrs. Casey?" he asked after a while. "I have letters from my mother, and sometimes when I read them, it helps me remember her voice and her smile."

"Yes." She pulled away to look up at Silas. "I have all of his letters. Every one he ever sent. He talked so much about the things he saw in Virginia and the horrible way that the slaves were treated. It made him want to fight all the harder for them."

"He sounds like an amazing man, Mrs. Casey."

By the time my grandmother came home, Aunt Birdie's tears had finally tapered off. But I knew Grandmother would see our red, swollen eyes and soggy handkerchiefs and know that something was wrong. I jumped up from the sofa and drew her aside.

"What happened, Violet? Is Birdie all right?"

"Louis Decker told her the truth about the war," I whispered.

"Louis did? But why?"

"He said that Satan is the father of lies." I was still furious with Louis and I wanted Grandmother to be too.

"Oh, dear. Come here, Birdie, dear." Silas helped Birdie to her feet, and Grandmother led her upstairs to her room. I drew a shaky breath and faced Silas. When I recalled everything he'd said to comfort Birdie, I could only stare at him, dumbfounded.

"I don't know what I would have done without your help. You knew exactly what to say. Thank you."

Where had all of his beautiful words about Jesus and heaven come from? Were they simply a memorized spiel, like his sales pitch for Dr. Dean's Blood Builder? I didn't think so—Silas had spoken as if he'd meant them. But then why did he consort with thieves? Why hadn't he revealed this side of himself before? Was he still being the professional con-artist—even now?

"Say, listen—I should go," he said, edging toward the door.

"Wait. Didn't you say you had something to show me? Was it about my mother?"

"It's nothing definite. It can wait until tomorrow night."

"You came all the way over here, Silas. You must have learned something definite." He rubbed his forehead as if it ached. He took a long time to reply.

"Your aunt kept saying that your mother loved the theater, and I began to wonder if maybe she was an actress or something. So I looked into it and found a showgirl who goes by the name of Angelina. No last name. I didn't speak with her, but I was able to take a photograph of her. I was going to show it to you and see if you recognized her, but . . . this isn't the time."

"I want to see it." He seemed very reluctant to hand it over. When I finally convinced him to show it to me, I immediately understood why. The woman wore a harem costume that looked like an illustration from the Arabian Nights. Her midriff was bare. She was very beautiful and had dark, curly hair like mine, but my heart rebelled at the idea that she was my mother.

"I didn't say anything to this woman about you," Silas continued, "because I didn't think it was a good idea to barge into her life until we're certain that it's her. If you want me to, I'll go back and talk to her."

"No, I don't want her to run away again. Please tell me where she is. Tomorrow might be my last chance to see her before my father comes to take me home."

"I don't think you should go there—"

"Why not? I've been to the tenements and the slums with my grandmother and to the Jolly Roger with you. . . . Can you go with me tomorrow?"

"Violet, it's not the neighborhood I'm worried about." Silas' smile was gone. He looked sorrowful. "I doubt that it's your mother."

"Why? What aren't you telling me?"

He hesitated a long time before saying, "This woman dances at a burlesque theater."

I should have been prepared for the truth after what the old Bohemian woman had told me about my gypsy ancestors, but I wasn't. I was sorry I had ever come to Chicago in the first place. I never would have tried to find my mother if I had known it would hurt this much. I was better off living with a lie, the way Aunt Birdie had.

"It can't be her!" I cried out. "It isn't my mother!"

I thought I had run out of tears, but I couldn't stop them from falling. I covered my face with my hands and wept. The next thing I knew, Silas had pulled me into his arms to console me the way he had consoled Aunt Birdie. He smelled like bay rum aftershave. I buried my face in his shoulder and sobbed.

I don't know how long we stayed that way before my good sense returned. My behavior was highly improper. I squirmed out of his arms and looked away, embarrassed. He handed me his handkerchief to dry my eyes.

"I'm sorry," I sniffed. "There has been entirely too much weeping here this afternoon. I'm sorry for subjecting you to it."

"No, I'm the one who's sorry, Violet. I never should have shown you the picture when you were already so upset. We don't even know if it is your mother. It might not be, you know."

"It isn't," I said, although I knew that it was.

"Anyway," he said with a sigh, "I should leave now and let you and your family recover. I guess I'll see you at the fair tomorrow night with your fiancé?"

"Nelson isn't my fiancé."

"I see." Silas was trying not to grin, but I could tell that the news delighted him. "Well, we can talk more tomorrow night."

"Thank you again for helping my aunt. I don't know how I will ever repay you."

"It isn't necessary."

He retrieved his hat, then turned to me, studying me for a long moment. I could only imagine how awful I looked with my bloodshot eyes and reddened nose. But his tender gaze told me he hadn't noticed.

"Good-bye, Violet."

"Good day, Silas."

When he was gone, I took the photograph over to the window and pulled back the lace curtains so I could see it in the light. Eleven years had passed since the last time I'd seen my mother, but she looked the same. I fought back my tears so they wouldn't blur my vision. If only Silas had told me where he had found her.

I decided to study the background for clues. That was when I spotted the familiar-looking steel girders and support trestles that held up Mr. Ferris' wheel. They were unmistakable. I also saw something that resembled a camel, half-hidden behind my mother's arm, and I remembered seeing the Bedouin Arab with his camel on the day I had visited the Midway with Silas. Herman Beckett had refused to tour the Midway because of the exotic dancers, improperly clothed. Misery Mary had called them hootchy-kootchy dancers.

This photograph of my mother had been taken on the Midway at the World's Columbian Exposition. I was certain of it. Tomorrow night, when Nelson took me to the fair, I would go over to the Midway and find her.

I hurried upstairs to splash water on my face and try to recover from all of the events of the day—and realized that I still had Silas' handkerchief in my hand. It was made from the finest quality linen, monogrammed in blue silk thread. But the letter wasn't an *S* for Silas or an *M* for McClure. It was monogrammed with the letter *A*. Silas had stolen it, no doubt.

He had so many wonderful qualities—why did he have to be a thief?

Chapter

34

Friday, July 14, 1893

On my last full day in Chicago I stayed home. It would be my last chance to make social calls with Aunt Agnes, but I'd seen all that phoniness for what it was. I received a note of apology from Louis Decker, asking if he still could meet my father on Saturday, but I was too disappointed with Louis to face him.

My grandmother left for the settlement house, promising to bring Katya home with her. Aunt Matt and I remained home to help console Aunt Birdie.

"How long will it take for her to forget again?" I asked Aunt Matt as I helped clean up the breakfast dishes.

"It varies each time. Maybe a week. We can hope and pray that it's sooner."

"I'm so sorry, Aunt Matt. I feel like it's all my fault."

"Sometimes the truth is very painful, Violet. I want you to remember that if you do find your mother someday. I would hate to see you get hurt."

I nodded and swallowed back my tears. I already knew that my mother was a dancer at a burlesque theater.

That afternoon, my grandmother brought Katya home with her. I was in the kitchen fixing a tea tray for Aunt Birdie and Aunt Matt, but I poured a cupful for Katya and myself.

"Let me take this tray upstairs to my aunts," I told her, "then we'll talk. Please go into the parlor and make yourself at home." She was still standing in the kitchen when I returned. I picked up our two teacups. "Let's go sit down," I repeated, gesturing to the parlor with a tilt of my head.

"Oh no. I could not do that."

"Why not?" I thought her hesitation came from mistrust, but her reason surprised me.

"It is not right for a person like me to sit in your parlor. I am only a servant."

"Katya, it's perfectly proper if I invite you."

She shook her head vigorously. "No, no, I could not."

"Okay, fine." I set our cups on the kitchen table and sank down in a chair, gesturing for her to sit. She hesitated, and as much as I disliked doing it, I knew I would have to command her as I would a servant. "Sit down and drink your tea, Katya. We're going to talk."

I offered her milk and sugar but she refused, obviously uncomfortable with being served by me. She seemed as fearful and skittish as a sparrow.

"Katya, please sit back and relax. I want to be your friend. I meant what I said the other day. I want to help you and Nelson."

"But why would you help me? You are going to marry him."

"No. I'm not going to marry Nelson. I want to help you because . . . because love is so precious and perhaps so fleeting that we need to hang on to it tightly when we do find it. My aunt Birdie taught me that lesson. Her husband died nearly thirty years ago and she's still mourning for him. So I made up my mind to help you and Nelson find a way to be together."

Tears filled her eyes. "But I am not a good wife for him—"

"Stop right there. You're wrong. The best wife for Nelson is the one who will bring him love and joy. You need to forget that you ever were a maid and start thinking of yourself as a woman—a very lovely woman. The only difference between you and me is where we were born, and birthplace has nothing to do with who we are on the inside. If I can learn all those fancy manners, so can you—if you want to, that is. Do you want to?"

"I will do anything for Nelson."

"Good. Then pick up your teacup and come into my parlor. We're going to sit down in there like two proper young ladies and drink it." I rose from my chair and led the way to the parlor, gesturing to Katya to sit on the sofa beside me. She did so, looking stiff and uncomfortable.

"Just watch me and do exactly as I do."

"I am always watching the fine ladies when I am serving the food."

"That's good. Pretend you're one of those fine ladies. It's all an act anyway."

"I do not know that word, 'act.'"

"It means make-believe, like a show in a theater. Everyone is pretending to be someone they aren't." I was confusing her. "Look, you had to learn the rules for being a good maid, didn't you? Being a lady is simply a matter of learning all new rules. Tell yourself that you are a lady, copy what the other ladies are doing—and pretty soon you'll begin to believe it." I lifted my teacup and sipped daintily. Katya did the same, but I saw the cup trembling in her hand.

"Tonight we'll be going to a private club at the fairgrounds. Nelson is coming for us, and—"

She gasped. "Does he know I am here?"

"Not yet. Look, this will be an experiment." Again, she seemed confused by the word. "What I mean is, tonight you and Nelson will have a chance to try being together in his world—the way you would

---

try on a dress to see if it fits you. If you decide to get married, then you'll be going with him to fancy places all the time. Now finish your tea and we'll go up to my bedroom and try on some clothes."

"I cannot go up to your room! Maybe there is a room down here to dress? Where your servants stay?"

"Did you forget your first lesson already? You have to get rid of the idea that you're a servant. Someone told me yesterday that when we love somebody we are changed—we become better people. Let your love for Nelson change you, Katya. Tell yourself that you are the same kind of woman that I am. Now, come on."

I dragged her up the stairs and into my bedroom. We were nearly the same size, so it was easy to dress her in one of my gowns. She was so naturally elegant and graceful that she would never need to practice with a book on her head. I helped her arrange her fine, wheat-colored hair in an elegant, upswept style, then took her downstairs to look at herself in the hall mirror.

"See? You look beautiful, and as fine as any lady."

"But everyone will hear that my English is not so good."

"Stay beside me. I'll answer everyone's questions for you. Besides, for all they know, you could be an elegant European lady visiting Chicago to see the fair."

"I am scared. What will Nelson say when he sees me?"

"I don't know, but we'll soon find out. Listen, this night may not turn out the way we're hoping it will, but don't you want to know the truth? Don't you want to see if he loves you enough to try to make things work?"

As it turned out, Nelson was so stunned when he came to the door and saw Katya that he couldn't utter a single word. He didn't have to. The tender look in his eyes spoke for him. I saw the deep love he and Katya shared written on both of their faces, and I envied them. I'd had three marriage proposals, but not one of my suitors had ever looked at me that way.

"I think we should take your carriage to the fairgrounds," I told Nelson.

He nodded absently. He hadn't taken his eyes off Katya. I could have suggested that we walk to the fairgrounds in our undergarments and he would have nodded the same way. I explained my reasons, even if he didn't hear them.

"If we drive we can avoid running into the pea pods onboard the ship. They might ask too many questions. And if I know the pea pods, they'll be lining up to court Katya before the ship leaves the dock."

"What is that word—pea pod?" Katya asked.

"That's what I call Nelson's look-alike, act-alike, think-alike friends. They're like vegetables, like peas in a pod, all the same."

She nodded, but I could see that she still didn't understand. Playing fairy godmother in this Cinderella act might be more difficult for me than I had imagined. I thought of my mother, trying to adjust to life in Lockport. It must have seemed like another world to her.

We climbed into Nelson's carriage and started on our way. Nelson sat close to Katya, holding her hand all the way there. I sat opposite them, issuing instructions the way that my aunt Agnes had whenever she'd taken me places.

"I'll introduce Katya as a friend of mine. It's true enough, for now. But you'll have to escort me into the casino, Nelson, not her. Your friends will get suspicious if you arrive with another woman on your arm after courting me all of these weeks."

"I'm sorry," he told Katya. "I hate pretending."

"Your life is all about pretending!" I said. "It's knee-deep in phoniness! Remember how we talked about that? And how much we both hated it? You're not giving anything up, Nelson. You're gaining a real life. And true love."

Nelson grew increasingly nervous as we neared the fairgrounds. So did Katya. She had proper manners to worry about, but he had a pile of his father's money to win back.

"Are you sure this McClure fellow will show up?" he asked me.

"He said he would. I have no reason to doubt him."

"But will he have the money? I have to have the money, Violet."

"Listen, if he does give you a loan, I think you should use it to repay your father instead of gambling it all away again."

"That's impossible. I need to win enough to repay my father and have some left over so I can be my own man. Make my own rules."

"But you could also lose it all and end up in twice as much trouble as you're in now."

He shook his head. "I have to do it. For Katya's sake."

"If people respect you, Nelson, they'll respect your choice of a wife. The ones who don't accept Katya aren't worth having as friends. Let her be herself, not a copy of Haughty and Naughty. You fell in love with her, remember? Not them. You and I can both play the game and act phony, but we're much happier when we're ourselves."

That was what my grandmother had been trying to tell me. *"You be exactly who God created you to be, and don't let anyone tell you otherwise."* I still wasn't sure what I wanted to do with my life, but I was narrowing it down and eliminating several possibilities. I didn't want a life in Nelson's social circle, living with all of the suffocating rules and manners I'd learned at Madame Beauchamps' School for Young Ladies—no matter how wealthy my husband was. Money meant nothing if I'd never be allowed to be myself.

As for settling down in Lockport, I didn't think I was cut out for that life any more than my mother had been. And after what had happened with Aunt Birdie yesterday, I didn't want to be part of Louis' world either, always under scrutiny as a minister's wife, suffocating under a church board's expectations. Those rules and limitations were as foreign to me as mine were to Katya.

We got out of the carriage at the entrance gates. I glanced at Katya's face and saw her wonder and delight as she glimpsed the fair for the first time. Cinderella, arriving at the prince's ball, could not have been more awestruck. Nelson was watching her too, and I could hear the excitement in his voice as he described the pavilions as we strolled past them. I followed behind like a chaperone as we made our way to the casino, allowing the two of them to be alone for as long as possible.

I was as nervous as Nelson and Katya, but for a completely different reason. My mother was here at the fair. After eleven long years, I might find her tonight. But did I really want to? It would mean facing the truth about who she really was and why she had left me. I had seen firsthand how deeply the truth had hurt Aunt Birdie. Did I really want to uncover all of it? I had the next few hours to make up my mind.

Silas and his friend were waiting for us in front of the building. I didn't even recognize Silas at first. Dressed in an elegant tuxedo with a bow tie and white satin vest, he looked like a completely different man from the sleazy one I'd first encountered on the train. I decided Katya must have cinched my corset too tightly; I could scarcely breathe.

I was wearing the gown that Aunt Agnes' seamstress had made for me, and when Silas saw me, his smile faded to a look of awe. I saw love in his eyes. Love! He looked at me the same way Nelson had looked at Katya. But any future between us would be even more impossible than the future they faced. I remembered the monogrammed *A* on his linen handkerchief and wondered who he really was. For the first time, I felt relieved to be leaving Chicago tomorrow. I couldn't risk meeting up with Silas McClure ever again.

"This is the way we'll do things," Silas told Nelson. "I'll give you a small stake to get you started. You place the bets while my friend Jackson studies the dealers. If things are on the up-and-up, we'll talk about a loan."

I took Nelson's arm as we entered the private casino. Silas and his friend escorted Katya. I felt absurdly jealous.

Cigar smoke filled the opulent room, making it seem dingy. The atmosphere seemed darker and more oppressive than I'd remembered from last time. Perhaps it was because Nelson was so on edge. I felt sorry for him. He had more at stake than ever before—not only his father's money, but also his happiness with Katya. I followed him to the dice table and watched as he placed his first bet. He held out the dice to me.

"A kiss for luck, Violet."

I backed away, shaking my head. "Let Katya be your good luck charm."

I tugged on her arm. She had been holding on to Silas, but she let go as I nudged her forward. Silas' friend was watching the game, but Silas was studying the three of us.

I turned my attention to the game. Nelson's forehead shone with sweat, even though the room didn't feel at all warm to me. Katya looked as frightened as a doe in hunting season. Silas and his friend seemed very intent on the game, and I thought I saw them exchange knowing glances and sly hand signals from time to time.

I watched each roll of the dice until I could no longer stand the tension, then I turned away and watched all of the other well-dressed partygoers gambling away their money. A group of cigar-wielding men waved wads of it around like it was so much paper. I suddenly had a horrifying thought. What if Silas and his partner had used Nelson to get inside because they intended to rob everyone? What if they weren't watching for crooked dealers at all but for a chance to steal every last dollar in this place? Just because Silas had shown me a harmonica instead of a gun didn't mean he was unarmed tonight.

Why had I ever trusted him? I knew that his friends had committed robbery before—right here at the fair! I had to warn Nelson. I inched my way over to his side and bent to whisper in his ear.

"Nelson? May I have a word with you, please?"

"Not now." Sweat trickled down his brow.

"It's very important—"

"Shh!" He waved me away.

I'd had enough. My father was coming tomorrow, and I'd wasted six weeks on Nelson and his nonsense. It was his own stupid fault for being in this situation. Besides, he didn't have any money to steal. Who cared if Silas and his friend robbed everyone in this place? I didn't.

I slipped away from the gaming table and merged into the crowd. Everyone was occupied with money. No one cared where I went or what I did. My anger and disappointment made me courageous. My mother was at the fairgrounds, a short distance away. I needed to face the truth.

I left the smoke-filled casino and went to find my mother.

Chapter

35

I stopped outside the pavilion to get my bearings. I was alone, but I didn't feel at all afraid. The well-lit streets bustled with people, and colored searchlights crisscrossed the sky, lighting up the fair's golden domes and towers. The World's Columbian Exposition was beautiful, and I was seeing it for the last time. Tomorrow I would leave Chicago. In another three months all the grand pavilions would be torn down and the White City would disappear. Everything would change. That was the lesson I'd learned this summer: Life was all about change.

I scanned the horizon and saw the giant wheel, revolving slowly in the distance. I began walking in that direction, following the clues I'd found in Silas' photograph. I remembered that the entrance to the Midway was near the Woman's Pavilion, and I could see that graceful building across the lagoon.

Finding my mother's theater turned out to be easier than I'd expected. The turbaned Arab and his camel stood right in the middle

of the Midway Plaisance, drumming up business for the Arabian
Nights Show. The billboard outside the theater featured a woman in
a harem outfit just like the one my mother wore in the photograph.
According to the scheduled times, I had more than an hour to talk
with her before the next show began.

I left the pathway and walked around to the back of the theater
as if I knew exactly where I was going. It was what Louis had done
when he'd led me backstage at the theater the other day. No one had
stopped him then, and no one stopped me now. A sign above the
backstage door read *Employees Only.* I tried the knob and found it
locked. I drew a breath for courage and pounded on the door. It
opened a crack, and a bearded man with oily hair peered out.

"What do you want?"

"I'm here to see Angeline . . . um . . . Angelina. She's expecting
me."

He looked me over from head to toe like a greedy child eyeing
an ice-cream cone. He didn't seem inclined to let me in.

"Angelina said she might have a job in the show for me," I added.

His lips curled into a smile. He opened the door very wide. "Second door on the right," he said, pointing.

My knees shook violently as I walked down the short corridor. I
quickly knocked on my mother's door before I lost my nerve.

"Come in," someone called from inside. I turned the knob.

The scent of roses overwhelmed the tiny dressing room. I knew I
had found my mother.

She sat before a mirror at a lopsided dressing table, brushing her
dark, loose hair. I had loved to watch her do the very same thing in
her bedroom in Lockport. She looked up at my reflection in the
dingy mirror and knew in an instant who I was.

"Violet," she whispered. She stood and turned, and we rushed
into each other's arms.

"Mama!" I wept. "Mama, I found you!"

Memories from childhood flooded back as I felt her familiar arms surrounding me and heard her murmuring in her native language. I don't know how long we remained that way. I only know that I had missed her embrace, her voice, her love, for eleven long years. I needed to make up for all that lost time.

"I've missed you so much, Mama!"

"And I have missed you, *ho-cheech-ka*," she cried. "You will never know how much!"

At last Mother released me. She held me at arm's length and gazed at me, her eyes brimming with love.

"Look at you," she murmured. "You are beautiful! And such a lady! A proper young lady, just as I hoped you would be."

I thought she would hug me again, but instead she turned away, tightening the belt on the ragged bathrobe she wore over her costume, drawing it closed. I saw shame in her eyes and in her manner as her gaze flitted around the shabby room, seeing it the way I would see it.

"I am sorry that you found me, Violet. Sorry that you see me this way."

"No, Mama, don't be sorry. I'm not—"

"Shh, shh . . . Listen, my darling. You must go back home. You must not let anyone see you here with me."

I shook my head, swallowing the lump of emotion in my throat. "But I want to talk to you. I want to know—"

"Shh . . . No, darling. No one must know that I am your mother. I do not want to tarnish you."

"You could never do that! I love you, Mama!" I moved toward her, longing to embrace her again, but she shook her head, holding up her hands to keep me away.

"You are very young, Violet. You do not understand how the world is."

"Then explain it to me." I sank onto her chair, wiping my tears as quickly as they fell. "I'm not leaving until you tell me everything I want to know. Why did you marry Father? Why did you have me?

And why . . . why did you abandon me?"

"Then will you go?"

"If you want me to." I couldn't understand how she could hold me in her arms and weep one moment and push me away the next. "I know that you and Father met on the night of the Great Fire. I know that he rescued you, but I don't know how."

She paced the cramped room for several moments as if gathering her thoughts, searching for a place to begin. I was struck by how lithe and graceful she was—and how beautiful. She looked very young to me, not yet forty, and I realized that she had been younger than I was now when she'd married Father. My hapless, straitlaced father must have been as attracted to the exciting young Angeline as stuffy Herman Beckett had been attracted to me in bloomers.

"Listen, I came to this country with my family when I was only a small girl," she began. "We were a family of gypsies—do you know what that means, what kind of life we led?"

"I-I think so." Thieves. Like Silas McClure.

"My father and older brothers started a theater here in Chicago. It was not a very nice place, and they made my sisters and me . . . We had to do whatever they said. I wanted to get away and have a better life, but they forced me to stay. My brothers locked me in my room every night with no shoes and no coat so I could not get away. I was their prisoner.

"That is where I was, locked inside, when the fire began. My brothers saw that the city was burning, so they left me there and went out to steal things from other people. I would have died that night if John hadn't saved me. He and his brother smashed down my door and helped me get out. Then John's brother ran back inside to save more people—but he never came out. The building fell into the street, and we had to run and run to get away.

"I hope you never have to live through a night like that one, *ho-cheech-ka*. It was worse than any nightmare I have ever dreamed of. The flames roared like a hundred trains, and buildings crashed to the ground. The sky was as light as daytime, the heat as warm as a summer day. We ran from the smoke and from the hot sparks that blew over us like snow. The cinders stung our skin, blown on the wind that howled in our ears. Some of the burning coals were as large as chestnuts.

"We ran as fast as we could, but the fire chased after us, a towering wave of flames that rolled toward us, trying to drown us. The streets were full of wagons and horses and screaming people trying to escape. They would leave things behind, dropping furniture and belongings to lighten their load until we had to climb over mountains of baggage just to get away. Behind us the flames leaped hundreds of feet in the air and swallowed buildings in one gulp. No one was fighting the fire. They could only watch helplessly as everything burned.

"John and I walked for miles and miles. My throat hurt from the smoke, and my feet ached because I had no shoes. John carried me on his back much of the way, like a child. We finally got to where all the streetcars had stopped. The men had driven them as far away as they could to get them out of the fire's path. They let us sit inside them to try to rest or maybe sleep.

"The city burned all night and all the next day. When the rain finally came and the fire stopped, my old life had all burned up. I could start all over again in a new place. John took me to his father's church in Lockport. I had never seen such a nice, quiet town.

"I fell in love with John, with his kindness and gentleness—and he loved me. But it was a terrible mistake to get married. I did not belong like all of the other people in that town. John's father disliked everything about me. The clothes I wore had too many colors. My hair should be put up, not hanging loose. I smiled too much; I was too foolish; I loved to dance. Everything was always wrong, and he said that I was turning you the wrong way too. He said I should not dance with you. And so I began to feel very sad. I stopped going out of our house. But I still had you and John. You brought me so much joy, Violet. I don't have enough words to tell you how much."

"Then why did you leave me?"

"After you were born, *ho-cheech-ka*, I had two more babies, but they died while they were still inside of me. Your grandfather said that God was punishing me for some sin in my life. I grew afraid that God would harm you or your father in order to punish me even more. I loved you both too much to let you suffer because of me."

"But that isn't true. God doesn't do things like that. And Father knows it isn't true. Why did you listen to Grandfather?"

"Do you remember the game we used to play together?"

"I don't remember very much . . ."

"I would ask something like: 'If you could choose, would you rather be a butterfly or a firefly?' And then you would have to choose."

I closed my eyes as tears flooded them.

"If you could choose, Violet, would you rather live on the moon or under the sea?"

"Mama, listen . . ."

"No, you need to listen to me, *ho-cheech-ka*. In the end, it was no longer a game for me. I had to make a choice and it was a terrible, terrible one—like choosing whether to be blind or to go deaf. Except that I had to choose between staying with the man I loved, the daughter I loved more than life itself, and ending up destroying them—or choosing to go away so they could live."

"I don't understand—"

"Have you ever been in love?"

I shook my head, trying not to think of the tender look I'd seen in Silas' eyes.

"Come back and talk to me when you do fall in love. Only then will you be able to understand."

"But I need to know now. I won't leave until you tell me everything."

I could see her frustration and her reluctance. But I had waited too long and searched too hard to leave my mother now.

"Very well," she said, exhaling. "Do you remember how I used to tell you tales about a princess who battled evil sorcerers and monstrous dragons and finally married a handsome prince? That was my life, Violet. My brothers were evil men, monsters who held me captive until a handsome prince came and rescued me. I did some very bad things before I met John Hayes. My father, my brothers—they were not good people, and they made me do bad things. John knew the truth about my past. When I told him, he said that Jesus forgave a woman in the Bible for the sinful life she lived, and He would forgive me too. But we never told John's father the truth.

"Then one terrible day my two older brothers found me. They came to our little town and told John's father. My brothers demanded a lot of money from him to keep quiet about all the things I had done. Your grandfather hated me even more for bringing this shame upon his family. Everyone in his church and in the nice little town would hear the truth unless he paid the money. I knew that my brothers would never be satisfied if we paid one time. They would always come back for more and more and more. So I chose to leave and go with them instead."

"Father told me you left because you didn't want to feel tied down anymore."

"That's what I told him. I wanted to make him angry with me so he would not follow me and beg me to come home. I left so that you and John could have the best possible life, not stained by my past. And look at you! You are beautiful. You look like a princess in your magnificent gown. You must have many rich young princes who want to marry you. And that is what I wanted most of all for you. A life of love and happiness—not a life like mine. The only way I could give that to you was to leave. I did it for you and for John. And now you must go and marry well, live well. You must forget all about me."

"But I can't forget you, Mama. I love you! I don't care about your family. I want to stay with you."

"No. That's not possible. Don't you see what I am?"

"Please, Mama. I could—"

"I don't want you here!" she said harshly. "You need to leave! It's time for the next show!" She opened the door and pointed to the hallway. Exotic music had begun playing in the background, and I heard drums pounding in the distance. "If you love me, then live the rest of your life without me, Violet. . . . Go!"

I didn't move.

She untied her ragged bathrobe and let it drop to the floor, revealing her flimsy costume. Then she turned her back on me and hurried away in the direction of the drums. The scent of roses trailed behind her. I ran outside, blinded by tears.

And I ran straight into Silas McClure.

Chapter

36

ey, hey—whoa!" Silas said as he caught me by the arm.

"Let me go!" I wanted to run and run and never stop, but he didn't ease his grip.

"There's no place to go, Violet. Just take a minute, okay? Take a deep breath." I did what he said. I had no choice. He wouldn't let go of me. I could hear the music from my mother's theater drifting faintly through the walls along with the relentless drumbeat.

"W-what are you doing here?" I asked when I could speak.

"I saw you leave the casino all alone, and I followed you. I was afraid you'd do something crazy like come over here. I figured I'd better come after you."

"I found her," I said, my voice shaking. "I found my mother. The woman in your picture—"

"I figured as much. There's a very strong resemblance."

"But she sent me away!" My tears started falling again.

Silas relaxed his grip on my arm and reached for my hand. "Come on. This is a lousy place to talk."

He led me around the building to the Midway's main street. The noise and bright lights and activity made my head swim. I was afraid that Silas was going to take me back to the smoke-filled casino, and I didn't want to go there. But he led me in the opposite direction and stopped at the base of the giant wheel. He bought two tickets. A few minutes later we were slowly rising above the bustle and confusion. Silas was a strong, silent presence at my side, saying nothing as we ascended. Lights twinkled below us and in the starry sky above us, and I felt my sorrow slowly ease. By the time we stopped at the very top, my tears were under control.

"Do you want to tell me what your mother said, Violet? I'm sure there was a very good reason why she sent you away."

The glorious wheel had worked its magic, and I was able to see past my bruised feelings and recall her words. "She left home because she loved me. She wanted a better life for me than the one she'd had. She thought I would be better off without her."

"And is that why she sent you away now?"

I nodded, remembering her shame as she'd pulled her robe closed over her costume.

"Violet, I'm so sorry," he murmured.

"My mother loves me. I finally understand that. She loves me so much she gave up her happiness for mine."

By the time we reached the bottom again I was calm. "Thank you for finding her for me."

"You did as much of the work as I did."

I felt drained as I stood in the bustling Midway, hearing the excitement and laughter all around me. "I guess we can go back to the casino now," I said with a sigh.

"No, Violet. I'm taking you home."

I wondered if he and his friend had already robbed the casino and he was using me to make his getaway again.

"What about Nelson and the others?"

"I'm sorry to say that your friend is a fool. That casino is as crooked as a witch's nose. If he borrows money to gamble in that place, he'll lose it all. He might as well toss his money into Lake Michigan."

"But what else can he do? He has to pay his father back."

"Well, my advice to him was to tell his father the truth and suffer the consequences. From what I hear, his father will never miss a few hundred bucks. I'm not sure your friend was listening, though."

We walked to the entrance gate, and Silas flagged down a cab. He helped me climb inside and sat opposite me. I couldn't stop thinking about love on the long ride home, and what a truly powerful force it was. It made people take enormous risks and make huge sacrifices. There was so much more to it than what I'd learned from reading Ruth's romance novels. Aunt Birdie had been the wisest of all the Howell sisters. I needed to make certain I married for love. And none of the three men who had proposed to me had loved me—the real me.

Now my time was up. Father was coming tomorrow. I would have to join Aunt Matt's suffragettes and remain a spinster because I didn't want to marry Herman Beckett or Nelson Kent or Louis Decker. I had thrown away my chances with any of Aunt Agnes' other suitors, even if I had wanted to live that phony life.

My parents had truly loved each other, but like Romeo and Juliet, interference from their families had doomed them. Katya and Nelson would likely face similar opposition from their families. Even so, I would be rooting for them to overcome all of their obstacles. I remembered the kiss they had shared and sighed.

What would it feel like to be kissed that way? Too bad none of my suitors had ventured to steal a kiss from me. At least I would have something to remember in my old age. I wondered if Aunt Matt's beau had kissed her before she'd learned the truth about him. Did she have the memory of that one kiss to see her through the lonely nights? If only there was a way I could experience a kiss—just once—before I gave up men forever.

Silas didn't say a word on the journey home. I noticed that he was no longer smiling. He paid for the carriage and let it drive away, then walked with me to the front steps.

"Are you still planning on leaving tomorrow?" he asked, pausing outside our front door.

"Yes. My father is coming to take me home to Lockport."

"Listen, before you go, I need to tell you the truth about myself."

"I already know the truth, Silas."

"You do? How did—?"

"I found out about the robbery on the day we went to the fair because my aunt works in the Woman's Pavilion. She told me the guards caught one of the thieves but that the other one got away. It wasn't hard to figure out."

"That was a real mess. I'm sorry—"

"Josephine and Robert were in disguise, weren't they?"

"Violet, I'm so sorry about all of that. I didn't know where else to get a chaperone, and I wanted to take you to the fair so badly."

"I understand."

"Just so you know, they were working the fair that day, but I wasn't."

"But you were working on the train the day we met, weren't you?" If I had learned anything at all this summer about being a detective, it was to plunge right in and pretend I knew the truth, then wait and see what people told me. "That's why you were in disguise on the train. I know all about that too, Silas. And that you aren't a salesman."

"Guilty as charged," he said, holding up his hands in surrender. "Listen, I'm sorry that I didn't tell you the truth about myself sooner, but I was afraid you would tell me to get lost—and I wouldn't blame you. I know I'm unworthy of you. I was going to tell you the truth last night when I brought you the photograph, but then your aunt was so upset and—"

"You really helped her, Silas. I want to thank you again for being so good with her."

"I don't suppose you'd be willing to reconsider—?"

"It's not a good idea. Besides, I'm leaving Chicago, probably for good. But thanks for helping me find my mother."

"If there's anything else I can ever do for you, just ask, okay?"

I had nothing to lose. I didn't want to die an old maid who had never been kissed. It was just an experiment, I told myself. Silas was a confessed thief, but in his fine tuxedo and white bow tie, he was a very respectable-looking one. If he could pretend to be a gentleman for an evening, then I could pretend that he was one.

"Now that you mention it, I would like to ask one more favor of you, Mr. McClure, but I hope you won't get the wrong idea about me. I would like . . ." All of my courage fled. I couldn't go through with it. I turned away. "Never mind."

"No, wait." He caught my arm. "I'll do whatever I can, Violet. And I could never think ill of you. Please tell me."

I made the mistake of looking into his eyes. The tenderness and love that I saw in them began to hypnotize me. I couldn't seem to look away.

"You're right about Nelson being a fool. My other suitors turned out to be disappointing too. And so it is starting to appear that I will never marry."

"Never marry? A girl as smart and as pretty as you? I don't believe it."

"It's too complicated to explain. But the truth is . . . you see . . . I mean, the favor I would like to ask . . . if you wouldn't mind . . ."

"Just ask me, Violet."

"I have never been kissed, Mr. McClure. And I would like to be—kissed, that is. Just once. So I could see what it's like."

"And you want me to be the one?" he asked breathlessly.

"I-if you wouldn't mind."

"Whoa," he said, exhaling. "I never saw that coming! But I would be honored." He looked into my eyes for a very long time as if trying to steady himself. "Are you ready?" he finally asked.

"Yes," I whispered.

Silas leaned toward me. I closed my eyes. His lips touched mine, as softly as a butterfly landing, and rested there for a moment. Then he moved closer and his mouth seemed to melt into mine as he kissed me. It was the most wonderful sensation I had ever felt. It started where his warm, tender lips joined mine and traveled slowly through me like a wave of warm water.

Much too soon, the kiss ended. Silas moved away.

"How was that?" he murmured. In the moonlit darkness, his eyes looked as though they were made of navy blue velvet.

"Oh my . . ." I breathed. "I had no idea that a kiss traveled all the way to your toes."

"Yeah. I felt it too."

"Why are we whispering?" I asked.

"I don't know."

He moved toward me again and this time he took my face in his hands. He was going to kiss me again. And I wanted him to.

The second kiss was much firmer and lasted much longer. I felt the stubble of his chin as his face brushed against mine. This time the sensation that washed over me was like falling into a raging river and being swept downstream. The power of it came not only from the touch of his lips against mine but from the warmth of his hands on my face and in my hair. My knees turned so weak I thought I might fall over. He finally pulled away once again, but I didn't want him to.

"That . . . that was even more wonderful," I whispered.

"Yeah . . ." We both sounded like we had just swum across a river and collapsed on shore. "Violet? May I. . . ?"

"Yes, please . . . one more . . ." I closed my eyes. This time his arms encircled me, and he pulled me close. I clung tightly to him, no longer simply being kissed, but kissing him in return. It was every bit as passionate as the kiss Nelson and Katya had shared—but I wasn't observing this time. I was drowning in it.

The sensation was the most amazing, terrifying, wonderful,

frightening one I had ever felt. All of it—the feel of his strong arms around me, his sturdy body close to mine, the way he breathed, the way his skin caressed my skin, his scent. As his warm lips melted into mine, I decided that a kiss was the most wonderful thing in the world. And now that I had experienced one, I didn't want to spend the rest of my life without another. No wonder Aunt Birdie hugged every man she met.

When our lips finally parted, Silas crushed me against his chest for a moment. I was glad that he did. I felt so weak and breathless and dizzy that I could barely stand.

At last my strength returned and I pulled away.

"Thank you." I still was able only to whisper, for some reason. "Now I know what it feels like and—"

"I love you, Violet."

I couldn't speak. Tears filled my eyes.

"It's the truth. I love you. I've never been in love before, but I've fallen in love with you. I don't suppose I could get you to change your mind? About never getting married? Because I don't think I can live without you."

I longed to ask if he loved me enough to change; enough to give up stealing and find a legitimate occupation. But I remembered Nelson Kent's indecision when I'd asked if he would surrender all of his wealth for Katya, and I was afraid to ask. If Silas hesitated, if he was unable to decide—or if he lied to me—it would break my heart. He would have to choose to change on his own.

"No, I won't change my mind. Good-bye, Silas."

"Violet, wait—"

"I'll remember that kiss for the rest of my life, but now I have to go." I was going to burst into tears, and I didn't know why. I fled into the house and up the stairs to my room.

As soon as I closed my bedroom door, I took off my dress and unlaced my corset. To my despair, all of the symptoms of love that every romance novel had ever described were still there. My heart raced wildly. I was breathless, weak, dizzy. His last kiss had left me so dizzy, in fact, that I had leaned against him to keep from falling over. And the symptoms were still there, even after I'd torn off my corset and tossed it onto the floor. I was in love with Silas McClure. I had fallen in love with a thief.

True love was much more devastating than in a romance novel. More devastating than the Great Chicago Fire. The flames of love were all-consuming, and there was nothing you could do to stop them or hold them back. You either saved yourself or ended up destroyed.

I cried inconsolably.

After a while, I heard my bedroom door creak open. Aunt Birdie floated into the room in her nightgown and gazed down at me, her head tilted to one side in sympathy.

"You must be in love," she said. I could only nod. "Make certain you marry for love, dear."

"I know, Aunt Birdie, I know!" I sobbed as her arms surrounded me. "I want to marry for love, but he is completely unsuitable. He's a thief. He even confessed that he was one tonight. My father would never approve of him, even if I got up the nerve to ask him."

"Your father, of all people, would understand."

"What do you mean?"

"Well, he defied his father, you know. Angeline was totally unsuitable too. But he married her for love."

The mention of my mother brought another flood of tears. "I found her, Aunt Birdie. I found my mother tonight."

"Oh, how nice."

"And she didn't abandon me after all. My mother left me because she loved me."

"Well, then," she said as she hugged me tightly. "That says it all, doesn't it."

Chapter

37

I was packing the last of my things on Saturday morning when I remembered the journal I'd stuffed beneath the mattress. I took a moment to leaf through the record of my time in Chicago and paused when I found my entry from June twentieth.

I had written *Mysteries to Solve* on the top of the page. I had arrived in town with two of them and had added several more. Now that I was going home, it surprised me to see how many of them I could cross off.

1. Why did Mother leave us? Where is she?
2. Did Maude O'Neill murder her first husband? How can I stop the wedding?
3. Why did Father change from being one of Mr. Moody's Yoke-fellows to being indifferent about religion?
4. Why are Grandmother and Father estranged? What were the "sorrows" she mentioned in her life with my grandfather? Why won't Father let her talk about my mother?

5. Was Aunt Matt's fiancé, Robert Tucker, really a thief, or was Aunt Birdie simply rambling? Did Mr. Tucker get caught? Is he in prison?

6. Does Nelson Kent really love Katya, or is he using her? Is he using me?

7. And speaking of being used—is Silas McClure using me, or does he truly have feelings for me?

The last question brought tears to my eyes. Silas was the only man I'd met this summer who had truly loved me. And I loved him. I dried my eyes with his handkerchief, which still bore his faint scent. I finished packing my trunk, then went downstairs to wait for my father. I had just reached the foyer when Aunt Agnes burst through our front door without even knocking.

"Violet! Oh, you poor dear," she said breathlessly. "You had better sit down. I'm afraid you're in for a terrible, terrible shock."

"What's wrong?"

"I have scandalous news. Outrageous news! Nelson Kent eloped with his grandmother's serving girl last night!"

"Good for him." I couldn't help smiling.

Aunt Agnes gripped my shoulders. "But, my dear, aren't you positively heartbroken? He proposed marriage to you!"

"And I turned him down. He's in love with that serving girl, Aunt Agnes, and I'm thrilled for both of them. I hope they figure out a way to make it work."

"Oh, my dear," she moaned as she pulled me into her arms. "You must be in shock. I'm sure the truth hasn't sunk in yet. I feel so bad for dragging you into this mess."

"You don't have to feel bad at all." A giggle escaped from my lips, and Agnes pulled away to stare at me.

"I knew you'd be upset," she said. "You're hysterical!"

"I'm not. Please believe me, Aunt Agnes. I know all about Nelson and Katya. I loaned her the gown she eloped in."

Agnes pulled a collapsible fan from her handbag and flicked it open. She fanned herself vigorously, causing the papers on the hall table to flutter in the breeze.

"Oh, Violet, I'm so sorry."

"Listen, I had a good time with you and your friends. I learned a lot. You helped me decide some things in my life."

"I'm acquainted with plenty of other young men from good families. I could make introductions for you."

I smiled, wondering what she would think of the nickname I'd given them: pea pods. "I have to go home today, Aunt Agnes. But who knows? Maybe I'll visit Chicago again someday."

"What's all the fuss?" Aunt Matt asked as she marched out from the kitchen. "What's going on?"

"I've come with dreadful news," Agnes said. "Violet's beau eloped with another woman!"

"He wasn't my beau—"

"Oh, is that all?" Matt asked. "Will you be staying for lunch, Agnes?"

"Not today. I must go and comfort my dear, dear friend, Sadie Kent. She is simply devastated that her Nelson would do such a thing and run off that way. The family is worried sick about a breach of promise suit, so I offered to come over and talk with you, Violet." She sniffled as Aunt Matt stomped back to the kitchen, shaking her head.

"I'm not going to sue anyone, Aunt Agnes. I never accepted Nelson's proposal."

"Oh, thank goodness. The Kents will be so relieved. Disappointed, mind you, but relieved to know they won't face a lawsuit. I'd better go and tell them right away. *Au revoir*, my dear. And give my apologies to your father. I'm afraid I've failed him miserably."

I watched Aunt Agnes hurry away to comfort Mrs. Kent and realized that while many things in her life were superficial, the friendships she shared with the other women were not. There was a solidarity in their lives that I had experienced only at school with

Ruth Schultz. I no longer wanted a life like Aunt Agnes', but I admired her a great deal. She had taken her sorrows and tragedies and allowed good to come from them, just as Grandmother had advised me to do.

I went into the parlor and found Aunt Birdie seated on the sofa, reading a letter from Gilbert. I could tell by the faded ink and tissue-thin paper that it was many, many years old. I still hoped she would forget that Gilbert was dead, but for now she had found comfort in his letters. She looked up when she saw me and smiled through her tears.

"Your young man was right, Violet. I hear Gilbert speaking to me."

I couldn't reply around the lump in my throat. She had referred to Silas as "my young man." I wondered how long it would take for me to forget him. Did people ever find true love more than once in a lifetime? Birdie and Aunt Matt never had. I hoped I would.

I heard my grandmother puttering around in the kitchen with Aunt Matt, fixing lunch, and I wandered out to talk with her. She stood at the kitchen stove, stirring a pot, and I slipped into place beside her.

"I hope you aren't too disappointed that things didn't work out for Louis Decker and me."

She circled her arm around my waist and laid her head against my shoulder. "Not at all, my dear. You would make a dreadful minister's wife. You're much too high-spirited and unconventional. There are people in the church, I'm sorry to say, who would try to put you into a mold and squeeze your wonderful imagination right out of you. God has a purpose for your life. You would be wrong to marry Louis for my sake."

"And there is much more to life than getting married," Aunt Matt added. "But if you do get married, Violet, make sure you and your husband want the same things in life."

"I know. I want to do something useful with my life, the way both of you do. I'm just not sure what that will be. I'll never forget all those wonderful displays you showed me at the Woman's Pavilion, Aunt Matt. You really inspired me. You both did."

Father arrived in time for lunch. I listened as he chatted with Grandmother at the dining room table, and it seemed to me that they had reconciled a bit. He kissed her cheek when it was time to go.

"Good-bye, Mother," he said. "I trust I'll see you in Lockport for the wedding?"

"Of course, dear. And don't be a stranger, John. Bring Violet back to see us once in a while. We love her dearly, you know."

We all wept as I said good-bye. Even Aunt Matt brushed a tear from her eye. Father finally pried me out of Aunt Birdie's arms and towed me out to the waiting carriage, grumbling about missing our train. We chugged away from Union Station an hour later, but my tears didn't stop falling until we reached the outskirts of the city.

We would be back in Lockport in another hour, so I drew a deep breath to gain control of my emotions. I still had a few things that I needed to discuss with my father. He was engrossed in the newspaper he had purchased from one of the street urchins at the train station, but I cleared my throat, signaling for his attention.

"I know why Grandmother came to Chicago after her husband died," I began. "And I know why she didn't come to live with us." He folded his newspaper and laid it aside, frowning.

"It was because your Aunt Bertha—"

"No. She came here to search for Mother."

His frown deepened. "Did she tell you that?"

"Yes. She started working in all of those poor areas so she could look for Mother and convince her to come home to us."

"She promised me that she wouldn't talk to you about your mother."

"And she didn't break that promise. I learned everything on my own. I came to Chicago to find Mother too."

"You what?"

"That was the real reason I asked to visit the city—not to see the fair. I needed to know why she left me."

"Violet, I already told you—"

"I found her. And now I know exactly why she left. I know the truth about her past—that her family were gypsies and that she worked in a burlesque theater."

He closed his eyes. When he finally opened them again, he gazed out of the window not at me. "How is she?" he asked quietly.

"Still beautiful."

He nodded silently.

"Mother told me the whole story, her side of it. She didn't go away because she was discontented with you. She left because she loved you. Your father told her that the reason her babies died was because God was punishing her. She didn't want anything bad to happen to us because of her. Then her brothers found her and threatened to expose her past to all of Lockport if Grandfather didn't pay them money. She was afraid the scandal would ruin you and me. So she left."

Father's lips drew into a tight, angry line. "So it wasn't just Philip who my father destroyed."

"I know how strict your father was and how he made your brother run away. But I would like to hear your side of the story. All of it. Starting with the night of the fire when you and Mother met."

He was silent for so long that I began to believe he wouldn't speak. But at last he started talking, hesitantly at first. His voice was very soft.

"I was in Chicago that night with Philip. I found him in the saloon that he and Lloyd O'Neill ran together. Philip wanted to become an actor, and he enjoyed the theater and all of those other vices that our father railed against. I made a deal with Philip to come to Dwight Moody's church with me—just once—so he could see how the Gospel was supposed to be preached. I kept telling him that Mr.

Moody's portrait of Christ was much different than our father's. I convinced him to come, promising that I would never ask another thing of him if he did. And Moody's sermon didn't disappoint me. I remember they sang a song that night called 'Today the Savior Calls.'"

My father began to sing softly, surprising me with his beautiful tenor voice:

"Today the Savior calls
For refuge fly
The storm of justice falls
And death is nigh."

"We had no idea how true those words would be," he continued. "Mr. Moody was still preaching his sermon when fire engines started thundering past and the bell in the old courthouse began to toll nearby. Everyone grew restless, and there was so much noise and confusion in the street outside that Mr. Moody decided to close the meeting. He didn't invite the congregation to come to Jesus—so I never knew if Philip . . ."

I took my father's hand in mine, waiting until he could continue. He had suffered more losses in his life than I had ever realized.

"Philip was worried about the saloon, worried that his friend O'Neill would be too drunk to get himself out of there with his bad leg. O'Neill had saved Phil's life during the war, so I went along with him. The fire was spreading very close to the saloon, and we found it empty except for looters who were stealing as much liquor as they could carry. I told Philip it was time for both of us to get to safety, but he wanted to go to the theater first and make sure his friends had all escaped.

"On the way we passed a building that had just caught fire. Your mother was leaning from a third-story window, screaming for help. Her father had locked her inside. Philip and I broke the door down and I carried her out. But then he went back inside to make sure no one else was trapped."

Father paused. I saw him struggling to compose himself.

"Philip never made it out. I watched the place collapse on top of him."

"He sounds like a great man," I murmured. Father nodded wordlessly, then cleared his throat.

"Our church in Lockport was taking in refugees, so I brought Angeline home. I was grieving for Philip, and she helped me through it. She always said that I saved her, but she saved me too, Violet. I fell in love with her.

"Looking back," he said, after clearing his throat again, "I can see how hard it was for her to adjust to Lockport. She didn't fit in. Her family were gypsies—thieves and rogues—and she didn't know what a real family was supposed to be like. She loved you though. You and I were her life, especially after she stopped trying to find acceptance in town. I never knew that my father was the one who drove her away . . . just like he drove Philip away. She never told me what he'd said about our children dying. I wish she had. And I never knew that her brothers had found her. . . ."

He turned to gaze out of the window at the flat prairie land we were passing. I could see his reflection in the window. There were tears in his eyes.

"If I could offer you any advice, Violet, it would be to marry someone who comes from the same background as you do and has the same values. That's why I want to encourage you to consider Herman Beckett. He's a nice young man. Bright, capable . . . I offered him a job with me if he does marry you."

"You—*what*? When did you tell him that? Was it before the Fourth of July?"

"Well, yes it was, in fact. He came to see me the day after he took you to the fair. He told me that the outing had gone very well and that he had grown fond of you."

"Don't you see? That's the only reason he proposed to me. He wants a job with you!"

"Well, why not? I don't have a son to inherit my business."

"Take away the job offer and see if he still wants me. Go ahead, I dare you."

He stared at me in surprise, then murmured, "You're so much like your mother."

"And that's another reason why I can't marry Herman Beckett. I want more than a life in Lockport. Maybe it's my gypsy blood, I don't know, but Herman and I have nothing at all in common. Besides, I don't love him. Please don't make me marry a man I don't love."

I was still holding my father's hand, and he squeezed mine gently. "I know what it's like to have a father who tries to control your life," he said. "It's just that I'm concerned about your future—but perhaps my father felt the same way."

We traveled in silence for several minutes. "You need to finish your story," I finally said. "Tell me about Maude and Lloyd O'Neill."

Father exhaled. Again, he took a long time to reply.

"O'Neill lost his leg during the war while saving Philip's life. That's why I wanted to help him, even though he was a drunk. He would dry up for a little while and get a respectable job, but he always returned to the city to start drinking again. Whenever he got drunk he would go after Maude and start beating her. She would send the children down into the cellar because he had a wooden leg and couldn't manage the steps very well. That's what happened the day he died. He was drunk, and he came after her and the children. She fled into the basement with them, and when he tried to follow, he fell and cracked his skull. Maude and her children have been through so much, Violet, and seen so much. I would like to provide them with a peaceful home."

"Do you love her?"

"I married for love the first time. Now I simply want companion-ship."

"Well, I want to marry for love. I want to fall madly, passionately in love with someone, and I want him to love me the same way in return, and—"

I had to stop or I was going to cry. We were nearing Lemont, where Silas McClure had boarded the train and I'd seen him for the first time. Father wrapped his arm around my shoulder and pulled me close.

"I won't make you marry Herman Beckett—or any other man— unless you want to. But please think about what I said. Two people need more in common for a good marriage than passion."

"I know. I've learned a lot in these past few weeks. I'm not the timid, fragile girl I used to be. When I first arrived in Chicago and no one was there to meet me at the train station, I had no idea what to do. Madame Beauchamps' School for Young Ladies never prepared me for real life. I was scared and foolish and much too sheltered." I recalled how I nearly had gone off alone with Silas that day and shuddered. "But I've grown up since then. I don't need to be protected and sheltered from bad news anymore. And I don't want to hide away in Lockport living a safe, comfortable life. I want to live. I want to discover new things about myself and see new places."

"I wish you would take time to get to know Maude since she's going to be your stepmother."

"All right, I will." I finally accepted it. "But then I want to go back to Chicago and find my place in life. I don't want to look for a husband right now. I won't be twenty-one for nine more months. Just give me some time to figure out what I'm supposed to do with my life, okay? That's what we're put on earth for, isn't it? I need to serve God in my own way, just like you and Uncle Philip had to find your own way."

"Are you going to see your mother again?"

"I want to see her, if she'll let me. Someone needs to tell her that all those things Grandfather said were wrong. I think she should know the truth—even if she never does come home to us. Maybe she and I can learn together."

"You're so much like her," he said again. "So lively and dramatic. That's why I worry so much about you."

"I don't want to be an actress," I said, smiling. "And I'm not going to marry one of Grandmother's religious zealots or be brainwashed by Aunt Matt. I want to be my own person. I know that worries you, but remember how your father tried to put you into a box that didn't fit? Remember what it did to Philip? And to Mother? Let me find my own box. I'll be okay—I promise."

He tightened his grip on my shoulder.

"I'll stay home with you for a few months," I told him. "I'll be nice to Maude and her children. I'll stay until after the wedding. But please let me go back to Chicago in the fall. I have so much more to learn."

"All right, Violet," he said with a sigh. "You can go back."

Chapter

38

Saturday, September 9, 1893

On the second Saturday in September I stood in the train station in Lockport, saying good-bye to my father once again. He was allowing me to return to Chicago with his blessing, as he'd promised. Maude and her imps were at the station too. Her wedding to my father had been simple and brief, and she had moved into our house on the same day. I no longer resented her for coming between my father and me now that I had my own life to look forward to.

I settled comfortably in the seat as the train began to move, excited to be on my way back to the city. I would have two more months to revisit the World's Fair before it closed, to see all of the sights I had missed. I was especially eager to attend the festivities on Chicago Day, October 9—the anniversary of the Great Fire. It still amazed me to realize how quickly the city had risen from the ashes after that tragedy twenty-two years ago. It was a good lesson for my own life. Tragedies can mean a new beginning as well as an ending.

Within minutes the train was moving fast, chugging past the

boring Illinois terrain. Some of the leaves had begun to change colors, but not enough of them to make the view a scenic one. I had a book to read in my satchel, but my thoughts were racing much too quickly to be able to concentrate as I anticipated all of the new discoveries that lay ahead for me. I would visit my mother again—of that much I was certain. And I would try to discover what God wanted me to do with my life.

Some time later, I felt the locomotive slowing down as it prepared to stop at the station in Lemont. Silas had boarded the train here the last time I had traveled to Chicago, wearing his garish plaid suit and hauling his satchel full of elixir. I closed my eyes to erase that image of him, preferring to remember Silas the way I last had seen him, wearing a tuxedo and bow tie and white satin vest.

"Is this seat taken, Miss Hayes?"

I opened my eyes, and there he was! Silas McClure! I blinked, wondering if I was dreaming.

His grin was as brilliant as the electric lights at the White City. My heart began thumping. I stared up at Silas in surprise, then quickly looked away, remembering the kisses we had shared. He was a rogue, stalking me, hoping to seduce me into kissing him again. I never would have asked him to kiss me in the first place if I had known we would meet this way. I had been certain that our paths would never cross again.

He stood beside my seat, waiting for me to answer his question. But first I had one of my own.

"What are you doing here?"

"I'm going to accompany you to Chicago."

"I'm sorry, Mr. McClure, but my father would never allow you to do that."

His brow furrowed in confusion. "Violet, your father is the one who hired me."

"Hired you. . . ?"

"Yes, just like he hired me the first time. Well, not me specifically—either time—but since I ended up with the assignment last June, I was able to arrange things so I could accompany you again."

"What are you talking about?" The train lurched as it pulled out of the station. Silas gripped the back of the seat to keep from losing his balance.

"May I sit down?" he asked again, gesturing to the seat beside mine. I nodded. My heart raced much faster than the train. "Violet, you said you knew the truth about me."

"Yes, that you're a thief."

"A what?"

"You know . . . the robbery at the fair, your trial at the courthouse, all your underworld connections to find my mother—I know that you're a thief."

"Violet, I work for Pinkerton's."

His words seemed to hang suspended in the air between us. I couldn't comprehend them.

"The . . . the detective agency?"

"Yeah. You said that you knew."

"You mean . . . you don't commit crimes? You . . . you solve them?"

"Well, we do a lot more than solve crimes. And some of our work is pretty routine. A law firm might hire us to conduct an investigation or serve a subpoena. And I've also been hired to guard payrolls or to travel by train undercover to watch for thieves. That's what my salesman garb was for. It was pure chance that I got picked to accompany you that first day. . . . And I have to say that I never expected you to be so beautiful. I figured I'd be accompanying an ugly old spinster—not you. That's why I couldn't stop staring at you that day. And why I was horrified to be seen wearing that corny getup and—"

"Wait a minute. Back up. . . . My father hired you to spy on me?"

"Well, I wouldn't want to call it that. Our company has done security work for your father in the past and—"

"That's outrageous!"

"Hey, don't get mad at me," he said after I punched his arm. "He cares about you. He wanted to make certain you arrived safely. He was afraid you'd meet up with someone unsavory or unscrupulous."

"Like a sleazy elixir salesman?"

"Exactly."

"And now my father hired you to keep track of me again?"

"If not me, then it would have been someone else," Silas said with a shrug.

"Were you being paid to follow me all around Chicago too? Is that why I kept running into you and—?"

"Hey, no! Not at all! Just to the train station. After that, it was my own idea to keep track of you."

"Then the robbery at the fair . . . Your two friends must have been the *guards*, not the thieves!"

"Right. Joe decided to pose as a woman to try to catch the thieves who were snatching purses at the Woman's Pavilion. Robert caught one of them and had to testify in court the day I met you downtown."

"So that's how you were able to find my mother. You're a detective!"

"A pretty good one, eh?" He couldn't help grinning.

"What about the night at the casino, with Nelson? Were you working then?"

"The fair administrators knew about the gambling and suspected a scam, but the room was rented privately. Admission was by invitation only, so they couldn't gather any proof. Thanks to your friend, we were able to get inside and check it out for them."

"I understand the dealers were all arrested. I read about it in the paper." When I saw his look of surprise, I added, "I read the newspaper every day now. My aunt Matt is right. You can learn a lot about the world that way."

"Well, thanks to you and your gambling friend, I got a nice bonus from the fair's administrators for my night's work."

"Does that mean you won't have to sell Dr. Dean's Blood Builder anymore?"

"That's right—and it's a shame too, because our specially patented formula is made from the highest quality beef extract, fortified with iron and celery root. If you're suffering from extreme exhaustion, brain fatigue, debility of any kind, blood disorders, or anemia, our blood builder will enrich your blood and help your body throw off accumulated humors of all kinds. You should try it, Miss Hayes. It's guaranteed to stimulate digestion and improve your blood flow or we'll give you your money back."

I laughed and laughed—so hard that I could no longer sit up straight. Silas laughed with me. It was a wonderful sound.

"May I ask you a question?" I said when we finally paused for breath. "When you comforted my Aunt Birdie and you talked about heaven and Jesus . . . do you . . . are you. . . ?"

"I'm a believer, Violet. My saintly mother made sure of that."

"I see." I couldn't stop smiling. "Me too. And one more question? What does the *A* on your monogrammed handkerchief stand for?"

"It's an *A* for agent. It's so we can recognize each other when we're working undercover. It's less obvious than *P* for Pinkerton's."

"But suppose there's an innocent bystander whose name just happens to begin with an *A* and he—?"

"You've asked enough questions," he said, putting his fingers over my lips. "Now it's my turn. Tell me, if you loved someone, and you had never fallen in love before, and you couldn't stop thinking about her day and night, would you let her walk out of your life or would you follow her to the ends of the earth and fight to win her hand?"

I didn't think my heart could pound any harder or faster but it did. "I-I'd fight to win her hand."

"I was hoping you would say that." He grinned and took my hand in his, twining our fingers together. "Okay, now it's your turn to ask me one. I love your questions, you know."

I was so rattled I couldn't think. I asked the first one that came to mind. "If you could choose, would you rather be a butterfly or a firefly?"

"I'd rather be a moth."

"Ugh!" I shuddered. "I hate moths."

He leaned his head back and smiled. "Now that's a mystery I'll never understand. A moth is just a butterfly without the fancy clothes, isn't it? But if a moth flutters around your head, you women scream and shoo it away like it was some kind of monster. If a butterfly does the same thing, you're entranced. You say, 'Oh, how lovely!' and you stick out your finger and try to get it to land there. It's the same insect, isn't it? Except for the color?"

"Yes, I suppose it is," I said with a smile. "So why would you choose to be a moth?"

"Because I'd like to make my way in life without all the fancy colors and be judged by who I am, not by what I look like from the outside."

"You're right," I said, grinning as broadly as he did. "One should never judge someone by outward appearances. I'll remember that the next time an elixir salesman in a baggy plaid suit boards my train."

And that, dear reader, was how I solved my first *True Crime* and found *True Romance* in . . .

❧ The End ❧

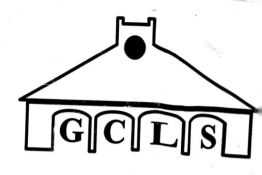

Gloucester County
Library System